Love, Charleston
Beth Webb Hart

Seaside Letters
Denise Hunter

THOMAS NELSON
Since 1798

NASHVILLE   DALLAS   MEXICO CITY   RIO DE JANEIRO

Published in Nashville, Tennessee, by Thomas Nelson. Thomas Nelson is a registered trademark of Thomas Nelson, Inc.

Thomas Nelson, Inc., titles may be purchased in bulk for educational, business, fund-raising, or sales promotional use. For information, please email SpecialMarkets@ThomasNelson.com.

Unless otherwise noted, Scripture quotations are taken from the HOLY BIBLE: NEW INTERNATIONAL VERSION® NIV®. Copyright © 1973, 1978, 1984 by Biblica, Inc.™ Used by permission of Zondervan. All rights reserved worldwide.

ISBN 978-1-5955-4774-3

Printed in the United States of America

11 12 13 14 15 16 HCI 6 5 4 3 2 1

Love, Charleston

Other Novels by Beth Webb Hart

Grace at Low Tide

Adalaide Piper

The Wedding Machine

Sunrise on the Battery (available October 2011)

Lovingly dedicated to my sisters,
Peggy and Libby

He restores my soul.

PSALM 23:3

Chapter 1

THE REVEREND ROY JESSUP SUMMERALL JR.

April 3, 2008

Roy's right eyelid began to twitch when he sat down in the small antique chair across from Bishop Boatwright. He pulled at his stiff white collar. It was an XXL, but it fit his thick neck snugly, and he often undid the metal tab toward the end of the day to give himself a little relief. He repositioned his broad frame, and the small chair creaked. Then he rubbed his wide, sweaty palms on his khaki pants and looked up to meet the bishop's gaze.

"Church of the Good Shepherd is thriving, isn't it?"

Roy nodded his head. "I can't tell you what a blessing it is to serve in my hometown, Bishop. It couldn't be better for me and Little Rose." Roy had a thick South Carolina sand-hills accent, very different from the slow, round tidewater drawl of Charleston. The sandhills accent was clipped and most of Roy's *e* and *a* vowels made the short *i* sound so that the word *heck* or *hack* both sounded like *hick*. It was the kind of accent folks in the metropolitan areas of the state called country or redneck, and he tried to temper it when he met with the bishop, whose office was at The Cathedral of St. Luke and St. Paul in the center of downtown Charleston.

"Why do you think it's going so well?" The bishop's question seemed more directed to the stack of papers on his desk than to Roy. The old man tugged at his white mutton-chops before looking up.

The young priest cleared his throat and puffed up his broad chest. "Well, we keep it simple, I guess. I stick to the Gospel in the pulpit every Sunday, and we pour all that we have into our Alpha Course, which folks have attended from as far afoot as Darlington, Hartsville, and even Florence."

The bishop patted the left pocket of his pressed purple shirt. He wore a large and ornate gold cross around his neck that he kept tucked in his pocket when he wasn't decked out in his heavy robe and ruffles.

Roy looked out of the thick glass panes of the third-floor corner office. It was a Holy City view if he ever saw one, with the largest, most historic steeples in the country dominating the skyline—St. Philip's on Church Street, St. Michael's on the corner of Meeting and Broad, St. Matthew's on upper King, St. John's on Archdale, and the Unitarian church right next door which he had forgotten the name of.

He smiled when he thought of his simple red brick sanctuary, circa 1967, back in Ellijay, with the lettered marquee in the front. This month it read, *Distressed? Try This Address! (Every Sunday at 10 a.m.)*

He turned back to the bishop, who watched him steadily as if he wanted him to say more. "It's my kind of people at Good Shepherd, sir. The kind I grew up with, and we speak the same language, you know?" He tugged at his collar and smiled. "They trust me, and I know just where they're coming from. Then it's not long before one or another brings in a friend or a neighbor or coworkers . . ." The chair creaked as he sat back. "And that's why we've grown, I reckon. 'Cause we know and understand each other."

Bishop Boatwright made a steeple with the tips of his fingers, then he raised his white bushy eyebrows, forming two symmetrical arches. "I called you here because I have a new position I'd like to recommend you for, Reverend."

The twitch in Roy's right eye turned into a flutter. He reached up and rubbed it, then he leaned forward, resting his elbows on his wide knees. "Bishop, you know it's been a tough few years for me personally."

"Of course I do." The bishop squinted. His pale blue eyes shot a sharp look that Roy recognized as a complicated blend of love, concern, and most striking of all, appraisal.

He kept on. "And now Rose and I are hunkered down in Ellijay. She loves her school, and my mama sold the farm and bought a house just down the road from us. Plus, my brother is only ten miles away over in Robbin's Neck." Roy bit his bottom lip hard. "It's been real good for me to be back in my old stomping grounds after losing Jean Lee." He patted the left side of his chest. "I feel like the Lord's had his hand on my heart, and he's been binding it up."

"Undoubtedly." The bishop balled his right hand into a

fist, his large, gold ecclesiastical ring catching the afternoon light. Roy had been a second-string offensive guard for Clemson University before he became an Episcopal priest, and the bishop's gold band always reminded him of a Super Bowl ring. This made him chuckle a little, imagining Bishop Boatwright at the ten-yard line giving some defender the Heisman before running toward the goal.

Bishop Boatwright held out his fist and leaned forward. "You know what happens after you receive healing, son?"

Roy wasn't sure how to answer this. Was it a theological question or a personal one? He wasn't bookish like the bishop; he just knew the Holy Spirit and felt its daily presence like the air his lungs inhaled or the soft light that fell on his face on his morning walk to work.

"Sir?" he said.

"It's been my experience these short seventy-six years"— the bishop pounded his fist twice on the arm of his chair—"that after you receive healing, the Lord calls you *out* to a new frontier." He pursed his pink lips and leaned forward. "He takes that fresh strength and puts it to a new test."

Roy tilted his square chin. He was a big, handsome fellow with a head full of thick brown hair and dark brown eyes to match. Bishop Boatwright had confirmed him when he was twelve years old. And he'd ordained him the same year his wife died some fifteen years later. Both times he had laid his stubby hands on Roy's head full of hair, his gold ring rubbing against the boy's scalp, blessing the holy ceremony with the presence of the Almighty One he represented. The truth was, this man was in authority over Roy, and like Saul on the road to Damascus, there was no use kicking against the goads. He exhaled and uttered a prayer of mercy. "What did you have in mind, sir?"

"Phil Rainey is retiring this spring."

Phil Rainey, Phil Rainey, Phil Rainey. Roy ran the vaguely familiar name through his mind as he thought about the other churches in the middle part of the state. The only Phil Rainey he knew was the rector of St. Michael's in the center of downtown Charleston. The fancy old church on the corner of Meeting and Broad where his Aunt Elfrieda used to drag him during his miserable summer visits.

Roy reached up to steady his right eyelid again. "I'm . . . you don't mean . . . ?"

Bishop Boatwright nodded. "Yes. St. Michael's here in Charleston. I'd like to recommend you to their search committee." He looked toward his desk as if his mind had already concerned itself with his next appointment. "I think you could be the man for the job, Reverend Summerall."

Roy felt the burn of perspiration beneath his arms. He blinked several times and set his jaw. "With all due respect, Bishop, I'm not the kind of fellow that can lead a Charleston church, especially a South of Broad one." He looked around the room at the shelves and shelves of books as if to find proof. Then he pointed to his mouth. "Just listen to my accent."

The bishop turned back and cocked his head in curiosity.

"Or this." Now that Roy had the bishop's attention, he smiled and pushed a little bit of his tongue through the gap between his two front teeth. "I need braces."

The bishop furrowed his bushy brows and Roy continued, counting off the examples like a verdict.

"I drive an all-terrain vehicle on the weekends, I go to the races for fun, I wear gold jewelry. Heck, I even vacation at Myrtle Beach by my own choice." Then Roy said with a firm whisper, "Bishop, did you know that I have a *tattoo* of a Clemson tiger paw on my right shoulder?" He rolled his shoulder forward at the mention of it. He had dislocated it his junior year, and his senior year he had torn so many tendons that he had to have an operation. It still gave him a fit. "Sir, I wouldn't know the first thing about ministering to those 'mind your manners' and 'just where do *your* people come from?' folks."

The bishop took his time standing up, then ambled over to his desk where he thumbed through his stack of papers. "You spent your boyhood summers in Charleston, as I recall." He glanced toward Roy, who was peering out of the window at St. Michael's massive white steeple with its clock tower and weather vane and one-ton bells that had called the city to worship since before the Revolutionary War. He remembered reading about how the steeple was painted black during those days so the British ships wouldn't spot it. Only it backfired. The black made the church all the more noticeable from the harbor, and the troops were quick to ransack it.

"They were the worst summers of my life." Roy rotated his right shoulder again. "My brother, Chick, and I were treated pretty harshly by the local kids." Roy could still hear Heyward Rutledge calling him a "Neanderthal" when he asked the fellow's crush to dance at one of the Friday night parties at East Bay Playground. He'd had to go home and look that word up in Aunt Elfrieda's encyclopedia, and then he had to take the scientific definition and translate it into the slang.

The bishop chuckled. He sniffed the air and scratched his muttonchops.

Then he looked down at Roy and whole seconds passed before he nodded once. "You might be just the man for the job, Reverend. I want you to be open and trust me in this. I'm going to recommend you to the search committee and the vestry, and you'll be hearing from them."

Roy sat back in his chair as though he had been hit by a three-hundred-pound nose guard. The chair seemed to waver, and for a moment, he thought it might collapse under his weight. He pictured Rose, his five-year-old daughter, curled up in Mama's lap on the front porch this morning. Charleston was the last place he wanted to raise her. Jean Lee was gone. Why in the world would the bishop, why would the Lord even, want him to entertain this outlandish idea?

The bishop bowed his head and started to pray, but Roy didn't hear the words. When he heard the old man say, "Amen," he stood and firmly shook the bishop's hand. Then he got back in his pickup and drove quickly down Interstate 26 toward Interstate 95 where the live oaks and palmettos gave way to the scrub pines and the flat lands of the only place, this side of heaven, he ever wanted to call home.

꘡

"What did high-and-mighty have to say?" His mama was sporting her new rhinestone-encrusted flip-flop heels and white shorts too short for a sixty-five-year-old woman. She was flipping pancakes on his griddle while her new husband, Donny, and Roy's office manager, Skeeter, sipped coffee at the kitchen counter.

"Breakfast for dinner, Daddy!" Little Rose abandoned her piano-playing in the den and ran into his arms. He picked her up and squeezed her tight, overcome as he often was by how her little embrace soothed his very soul like the balm of Gilead.

Mama turned down the eye of the stove and stacked three fluffy pancakes on a plastic Dora the Explorer plate. She coated each one with a thick pat of butter and set them on the little round table in the corner of the room.

"Enjoy 'em while they're warm, Rosebud," she said. "This is a one-plate-at-a-time meal, and I'll do your daddy's next so y'all can overlap."

"What's news around the church house?" Roy massaged his bum shoulder and looked to Skeeter, who blew a bubble with the pink gum she always seemed to be gnawing on. He watched the bubble deflate as she pulled four white slips from her Day-Timer. "Here are the messages, but the most pressing matter is Brother Jackson."

Roy winced, his dark brown eyes narrowing. "He looked real good a couple of days ago."

"Well, hospice told Mrs. Jackson that they figured that was a last burst of energy. They think the end is near."

Roy nodded and looked at his watch. "I'll take him the Eucharist tonight."

"Can I go too?" Rose said. She was dipping a fork-full

into a pool of syrup she had poured right on Dora's over-sized head.

Rose loved Mr. and Mrs. Jackson, who used to sing in the choir until they found cancer in his pancreas. And she often made sick visits with Roy. She was no stranger to Ellijay Memorial and the Darlington County Hospice Center or the Robbins Neck Funeral Home for that matter, and the nurses and caretakers usually set aside a lollipop or some other little trinket from the dollar store in anticipation of her next pastoral visit.

He nodded yes as Mama handed him a stack of pancakes.

"What did Bishop Boatwright want, son?"

"He wants to recommend me for a job . . ." Roy shook his head in disbelief as his kitchen got real still. "In downtown Charleston, of all places."

Mama's eyes widened. "The Holy City!" She clicked her long, silver fingernails together and winked at Rose. "Now wouldn't that be something!"

"Charleston?" Rose's eyes lit up. Her granny had taken her there once and bought her a pair of red, glittery shoes. "Oh, that's my dream city, Daddy!"

Roy pushed his pancakes aside. He turned to Donny. "Why do all females go ga-ga at the mere mention of Charleston?"

Donny shrugged his shoulders and smiled.

Jean Lee used to love Charleston, too, Roy now recalled. She'd begged him to take her to some historic bed-and-breakfast on their first anniversary, and he had complied, though he didn't care much at all for the squeaky old bed or the ridiculously high rate or the bathroom down the hall that they had to *share* with four other guests.

"Don't get too excited, gals," he said. "I don't think the bishop has really thought this thing through. And if it was up to me, we'd *never* leave Ellijay." He gently laid his paper napkin over his plate. "I'm going to run over to the church to get what we need for Brother Jackson's Communion."

"Well, who is it up to?" Rose said. Skeeter popped her bubble gum and Mama cocked her head, her big, amply-sprayed hair shifting in one cohesive clump.

Roy shook his head like an exasperated teacher and pointed upward with his index finger. "Now who do y'all think?"

Late that evening after administering the Eucharist to Mr. Jackson, who the hospice folks predicted would meet his Maker within the next forty-eight hours, Roy lifted Rose out of the pickup and tucked her into bed.

Then he went to the hall closet where he kept Jean Lee's stuff. He often came in here late at night and took comfort in the touch of her shimmery blouses, her cowboy boots, and the sweaters folded neatly on the shelf above that still contained just the faintest hint of her sweet and powdery scent.

He thought about Bishop Boatwright and his surprising request to submit his name to the search committee of what was arguably one of the oldest, stuffiest, most affluent churches in the whole diocese. He didn't want to minister in some historic monument where the parishioners might shudder with disdain at his country accent or shoo him out with the business end of the broom the way Aunt Elfrieda did when he forgot to put the napkin in his lap during one of her Sunday afternoon dinners. Truth was, he couldn't even imagine relating to those folks. It was a ridiculous idea. Maybe Bishop Boatwright was slipping as he tilted toward retirement. Maybe he was downright delusional.

Roy tucked his hands into the satin-lined pockets of the pink leather jacket Jean Lee bought on a vacation they took to Six Flags in Atlanta. She had stood in front of the three-sided mirror at one of those strip malls on the outskirts of the city and said, "Tell the truth now, Roy. Is this too much for a future priest's wife?"

"Nah," he said. "It's you, baby." And it was. It fit her in all the right spots, and he knew in his heart that God wanted her to be herself—lipstick, teased bangs, and all—like the first day he laid eyes on her in the parking lot of Ellijay High just days after his sixteenth birthday.

It had taken years to get used to life without her. And he was just beginning to feel (after much urging from his mama and daughter) that he could maybe meet someone one of these days. He had even thought about asking Skeeter out but the bubble gum bothered him, and he just never seemed to get around to it. Maybe now was the time. Or maybe now he was ready to meet some of those daughters and nieces the ladies at church kept trying to introduce him to.

Roy's unspoken hopes were becoming clearer in his heart and mind. And they were these: that he might love again and expand his family right here in Ellijay with his mama down the street and his brother, Chick, and their lively brood just a few miles away.

"My life is here, Lord," Roy said as he buried his face in the pink leather jacket. "Don't allow this to be taken away too."

Chapter 2

Della sat in the corner booth next to her cousin, Anne, smacking one of her gold gladiator sandals on the floor. They were at Earthfare, a whole-foods grocery store and café just over the Ashley River where they met to catch up every other Saturday along with Anne's sister, Alisha, whom everyone called Lish.

"Wonder where she is?" Della glanced at the clock on the wall, then reached across the table to squeeze Anne's wrist. "I don't want to ask you how you're doing because you'll just have to repeat it when she gets here."

Anne grimaced and repositioned her remarkably long frame. "Don't I wish I had something new to tell you?"

Della's eyes softened and she rubbed the top of her cousin's long, freckled hand. "Remember what Nana used to say?" Anne wrinkled her brow and shook her head no.

Della took a bite of her tabouleh and pointed with the prongs of her fork. "Sometimes no news is good news."

Just as they relaxed into a chuckle, Della spotted Lish and her family in the bakery section. "Well, looky here." She peered beyond Anne's shoulder. "If it isn't the Doctors Sublime."

Lish's tall husband was somehow both sporty and distinguished-looking as he pushed the grocery cart with their three-year-old daughter gnawing the handle and their five-year-old son riding on the back, reaching for a sample of a vegan oatmeal cookie.

Lish was seven months pregnant with her third, a subject she'd written about all spring in her "Dr. Sutton Comments" newspaper column. She'd covered morning sickness, prenatal nutrition, heartburn, genetic testing, leg cramps, mood swings, gestational diabetes, and Braxton Hicks contractions.

The handsome, fertile duo were both in scrubs, ready for the morning they would spend at the Holy Cross Free Health Clinic where they volunteered on weekend afternoons.

As Lish turned and tousled her son's brown locks, Della watched Anne gape.

"Yeah." Della leaned in to whisper. "I know what you're thinking. It's hard to believe she still has seven weeks to go. Is it me, or does she seem almost *twice* as big this time?"

"C'mon, Del," Anne muttered. "She's not *that* big."

Little Andrew spotted his aunt and cousin in the corner booth of the café and ran over to embrace Della, who tickled him hard beneath the arms before kissing his rosy cheeks.

"Cousin Del," he said. "Will you get me a cookie?"

Della scrounged around the bottom of her pocketbook. She pulled up four pennies, half of an old Cheerio, and a ball of lint.

Anne waved a five-dollar bill and Andrew snatched it.

Then he looked up through his long, dark lashes and smiled at Della. *What a knockout*, she thought.

"Thanks, Aunt Anne!" he said in the direction of the baked goods. He ran over to his daddy, who shook his head in surrender and opened the cookie bin.

Della felt Anne turn to her. "Why doesn't he embrace me like that?"

"I've seen him hug you lots of times."

"When his mama tells him to." Anne rested her narrow chin on the palm of her long, thin hand. "I suppose it's my height. It probably scares him as much as it does all the other men in Charleston."

"Anne." Della groaned before gently punching her cousin's shoulder. "I want you to stop waiting around and get out there and take hold of what you want." Della, who was more than a foot shorter than Anne, had been ordering her cousin around since they were children, and it was hard to stop now. The three had spent their childhood summers together at their grandmother's house in downtown Charleston, roaming the streets until dark. They'd climbed trees at White Point Gardens and reenacted duels in Stoll's Alley. On allowance days they'd snuck down to the old market for a praline or a sliver of fudge, which they devoured quickly before pestering the boys who fished treasures out of the restaurant trash bins, or spying on the longshoremen who stumbled out of the local bars and down the cobblestone alleyways singing songs.

Lish waddled toward them, then turned back to wave good-bye to Drew, who usually walked the kids over to the public library to pick out a book so she could have her girl time.

Della stood to give her a hug.

"Cute shoes," Lish said.

"Goodwill." Della did a few steps of the fox-trot they learned at Cotillion when they were kids. "I've made friends with a gal who works there, and she calls me whenever some South of Broad size 5½ drops off a shoebox."

"Savvy," Lish said. She heaved herself into the booth next to Della. "So what did I miss?"

Della fished for a tomato in the corner of her to-go container. "Well, Anne was just about to tell us about her secret life as a dancing bartender at the Harley-Davidson Pub in North Charleston."

Anne spit out a mouthful of her peach protein blast, and Lish laughed.

"You know, maybe I've missed my calling." Anne stood up for a moment to grab a napkin from a neighboring table, and it seemed as if the whole café turned to examine her striking height. She was six foot two with thick, wavy red hair that added at least another inch, and she had the longest, most narrow hands and feet Della had ever seen. "Maybe God didn't say, 'Stay and wait' that day in the bell tower." Anne winked at Lish. "Maybe he said, 'Buy a leather mini and learn to mix a drink.'"

Della cut her eyes at Lish. From time to time since they were kids, Anne claimed to have *heard from God*, but Della was skeptical. Her most recent claim was that one winter afternoon a few years ago in the bell tower of St. Michael's, where she served as the cocaptain of the bell ringer band, she'd heard from God regarding her desire to find a mate. She said that just after she took hold of the rope and called out, "Treble's going. She's gone!" to her team of eight, who stood in a circle ready to practice their rounds and change ringing, she had asked God if she would ever marry. He said as clear as the copper tongue of the treble clanging against the bell's side, "Stay here and wait." In fact, she had even stayed in the drafty tower until midnight that night, hours after all the bell ringers had departed, until she remembered that verse about a thousand days being the blink of an eye for God. She decided "Stay here and wait" could be a little longer than that very day.

Della often reminded her thirty-six-year-old cousin that "Stay here and wait" was not a clear-cut "Yes." And as for Della, she couldn't imagine God *speaking*. The thought of it kind of disturbed her because, in truth, she wasn't sure that he existed.

Couldn't it have just been the sound of the bells? And if he did actually *speak*, wouldn't we humans (Anne included) be apt to misunderstand whatever he was trying to communicate? And c'mon now, if God did actually exist, would he really be upset if Anne, say, went out on one of the set-ups Della had tried to arrange with the tallest men she could find? Or would he be disappointed if the single accountant/bell tower cocaptain (who was getting way too obsessed with her tabby cat for Della's comfort level) signed up for one of those Internet dating services?

"You know, Anne"—Della bit her lip—"we're not getting any younger. Don't you think—"

Anne held up her hand. "Don't say it today, Del." She swallowed hard. "Yes, I've thought about it. Maybe I didn't hear it right." She put her head in her hands for a moment. "You know, the Central Council of Church Bell Ringers outside of London has invited me to apply for a six-month training program where they'd place me in a few English churches for method ringing training in order to prepare me for the full peal we hope to attempt next year at St. Mike's." She shrugged her shoulder. "I was thinking maybe I should apply."

"Are you kidding?" Della said. "I think you should absolutely go for it."

Anne grinned and straightened her shoulders. "Remember how much I loved that semester in London when I was in college?"

"Yeah, I do." Della and Lish said in unison. Then Della pounded the table once. "You know, the truth is, you're not in that bad of a place, Anne." She reached out and put her hands firmly on top of her cousin's. "You can start over. Your whole adult life. Do you realize how many people wish they could do that?"

Anne pulled back into the cushion of her booth. "Yes, I know what you're saying." She gently crossed her thin arms. "I'm lucky not to have married the wrong guy or anything. But I can't say I agree with you that I'm in a good place, Del. I'd give anything to have what you and Lish have. You know that."

"Yes, we know." Lish stretched out her swollen hands. "But your life's not over yet, Anne. You're probably not even halfway there, so maybe Della's just saying that going off to England with a clean slate is pretty exciting . . . provided you don't stay over there too long."

Della swallowed hard. "Thank you for putting it so diplomatically, Lish." She turned to Anne and winked. "That's what I'm saying. And I'm also saying that I bet there are some pretty tall chaps on the other side of the pond, and maybe you can swipe one and bring him back."

Anne smiled. "We'll see."

"Good," Della said as she felt both sets of eyes turn to her.

"Your turn to spill it," Lish said.

Della shrugged her little shoulders. "Well, in my case no news is *bad* news."

"Hard times?" Lish tucked a piece of Della's thin, dirty-blonde hair behind her ear.

"Yeah." Della scoffed. "Peter hasn't had a commission in five months, so we're pretty much surviving on my teacher salary, and we've got to come up with a big chunk of change next month to pay a portion of Cozy's tuition."

"What about the new novel?"

"I'm cranking it out as fast as I can, but it will be a good six months before I get my advance. And you know it's not that much."

"You'll ask for help if you need it, right?" said Lish.

Della looked down at Lish's belly. "Yeah." She thought she could almost see the baby kicking beneath the taut blue scrubs. She met Lish right in the center of her bright blue eyes and pointed to her abdomen. And just as she was about to say, "And you know I'm dying for another one of those," Lish jerked forward and opened her eyes wide.

"You okay?" Della jumped.

Lish grabbed her belly. "Just a Braxton Hicks." She squinted her eyes. "I've been having them a lot this week."

"That one looked like it hurt." Anne wrung her hands.

"It kind of did." Lish raised her shoulders as if to shake it off. She looked at her watch. "Okay. I've got fifteen minutes before the kids get bored at the library. Give me the rest of the lowdown."

After Anne grumbled about a coworker who sent her a nasty e-mail, and then told a lengthy and detailed story about her heroic cat who saved her from a bat who flew into her kitchen last week while she was eating a bowl of Special K at the sink, Della turned to Lish and said: "So what about you, Dr. Sublime?"

Lish sucked her teeth and blushed. She looked back and forth at Della and Anne, then said, "The CDC is still courting Drew even though he turned them down last month. He knows how I feel about leaving Charleston, and he says he'll turn them down again." She gently patted her belly button, the outline of which could be seen through her scrubs. "And

I'm not at all ready for this baby, y'all. Mary Jane is still in the crib *and* she's refusing to potty train. I haven't washed the infant clothes in Dreft yet. I'm not even sure where my breast pump is. The room's not set up. And worst of all, Drew and I can't agree on a name. "

"Wait." Della leaned in toward Lish. "Are you telling us that you are human?" She tapped Anne's foot under the table. "If this is true, I can stop fantasizing about finding an off button in the back of her head."

Anne smirked and Della squeezed Lish's shoulder. "You've still got seven weeks. It'll come together. You're a pro at this whole thing."

Lish nodded. "Yeah, I guess so."

Just then Drew knocked on the window and pointed to his thick, black waterproof watch at the end of his tan and muscular forearm.

Lish held up her index finger and mouthed, "One more minute." She turned back to Della. "Guess who I ran into yesterday?"

"Who?" Della fished at a piece of parsley in the back of her mouth.

"Todd Jervey," she said. "He just moved back to town, and he was all asking me about you. Do you know he's read all of your novels?"

Della had been engaged to Todd before she met Peter, her husband. Todd went on to be a successful psychiatrist, and she read in the paper a few months ago about how the Medical University of South Carolina just hired him to be the chair of the Psychiatry Department.

"He's never married?" Anne asked.

"Nope," Lish said.

Della tapped her fingers on the rust-colored Formica table. It wobbled.

This time Drew rapped on the window with both fists while the kids clung to his legs.

"Gotta go," Lish said. She leaned forward and kissed them both on the forehead.

"Todd Jervey." Anne shook her head in disbelief. "Back in Charleston."

Della shrugged her shoulders. "Yep."

Anne bit her bottom lip for a moment. "I wonder if he ever got over you, Del."

"It was seven years ago." Della readjusted the table to correct the wobble. Then Anne recounted a story of Todd getting his johnboat stuck on a mud bank one day when he had taken all the gals out for a boat ride just off of Edisto Island. They'd had to wait six hours for the tide to go all the way out and back in again before they could get home.

Just then Della looked down and noticed a pool of blood on the seat beside her.

"Oh no!" Anne shouted, pointing out the window. Della stood and stared out into the parking lot. A crowd was gathered around her cousin, who had collapsed and was lying on her side on the hot, black asphalt.

Chapter 3

July 12, 2008

"Hi, there." A trim, clean-cut man in a light blue seersucker suit and bow tie met Roy at the door of the St. Michael's parish hall. The man shot out his hand. "I'm Heyward Rutledge, senior warden."

"I think we met as kids." Roy held out his hand and returned the firm handshake. "My brother, Chick, and I spent our summers on Legare Street with our aunt, Elfrieda Summerall."

Heyward cocked his head and Roy thought he could detect a sudden recognition in the man's pale green eyes. "Yeah." The man nodded. "Maybe so." He gestured toward the large meeting room just off of the kitchen. "Well, come on in. The search committee has a little lunch prepared, and we can grab a bite and get right into the interview process."

Roy met the five members of the search committee,

which included two other men who could be Heyward's clones, give or take ten years. They were both fresh-shaven, dapper attorneys with boyish faces, clean hands, and freshly clipped fingernails. There was an old and decorated naval commander with a black patch over his eye; and the smallest, most regal little lady Roy had ever seen. She sort of reminded him of a miniature Queen of England dressed just so for a high-tea party.

"I'm Eliza Belser." She smiled and took his hand. "But everyone calls me Ms. B. And I knew your Aunt Elfrieda." Ms. B.'s hand was cold and soft, and he imagined it smelled both sweet and clean, like the miniature hand soaps his aunt used to display in a gold-rimmed china dish in her guest bathroom.

"Let me show you to the buffet." Ms. B. led him over to a long antique table full of food. "Everything here is from *Faithfully Charleston*, our St. Michael's cookbook."

"What a feast." Roy's mouth, which had been dry during his nervous drive down I-26, literally watered when he took a gander at the spread. There was a tomato pie, a sweet onion pie, pickled shrimp, and pimento cheese finger sandwiches. And there were ham biscuits and cheese straws, a blue crab dip with little white round crackers, and a hummingbird cake with cinnamon and pineapple and pecans like his Aunt Elfrieda used to make for their Sunday dinner. (It was the only day of the week during his stay with her that he could remember looking forward to.)

He thought back to his interview at Church of the Good Shepherd five years ago. The search committee consisted of

Bubba Jones, Brother Jackson, and Skeeter's mama, Donna Mead. They'd taken him over to the Quincy's by the highway exit, and he'd ordered a hamburger steak that was burnt to a crisp. He'd had to douse it with a lot of Heinz 57 to get it down.

"Did you make all this?" he asked the miniature lady. She tugged at her beige suit jacket and corrected her posture.

"Yes, she did." Heyward came over and patted him on the back. "The first thing you need to know about St. Mike's, Roy, is that Ms. B. runs the show. She's got more power than the vestry and the rector combined. I bet she'd even put the archangel in his place if need be."

"Oh, stop." The lady nudged him in the side. "Don't listen to that. I'm just here to help. I lost my husband fourteen years ago, and my children said to me, 'Mama, pour yourself into something you love,' and I've been helping out a little at the church ever since."

"Helping out a little?" Heyward said. "I don't think I've ever been in this building when this lady wasn't cooking up something or running a meeting or folding and addressing the newsletter."

Roy smiled. He had a lady like Ms. B. back at the Church of the Good Shepherd. Her name was Candy Mills and she was always organizing the kitchen and sprucing up the after-church coffee hour with sweet rolls or brightly colored cupcakes that the kids devoured. Candy Mills was short, too, but she was as wide as she was short and she had these little gray whiskers on the tip of her chin. Roy glanced at the narrow swinging door that led to the St. Michael's kitchen.

Candy Mills might not be able to make it through that entryway.

After everyone helped themselves, Ms. B. gave a brief and impressive history of the church, and Heyward laid out their current status: 1,658 registered members, 450 of whom were active volunteers and financial contributors, a capital campaign project for the new office and bookstore on Broad Street that was in its final stages, and a need to reach out to the younger families who came in for a few months or years and then tapered off.

The room was dark and cool with burgundy walls and a dark Oriental rug, and on the walls there were ornately framed paintings and sketches of the sanctuary by various artists over the last three centuries. Roy pushed up the sleeves of the navy blue blazer his mama had driven him to the Marshall's in Darlington to purchase last week. He had not had time to get the arms of the jacket taken up, and his right cuff kept brushing the crab dip on his plate every time he reached for his iced tea.

"Reverend Summerall," the one-eyed commander asked, "what is your vision for a church like ours?"

Roy cleared his throat and rotated his right shoulder. After three months of prayer, mostly of the "Let this cup pass from me" type, he had no desire to impress these folks. Of course, he wished the best for this body of worshippers, but in his heart he felt that a church with such privilege and history wasn't the kind that he was built to lead. He suspected that a place like this wasn't desperate enough to *cling* to the Gospel as if its life depended on it. Was he judging on appearances? Yes, he was. Was he judging because of his own miserable Sundays here, with his aunt clucking at him and Chick if they so much as repositioned themselves in the hard wooden box pews? It was a strong possibility. *Forgive me*, he prayed as the Lord convicted his heart. Judging was a particularly toxic sin, and he knew it.

Then as the table stared him down, he opened his mouth and the words came spilling out in a way they did sometimes when his sermon took a Spirit-led detour. It was moments like those that he laid aside his notes and became a vessel, empty enough to be spoken through, if for just a little while.

"We can't assume folks know the Gospel." Roy sat up and let it come. "Even folks that have been coming here for decades. Or generations, for that matter." He rubbed his hands together. "So I think it would be wise to offer the Alpha Course. It's sort of a Christianity 101 that came out of this really fired-up church in London, and it breaks the whole thing down with real basic questions like 'Who is Jesus?' and 'What does his death have to do with me?' You know, that kind of thing."

"Ah," the group seemed to say. These Charleston folks were all Anglophiles, he reckoned. In fact, this church was formed thanks to the support of England when Carolina was still a British colony. He hadn't intended to hit a sweet spot. He felt the Spirit again and kept on.

"Anyhow, I would want to make sure everyone here knew the Gospel, first. That Christ died for their sins and that all they have to do is repent and believe in order to be saved. I want them to have a genuine faith and be able to tell others about it. I want it to burn in their guts and in their hearts." He patted his thick, dark brow. "That's my prayer for Church of the Good Shepherd, and that would be my prayer for wherever I was called."

Heyward sat back in his chair and narrowed his eyes. The naval commander nodded sternly, and two of the other lawyers gave one another a knowing look.

Too heavy-handed? Roy wondered. *Heck, this was the crux of the call on his life, and he wasn't going to soft-pedal it.*

"Go on, Reverend Summerall," Ms. B. said. She wasn't smiling, but her eyes were warm, and they caught the soft lights of a brass chandelier overhead.

So he did. "As for the young families, well, they need support. I'm a single parent, and it's tough out there. And while I was only married four years before my wife passed, I know married life can be a challenge. I guess I'd try to teach about how to stick by one another and how to raise kids up in the knowledge and love of the Lord." He pointed his thick finger on the table. "Kids can come to church here, but it's what's happening at home that counts the most. Our homes need to be a haven of blessing and peace. I'd drive that message home right from the pulpit, and I'd try to find ways to support couples as they create these havens of ministry for each other, for their children, and for the needy people the Lord puts in their path."

One of the attorneys raised his eyebrows, and Roy didn't know whether to take the look as astonishment or consideration.

Roy took a sip of his iced tea. It wasn't as sweet as the kind that Jean Lee or Mama made, but his mouth was dry and it was refreshing. Plus, Ms. B. had put fresh mint in there and that made all the difference. He was a little warm so he took off his jacket, and the thick gold bracelet Jean Lee had bought for him at the Costco in Florence tumbled down from beneath his black shirt. He shrugged his shoulders and thought of one of the sermon critiques he'd received from Dr. von Hasellyn in seminary. The critique had blasted his grammar—specifically the improper use of prepositions at the end of sentences, but it had concluded on an up-note with a list of positives about the shape and meaning of his teaching, and a truism Roy thought of quite often: *One must be oneself.* And so he smiled at his chain and thought of the gap between his teeth and kept on.

"You know the people at my home church are hurting right now. Ellijay is an old mill town that's been dying a slow death ever since the textile industry uprooted itself when I was a kid, and this new recession is going to set us back even further. I know Charleston has the two extremes in terms of wealth and poverty. And I can't think of a better mission, beyond teaching the Gospel to the ones that are already coming through our doors, than to reach out to those on the other side of the community's spectrum."

Ms. B. dabbed at the corner of her mouth with a linen napkin, and the commander rubbed at his eye patch. It must get awfully itchy beneath there, Roy thought. He sent up a prayer of comfort for the man.

"Well,"—Heyward bit the inside of his cheek—"who do you mean exactly?"

Roy thought of his descent into the Holy City from the

highway ramp. He had noticed the crumbling houses by the highway and the face of a coal-skinned man staring him down from a doorway as he turned toward the tip of the peninsula.

"How about those folks who live on the other side of the crosstown? Are we directly ministering to them?"

Heyward looked to Ms. B.

"A little," she said. "Some of our parishioners volunteer at the homeless shelter. But we could do more."

The group took a collective sigh, and after a few moments Heyward stood up straight and stuck out his hand. "I think we know where you're coming from, Reverend Summerall." He reached across the table and waited for Roy to stand and meet his shake. "We've got two more gentlemen to interview, and we'll let you know where we stand."

Roy stood and smiled and accepted the firm grasp of each member of the St. Michael's search committee. Had he dodged this bullet? He supposed so. And he hadn't had to do anything but speak from his heart. Simple enough.

He grabbed his navy blue blazer, and just as he was about to turn and head for the car, Ms. B. grabbed his elbow. "Now for the sanctuary tour!" He looked down at her expectant face and nodded in defeat, and the lady led him out of the meeting room and closed the door with a gentle click; he could almost feel the committee observing his exit.

Ms. B. led him with all the authority of a colonial historian around the outside of the white, stately sanctuary that had been built in the traditional 18th-century English design, with a grand four-columned portico and a massively proportioned 186-foot-high steeple, a clock tower, bells, and a seven-foot-wide weathervane. According to Ms. B., the building had survived hurricanes, wars, fires, an earthquake, and even a cyclone with very little damage. Roy was impressed (in the way you would be impressed by a tour of Mount Vernon or the Biltmore House) by the beauty and history of the oldest church building in Charleston, not to mention one of the finest colonial churches in America.

The inside of the sanctuary was just as he remembered, dark with a three-sided second-story gallery and cedar box-pews that were available for purchase by the local gentry when the church first opened its doors in 1761. Ms. B. pointed out (as his Aunt Elfrieda had done when he was a boy) pew number 43 in the north center aisle where both George Washington (in 1791) and General Robert E. Lee (in 1861) had worshipped. And then there was the colossal handcrafted pulpit, near the foot of the south central aisle that had a heavy-looking top supported by two Corinthian columns. The top was adorned with a large, hand-carved pineapple that Ms. B. reminded him was the symbol for welcome and hospitality.

"How did that not topple over in the earthquake?" He pointed to the precarious top that would surely crush a priest's head in mid-sermon if another quake hit on a Sunday morning.

Ms. B. had just finished telling him about the church roof and how it had not only been melted down to make bullets in the war against the British, but the earthquake of 1886 had ripped it right off.

"God's grace, I suppose." She nodded and then took him down the center aisle to the Victorian-style altar where the Tiffany stained-glass window designed after Raphael's own painting of St. Michael served as the focal point.

Roy took a good look at the Almighty's archangel—the warrior, Michael, who in this image was casting out the dragon, Lucifer. At first glance, Michael looked a little too angelic for Roy's taste with his pink skirt and his gold scarf billowing in the breeze. But all you had to do was take one good look at his biceps and the way he gripped the spear and pointed it at the weaselly beast to know this angel was not to be messed with. Raphael got it and so did Roy.

When the bells started to ring, Ms. B. clapped her hands and looked up at him. "Oh! They must be practicing. You must see the bells." She brought her little clasped hands toward her pointed chin. "They are one of the city's most beloved treasures, Father Summerall. Do you know what they've been through?"

Roy had to give Ms. B. an A in the enthusiasm department. He'd never seen a person love a building so much. He tugged at his collar. "Well, they went through two wars, right? But I'm ashamed to say I don't know the specifics, Ms. B."

"Let me tell you then." Her little gray eyes gleamed, and she puffed up her chest like a mourning dove. "The bells were imported from England in 1764. During the Revolutionary War, they were seized by the British as a war prize and shipped back across the Atlantic. Then a sympathetic London merchant—a good Samaritan of sorts—recognized them. And he purchased them and returned them to Charleston."

Roy nodded. It was a pretty amazing story. He watched Ms. B. raise her finger, and he figured there must be more to it.

"Then," she said, "during the Civil War, the bells were sent to Columbia, but they cracked in a terrible fire there in 1865." She looked at the marble floor beneath her and shook her head, then she lifted it back up in triumph and met his gaze.

"So then what happened?" Roy couldn't help but be hooked now.

"Well," she said, "the metal fragments were salvaged from the fire and sent to England to be recast in their original molds and rehung. And that's what you're hearing right now."

"Wow," he said. "There's a resilient spirit here, I have to say."

"That's it," she said, and she pointed him down the aisle toward the front doors of the church. "But a church isn't really the building, is it?" She squeezed his elbows with a strength she didn't look like she could muster. "No matter how impressive the history."

"Not to me, Ms. B.," he said.

"Well, what would you say it is, Father Summerall?"

He smiled and gently patted her tiny bird-like shoulder. "The people."

After a tour of the clock tower where he met a few of the ringers as they trickled in, Ms. B. led him through the bookstore, bought him a Coca-Cola, and bid him farewell on the slate sidewalk of Broad Street.

It was a hot summer day, like the kind he remembered when he was a kid, with the syrupy smell of wisteria and overripe loquats hanging in the air. He was feeling a little nostalgic after Ms. B.'s history lesson and he decided to amble down Meeting Street, hanging a right on Lamboll as he made his way to the corner of Little Lamboll and Legare where Aunt Elfrieda's former home still stood, a pale yellow single house with a little lean despite the obviously major renovation job. He couldn't get over the polished quality of the place—the crisp new driveway with bricks and oyster shells where he used to park his bike, and the piazza with freshly painted floorboards that looked too new to creak or buckle or gather love bugs in its cracks the way they did when he was a child. How many times did he and Chick have to navigate those floorboards as they crept out in the afternoon to run their paper routes during Aunt Elfrieda's daily snooze?

When a peppy woman suddenly popped out of the front door and hopped in her BMW convertible with Pennsylvania plates, he thought he could hear Aunt Elfrieda rolling over in her grave on the edge of Magnolia Cemetery. She didn't hold people "from off" in the highest of regard, and the only thing that unnerved her more than two adolescents from a podunk midlands town she had to house and attempt to cultivate for three months out of every year was an ostentatious Yankee.

Roy chuckled, took a sip of his warm, flat Coca-Cola, then headed up Legare toward Tradd, where he recalled the rough-and-tumble Campbell boys at #27, who threw water balloons at cars from behind their gates, and then the three pretty girls at #18, who he could hear giggling and talking as they picked loquats and lounged beneath the shade of their grandmother's leafy tree. He remembered watching one of them slip over the rail at The Battery when he was on his paper route one hot afternoon. She'd sliced her shin pretty bad on the oyster banks, and he and Chick pulled her up, took off their shirts, and fastened them around her leg with some rubber bands to stop the bleeding. The girl's grandmother was so thankful when Roy delivered her home in the front basket of his bike that she gave them a bucket of ripe loquats that he and Chick delivered to Aunt Elfrieda, who said, "Well, good." She clucked her tongue. "I suppose Cozy Brumley will spread the word that you two aren't complete hooligans like those Campbell boys." She put her hand on her hip and smiled thinly. "Stay out of trouble this week, and I'll make you a chocolate chess pie for Sunday dinner." (He felt guilty for thinking it, but he couldn't say he missed Aunt Elfrieda.)

After a good stroll down Tradd, he headed back over to St. Michael's alley where he hopped in his pickup and pulled out onto Meeting Street. He pulled over for a moment in front of the sweetgrass basket weavers on the corner to utter a prayer.

When he looked up a few moments later, he heard one lone bell sound, and he examined the grand portico of St. Michael's where he pictured Ms. B. pointing out yet another reason why the sanctuary had become a city landmark.

"Robert Ripley came through here in the 1930s," she'd said. "He took a look at this intersection, with St. Michael's here on the southeast corner, City Hall on the northeast corner, the County Courthouse on the northwest corner, and the

Federal Court on the southwest corner, and he coined a new phrase—"

"The Four Corners of Law," a carriage tour guide had stolen her thunder as he pulled the reins of his horse in front of the portico and pointed out the corners of the intersection—"municipal law, state law, federal law," and then right to Roy's white collar, "God's law, all represented on four corners. Now isn't that something?" The tourists had smiled at Roy and waved. Ms. B. had waved back.

Now as Roy bade farewell to the church before pulling back out onto Meeting Street, one of the large wooden side doors of the sanctuary opened, and a striking woman in a long white vestment stepped out gently and loosened her red, wavy hair from its twist. She was the tallest, most lovely woman he thought he had ever seen, and as she rounded the opposite corner, the sun illuminating her hair before she disappeared behind the huge, white edifice, he thought of Mr. Jackson who had held on longer than anyone expected, passing only ten days ago.

The second time Roy and Rose had delivered the Eucharist, the man had pulled Roy close and said: "I saw some angels pacing around here last night. They looked a lot like us only taller, much taller. And more pleasing to the eye."

That night after returning from the Holy City, Mama and Rose asked him a million questions with an excitement he tried to deflate. Later he fell asleep in an uncomfortable position in Rose's lavender Barbie bed where he had been reading her *Heidi* for the third time that summer.

With his neck at an awkward angle against the Formica headboard, he dreamed in a way he had only dreamed a few times before. In his sleep, he was flying over an urban area. He eventually recognized the steeples and slate roofs as belonging to Charleston, and he was headed from upper Meeting Street toward the High Battery. The bells were ringing loudly, but there was no movement in the streets. It was dusk or maybe sunrise, and while the lights were turning on in the windows North of Broad, the neighborhoods surrounding the St. Michael's parish were completely still. When he looked down to the windows below, he saw only a blackness, as if everyone had vacated the neighborhood. The darkened panes of the tall windows reminded him of loneliness. And suddenly he found himself standing on a third-floor piazza where he peered into one of the large black rectangles only to find the shadowy figures of a man and a woman, fully dressed and lying down on top of a made-up bed. They were still as stones.

He woke up in a cold sweat with a sharp crick in his neck. Rose was facing him, curled up like a satisfied kitten, her lids gently shut, her little chest lifting up and down with each slow, deep breath. She looked like a smaller version of Jean Lee, the Peter Rabbit bedside lamp shining on her black hair, her red lips like a doll's as if they were painted on her face. He stood, leaned over to kiss her, and turned off the light as he rubbed his neck, then turned toward his room.

After dressing for bed, he couldn't shake the dream and he sat on his den sofa for several hours, wide-eyed, picturing those long dark rectangles. Roy Summerall had a feeling he was stiff-necked in more than just the literal sense, but he didn't dare let his mind or his heart acknowledge the sign that the dream seemed to be.

Chapter 4

Della pulled into her dirt driveway in the twenty-year-old Honda Prelude her father had given her eighteen years ago on the eve of her high school graduation. She lived with her husband and six-year-old daughter on the corner of Radcliffe and Smith Street, three blocks north of Calhoun in the middle of the peninsula. Their place was the first floor of a rundown single house that leaned a good fifteen degrees to the left from the wear and tear of more than one hundred years of heat, humidity, and flooding from the storms that hit at high tide. The house was painted a reddish purple that must have been a fun and flamboyant choice in the late '70s. But today the place looked like a rotting plum, the dirty strips of paint peeling off in jagged strips across the clapboards. They had bought the house with Della's portion of Nana's inheritance in hopes that the neighborhood was on its way up, but eight years later she could still spot the guy who sold pot to the college kids on the northwest corner leaning against the Cash and Carry convenience store with a bulge beneath the left side of his baggy jean jacket. Though she had never seen a gun, she'd heard a shot more than once in the middle of the night, echoing down the corridors of the disheveled streets of her neighborhood.

When she opened the front door, the steamy air from her un-air-conditioned house smothered her. The thermometer read ninety-four degrees just inside the door. She took a slow, hot breath as if she was pacing herself for an hour in a sauna. A muffled laughter came from behind the closed door of her daughter's room—the one place in the house where they had broken down and bought a window unit.

Peter and their daughter, Cozy, were playing a game. They had built a tent by draping a fitted sheet over her bedposts, and they had brought in food from the kitchen and sticks from the backyard to simulate a campout. Peter, dressed in a black t-shirt and jeans, was wearing the gorilla mask he had bought last Halloween. He was crouched in a make-believe bush behind the bed. Cozy squealed with joy. She loved the element of surprise—that the gorilla was hiding, waiting to lurch at her when the moment was right.

Through the window, Della saw the heap of scrap metal and the blowtorch and face mask, resting on top of a headless shrimp who squatted slightly, his front legs playing a copper cello. Peter was a metal sculptor whose medium was crunched copper treated with a blue-green patina. The shrimp had sort of become his signature—he had a knack for giving each crustacean a kind of human personality just in the way they curled their tails or positioned their bulbous eyes. But he'd been known to sculpt frogs, sea turtles, palmetto bugs, mosquitoes, pelicans, and herons as well. In fact, the South Carolina Aquarium had two of his creations greeting every tourist who walked in the door, a six-foot toad holding a lantern and a ten-foot sea turtle in mid-flap with what almost seemed like a smile at the bottom of his round, prehistoric skull.

You could also see his work at the Children's Museum in Columbia and the Governor's School for the Arts in Greenville, and even farther afoot at the Bronx Botanical Gardens and the Peabody School of Education at Vanderbilt University. But commissions had been dwindling for the last couple of years. Art and books were the last expenses folks with means considered incurring when the economy turned south, and Peter and Della were both feeling the beginning of the recession. They had always scraped by more or less with the meager advances from Della's publisher, her occasional teaching gigs, the periodic grants, and the sculpture commissions that seemed to always materialize just when it looked like one of them would have to forsake their craft and start selling insurance or something.

Della had suffered a change of heart about their lifestyle ever since Cozy was born. A woman can change when she has a child. Her whole notion of what life ought to be can be altered. The conventions and lifestyles she used to disdain become the ones she desires most. Oh, she wanted so much for her child. Not necessarily material things, but the rudimentary basics of a decent life—safety, comfort, a clean home, and a solid education. A woman can read one of those desperate-housewife novels like *Revolutionary Road* and say, "What is April's problem? Does she know how lucky she is to have a husband who brings home a decent paycheck? What's so evil about being a salesman? What's so philosophically wrong about making a steady living?" Della, even though she would have never predicted it, was becoming one of those women.

Then Peter lunged at Cozy, and she gave the requisite shriek before he hurled her onto the bed, where she bounced and shouted with delight. He lifted his mask so that the gorilla was face-up on the top of his head. "How's Lish?"

Della turned the window unit up a notch and said over its mechanical drone, "They're trying to stop the contractions. We may have to go over to Legare Street and stay with the kids."

"Why not bring them here?" Peter lifted his large hands, palms up as if he was making an offering.

Della was frequently taken aback by how fantastic-looking Peter was: six-five and absolutely chiseled with broad shoulders, a sharp jaw line, a tan that accentuated it all, and pale green eyes beneath dark, bushy brows. Once at a cocktail party, a flamboyant art dealer told her she'd married an Adonis. She'd blushed and nodded. But what was even stranger than Peter's Greek-god looks and their ability to stun her, even now after eight years of marriage, was her lack of desire for him—her utter lack of passion or attraction in the face of the undisputable fact that he was an eyeful.

Della could hardly stand the deep hum of the air-conditioning unit, but she walked over to it and let the cool air lift her hair off of her neck as her daughter came over and leaned in toward her. She rubbed Cozy's back as the sun caught the golden crown of her small, perfectly round head. Della turned back to her husband. "We can't bring them here because we have one bathroom and it's under construction, and our backyard is full of shards of metal and electrical wires and rusted nails."

Cozy turned to him and added, "And we don't have Rosetta who cooks and cleans, right, Mama?" Della nodded.

"All right. All right." Peter held out the heel of his right hand. "Don't you two gang up on me now."

Cozy grabbed the gorilla mask and put it on. "Me hungry," she called, then she ran back toward her mother, and all Della could see was a blur of black fur, tan little arms, and the flap of a yellow sun dress with white polka dots.

"I've got you, Mama!"

Then Della picked her up and spun her around and gently dropped her on the unmade bed where she kissed each pad of her soft little fingers. She gazed into her daughter's deep brown eyes. Next week she'd start first grade at The Pinckney School for Girls, an old and prestigious single-gender school where Della, her mother, and her grandmother had graduated from. The public schools in their district were failing, and while they tried for the magnet option, they received the last number in the lottery; they never even had the opportunity to test. The Pinckney School tuition far exceeded their budget, so Della had put her writing career on hold to serve as a full-time teacher in the middle school in order to make the payments.

"How would you like to spend the night with Andrew and Mary Jane?" Cozy's eyes widened and she tossed back her golden hair and sat up straight. She cupped Della's face in her delicate hands. "I would love it, Mama!"

Peter wrapped his arms around his wife and child. "Let's get packing, girls."

At the hospital Della spotted Drew in the hall, chuckling with two other doctors. They looked familiar and the closer she got, she realized that they were the infectious-disease fellows who rented the carriage house at 18 Legare. There was Rob, a stubby guy who started an herb garden beside Nana's old loquat tree, and Melanie, a towering blonde who could almost give Anne a run for her money in the height department.

"Things must not be too bad." Anne intercepted Della in the hallway. She nodded toward Drew and took a deep breath. "I mean, if he has time to shoot the breeze with his apprentices."

"True." Della reached up high and put her arm around her cousin.

Drew seemed to catch them out of the corner of his eye. He stepped away from the fellows and turned to them.

"What's the status, Dr. Sublime?" Della said.

"We're in a 'wait and see' mode." He raked his fingers through the thick curls of his salt-and-pepper hair. "They're going to stop the contractions long enough to do an amnio to gauge lung development. If it comes back strong, we may deliver as early as tomorrow night."

"How's she doing?" Anne whispered.

"A little anxious." He rubbed his stubbled chin. "You know how she likes to plan these things out."

"We know." Della grinned. "Maybe her next column in the paper can be 'Expect the Unexpected.'" They all chuckled, then she knocked his elbow. "Peter and I would be happy to stay with the kids tonight, and we'll get the nursery ready."

"That would be great, Della." Drew rubbed his hands together. "Rosetta's with them now, and she'll be back first thing in the morning to take over."

Della nodded and looked at the closed door where someone had scrawled the name Sutton with a black Sharpie.

"Can we see her?" Anne said.

When they entered, Lish sat up without fully taking her eye away from the baby's heartbeat on the screen. She was sitting on top of the bed in a hospital gown, and Della noticed—as she did every time she saw Lish's bare leg—the scar that ran down her shin from the time she fell off The Battery rail and into the oyster beds.

Della and Anne took their places on either side of her

bed and Lish patted both of their knees as if to reassure them. "Drew give you the update?"

"Yeah," Anne said.

"Not exactly what I had planned for today." She turned to Della. "You okay to keep the kids?"

"We're already packed and Cozy's about to do back-flips, she's so excited."

Lish reached for a notebook on her bedside table and handed it to Della. "Here's the bedtime routine and the church schedule as well as their day camp that starts on Monday in case I'm here for a while. Rosetta will get their outfits ready."

Della showed the thorough notes to Anne. "Are you believing this?"

Anne turned to Lish. "Put me to work, too, okay?"

Lish scanned her list.

"I've got tomorrow off." Anne gently pulled the notebook from Lish's hands. "Give me an assignment."

She quickly read the list and handed it back to Lish. "I'll make the trip to Babies R Us. How hard can it be to pick out a car seat and a few pacifiers?"

"You don't mind?" Lish leaned forward and picked at her plastic hospital bracelet.

Anne nodded emphatically. "I can handle it. And I can do more. So call me when you think of something else."

"Thank you." Lish smiled. "I will."

Della bit at the tip of her index finger. "So what are the doctors saying?"

Lish tucked a strand of her thick brown hair behind her

ears. "If all goes well for forty-eight hours, then I can go back home and stay on bed rest for a week or so. If the contractions continue, they may have to deliver early."

"Well, you're in good hands," Drew said as he entered the room. He stood at the foot of the bed and crossed his arms. "As far as I can tell, our biggest problem is settling on a name."

"Here." Lish handed them a list of girl names. "We've picked the boy name, but we don't have one for a girl, and I just heard the nurse slip and say, 'How's *she* doing?' when she examined the monitor."

"Oh." Anne took the list and glanced at the names. "You just want an opinion?"

Lish nodded. "Yeah, I'm just not drawn to one the way I usually am." Della looked over Anne's shoulder. The list read:

Emma Louise Sutton

Jane Brumley Sutton

Cecilia Elizabeth Sutton

"They're all beautiful," Anne said. She handed the list to Della. "I couldn't possibly choose—"

"Cecilia." Della nodded her pointed chin once. "How can you not hear that name and think of dancing at two a.m. at the frat house of your choice with Paul Simon's voice belting through the speakers, 'Ce-cil-ia, you're breaking my heart. You're shaking my confidence lately . . .' It's a completely upbeat name."

They all chuckled and Della leaned in to peck her cousin on the forehead. She sensed Lish's desire to have more time to flesh out her list. "We'll take care of everything!" Della took Anne by the arm. "Just rest and tell Cecilia to take a chill pill."

On the way to the parking garage, a voice called behind them, "Della? Anne? Y'all wait up!"

Della turned to see a tall, thin, bearded man in tortoiseshell glasses and a white physician's coat walking toward them. "I think that's Todd," Anne said. "Todd Jervey." He pressed a button on his key chain and one of those snappy little BMW convertibles lit up and beeped behind him.

"Della!" He waved his arm and slowed down when he got close. He stretched up and kissed Anne on the cheek and then leaned down and did the same to Della before stepping back to take her in. Della was in the thin gauzy white sundress she wore when the temperatures topped ninety degrees and her gold designer gladiator sandals care of Jodie at Goodwill.

"You look fantastic," he said. "How are you?"

"All right," she said. "Welcome back to town."

"It's great to see you." He grinned and shook his head as if he was trying to fight off a chill. "I've read your novels. All four of them. My mom sent me the first one, then I tracked down the others."

"Good for you," she said. "You're in a very small fan club. You and twenty of my closest family and friends."

"Not true," Anne interrupted. "She's been nominated for an award, and thousands of people have read her books."

He grimaced. "Your voice is unmistakable, and your descriptions are dead on. They really bring me back to Charleston. Kind of make me homesick, even."

Della grinned. "Well, good. We need a decent shrink around here."

"So you've settled down. Have a child, right? I read that in your bio."

"Yes. A daughter. Cozy."

He smiled. "After your grandmother. Nice."

Della scanned his left hand. No ring in sight. He always wanted a boatload of kids.

"You?"

"Nah," he said. "This medical research thing has kind of sucked me in for the last ten years." He bit his lip, then readjusted his glasses. "So what are you two doing here?"

"Lish is in the hospital."

"What for?" The lines formed above his fair forehead.

"She's pregnant, and she started going into labor this morning."

"How far along is she?"

"Seven and a half months," Della said.

"Mmm." He narrowed his eyes and nodded. "I'll check in on her."

"No need," Della said. "Drew's got her surrounded by the top doctors in the state. But she'd probably love to see you."

He smiled and nodded. He leaned forward as if to give a good-bye kiss, but he stopped and took a side step toward the elevator.

"Well," he said, "I'm glad I ran into you two. It's been too long."

Anne grinned and waved. "Take care, Todd."

Della nodded and before she decided on what to say, he had turned and was heading toward the exit.

❧

A sharp rush of brisk central air-conditioning greeted Della and her family as they walked through the front door of 18 Legare Street and into the grand home of her childhood. It must have cost a fortune to cool down the three-story home with its tall ceilings and wide, creaky floorboards.

Installing the central air system was only the beginning of the changes the Suttons had made to the place, and Della couldn't help but be taken aback when she discovered each new attempt to modernize the old home in which her grandmother had raised her. Last year it was the skylights and the hot tub on the third floor, this year it was the refurbished kitchen—the large stainless steel appliances and dark granite countertops whose surface shimmered like asphalt on a hot day.

The oven and fridge seemed like they took up too much room in the long, narrow galley kitchen where Della still pictured Nana beating eggs, frying fish, and canning loquats by the screened door. How many hours had Della and her cousins harvested the Japanese plums for Nana? They'd play a game called "Who's he gonna be?" where they'd twist the stem and count how many times it took for the loquat to release. With each twist, they ran down the alphabet. A, B, C, D and wherever it finally popped, that would be the initial of the man they would marry. Once they thought of a boy's name with the corresponding letter, they'd paint a vivid word picture of a beautiful life with the lucky boy that involved many children, a swimming pool, a trampoline, and some sort of red or white sports car.

Della sniffed the air and closed her eyes. The one thing the Doctors Sublime couldn't get rid of was the unmistakable smell of the old house. Despite the refinished floors and the fresh coats of paint and the new furniture their pricey decorator had brought in, the house still retained the faint scent of mothballs, mud, mold, and what Della could only describe as history. Age. Like Papa's pillow on a hot summer day when she snuck up to his nook on the third floor and lay down to read a book before he came home from work.

Now she took a look at Peter and Cozy and had to laugh. They looked like three hobos from significantly north of Broad Street with their mismatched bags full of clothes and toiletries: a dusty tennis bag meant to hold a racket and balls, an old canvas boat bag of Nana's that she used to pack Della's girlhood picnics in, a My Little Pony backpack, and soaps and toothbrushes in plastic Food Lion sacks.

Cozy opened wide her arms. "Wow, it feels good in here."

Andrew ran out from the kitchen with his face smattered with ketchup. He nearly toppled Cozy over with his big hug.

"You're spending the night!" he said.

"Yep," she said, grinning back at her parents. "I am."

After Rosetta served a delicious Cuban meal of seasoned pork tenderloin, fried plantains, beans and rice, and a tomato salad, Peter took the kids in the back garden where they played hide-and-seek, climbed the loquat tree, ate the plums, and had a pit-spitting contest just like Della and her cousins had done when she was a child. Then she hosed them off one by one on the piazza and sent them to their rooms to put on their pajamas. Mary Jane was having a hard time going to sleep after Peter read them *Paddington at the Circus* three times. When Della went to tuck her in, she whispered, "My mommy lies down with me sometimes."

Della grinned and wiped a strand of hair out of her mouth. "Does she?" she said. Then she lay down beside her and pulled the little girl close, relishing the crisp, clean, all-cotton sheets and the cool air from the vent above as it quietly poured down on them.

An hour later Peter gently woke her by massaging her shoulders. Her neck was stiff from squeezing into Mary Jane's little bed. When she stepped into the lighted hallway, she saw that he had two small fluted cordial glasses of Madeira on the window sill he must have poured from the wet bar in Drew and Lish's bedroom. He offered her one and nodded toward the third-floor piazza.

Della rubbed her eyes, accepted the glass, and followed him up another flight of stairs onto the porch where she leaned against the rail, surveying the familiar rooftops, chimneys, and gardens of their neighbors. The after-dinner drink was thick and sweet and tasted almost chilled from the cool house. "Mmm," she said. "Thanks."

He came quietly up behind her and softly kissed her earlobe. His stubble tickled her neck. "Wanna fool around?"

In the historic beauty and new creature comforts of her grandmother's refurbished home, Della felt the contrast between her life and her cousin's. On paper she had what she thought she always wanted—an artist husband who loved her and their child. A truly great man. An inspired and devoted one. And a magnificent-looking guy to boot.

But this eking out a life as a writer and an artist was getting to her. She thought it would be romantic and meaningful and exhilarating, but it had actually turned out to be the opposite. She'd be thirty-eight in a few weeks, and she wanted more children, a house full. And she envisioned her brood attending above-average schools and dwelling in a clean, safe place with bedrooms like Mary Jane's—coordinated sheets and pillows, Madame Alexander dolls, and that crisp, cool air preserving it all.

Peter, on the other hand, could live this way forever. He loved their life. Their home. The way they made their little living. From the moment she met him, he had not changed. *She* was the one who had. She didn't set out to, but it happened, and she couldn't reverse it now.

When he pecked her shoulder, she froze. He let out a deep breath and cleared his throat. "Worried about your cousin?"

She fibbed with a nod and a "Mmm-hmm." Della used to tell Peter exactly what was on her mind. He used to be her confidante until she started to wish for another life for her daughter. Now what was on her mind would wound him. Maybe for good. And she couldn't stop the resentment or the fantasy of what could have been had she not broken things off with Todd to pursue a degree in creative writing. Had she not eyed Peter a year later across the Wells Gallery at the "art walk" while he shook hands with art collectors and posed for pictures for the style section of the paper beneath the beak of one of his enormous copper pelicans. She'd walked right up to the artist and flashed the broad smile that had cost Nana and Papa thousands of dollars at the orthodontist's to perfect. "Hi," she'd said, cocking her head. She had eyed the pelican and then the tall handsome man. "Stupefying."

He had grinned and given her a quick once-over. "Now that's an adjective you don't hear every day."

Now as she felt her husband's warm breath on the back of her neck, she couldn't help but think of Todd Jervey, stable and as predictable as the tide. And could she admit it to herself? Yes, financially sound. Why was that such a bad thing to want? It was wrong to think this way. It was dangerous. But it was difficult to stop.

Peter squeezed her shoulders. "Drew called while you were napping and said everything looks good. He predicts she'll be home tomorrow." He gently kissed the crown of her head and stepped back. Della looked out into the night. She was sure there were stars to be seen above, but the humidity kept the sky a kind of thick ash gray.

"I woke up," a groggy little voice behind them called.

Della turned to see Mary Jane standing at the top of the stairs in her monogrammed nightgown, rubbing her eyes.

"Coming," Della handed Peter her half-empty glass and walked Mary Jane down to the second floor, relieved to curl up beside the little girl beneath her pink striped sheets for the rest of the night.

Chapter 5

Dr. Alisha Brumley Sutton

The monitor felt tight on Lish's belly. Her doctor suspected a mild placental abruption, a slight pulling away of the placenta from the uterine wall. Sometimes blood could pool in the space between the two and that was why she was bleeding yesterday. It had been almost twenty-four hours and the baby's heart seemed steady and strong, but Lish could still feel her abdomen tighten every few minutes, and she had a localized pain on her left side that must be where the abruption was.

She knew enough about obstetrics from her medical school rounds on these very halls to know that if the baby continued to look strong and the pain subsided, she'd be able to go home late today. If the baby fluctuated too much, she'd be here until the fetus was strong enough to be delivered. Of course, if the child went into distress, that was another story altogether. One she didn't want to think about.

The steady sound of the baby's heart rate as it moved across the monitor reassured her. Each child she had delivered had been strong and fully developed—able to hold on her chest, skin to skin, and nurse within minutes after their routine deliveries. In fact, she had practiced her Kegels so much with Mary Jane that she didn't even need an episiotomy. What a relief. She was jogging around The Battery within two weeks after that delivery, and she could wear her size four jeans by the end of the first month. As a pediatrician who had treated many sick babies, Lish understood how fortunate she was. With both Andrew and Mary Jane, her milk production was plentiful and her children seemed to thrive from the moment they left the womb.

Stronger than the contractions and the localized pain was the emptiness in her belly. With the exception of half of the last third of Mary Jane's waffle, she hadn't eaten anything in almost twenty-four hours.

"Darla," she said to the nurse who came in every hour or so to check the monitor and take her temperature. Lish made it a point to learn the nurse's names right away. They are the ones who are on the ground doing most of the work; they are the ones who are around to save your life at a moment's notice. "I'm starving."

Darla gently cocked her head to the side. "You know you can't eat anything until we've observed the baby for twenty-four hours." She checked her watch. "You've got six to go."

"I know," she said. "But how about a Popsicle or even a few ice chips? I'm afraid I'm going to be sick if I don't eat."

Darla grinned and nodded as she walked toward the door. "Let me see what I can do."

Drew should have been back by now. He had to make his rounds and check in at the lab, but he had traded schedules with Dr. Willis so he could be off for the next day or so. Where was he?

Lish was thankful that Anne had offered to go to Babies R Us. She knew Della was aching for another child, and she didn't want to have to send her to the baby store. But if the baby came this week, Lish needed a car seat to take her home in. Mary Jane had had reflux so bad, she must have spit up on their old car seat a hundred times. The cover was worn out from all of the washing, and Drew insisted they throw the whole contraption away when she graduated from the infant seat into a forward-facing one.

Now Lish closed her eyes for a moment. She was thankful for Della too. Della could handle the kids. She could handle them for a year if she had to. Poor Della. She was the brightest and most capable person Lish knew, but she and Peter had trouble making ends meet.

She checked the "labor and delivery" file Drew had brought from home. In it was the article she wrote for the paper about the importance of creating a birth plan. She had delivered both Andrew and Mary Jane without any anesthesia, and she'd avoided the usual grogginess and headaches some of her friends had complained of postpartum. With each birth, Drew had had one of the nurses immediately snap a photo of the mother-child bonding after he rested the baby on her chest, and these photos were framed and hung in their bedroom as a reminder of the momentous occasion.

Besides her husband, she didn't want any family in the room for several hours. They would both need time to connect with their beloved little one. Then, by the afternoon, the rest of the family could meet the new arrival. First her children, who would be anxious to meet their younger sibling. She wanted Drew to take a photo of their faces at their first sight of the baby; she would put them in a frame she found at Metropolitan Deluxe that read "my family" and hang them in the nursery as well. Now she read the closing of her column,

> While I've encouraged you to go with the flow during much of your pregnancy, in this particular case, you can't plan or be specific enough. If you don't have a vision, you will be frustrated and powerless, and your first hours with your baby will be decided by well-meaning medical professionals and family members who may not fully realize what this initial bonding means to you and your child.

Lish put down the article and looked out the window as an extremely sharp contraction began. She heard the baby's heart rate slow on the monitor and there was suddenly a warm pool beneath her. Blood. She pressed the call button for the nurse just as Darla walked in with a Popsicle on a tray.

Darla dropped the tray and ran out in the hall. "She's

hemorrhaging!" she called down the hall to the nurse's station.

Lish's eyes clouded over, but she could still hear Darla and the others.

"Fetal distress," Darla said, her voice trembling as two other nurses crowded around and checked the vitals.

"Get Dr. Hunter and Dr. Chang," another said. "This is going to be a crash C-section, and it may have to happen right here."

"We're with you, Dr. Sutton. You're going to be okay." Lish nodded, but she couldn't open her eyes. The sound of her baby's heart in distress was deafening. She heard a nurse paging Drew, and she was aware of a cool swab being rubbed across the lower half of her belly. The last thing she felt was the tube scraping the back of her throat as the anesthesiologist shoved it in.

Chapter 6

DELLA

Della stared at a wall of car seats in aisle five of Babies R Us in a North Charleston strip mall. Anne had called earlier that morning and said that she had to stand in for a Sunday bell ringer who was sick.

"No problem. I'll go," she'd said to Anne, though in truth she feared she might have an out-and-out breakdown winding her way through the aisles of a baby superstore where all those infants would beam at her from the boxes of merchandise, their Gerber-like faces so perfectly round and sweet.

Della decided not to read about all the bells and whistles of the car seats. She simply bought the most expensive one, which was beige and remarkably bulky, grabbed three different brands of pacifiers, and headed to the checkout without looking one single baby picture (or real-life baby, for that matter) in the eye.

Peter had given his blessing for her to make a morning of it, so she stopped in Starbucks to crank out a chapter of her novel. The manuscript was due to her editor in four short months, and once she started teaching full time, she would rarely have more than thirty minutes in one sitting to work on it. She bought a venti Frappuccino and settled in with her laptop.

It was kind of nice to be off the peninsula on a Sunday. The bells, which Anne described as jubilant, always made Della sad somehow. Sometimes she would even put on Peter's old Walkman with the Springsteen cassette (stuck there for years) to tune them out. Last week she'd spent a good twenty minutes stomping around the house, screaming, "Born in the U-S-A!" until Cozy walked by with her fingers in her ears.

Just then the guy behind the counter called out, "Is there a Della Limehouse here?" She saw him clutching the receiver to his chest. She blushed, partly because now all of Starbucks knew that she didn't own a cell phone, and partly because she'd told the man at the counter that her name was Felicia when she ordered her coffee. (She was trying to get into her character's mind, so she thought she'd try her name out.) She ran over, grabbed the receiver, and pressed her finger to her other ear to block out the jazz music. "Hello?"

"Something's gone wrong with Lish and the baby," Peter said from the other end of the line.

"What do you mean?"

"Drew's beeper went off a few minutes ago. He ran to the car saying something about a crash Caesarian."

Della could hear Andrew and Cozy squealing in the

background. "How many weeks is she?" Peter whispered.
"Thirty-two."

Now Della let out a deep breath and her stomach turned. She looked out to her car where the fancy car seat rested against her passenger side window.

"I haven't said anything to the kids," he said. "You better call Anne and get to the hospital."

When Della arrived on the fifth floor of MUSC, she found Anne sitting next to Phil Rainey, the head priest from St. Michael's. They were both still in their vestments, holding hands in a prayer. Drew was in full scrubs and a face mask, pacing in front of the doors of the operating room.

Anne looked up and reached out to grab Della's hand. "They won't let him in."

Della looked at Father Rainey, who used to come to her nana's house and deliver Communion when Papa was having a tough Sunday. He had given Della her first Communion when she was ten, and he had married her and Peter on a a mild October evening nine years ago. His wife had even sewn Della a tiny, beautiful embroidered day gown when Cozy was born. That had meant a lot to Della. It was something Nana would have done had she been alive. She christened Cozy in it after much pressure from Anne, Lish, and Peter's folks. Then she tucked the gown away in the bottom drawer of an old bureau, and she had not looked at it (or darkened the door of church) since. She had nothing against this kind, older man. But she did have a bone or two to pick with God.

Lish and Drew were active at the old affluent church of her childhood, and Anne, who inherited Nana's unwavering faith, had served for a decade as a bell ringer. It wasn't so much that Della blamed God for her current struggles. (She knew she only had herself to blame for her adult life.) But she did have a lot of questions about her childhood.

In the same way that she couldn't bear to go to Babies R Us, she couldn't bear St. Michael's. She could hardly abide the sight of the beautiful, well-heeled families dressed to the nines and kissing one another on the cheek during the passing of the Peace. Those families seemed whole and content in a way that broke Della's heart each time she laid eyes on one. She'd had to turn away from Lish's kitchen window this very morning, even as a couple of these families strolled by on their way to worship as the bells rang out their forlorn toll.

She knew she was both self-centered and pitiful. And she didn't actually want the church families to be ugly and unhealthy, did she? No, no, no. These were the thoughts that ricocheted around the walls of her mind on Sunday mornings as the bells pealed from the top of the steeple in her exceedingly North of Broad life.

"Good to see you, Della," Father Rainey said. "I'm sorry it's under these uncertain circumstances."

Della nodded. "Me too." She took a seat by Anne and tapped her foot so fast and furious that Anne had to reach out, hold her knee, and ask, "Trying to wear a hole through the floor?"

Finally, Lish's young obstetrician walked out of the operating room and lifted his mask above the Phish do-rag he had over his head. There was a swath of dried blood on the back side of his forearm, a spot he must have missed when he scrubbed his arms moments before. Della dragged Anne over toward Drew. The doctor nodded and put his hand firmly on Drew's shoulder. "Congratulations, Dr. Sutton. You have a new daughter and one hell of a survivor for a wife."

Drew let out a deep breath and nodded. He looked to Della and Anne and grinned. "Thanks be to God!" Anne clapped her hands together and bounced on the balls of her long feet. Father Rainey shuffled over and patted Drew on the back. "Yes, indeed, son!"

"The pediatrician will meet with you shortly, Dr. Sutton," the OB said. "The baby is well, but she'll need to be on a breathing machine for the next few days or so until her lungs are fully developed. And we're going to have to observe Lish for several hours. She should be waking up any time now."

Drew stepped back as the baby came out in a warming crib with thin tubes of oxygen stuffed in each tiny nostril. Her pinkish hands were no larger than a benniseed wafer, but they were perfect as a doll baby's, each with their own little rounded fingernail. Anne gasped and Della swallowed her tears and cheered as two nurses rolled the infant down the hall toward the Neonatal Intensive Care Unit. Drew walked alongside his infant daughter, his hand clutching the edge of the plastic bassinet.

Della and Anne stood in the hallway as they rolled Lish over to the observation room. Her cousin looked as though she was sound asleep, but her fingers were swollen and her ankles and toes were streaked with dried blood. The two women took a seat by her gurney at the nurse's invitation and sat for several minutes watching Lish's chest rise and fall.

Della should call Peter to let him know that he was an uncle again, but she couldn't move. Neither she nor Anne could stop studying their closest relative and friend who never failed to possess a kind of valor and grace no matter how gritty or challenging the circumstances. While Della and Lish were born a few months apart and (with the exception of grad school) they had always lived less than a ten-minute walk from one another, Della felt as though they inhabited different universes. One of the hardest things about her current struggles was that they were further evidence of what she had suspected since they were adolescents planning their lives beneath Nana's loquat tree—that Lish's life was on a trajectory out of her reach. One she was either incapable of possessing or simply didn't deserve, for a reason she couldn't or wouldn't ever know.

"What are you thinking about, Del?" Della turned and realized Anne must have been studying her for a while.

Anne reached out and touched her clenched hands.

Della had written some love poems for a therapist friend who was trying to woo a woman in his yoga class, and he'd given her five free sessions where she'd tried to work out some of what was stirring inside of her. "You know the other day my therapist made me tell him about what it was like for me when your daddy died."

Anne shook her head. Della and Lish were in second grade and Anne was only in first when Nana delivered the news during a summer swimming lesson at the YMCA.

"I can't remember a worse day." Anne bit her lip.

Della nodded. "I remember the visitation, standing in front of the casket. When Nana and Papa entered the room, I ran over and asked Nana to hold me. I wanted to be in her arms so bad."

"She was everyone's favorite," Anne said.

"Yeah." Della felt her ears redden and she tapped the floor again. "Anyway, Lish pulled me back and held me tight. 'Let Nana and Papa see their son,' she'd said. 'You stand here with me.'"

Della looked back at Anne, who was studying her intently. She bit the inside of her cheek and added, "Lish was always showing me things like that—even on the day her own father was being laid to rest—things that I'd never thought of. You know?"

Anne gave Della a sympathetic smile. She just didn't seem to have the anger or grief that surrounded Della like the humidity itself, thick and stifling. Anne must have made peace with it a long time ago, Della thought.

Yes, Lish had her act together, Della thought, gazing at her cousin with a kind of wonder and curiosity. Lish's eyes fluttered for a moment before she settled back into her sleep. Her cousin was bright, conscientious, organized, and coolheaded. She knew when to keep her mouth shut, what to keep personal. While Della was usually complaining about her marriage, Lish rarely uttered a negative word about

Drew. Was this discretion or satisfaction? Either way, it created a sense of otherworldliness about their marriage. As if it existed on a plane far beyond Della's.

The truth was, Lish had had her choice of men to marry, and she'd chosen wisely. And now her body had produced three perfect, beautiful children, to whom she was dedicated to loving, teaching, wiping, and feeding day after day.

Della thought back to the sad day of her uncle's funeral. She had wept more than her cousins combined, and Lish had comforted her, giving her a piece of Dentyne from Nana's purse.

Drew came in just as Lish began to stir. He rubbed her hair out of her eyes and softly kissed her forehead.

"You did good, baby," he said. She opened her eyes and rubbed her neck. "How's the baby?"

"In the NICU, breathing strong. She looks like a Cecilia to me." Della smiled. She was earnestly happy for Lish and relieved that all had gone well. She loved her cousin deeply despite her inability to stop comparing their lives. She would do anything for her, and she knew the reverse was true.

"Hey, Anne, Del." Lish looked their way. "I didn't see y'all there."

Anne stood and walked over to her sister's side. "We're here." She took her hand. "Congratulations."

Peter jumped on the Doctors Sublimes' king-size bed with Andrew, Cozy, and Mary Jane while Della hung the freshly washed and pressed infant day gowns in the nursery. After Della stuffed the last little diaper into the drawer of the changing table, she walked into the master bedroom and leaned against the bedpost. "I've got good news, gang! Mama and the baby are coming home this afternoon."

"Hooray!" Mary Jane said, falling into Peter's brawny arms. He lifted her upside down and spun her around the room, chanting, "Mama's coming home! Mama's coming home!" before he gently tossed her in the center of the bed. Andrew cheered, then took off his pajama top and made the crude sound Peter taught him where you cup your hand in the opposite underarm and pump like a chicken.

"Stop that, man." Peter chuckled. "Your mama won't invite us back if she sees you doing that. Let's save that for when you're with the guys—your dad or me."

Andrew allowed himself two more pumps, his two flaw-less rows of white, square teeth showing in his full-out laugh.

"Why'd you teach him that, Daddy?" Cozy's hands were on her hips.

He pinched her rosy cheek. "Ah, come on, pumpkin. Loosen up and maybe I'll show you how."

Cozy looked at her mama and rolled her eyes. "Boys," she said.

Peter packed the clothes as Della bathed Mary Jane and Andrew and put them in matching blue gingham sailor outfits—a dress for her and a shorts suit for him. She settled them in front of an episode of *Curious George* while she continued to straighten up the house.

This used to be Della's home, the one she shared with Nana and Papa. She had spent every summer here until the ninth grade when Nana persuaded her father to let her move in for good and attend The Pinckney School for Girls. Her father agreed; nothing could persuade him more than education, and he was weary of getting in the middle of the fights between Della and her stepmother.

As for her mother, she was off living the life of a beatnik. Had been ever since Della was in grade school. She secured small fellowships and grants to teach or write all over the world, but the truth was, she spent much of her time experimenting with drugs and searching for a mate who could fund her habits.

When Della's mother was a senior in high school, she'd spent a year in Paris studying art history before attending college. A group of Columbia University students took her to an inn on the Left Bank that later became known as the Beat Hotel, a haven for young American expatriate painters, writers, and musicians. She met Allen Ginsberg and William Burroughs that year, and she became particularly close to a young beat, Gregory Corso, who helped get her first poem published in *City Lights*. She was now known as one of the few female voices of the time. It sounded implausible, a Charleston girl from South of Broad on the tail end of the beatnik movement. But that's precisely where she ended up thanks to a little bit of talent, a perspective that was particularly gothic, a spirit of adventure, and something that one could argue is even more potent than the aforementioned three: physical beauty. Not unlike Della, Kate Brumley knew how to woo a man. She was in control of her feminine charms, and she never hesitated to use them to her advantage.

Now Della stood at the large doorway that led to the front piazza and garden. She could recall waiting there for hours for her mother to come for a visit, every six months or so. She'd count raindrops, count cars, count mosquitoes and how many she slapped at as they attempted to nip her arms and legs. Usually her mother was several hours late. Occasionally she didn't show at all and would phone in the evening, having missed her train or flight. "I can't make it right now," she'd tell Nana. "Could Della come up to see me in a few weeks?"

Then Nana would bring two cups of hot tea—Della's was mostly milk and sugar—out to the front piazza and place them on the wicker side table. She'd pat a place next to her on the joggling board and hand her granddaughter the china cup with the blue Italian scenes of a bridge and a woman carrying a basket of fruit on her hip.

"Something's come up with your mama," Nana would say. The little girl would sip the milky sweetness and relax into her grandmother's soft side. Nana would gently scratch her arms and shoulders with the ends of her fingernails until Della had little goose bumps on each. They'd stay this way for an hour or so, Nana rubbing her back as Della listened to the cacophony of city sounds—cars, trucks, mourning doves, crickets, and restless fenced-in dogs that seemed to chant, "She's not coming. She's not coming this time."

She understood now that Nana was her true mother. She was there for her, and she offered a stable, genteel way of life. Nana provided everything for Della. Love, presence, even financial support. She knew her dad had sent a check each month, but Nana paid the tuition at The Pinckney School, purchased the fine wardrobe, procured the piano lessons, and hosted the grand debutant ball at Hibernian Hall for all three of her granddaughters.

Della wished she could rest against Nana on the joggling board right now. She had more ahead of her than she could manage—a full-time teaching job and a December deadline for her fifth novel, and she was only eighty pages in. The summer was racing by, and she knew there wouldn't be any time to write when school started. Worst of all, her heart ached for a second child. She'd be thirty-eight next month, and she knew her biological clock was ticking. She and Peter had talked about having two or three, but how? How could they manage and provide?

Suddenly, Mary Jane shrieked and then wailed. Della ran in to see if she was all right.

"Andrew pushed me!" Mary Jane's cheeks were red and streaked with tears.

Della looked to Cozy, who nodded to confirm the accusation.

Then Peter ran in. He heard the cry all the way from the driveway where he was tying Cozy's bicycle to the top of the old Prelude.

"C'mon, Andrew." Peter led him by the shoulders. "Into your room for a while."

As the Doctors Sublime drove up in their Volvo SUV, Della waved and called to the children. She saw Lish in the back seat retying a bow on the sleeve of Baby Cecilia's day gown. Drew helped Lish out of the car and gently pulled the baby carrier out. Lish turned toward the piazza and took a deep breath as Andrew and Mary Jane ran toward her. Cozy stayed on the piazza and leaned into Della, who rubbed her back up and down until the goose bumps formed.

"Hold me, Mommy!" Mary Jane lifted up her pudgy little arms to Lish.

"No," Drew said. "Mommy can't hold you for a few weeks, remember? She has a boo-boo that will get worse if she lifts anything heavier than the baby."

Lish bent down and pulled Mary Jane to her and then Andrew. "It's good to be home. I missed you both so much."

Della could see tears brimming in Lish's eyes as she took each of her children by the hand and walked toward her. "How can I ever thank you, Del?"

"Don't even." Della flapped her hand and kissed Lish on the cheek. "Rosetta's got lunch ready, and we're going to get on out of your hair. Call me when you need a break, and we'll come pick up the two little monsters." She pulled back and looked Lish in the eye. "Enjoy this sweet homecoming."

Lish nodded and Peter shook Drew's hand before Cozy jumped on his back and they walked toward the car. As Della waited for Peter to check the bicycle, she watched Lish and Drew and their three beautiful children go into their magnificent home, where the table was set and a warm quiche

Lorraine and fresh fruit salad were waiting for them on the dining room table.

When they drove up to their home on Radcliffe Street, Della noticed the weeds in the front yard and an unruly vine that had wound its way around the railing of the front steps. A random cat with a severed left ear lounged in the sun at the edge of the rusted screen door. The feline stretched when she saw them pull into the drive and then she slunk down the stairs and beneath the house as they headed toward the door.

Inside it was sweltering hot. Like walking through pudding or the inside of a giant oven. They all ran to Cozy's room, slammed the door, and turned on the window unit.

"Isn't it great to be home?" Peter grinned, reached for Della's waist, and pulled her close.

"Yeah!" Cozy shouted as she fell back on the graying sheets of her bed. They were Della's childhood sheets. The ones she slept on when she was growing up on Legare Street. When Nana died, she'd intercepted a bag of bedding and towels Lish was packing up for Goodwill. "We could use those," she'd said.

Now Della literally bit her tongue as a lump formed in the back of her throat. She wanted to grab her child and run back to Legare Street.

She stepped away from Peter.

"Well," he said. "That shrimp trio is waiting on me out there. I guess I better get back to work."

Cozy tugged on her mother's shorts. "Tell me a Binklemeyer story, Mama." The Binklemeyers were a family

Cozy and Della made up a few months ago. They lived in a town called Someplace Small, and Peachy and the kids, Burl and Bernice, walked to the ice cream store and rode their bikes down winding dirt roads that led to the forest where the occasional bobcat and even wild boar had been spotted. Burl had a lisp that made him a little self-conscious, and Bernice, while younger, often acted like a know-it-all (which grated on Burl's nerves). But all in all they got along pretty well and went on all sorts of jaunts that ranged from the amusing to the harrowing, including a romp through the peach fields, a climb up the local water tower, and a swing on a rope their grandfather had tied to the biggest tree on the edge of a nearby river.

Della nodded, and they curled up together and began their ritual. Cozy started with a line ripe with conflict like "The Day Bernice Lost Her Two-Dollar Bill" and Della worked to fill in a story with Cozy guiding her with a giggle or a "No, no, no. I was imagining something like *this* . . ." The story could go on for nights, and if it was really good they would act it out after it was finished.

"Okay," Della said, pulling her close. "Start us off."

Cozy nuzzled up to Della and nestled in the crook of her neck. She twirled her mother's thin golden hair around her fingers and squinted her eyes. "Burl Finds a Stray Pup in the Woods."

Della chuckled. Cozy had been wanting a real live pet ever since Andrew got a Boykin Spaniel last Christmas. She had sat and rubbed the dog's back whenever she'd had a chance over the last few days, and Della had overheard her asking Andrew if she could take him home for a spend-the-night party.

"I don't think so," she'd interceded. "You'll get a pet one of these days."

"When?"

"When we have a bigger yard."

Cozy had put her hands on her lips and shaken her head. Well, if she couldn't have her pet now, she'd give it to Burl and Bernice and watch them enjoy him in their safe and peachy world.

"Okay," Della said. "Burl was looking for insects for his science project one autumn afternoon when he heard a whimper coming from the bottom of the hollowed-out tree beyond the gates of the peach field."

Cozy inhaled and tried to suppress a grin. She gave a nod as if to say, "Go on."

That night when the house cooled down and Cozy fell asleep, Della sat at the kitchen table writing. After a dinner of frozen pizza, Peter had gone back out to work on his sculpture. They'd already spent the commission money on materials, a new set of tires for the Prelude, and three school uniforms for Cozy. Della could hear the faint scratching sound of a palmetto bug scurrying across the clean dishes that were drying on the rack in the sink, and she wondered how much it would cost to get someone to come and spray.

Her novel was based on a true story about a Latin teacher who was stalked by one of her students, a teenage boy who lived around the corner from her. The woman sympathized with the strange and lonely young boy who was a social outcast, but she would soon learn that he was more dangerous than she had ever suspected.

This manuscript was Della's second attempt to write a plot-driven novel with commercial appeal in hopes of "earning out" her advance and actually receiving a steady royalty check. She had tried this with the last novel when she wrote about a Charleston socialite who had an affair with her husband's ne'er-do-well brother, but it became more about the ne'er-do-well and his guilt over betraying his brother. His introspection and his childhood flashbacks took over the book, and *Publishers Weekly* had called it "character-driven and contemplative." Words her MFA professors would have applauded but not exactly the ones that stimulate sales. She knew reviews like that might seal her fate as a mid-list author, unable to make a living writing.

Peter came in shirtless with his blue jeans resting low on his hips. Sweat dripped down his neck and across his strapping chest. If she described his body in one of her books, her editor would say, "Yeah, right. Make him more realistic." He had worked construction to put himself through the Savannah School of Art and Design, and he couldn't have a better build.

He poured two glasses of water from the kitchen sink and put one by her side. The pipes were warm and the heat from the water clouded the tops of the glasses.

"Hey," he said. "How's it coming?"

She hit Save and looked up. "Okay."

He cleared his throat and talked through his plan to transport the shrimp he was sculpting for a new seafood restaurant in Asheville. They should be ready by the end of next week. His father, a shrimp boat captain in McClellanville, had an extra-long flatbed truck and was usually happy to lend it with enough advance notice.

"The café's going to put me up at the Grove Park Inn." He softly clinked his glass against hers. "I was thinking maybe we could drop Cozy off at your dad's and make a night of it. Maybe go out to dinner, come back to the room, enjoy the mountain air, and see if the five-star springs on the bed work."

She shifted in her seat. The back of her thighs stuck to the Formica chair. She shrugged her shoulder. "I don't know. We'll see."

He took a look around the kitchen, wiped his forehead, and turned back to her. He watched her for several seconds as she typed.

"What's going on, Del?" He leaned in close and she could see a drop of sweat dripping off of his nose. "You've been pouting most of the summer. And you haven't exactly warmed up to me more than once or twice."

She exhaled and shook her head. What should she tell him? Either the truth or another lie to get him off her back for a moment.

"I don't know," she said. Their windows were open, and she heard two men shouting in the distance; she couldn't tell if there was anger or elation in their tone.

"I think you do know." He stroked her hand. His fingers

were long and his joints were prominent. There were pro-truding veins on the tops of his tanned hands that worked their way all the way up to his elbow. "You need to talk to me, baby."

She rested her pointed chin in her small hand.

"Is it the job? It's going to be too tough to teach full time and make your deadlines?" He looked around the kitchen. "I don't see why we can't move out to Mount Pleasant to a decent public school district. Or even homeschool. My buddy, Tyler, and his wife are doing that, and their kids are already speaking Spanish fluently. They know all about ancient history, and they take these terrific field trips to archaeological digs and stuff."

"No." She scowled, then swallowed hard. "If we're going to give Cozy a decent shot, she needs an exceptional education. Plus, she's an only child. Only child plus home-school equals socially awkward adult. We've got to do right by her."

"We're doing right by her," he said. "We're here for her. We love her. What's more important than that?"

Della shook her head.

"Okay," he said. "Let's brainstorm. See if we can figure something else out."

"I want another baby." She pursed her lips. "How are we gonna figure *that* out?"

He drummed his fingers on the table. "Della, things are tough right now. We're in a recession. Let's give it a year or two and see where we are."

"I'm running out of time, Peter."

"You're thirty-seven."

"I'll be thirty-eight in August. The risks go up significantly after that. Also, it's not as easy to get pregnant."

"We'll give it a good try." He leaned in to her and nuzzled his damp forehead against hers. He smelled like salt and burnt copper. "Hey, I've got a thought. We can start practicing now."

She pulled away and looked at the computer screen. Then she started to type again as a car with a booming bass zoomed by.

He downed his water and cleared his throat. He watched her until she looked up at him.

"Things have been tough for too long now, and I'm tired of waiting," she said. "I feel like we've been waiting for our careers to take off since before we were married. I've stepped out and taken on work that wasn't ideal. What about you? I think we need to face reality."

Peter pulled on his fingers until his knuckles popped. "Della, I love what I do." He rubbed his bleary eyes and met her gaze. "You used to love what I do too. What do you suggest? That I start selling insurance? That I get my real estate license? That I try to get into med school with an art degree? What?"

"Insurance," she said and her voice gained strength. "Insurance would be dandy, Peter. My friend Michelle's husband sells life insurance, and they live in a roach-free house with air conditioning. They go to the dentist every six months. They take vacations where you buy a new bathing suit and get on an airplane. They drive a car that was bought after 1989!"

She took a sip of her water and slammed it down. "They have three children who they clothe and feed and educate. They have a backyard in a decent neighborhood, and a jungle gym and a dog and a membership to a swimming pool!"

He turned away from her and looked out at the window. "So *that's* what you want now?"

She held her head in her hands and didn't answer. *Yes*, she thought. *That's what I want now*. The nuclear family life. Heck, it could be at the end of a cul-de-sac in a cookie-cutter suburb. She didn't care! Why had she abhorred that life before? What a holier-than-thou artiste she had been before she had a child! How shortsighted. How unrealistic. How lacking in pragmatism. She was sick of it. Her life. Sick to death of it.

When she thought he was asleep, she climbed into bed next to him.

He was in his boxers, face up in the bed. It was too hot for sheets.

She lay quietly down and rolled away on her side.

"I don't understand it, Della." His face was outlined by the street light pouring through the open window and the sheen of perspiration.

"Mmm?" She turned back slightly.

He propped his head on his elbow. "Why it is that you suddenly act as though you've been gypped?"

He waited for her to respond, but she didn't. He sat up, slid on his shorts and flip-flops, and walked steadily out of the room and onto the back porch, where he flicked on the light and started to work again.

She closed her eyes, too tired to call him back, too confused to deny his supposition. She heard the scrape of his crimper against the copper. It formed a steady rhythm above the sounds of the city on a humid summer night—a horn in the distance, muffled voices, the click of a rusty bicycle chain as a stranger pedaled along the crumbling sidewalk.

In minutes, she was asleep.

Chapter 7

Roy

The week after his St. Michael's interview, Roy settled back into his routine of visiting the sick and jobless, setting up for the weekly Alpha program, studying the lectionary, and writing Sunday's sermon. His mama and Candy Mills were in charge of the upcoming Vacation Bible School, and they kept Rose busy making decorations and learning songs and the accompanying motions. They chose the "Beach Party" theme by Lifeway, and Roy had come home at night to a performance of his mama and daughter singing, dancing, and hanging ten on pretend surfboards as they sang, *"Beach party, surfing the Word . . . Beach party, surfing the Word . . . Beach party surfing the W-o-r-d of God."*

He had to chuckle watching Mama in her flip-flop heels and cut-off miniskirt as she squeezed her nose and did the twist all the way to the ground with Little Rose cheering, "Go Granny!"

Roy wouldn't describe his mama as a devout believer, but she sure did get credit for simply rolling up her sleeves and going to work. He had her and his daddy (who'd died of a heart attack less than a year after Jean Lee) to thank for getting him to church in the first place.

Back when Roy was a kid, his folks didn't have the purest of intentions when they decided to switch their membership from Robbins Neck Baptist to Church of the Good Shepherd. Truth was, his daddy had taken a liking to partaking of a cold Budweiser every now and then, after a buddy handed him an iced can at the Darlington Speedway one hot afternoon. And Roy Sr. decided he couldn't reconcile his Saturday refreshment with his Sunday worship at the Baptist church, so his wife suggested Good Shepherd where the Junior League ladies she greatly admired attended. Then off the family went with great hopes of climbing the social ladder while Roy Sr. savored an occasional Bud on a steamy day without remorse.

No, their reason for switching denominations wasn't all that pure, but God works all things for the good of those who love him, who have been called according to his purpose. It turned out there weren't many young folks at the Episcopal church, so Roy and Chick were called on to serve as acolytes nearly every Sunday. There was an older spinster lady, Miss Ruby Nuttall, who spent months preparing them for confirmation when they were in middle school. How often Roy recalled sitting in Miss Ruby's parlor on Wednesday afternoons breaking down the Nicene Creed line by line. Miss Ruby always had a large dish of caramel cubes within reach, and he still remembered relishing them one by one during her theological discourses about the Trinity, the virgin birth, and most thrilling of all, the resurrection, as a kind of warm and ardent yearning began to form in Roy's heart.

The following spring when Bishop Boatwright came and laid hands on his head during the confirmation cere-mony, Roy felt the presence of God. There was no denying it. It was like a surging heat that was both forceful and tran-quil. It started around the crown of his head and worked its way down to his fingertips and toes until his whole body felt like it had fallen asleep. It was all he could do to stop from laughing out loud when the heat concentrated itself in his gut, and he knew as soon as he felt the fire that he'd been called out of one world and into another.

He kept on being a regular boy during this sanctification process. He played football, delivered papers, listened to Garth Brooks, and got into the typical late-night trouble. But he also joined the Fellowship of Christian Athletes and became the president of the Clemson chapter by his junior year in college. And Jean Lee, whom he started dating the first day of high school—well, she went right along down this path with her hand in his as if there was no other plan for her life. She had gone to dental hygiene school in Anderson to be near Roy dur-ing college, and they married their senior year before he took a job as a youth minister in Winnsboro to get a feel for what it was like to work in a church day in and day out. After a few years, he was recommend for seminary, and they headed to Pittsburgh for a three-year program at Trinity. Jean Lee con-ceived during his third and final year in seminary, and a few months into the pregnancy she pulled aside the dentist she was working for to show him a funny white spot on her tongue that turned out to be cancerous. The doctors delivered Rosebud as early as they could and quickly began chemo, but Jean Lee was gone before their baby girl was three months old.

Roy didn't understand why some things turned out the way they did. He hated what had happened to his wife and his daddy, too, but he knew God wasn't out to punish him. It was just sin. Plain and simple. Roy traced its origins back to the garden where darkness and death first entered human lives—not by God's choice, but by man's. And Roy took heart in the fact that sin, whose end result is always death, was only half the story of this life. The narrative didn't simply end there like so many people thought. There was a whole 'nother half and it involved a way out of this predicament. Roy clung to Miss Ruby's belief that a provision had been made, a sacrifice on behalf of all mankind, and that's what buoyed him when his little girl climbed up in his lap and said, "Why did Mama die?"

It was just a week after Roy's trip to Charleston that he received the call.

"Reverend here," Roy announced into the receiver after Skeeter ran in and pointed to the flashing red light on line one.

"Hello, Roy, this is Heyward Rutledge from St. Michael's."

"Hi there, Heyward. Hope you're well."

"Well," Heyward said. "I don't want to beat around the bush, sir." Roy thought he could hear a pen being tapped on something on the other end of the line. He sat back and then Heyward said, "I'll be a whole lot better if you accept the call to be the rector of St. Michael's."

The words hit Roy like a blindside chop block. One might have thought with the dream about flying and the red-headed angel that this was the most obvious of conclusions, but Roy didn't see it coming.

After he caught his breath, he closed his eyes tight and said, "I didn't think it would be me."

"Well, it is," Heyward said. "It is you. The search committee, the vestry, the bishop—we're all in agreement on this."

How? he thought. *How in the world could y'all think this was a good fit?*

"I—" It was one of those rare moments when he didn't know what to say next.

"Well, don't sound so surprised, Roy. The timing is right—the bishop had us listen to a few of your sermons he had on tape, and I tell you, we believe you're just the man we need to light a fire under us."

Roy's ears popped when he swallowed. He heard Candy's husband, Milton Mills, cranking the lawn mower in the front yard of the church, and he could see Skeeter's shadow in the hall outside of the door as she listened in.

"Heyward, I've got to be honest." (He might have prayed right then and there, but he didn't.) "I didn't expect to be chosen, and I'm not sure it's right for me or for you."

There was a long pause and Roy imagined Heyward

looking up at the search committee, who it suddenly occurred to him might be gathered around the phone at this moment.

"Well, I don't know what would make you say that," the man on the other line said. "You're what we need. It was unanimous from our end. Why don't you . . ." There was a pause. "Take a little time and call me back in a few days?"

"All right," Roy said. "I appreciate you giving me some time. I'll call you by the end of the week."

"Okay, Roy," Heyward said. He cleared his throat, and Roy imagined the search committee leaning in to hear more. "We'll be looking forward to your call."

That night Chick and his wife, Nikki, came over with a pound of barbecue, some slaw, and a nice-sized watermelon. Ms. B. had called Roy's home, prematurely, to discuss the installation date and the reception to follow, and Mama was so excited about the idea of him moving to Charleston that she was just about to bust. She had looked up the church online and taken a gander at the three-story rectory on Meeting Street, and she and Rosebud were already picturing themselves there, sipping tea on an upper piazza.

"St. Michael's Church." Chick put a wad of tobacco behind his bottom lip and shook his head. They were on Roy's front porch watching Chick's twin boys, Buster and Jake, play monkey-in-the middle with Rose. The boys were only a year older, but they were nearly a foot taller than the little girl, and her effort to jump up and grab the football as they tossed it back and forth was all but hopeless.

"Supper's ready!" Mama called from the kitchen window. Jake softly threw the ball at Rose so she could win a round, and then Buster tousled her hair and led her toward the back door with his hand on her little shoulder.

"Yeah," Roy said after the kids slammed the screened door. "Isn't this the strangest turn of events?"

Chick nodded and turned to Roy. "Whatcha goin' do?"

"I want to say no," Roy said. "Every fiber of my being is saying, 'No, those folks are going to eat you alive, Bub.'"

"Yep," Chick said. He spit a little tobacco juice off the front porch just behind the azalea bushes. "I can't argue with you there, brother."

The only person who dreaded Charleston more than Roy was Chick. He had taken that Neanderthal comment to heart back when they were kids, not to mention all the times Aunt Elfrieda told them that their grandpa (her brother) had married beneath himself and that the ill effects of that would go on for generations unless they wised up, gave up an interest in farming and football and speed racing, and started acting and talking like civilized gentlemen. In fact, Heyward's old words and Aunt Elfrieda's were almost like a decree over Chick, and he seemed almost determined to live into them. His efforts to become the consummate small-town Bubba were made with a kind of fervor and bitter surrender that Roy didn't fully understand.

After a knee injury in college that gave Chick no prospects where pro football was concerned, he bought a patch of land off of Welsh Neck Road to farm and promptly let himself go. He gained a good forty pounds, stopped wearing shirts with sleeves, and had a profound disdain for anything that seemed remotely cultivated (and this somehow included church). When their mama offered to pay for voice lessons for Buster, who, according to the music teacher at school, seemed to have perfect pitch, Chick refused. "No. That's not for a boy like him," Roy remembered him saying one afternoon while his mama made a teary plea. "There's only one place outside of school for my kids—that's the speedway or the ball field."

"Boys, come on in and eat," their mama now called. She looked them both over and added: "And Chick, spit that tobacco out right now. You won't be able to partake of that when we visit your brother in Charleston."

Roy reached out and firmly patted her elbow. "Mama, please stop talking like this thing is a done deal."

She looked away from him, toward the little two-lane highway that ran in front of his house. An eighteen-wheeler was barreling by. It had a large bumper sticker on the back that read, "God is good. All the time!"

"All right," his mama murmured. She turned her back to him, the sparkles from her bright-green eye shadow catching the porch light. "But you and I need to talk."

Their leisurely supper ended with Nikki's homemade banana pudding and a history lesson about Charleston by Rose, whose granny had been pumping her with all sorts of romantic musings about horse-drawn carriages and hoop skirts and a row of houses as colorful as a rainbow. Chick and his brood headed home, and Roy tucked Rose in bed after a little more *Heidi* and the Lord's Prayer. As he turned out the light, she sat up and said, "Daddy?"

"Yeah, sweet pea?"

"Don't you want to move to a pretty city?"

He leaned his head against the door frame and crossed his arms. "You know, I'm not sure, Rose."

Her little head was tilted and he could see her pointing upward with her index finger. "Well, you said that God would show you, and now they've called and said they want you."

He nodded and the verse "You have hidden these things from the wise" blipped across his mind before he could fully tune it out.

"Maybe it's that simple, but somehow I don't think so. I need to feel like I'm supposed to go, sweet pea." He came over and sat next to her in the dark. "It would be a big change for you and me both. The kind of change that would affect our lives for years to come, and if I don't feel an absolute confirmation, I can't go."

She lay back down and he tucked the sheet and comforter around her side so that she looked like a burrito or a caterpillar in its cocoon.

"What's a confirmation?"

"A yes."

She nodded her head and lay back down. "Good night, Daddy."

When he went back downstairs, Donny, Mama's new husband, was watching the news in the den while Mama unloaded the dishwasher.

Roy poured himself a cup of coffee and sat down at the

kitchen table. He took off his collar and noticed he'd gotten a smudge of banana pudding on the top edge.

Mama sat down next to him, picked up the collar, and said, "I'll take this home and see if I can get that out with a little OxiClean."

He smiled at her. "Thanks, Mama."

She took a deep breath and reached over to grab his wrist. "You need to do something for me, all right?"

He nodded as the steam from his coffee rose between them.

"You need to be open to this call. I'm not saying this because Charleston is a nice place and the church is downright gorgeous, not to mention the rectory." She squeezed his wrist, and he looked up into her dark brown eyes. "I'm saying this because sometimes we're asked to go where we don't want to go. And it's not to torture us. It's because there's something there that only we can do. There's a purpose and a plan, and if we don't follow, we miss the blessing. And so does everybody else who we were supposed to love on."

He sat back and looked at her. She looked wise beneath the caked-on makeup and the orange tanning parlor glow. In her eyes there was a light, and it wasn't just the reflection of the overhead lamp.

"I underestimate you, Mama."

She smiled and the crow's-feet on the edge of her eyes that she worked so hard to conceal were more lovely than he could ever describe. She patted his hand, then took a sip of her own coffee. "We only get one go-around. Better make it count."

She stood, flipped the switch on the coffeepot, grabbed her gold purse, and said, "Sometimes you don't even need to pray or think on something. Sometimes you just know." She grabbed her keys, gave him a nod, and said, "Let's go, hon," to Donny who turned off the TV, took her hand, and nodded to Roy as they walked out the door.

Early the next morning Roy heard little footsteps and then the sound of Rose plinking on the piano. The summer sun was already blazing through the blinds, leaving a pattern of slats across his bed. He sat up and felt the same heat in his gut as the day the bishop placed hands on his head when he was twelve.

He took several slow breaths as the heat surged through his body, and he knew the Spirit was upon him.

"Show me the way, Lord," he whispered. "Show me, and I will follow."

When the tingling subsided, he went on down the stairs where Rose was playing one of the VBS tunes on the piano.

"Listen, Daddy," she said.

"All right." He sat down at the bench beside her and put his arm around her. Then they slowly belted out the song together. *"Beach party, surfing the Word . . . Beach party surfing the Word . . . Beach party surfing the W-o-r-d of God!"*

Chapter 8

LISH

In the living room sat four bouquets full of pink and yellow roses and hydrangeas and lilies. Anne and Della had left the tags in their plastic pitchforks, and now Lish opened each one and smiled. One was from the downtown neighborhood association, another from her editor at *The Post and Courier*, one from the infectious disease department at MUSC, and another from her book club. On the love seat, there was a pile of gifts to open, presents in slick white wrapping paper and pink satin ribbons with thick ecru tags bearing the names of the local children's boutiques.

She opened a gift from her next-door neighbor, a pale pink day gown with white smocking, and immediately wrote a thank-you note. Her stationary and stamps were set up on the side table along with her address books from the children's school, St. Michael's Church, the Country Club of Charleston, and the South of Broad Neighborhood Association. However, on the front of this envelope she wrote, "By hand" in the bottom left corner.

After she sealed the envelope, she opened the next box, a Charleston Bonnet from a friend in her Pilates class. As she reached for the next gift, her incision began to burn, and she leaned back and stuffed one of her grandmother's small satin throw pillows beneath her head.

The living room was the only room where she had not changed the furniture. Nana had left it to her—the pale yellow and orange Oriental rug, the yellow-and-white-striped Chippendale sofa, and the antique chairs Nana had bought during a trip to London. This was the room where she and Anne sat eating fruit salad and deviled eggs after their father's funeral when she was eight. She could still remember her mother and Nana standing at the doorway greeting the guests. Nana had put baby's breath and daisies in her granddaughters' hair, and Anne kept leaning over into Lish's bun to smell the flowers.

The year her father died, Lish became adept at holding back tears when need be. There were enough of those around Nana's home with Della's mother postponing her annual visit or their grandfather, Papa Brumley, shuffling home from his music store each day where he'd walk silently up to his room, put on a record (more often than not, the art songs of Richard Strauss), and stare blankly into the trees behind the piazza until the wetness formed in the corners of his eyes.

But despite the grief, Lish loved the summers she and Anne spent in Charleston with their grandparents. 18 Legare was a haven, especially compared to the naval bases they were dragged to after their mother married a naval commander the year after their daddy's death. Lish and Anne had moved three times in three years during their adolescence: Millington, Tennessee; Earle, New Jersey; Fort Worth, Texas. Each time, Lish missed the crumbling beauty and the thick, humid air of Charleston. The smell of low tide and sitting on the piazza listening to the rain hiss when it hit the ground, or the sound of the blind man who pounded the street with the top end of his merchandise, calling, "Brooms for sale," until someone came out of a house and bought one. Best of all were Nana's stories, which she told them at night in the hammock of the upstairs piazza. She'd recount tales about their father and Della's mother and the mischief they got into as children. And she'd tell them about their great-great-great grandfather, an old Charleston merchant for whom the street they lived on was named.

Now Lish could hear the tap of her husband's fingers on the laptop in the upstairs office across from their bedroom. He was e-mailing photos of the baby to their family and friends and uploading a new album onto his Facebook page.

As she rose from the love seat, she was astonished by the ache in her gut, and she shuffled to the kitchen to take another Tylenol with Codeine. Once the pill took the edge off, she slowly stepped up the stairs and made the rounds, retucking the children in for the night. She listened, as always, to Mary Jane's breathing. The toddler suffered from asthma from time to time, and Lish couldn't rest until she bent over and heard her breathe deeply in and out several times. Of course,

Andrew's room was a disaster—Tinkertoys, broken crayons, and plastic bowling pins were strewn across his floor. Della and Peter were great with the kids, but they left a mess here and there. She checked the Pull-up he still wore at night, kissed his forehead, and tucked the covers in around his sides. He rubbed his eyes with the back of his hand and rolled over.

On the back piazza, Lish sat for a moment and took in what she was feeling. A kind of overwhelming gratefulness. A relief that she and Baby Cecilia were all right. It could have been bad, but it wasn't. The chances of both a mother and child making it through a placental abruption were slimmer than she'd like to remember from her med school days. She felt blessed—undeservedly so. She sat back and let out a deep sigh. The truth was, Lish had all she ever wanted: a houseful of healthy children, a loving husband, a caring community, and the comfort of a familiar, beautiful home.

Drew, as if on cue, came out on the porch and rubbed her back. "How ya doing?"

She nodded. "I'm great. Come sit with me for a few minutes before I wake the baby to nurse." He took a seat on the wicker chair across from her and propped his foot up on the table. He leaned his arms back and stretched.

"So I got an interesting call today." He put his arms down and examined her.

"From whom?"

"The CDC."

"Again? Boy, they don't like taking no for an answer, do they?"

He cleared his throat. "The thing is, they've raised the

97

salary on the position by another $100,000, *and* they offered to pay the first year's mortgage on a house of our choice." He shook his head in disbelief. "I asked them if they'd change the title of the position to Director of Influenza Research, and they agreed." He sat up and leaned toward her. "I'd have a team of researchers at my disposal, Lish. I'd be in charge of my own lab, and the budget is practically limitless. We'd be working on improving the swine and bird flu vaccines, and we'd be on the front line of whatever comes next. Heck, we might even get a few trips to Capitol Hill out of it. Imagine that?"

"I don't want to move to Atlanta, Drew." She met his eye and spoke in a gentle, earnest tone. "Not now, with the new baby." When Lish reached for a mosquito that had landed on the back of her neck, a piercing pain shot through her side. She quickly returned to her original position. "Do you really want to uproot the kids and move away from our family? Our home? We talked this through a month ago." The incision throbbed, and she was wishing for another pill.

He bit the inside of his jaw and looked out over the landscaped garden. He rubbed his upper arm with the heel of his opposite hand. "This is my career, Lish. And it could be *the* opportunity of a lifetime." He tilted his head, and she met his eyes. "And not just that—we could be part of something huge. You know?"

She could hear the snorts of the baby in the nursery as she slowly roused. Cecilia let out a little whimper. The milk burned as it came in. It started in Lish's armpit and filled the ducts until her breasts began to drip.

Drew noticed the two circles of wetness on her night-gown. "You're tired. It's been an exhausting week, and the baby needs to eat. Let's talk about it in a few days. I can keep the CDC on ice for a little while."

After Lish fed the baby, changed her diaper, and tucked her into the bassinet, she went back onto the piazza. As she sipped the thermos of water she always kept by her side during the first weeks of nursing, she spotted the young doctors from Drew's fellowship program, Melanie and Robbie, to whom they rented the carriage house. They were coming back from their nightly run around The Battery after the city cooled off. Their bodies were young, taut, and muscular; their legs were long and they glistened beneath the street lights.

They were supposedly just friends, but she had to wonder as Melanie pushed Robbie's bare, wet shoulder and he chuckled. Lish saw residents and other young members of the fellowship program going in and out of their little house from time to time, and early one morning she had watched Melanie push the new ER doctor, Craig Michaels, down the stairs without his shoes on. She had thrown his loafers at him (or aimed them, rather), then slammed the door behind her. The doctor had stumbled out of the wrought-iron gates and into his Jeep, speeding off with no regard to the speed bumps or the Children Playing sign Lish had fought to put up on their street.

Now she remembered the days when she and Drew courted. She was living in the carriage house with Della and Anne before Nana died. She actually had a boyfriend she'd been on and off with since college who was trying to make it in the music world in Nashville, and Drew had a girlfriend in medical school at Vanderbilt. They would carpool together to see them. After the third trip, as they were approaching Nashville, he reached over, put his hand on her knee, and said, "Who are we kidding, Lish? Let's turn this car around and head back to Charleston."

They did just that, driving all night. They ran straight to Folly Beach, threw down a blanket, and watched the sun come up, imagining the messages on their respective answering machines from their significant others. They were married the following year and lived on ramen noodles and Kraft Macaroni & Cheese through residency. As soon as they both started getting a real paycheck (Lish joined a well-established pediatric practice downtown, and Drew accepted a prestigious job with the infectious disease department at the Medical University), she threw out her birth control pills.

Two months later she was pregnant with Andrew. It seemed absurd to leave Andrew every day so she could be with other children, so within six months of his birth, she left her practice and started to write a blog about motherhood. *The Post and Courier* found it and asked her to write a weekly column, which she'd been doing ever since. Wyrick Publishing had offered her a book contract, but she'd never found the time to get to that. Her family was her priority.

When her nana, Cozy Brumley, passed away just before Andrew was born, Lish and Drew were able to buy Anne and Della out of their portions of the house and move into 18 Legare Street, where an architect renovated the back portion with a large family room and vaulted ceilings. He also put in a small swimming pool, and the famous landscape designer, Benny Chestnut, updated the garden while preserving the old beauties: the magnolia, the rose bush, and of course, the loquat tree in the back corner where she and her kids harvested the fruit every June just like she did as kid. In fact, she had created a baby food with a little loquat in it a few years ago, and she sold it at the farmers' market downtown from time to time on Saturday mornings.

She could not imagine leaving Charleston now. After her father died, she spent the rest of her childhood and adolescence fantasizing and then strategizing about how to get back here. She hoped that Drew wasn't serious. He'd turned down the CDC offer twice before, and each time MUSC had lured him back with a hefty raise. He knew how she felt about raising their children here among her family and friends. These were her roots. Drew grew up in a suburb of Cleveland, and he always said he loved Charleston because of the sense of place, the history, and the realness of it. When he figured out a way for them to buy Nana's house, she'd said, "You've made my dream come true," and he held her, rubbed her bulging belly, and said, "That's what I like to hear."

The euphoria she was feeling an hour ago seemed to have dissipated, which was odd. She knew when she nursed, oxytocin was released, and she should be feeling it even stronger than she did before. Maybe it was the talk with Drew or the pain medication or simply the physical trauma of the emergency C-section. She rubbed her bloated belly and couldn't imagine it ever going back to normal. She was sure she'd never wear a bikini again. Good-bye youth.

She noticed a thump in her head. Right on the top as if she was standing beneath a dripping faucet. The baby cried out. Surely she was not hungry again. Lish gave her a few moments to settle down, but she got louder and louder, and Lish feared she would wake up the children.

Now she stood over the bassinet for a moment and watched the child kicking and snorting and wailing. Her face was red. Her gums looked hard and smooth.

Lish took the baby out to the wicker couch on the piazza. She winced as Cecilia latched onto her breast. She held her close so that she wouldn't wriggle and kick the sore spot below in her gut. Everything was tender. Achingly so. As the milk burned and released, Lish noticed the thump on her head strengthen. She had never felt it before. It was like a kind of Chinese water torture. *Hurry*, she thought as she rubbed the top of her skull. *Hurry up and eat so you can go back to sleep*. Then the unforeseen thought crossed her mind as she held the baby tight, *You could hold her so close that she wouldn't be able to breathe. A few minutes, pulled tight to your breast, and she'd be gone.*

Lish shook the thought off. She tousled her hair, but the pounding was still there.

"Drew," she called over her shoulder. "Drew, please go downstairs and get my pills."

Chapter 9

DELLA

August 29, 2008

Just as Della's planning period ended, the phone at her desk rang. She hoped it was Anne, who was on her way home from an interview in Atlanta for that bell ringing program in England, and since Della was the one who convinced her to make a move, she couldn't resist answering it.

"Hello, this is Della Limehouse," she said.

"It's me."

"I'm so glad you're taking matters into your own hands, Anne." Della balled her free hand into a fist. "How did it go?"

"Della," Anne said. "I need you to do something for me right away."

"Sure. What?" Della could hear Anne's old Saab rumbling down the highway.

"Listen to me," Anne said. "*Please* go check on Lish as soon as you can."

"Okay," Della said. "I mean, I don't get out of here until four this afternoon. Why do you sound so freaked out?"

"I don't know," Anne said. "It's just something in Lish's *voice*. Drew is at some conference in California, and she called me a little while ago, but she couldn't even get any words out. I don't have a good feeling. I just want you to go over for a little bit this morning if you can. I've got a five-hour drive before I'll be home."

"So you're telling me that something is going on with Lish that can't wait until four?" Della nervously rubbed her forehead as a large pack of seventh graders piled into her room just before the third-period bell sounded.

"That's my next class," Della said.

"Della, do this for me, okay?"

"Okay." Della exhaled as her students claimed their seats. "I'll see if I can get someone to cover for me here."

By eleven a.m. Della was knocking on Lish's front door. *Where is Rosetta?* she thought. There was no answer, but she could hear the screams of the baby from upstairs. The window was open, and the baby was calling in a chant that seemed both rhythmic and horrible. It rose and fell every few seconds.

When it was clear that no one was going to answer, Della lifted the urn of the potted ficus on the right side of the front door and pulled out the hidden house key. She had to try it a few times before the large brass lock slid back.

"Lish?" she called as she followed the screams of the baby up the stairs.

The baby was writhing beneath a soiled blanket in her bassinet. Her face was red, but her lips were pale. Lish sat in a glider chair on the other side of the nursery looking out of the window as though she hadn't heard a sound. Della looked out and saw that Mary Jane was half-dressed in only a shirt and underwear, sitting on a bench, trying to coax a lizard into a bucket while Andrew straddled one of the lower limbs of the loquat tree. He threw a Matchbox car down to the ground and it made a crashing sound.

Della grabbed the baby and pulled her close. "Lish?" She squeezed her cousin's shoulder as the baby continued its rhythmic wail. "Lish, what's going on?" Lish flinched, grabbed the top of her head with both hands, and shook it back and forth.

"Lish!" Della said. "Lish, look at me."

With her hands still grasping her head, Lish looked slowly up at Della as though she vaguely recognized her, then she turned away and shook her head again.

Della turned to the wailing baby, watched her pale legs kick furiously, and wondered what she needed. What could she do to calm her for a moment? She just needed a moment without the screams so she could get Lish's attention. When Della changed her small diaper, she saw that feces had dried around Cecilia's bottom, and beneath it was an awful rash the color of a cranberry. It looked like the bedsore she saw on Papa the day they discovered the nursing home had been neglecting him. As the baby wailed, Della examined her round, little mouth. Her gums were dry. Her tongue had no saliva on it.

Della gasped. This baby was dehydrated. Her heart started to race.

"Lish, talk to me," she called. She grabbed her cousin's knee. "Cecilia needs to eat. Do you have any formula?"

Lish continued to hold and shake her head. "I can't stand up. It will hurt too badly."

"Can you nurse her?" Della asked. She knew Lish was a purist; Andrew and Mary Jane were both breast-fed solely for the first twelve months.

Della tried to hand the wailing baby to Lish. Her tiny hands were curled into fists and her toes were spread out like little fans. She was so tense and miserable. Hungry. Della wondered when she had eaten last.

Lish pushed the baby away. She shook her head no and then she grabbed the back of her neck. "I can't make it stop," she said. "It's been hitting me over and over."

"What?" Della said. "Make what stop?"

"The pelts," she said. "The pelts on the top of my head."

The baby continued to cry. It was a dry, hoarse cry. Della could no longer bear it. She took the infant in her arms and ran across the street to Nana's old neighbor, Martha Emerson. Martha was bedridden, but she still had all of her help—a round-the-clock nurse and a housekeeper who cooked and cleaned every day.

"Please," Della said to the housekeeper. She suddenly remembered her name from childhood. "Miss Janie. Can you watch those children across the street? There's an emergency, I think. I have to get this baby some food."

"Sure," said the woman (who seemed elderly herself). She walked slowly across the street and toward the garden where Andrew was chasing Mary Jane with the lizard.

Della found Lish's car keys in the foyer, strapped Cecilia into the baby seat, and raced to the Harris Teeter, where she bought formula and a bottle as the baby wailed. Della's home was closer to the grocery store and it seemed time was of the essence, so she made a snap decision and raced to Radcliffe Street, pulled into her driveway, and ran into the house.

Peter was on the piazza, replacing a rotten spindle. "Hold her," Della said as she thrust Baby Cecilia into his arms. She filled the bottle with warm water, put two heaping scoops in, and shook, then she ran out to the porch and handed it to Peter. The infant girl began to suck at the plastic nipple as he took his place in the rocking chair and tilted the end of the bottle higher and higher with each ounce she gulped down.

He looked to Della, whose heart continued to pound. Who was only now aware of her hands trembling as she leaned back against the railing and breathed deeply.

"What's going on?" Peter did not take his eyes away from Cecilia. He must have remembered from Cozy's infant days that the nipple must be filled with milk or she'd take in air.

"Something's wrong." She looked at him. The top of his wide forehead, the protruding veins of his skilled hands, with some muck from the rotten wood of their piazza beneath his fingernails.

"It's Lish. She's not coherent or something." Della bit her bottom lip until it turned white. "She wouldn't respond to me or the baby crying, and the kids were running wild in the backyard." She tried to catch her breath and think clearly. "Drew's out of town. I've got to get back there, Peter."

He nodded. "I can call it a day," he said. "Leave the baby here, and go see about Lish."

She swallowed hard. Her mouth was dry. "Okay," she said. "Do you think you could pick up Cozy at three?"

"No problem." Baby Cecilia grasped his rough forefinger with her little hand. "I'll fish the old stroller out of the shed."

"And can you call my work and tell them there's a family emergency?"

"Sure," he said as he propped the baby on his shoulder and patted her back. She belched and relaxed. Then he walked toward the kitchen where the telephone was as Della raced out of the house and into her car.

Before she put her keys in the ignition, she ran back in the house. "One more thing, Peter!" she called from the foyer.

He was hanging up the phone and he turned around so she could see the baby against his chest.

"What's she doing now?" he asked.

Della looked at her little face. She pressed her hand gently down on her warm back. It was rising and falling slowly. "Snoozing, I think."

"Like riding a bike, baby. I've still got the touch." He grinned tentatively and swayed back and forth.

"If I'm not back in an hour, please give her some more formula. I'll call you if it's going to be longer than that." Della scurried toward the door and then turned back again.

"If she's wet, change her and use a clean dishrag for a diaper. She's got a terrible rash and should be changed right away."

He looked her way, put his finger to his lip to shush her, and nodded.

When Della arrived back at Lish's, the front door was wide open. She called to her cousin as she stepped inside. There was no sign of anyone—not the kids, not the housekeeper, not Lish.

In the kitchen, mold grew on three plates of what must have been lasagna from a few days ago. There was a bowl of curdled milk with a few bloated Cheerios floating on the surface. A couple of flies darted back and forth between the trash can and the moldy plates. The refrigerator door was slightly ajar, and as Della went to close it, she saw the thick droplets of condensation on an uncovered chicken carcass and an unclosed carton of organic milk.

Before she raced upstairs, she took a quick look out of the back door and spotted Lish curled up with her knees to her chest beneath the loquat tree. She rocked back and forth with her head face down.

Della ran out to her. "Lish?" She saw that she was in a

camisole and some flannel pajama bottoms. Her fingernails were bitten down to the nubs and her right thumb was bleeding. A mosquito landed on Lish's shoulder and started to nip her; she did not swat it away.

Della sat down, brushed the insects off, and started to gently rub her cousin's back. "I'm here. Talk to me."

Minutes passed and Lish continued to rock. Della noted a prominent vein protruding from the side of her cousin's long, thin neck; she watched the afternoon sun filtering through the loose strands of her rich brown hair. From across the street, Della heard Andrew and Mary Jane. As she craned her neck, she spotted them chasing one another behind the white picket fence of Mrs. Emerson's front yard. George, the gardener, sprayed them with the hose from time to time, and they shrieked with laughter. Janie was on the porch smiling and clapping.

On the opposite side of Lish, Della noticed a hole Lish must have dug with a stick in her pristine garden. It was a few inches wide and went down a good four or five inches. The soft, freshly dug dirt smelled like pluff mud and low tide.

It was humid and miserably hot. Probably still in the mid-nineties. The limbs of the tree seemed to sag from the heavy air, and the rotten fruit that had fallen to the ground was decaying on the grass around them. Della cleared her dry throat. "You've got to tell me what's going on, Lish. I can help. I'll do anything I can to help you."

Lish shook her head. She seemed unable to speak. She looked up once and her eyes were pink and swollen. She started to rub the top of her head with her dirty fingertips.

"There is a pounding on my head. It won't stop. I can't sleep." She turned to look Della dead on. "When I stand up, it's unbearable." She looked back down. "It's terrorizing me."

"A pounding?" Della's bright blue eyes raced back and forth as if she was speed reading.

Lish shook her head and then her eyes seemed to glaze over. She leaned back against the trunk of the tree and closed her eyes. "Leave me alone, Della. I need to sleep."

When Anne pulled into the driveway a few minutes later, Della was holding Lish's hand as she seemed to be in some kind of a waking trance beneath the tree. She put her cousin's hand gently down and ran out to meet Anne.

"Where is she?" Anne peered over Della's shoulder.

"She's in the back, in a kind of waking sleep, I think." Della's face was pale.

"What happened?" Anne asked. "When did you come by?"

"When I got here late this morning, the baby was screaming and the kids were running around the yard. Lish was just sitting in the glider in the nursery. It was like she wasn't really there." She reached out and squeezed Anne's hand. "The baby's mouth was *dry*. There was hardly any saliva. I don't know when she'd been fed last."

Anne's round green eyes bobbed up and down as Della stared into them. She turned her head from Lish to Della over and over.

Della followed her eyes to the backyard. She cleared her throat. "Anne, the baby had a rash that was worse than anything I'd ever seen. It was raw, and she was caked in feces."

Bile rose in Della's throat as she recalled it. She thought she might gag, but she took in a deep breath of the heavy air as Anne paced back and forth wringing her long, freckled hands. She closed her eyes and Della thought she might be praying. Then she looked up, tucking her red hair behind her delicate shoulders. "What should we do now, Del?"

"Okay." Della spread out her fingers, attempting to make sense of this and take charge. "I'll call Drew and you call Rosetta. We'll call her obstetrician, and if need be—" She paused and looked up to the carriage house, where the tall, blonde MUSC resident was bolting up the stairs in her white medical coat. "Todd Jervey."

Della hoped the young woman didn't see Lish in the backyard. She wanted to protect her somehow. She wanted to pull down a screen over 18 Legare, and she remembered Nana closing the shutters when Papa was weeping in the crow's nest. "He's having one of his spells," she used to say.

"Did she talk to you?" Anne asked as her eyes anxiously followed the medical resident into the carriage house.

Della nodded. "She says something is hitting her head." She exhaled as they watched the young woman in the carriage house throw off her coat and pull a wine glass down from the cabinet.

Anne unclasped her delicate hands and touched Della's bony elbow. "Maybe she just needs a decent night's sleep.

She probably hasn't had a consecutive eight hours for six weeks now."

Della nodded and turned back to Anne. "I think there's more going on here than that."

In Lish's Day-Timer in the upstairs office, they found the numbers they needed. Anne went to call Rosetta on her cell, while Della spotted Lish's fancy iPhone and attempted to call Drew. Della and Peter were the last people on the planet who didn't have cell phones. It used to be something they'd admired about one another. At art shows and book signings they'd say, *No one can track us down at a moment's notice.* Or they'd pipe up sarcastically when a friend or colleague gave an exasperated sigh when asking for their number, *How did we ever live before cell phones?* Now she found it rather embarrassing. It took her whole minutes to navigate this foreign device. When he didn't answer his mobile, she paged him. He called back ten minutes later.

"Why'd you page me, honey?" He sounded as if he was out of breath. "You knew my presentation was this afternoon."

"This is Della, Drew."

"Della?"

"Yes. Something's *wrong.*"

She heard him breathe in and out, in and out and then, "What do you mean? Are the kids all right?"

"It's Lish," Della said. "She's curled up in a ball in the backyard in a kind of catatonic state. The kitchen's disgusting. We don't think she's fed the baby for a while. Maybe *a day* even. How long have you been gone?"

He cleared his throat. "Three nights," he said. "I don't understand. Where's Rosetta?"

"I have no idea. Anne's trying to reach her now." She tightened her grip on the phone. "Something is truly amiss here, Drew. I think Lish needs some kind of medical help, maybe even *psychiatric* help. I don't know." Saying those words out loud made Della teary. She felt the perspiration burn beneath her arms, and she willed herself to keep her voice strong. "You need to get home right away."

"She's just tired, Della." She could hear him tapping rhythmically on something. He said a muffled, "Thank you. Yeah, see you there," to someone. Now he was back. "It's exhausting. Taking care of three. Don't go jumping to any drastic conclusions on me now, okay? Let me talk to her."

Della walked the phone out to Lish, whose eyes were now closed.

"She's sleeping, I think," she said to him.

"Don't wake her. Just have her call me as soon as she's up. I've got my final presentation tomorrow morning, then I'll catch the first flight out."

Della's ears popped as she swallowed hard. "You should catch the red-eye tonight. I don't think you understand what I'm saying, but you've got to believe me."

"Look, Della," he said. "I know you're concerned, and I appreciate you being there. Just have Lish call me when she wakes up, okay? I know how she works. It's exhaustion."

"No, it's more than that—" Della heard the click of his phone. "Drew?" He was gone. She was so angry and scared, she was seeing little black spots. How could he not hear the urgency in her voice? She looked down at the sleek, thin device. Where the heck was the Shut Down button? Should she shut down the phone? If she didn't get a cell phone soon, she was going to start feeling downright disenfranchised.

Anne stood in the doorway with three pronounced lines across her freckled forehead. "Rosetta said Lish kicked her out day before yesterday just after she let herself into the house like usual."

"Seriously?"

Anne nodded. "She said Lish pointed to the door and told her to get out for no apparent reason. The kids were crying and saying, 'Mama, we want Rosetta to make us pancakes.' She said they followed her out to the front gate and begged her to come back, but Lish kept saying no and pointing to the street corner where Rosetta catches the bus."

"This is nuts," Della said. "Did she say anything else?"

Anne lowered her voice. "She said Lish hasn't been right since she came home with the baby. That she's been sleeping a lot and letting the baby cry for a while before she nurses her. She's been short with the kids. Rosetta says she mentioned it to Drew a couple of weeks ago, and he said he would see about it."

"This is unbelievable." Della leaned against the wall, and one of the oil paintings of the Morris Island lighthouse tilted slightly. "Drew is convinced she's just exhausted. He wants her to call when she wakes up." She straightened out the painting and turned back to Anne. "I don't agree with him. I think it's something else."

Anne peered out the window at Lish and back to Della. "What should we do?"

Della looked up at the ceiling and around at the familiar crown molding of the upstairs hall. How many days had the three of them run up the stairs and down the corridor in a game of chase or hide-and-seek. "Settle down!" Nana would call. "Don't disturb Papa." Papa was often on the third-floor crow's nest, listening to an album on his old phonograph. He'd volunteered to fight in World War II, well into his mid-thirties, and when he came home, he was never quite the same. "He got real sad after the war," Nana had told them once when she was tucking them into the king-size bed in the guest room they shared from time to time. "And then when he lost his son, well, that about did it. He hasn't been able to shake it for more than a few days since then."

Now Della squeezed her eyes shut and then opened them again. "I'll get Peter to take Andrew and Mary Jane to our house for the night."

"I'll keep the baby," Anne said.

"Okay," Della said. "There's formula and a bottle at my house. I'll stay here with Lish until she wakes up. We'll call Drew. Then I'll see what kind of state she's in."

Anne nodded and they headed to the nursery where they found a well-stocked diaper bag to which they added blankets, baby soap, powder, a pacifier, and a pair of white pajamas with pink and green polka dots.

Della walked to the doorway and watched Anne zip up the bag. "Sometime you'll have to tell me how that interview went."

Anne sniffed the rank air of the nursery and shook her head. "It's not what's important right now."

❧

"Say something, please." Della grabbed Lish's shoulders. She'd woken up an hour ago, but she'd swatted away the phone every time Della handed it to her.

When Della called Drew back, he exhaled and said, "I've arranged to have my presentation moved up to eight a.m. I've booked a noon flight out. Don't do anything until I get home, okay?"

"Not okay," she said. "I don't think you're hearing me, Drew. Your wife needs you now. This is more than exhaustion, and it's scaring me."

Drew exhaled. "Della, I've seen this before with Lish. If you can just get her to have a good night's sleep, she'll be a new person tomorrow. I need you to hang in there."

Della was beginning to feel a little crazy. Could sleep be all Lish needed? Had this happened before?

"Call you later," he said before she could respond. *You're a lot of help, Drew. A real rock.* She shook her head in disbelief.

Della called the middle school principal and told her she needed a sub for tomorrow. She didn't offer an explanation, and she didn't pretend to be sick. She was thankful that she was not questioned.

"I'm calling your OB," Della said as Lish sat at the kitchen table and scraped at a cut on her shin with her unfiled fingernails.

The on-call physician, a Dr. Chang, called back. She had a kind voice, and Della explained it all to her.

"She may be worn out, or there could be another medical cause," the doctor said. "Let's see if she'll talk to me."

"This is the on-call obstetrician." Della handed the phone to Lish.

Lish managed to find her voice for a moment. Her hands trembled as she held the receiver to her ear. She answered "no" four times and then handed the phone back to Della.

"If she's not better after a good night's sleep, I'm sure her doctor would like to see her in the morning," Dr. Chang said.

"But—"

"Look, Ms. . . . I'm sorry. Tell me your name . . ."

"Limehouse."

"Ms. Limehouse." She cleared her throat. "I'm not sure I can discuss this with you. I'm not her physician, and you're not an immediate family member."

"I'm the only one here." Della tugged on the phone cord. "I need some guidance!"

"If you're that concerned, you should take her to the emergency room," Dr. Chang said. "They can properly assess the situation. All right?"

"Okay." Della nodded, and the doctor said a quick "Good-bye."

Outside a squirrel scurried across the wrought-iron fence, and two mourning doves took flight. They landed on the telephone wire and began their soft five-note coos.

Suddenly Lish scampered up to the nursery, holding her head; Della quickly followed her. She watched her pad around the room until she turned to Della and screamed, "Where's my baby?"

"Let me explain," Della said, but Lish ran past her and grabbed a silver letter opener at the desk just outside of the nursery. She turned to Della, her legs wide and firmly planted, her arm outstretched with the sharp end of the letter opener pointing toward her cousin. "Give her back!" Lish screamed, and she lunged at Della.

Della grabbed her wrist, but she couldn't stop the letter opener from cutting through the sleeve of her shirt and the surface of her shoulder.

She pushed Lish back, took a look at the wound, put her hands up and said, "Please, Lish. Listen to me." But Lish came right back at her with the letter opener, which Della dodged. When she saw Lish lunge again, she ran back down the stairs and out of the house. She jumped in her car and locked the door.

She grabbed the steering wheel as if to steady herself and watched her knuckles whiten. When Lish didn't come out of the house, Della reached for the cell phone, which she was glad she'd tucked in her skirt pocket. Without hesitating, she called Mrs. Jervey, who still lived in Todd's old family home on South Battery. Mrs. Jervey gave Della Todd's mobile number, and she dialed it right away.

"Hello?" a deep voice said before the third ring.

"Todd, this is Della." She sucked her teeth and continued to firmly grasp the steering wheel. "I need your help."

When Todd arrived, Lish was slumped against the bottom of the staircase with her head between her knees. She rubbed the top of her head as if she had just hit it on the corner of a table. She'd put the letter opener down a few minutes before when Della offered her a sip of water. Della had discreetly grabbed it and put it on top of a chest in the living room.

Lish took a small sip of water and looked up at Todd. Her eyes were puffy and bloodshot, and her pupils were dilated. Yet she looked him in the eye and seemed to recollect who he was.

"Todd?" she said. "Thank you for coming." She pressed her fingertips into her skull. "I can't find my baby, and I have this awful thumping on my head."

Della took a step toward her. "Remember what I told you about the baby?" She talked as calmly and gently as possible. "The baby is with Anne. She went for a little visit, and she'll be back soon. The children went to a sleepover at my house."

Todd helped Lish lie down. He put the glass of water by her side, stood up, and rubbed the back of his sunburned neck. Despite his beard and a couple of extra pounds, he still had his boyish look—a thin frame, fair skin with freckles, and strawberry blond hair.

When Lish closed her eyes, Della looked at Todd. It had been ten years, but his soft hazel eyes were familiar and comforting to her. He tugged at his bearded chin as if to think for a moment and then looked back at her. "I think we should take her to the emergency room."

Della swallowed hard. "I know Drew doesn't want that. He thinks she's exhausted. He wants me to wait until he gets back tomorrow."

Todd shook his head. "Della, if he saw her, he would want her to be checked out. We need to run an organic etiology—to rule out a medical cause for this. There could be a metabolic or thyroid problem." He looked at Lish and then back to Della. "It's pretty unlikely, but a brain tumor is another possibility." He grasped her thin shoulder. "And the letter opener incident shows that she could be a threat to herself or someone else."

Della had not considered any of those things. She was sure Drew hadn't either.

"Can we call Drew first?" she said. "Maybe if you talk to him . . . ?" She lifted her shoulders and threw her hands up as if in a plea.

"Sure," Todd said. He popped the knuckle of his forefinger. "I'd be happy to."

They paged Drew twice and waited for him to return the call. Della paced the floor and Todd walked around the house, noting Lish's framed articles and a high-profile cover story the local paper ran about the loquat baby food she'd created. Next to it there was a photo of the handsome couple in Venice at San Marco Square, embracing one another amid the pigeons.

An hour passed without a response from Drew. When Lish started to stir, Todd watched her intently from the foyer. Suddenly she sat up on the sofa, looked at Della, and said, "Get out of my house," then began to weep.

"Okay," Della turned to Todd. "Let's take her."

Lish didn't fight them, and she walked willingly into the emergency room. Right away, she was recognized by the attending physician and the head nurse, who whisked her out of the crowded waiting room and into a bed where they pulled a gray curtain around her.

Della and Todd told the attending doctor, a young guy by the name of Rob Suarez, what they knew. He nodded and seemed to give Todd a knowing glance. "We'll draw blood and do a metabolic panel," he said. "We should know in an hour or so if this is something organic. If the blood sugar and electrolytes are normal, I'll call in Dr. Swan, the attending psychiatrist, who may want to talk to you, Mrs. Limehouse."

Della nodded. "Okay. I'll be here."

Todd sat with Della in the waiting room, and they watched an obese woman pacing back and forth with a steaming cup of coffee in one corner and an elderly man holding the hand of a young girl in another. He was whispering to her in Spanish. Her eyes were big and nearly black, and when she looked up she met Della's stare head on. Della smiled at the beautiful girl. Who knew what they were waiting for? The girl looked back down to the pattern of her skirt—circles upon circles of lavender and yellow.

"Have you eaten?" Todd asked.

"No." Della became suddenly aware of her empty stomach.

He nodded toward the sliding door that led to the street.

"Let's pick up a quick sandwich. This always takes much longer than you might expect."

As he led the way next door to an all-night pizza and sub joint, she looked up at him and let out a nervous chuckle. "Well, I never thought we'd meet again under these circumstances."

He gave her a tenuous smile. "Listen," he said. "This is life. You take it as it comes."

He held open the door of the little dive. It smelled like beer, cigarettes, and pepperoni, and Della had a faint memory of eating there in the middle of the night when she was in college.

Todd pointed to the meatball sub on a menu. "This is good. Wanna try?"

After they got their food, they walked back to the hospital and took a seat on a bench in a little garden outside of the emergency room.

Della looked at the meaty sub, the parmesan cheese oozing out of the white bread. She took a sip of her Coca-Cola and looked at him. She wanted to ask him what would happen to her cousin tonight, and what he thought was really going on. But she decided to wait. She knew he wouldn't want to speculate until they ruled out the medical possibilities. She watched him unwrap his sub.

"So the whole eating-healthy thing hasn't made it onto your radar yet?"

He chuckled and took a hearty bite. A little smudge of tomato sauce was in the corner of his mouth, and he wiped it away with a thin napkin.

"Nah," he said. "I don't grind my own flour or anything yet. I've spent so many late nights in the lab or the psych ward that I've learned to survive on anything that's open after midnight, and that's not usually the unprocessed stuff."

Della nodded. The sub was surprisingly delicious.

"Yeah, we can't afford all of that stuff. It's great and all if you're wealthy, but one trip to Whole Foods and my *whole* paycheck is gone."

He nodded. "Oh, don't tell me the famous author doesn't make enough to buy organic?"

Della exhaled. "Famous? What's the definition of famous? Receiving a seventy-two-dollar royalty check, maybe, every four months?"

He popped open a bag of chips and his hands seemed strikingly familiar to her, the freckles across the knuckles, the scar on his thumb where she knew he once caught a fishing hook on a friend's bad cast. He looked up. "I don't know why you say that with a hint of disdain, Del." He took a bite, and she could hear the loud crunch. "You look to me like you've got the life you always wanted." He leaned forward. "I've seen your good-looking husband and your beautiful little girl. Mom sent me that article in *Coastal*

Magazine about you all, the one about artistic couples of the low country." He took a sip of his Sprite. "Plus, you're managing to do the thing you always wanted."

Della nodded. She noted a bat swooping between the corner of the hospital and the parking garage. A city bus lurched to a stop and a couple of third-shift workers exited its doors.

Della thought of her crumbling home just down the road. She thought of the finger-length roaches ducking in and out of her utensil drawer and the yard full of scrap metal and the stray cat lounging on the front stoop. She thought of her dinosaur of a computer and the novel she was only a third of a way through. She was too close to it to know, but she suspected it was the weakest of the bunch.

What made her think she could write about a stalker who committed murder? Had she ever stalked someone? Had she ever been a witness to a murder? Or shadowed a detective who arrived just after the scene of a crime? No, no, no. She was an idiot to try and write one of those kinds of books. And what were her intentions? To make money? To remake herself as a plot-driven novelist?

Her mother, if she were alive, would immediately peg the manuscript as her daughter's attempt to sell out. An unsuccessful one. But Kate Brumley, the highly anthologized poet, was an abysmal mother, Della admitted now. She never needed to worry about providing for her daughter because Nana was the present and responsible grown-up in Della's life. What did Katie Brumley know besides how to catch the eye of a strung-out beatnik at a shabby hotel in Paris with her well-proportioned curves and her piercing blue eyes? Or how to string a few words together so that they captured the kind of out-of-body experience one felt during an LSD trip? The older Della got, the more she disdained her mother.

She watched the third-shift employees in their hair nets, gray-green scrubs, and thick-soled shoes as they took their turns moving through the wide revolving doors.

Todd cleared his throat. "You've done very well. You can't deny it."

"Oh, yeah?" She looked at his gentle face, his hazel eyes glistening from the light of the street lamp. His head was tilted with a half grin, expecting her to agree with him. "Right now it feels like a façade." She exhaled. "I've got too much on my plate, you know? And none of it is what I really want."

"What's on your plate?"

"Well, I'm teaching English full time to middle school kids to make ends meet—grammar, sentence diagramming, recess duty, nasty parents, the whole nine yards. I love the kids, even the entitled ones, but it's tough working a nine-hour day, then coming home, taking care of a child, and writing at night. I have to write a book every twelve months that will sell only a few thousand copies. I sit at book signings where half the people don't even look my way—or worse, ask me for directions to the bathroom." A car honked in the distance. A radio blared suddenly and then faded. "I'm a mid-list writer. It's not exactly something an author aspires to. In fact, it's kind of a curse."

He balled up the empty paper bag from his meal and tossed it in the trash.

"Aside from making sure your cousin is okay, and I think she will be, what *do* you want?"

Yes, that was Todd. The consummate mental and emotional surgeon—aiming the scalpel at your heart when given the slightest opportunity. She remembered their long walks on the beach, how he would probe and probe her about her motherless childhood, about her desires, about how she felt when he took her in his arms. She used to find it wearisome. To answer all of those questions. She missed the spontaneity she'd had in previous relationships, and she was annoyed by his constant need for her to self-reflect.

But that was in her twenties. Tonight, just outside of the emergency room where her cousin (on whom she relied in a way she couldn't quite explain) was being poked and prodded in search of a medical cause for her mental state, Della was overwhelmed with the desire to take stock. She was about to turn thirty-eight, and she was not at all where she thought she would be at this point in her life. She wanted to tell someone how she really felt.

She took a deep breath and let it go. "The truth is, I just want to raise my daughter the best way I know how." She looked up into the night air above them. "And I want more kids. I love raising children. I know that sounds awfully 1950s, but it's the truth. It's the best thing I've ever experienced." She crossed her legs and tapped her foot as he waited for her to continue. "And I want time. Just a little time. Time to write a novel I can be proud of. Time to read. Time to take a walk." She shrugged her narrow shoulders. "And I'd settle for central heating and air and neighbors who don't deal drugs, you know?"

He nodded, peeled the lid off of his disposable cup, and tilted it up. Then he surveyed the street, looked back at her, and said, "You do have too much. You're going to have to think of a way to cut some things out."

She raised her eyebrows. "I'm all ears, Dr. Jervey. Tell me how to simplify my life and make twice as much money, will you?"

As she watched him rub his chin, Lish's cell phone rang. Della pulled it out quickly and looked hard for the Talk button. She punched it as soon as she spotted it.

"Drew?" She pulled the phone to her ear.

"No," said the voice on the other end. "It's Anne, Del. Where are you? How's Lish?"

Chapter 10

It hurt to swallow. The thumping was on her head and in her throat now, and she tried to wait as long as possible before she swallowed. She spit in the bedside pan a couple of times to avoid doing it.

The curtain was pulled back and the young attending said, "Dr. Sutton?"

Before she could stop herself, Lish swallowed. It burned, and she pictured the fire-breather she and Drew applauded at a Venice street show during their trip a few years ago. The man would put the flaming torch down his throat and hold it there for whole seconds before pulling it out and holding up its snuffed end with something between a wince and a smile on his face. Several in the audience, including Lish, would toss a coin in an empty hat, and the man would reach for a sword in the open case beside him and in he would plunge it, down beyond his tongue into the soft and tender shaft of his throat. Now Lish nodded and grasped her neck.

"Are you able to talk?"

She nodded again.

~

She had once been in this attending's same position a decade ago during her third year of medical school. She remembered making her worst rotations first in an effort to cross the particularly sad and miserable places off her career list: ER, Oncology Unit, Psychiatry Ward. She recalled one particular night in the ER, watching a doctor examine a woman who had been brought in naked from the downtown market in the middle of the night. Lish had draped a gown over her body as the rest of the staff rushed out to meet three ambulances in the driveway. (A bus had overturned on I-26 and there were five injured passengers who needed immediate help.) Lish remembered gently laying the gown over the woman who was curled up in the fetal position on the floor. She had recoiled at the woman's awful stench and the grime beneath her finger- and toenails.

"I can't find my puppy," the woman had said. "Have you seen a little black labradoodle around here?"

The attending physician rolled his eyes as he pulled Lish to the side. "Page the on-call psychiatrist," he'd said. "This one belongs on President Street. It's a tough night, and she needs to move on."

Lish wanted to ask, "Before you examine her?" but she knew better than to question an attending.

She had nodded and paged the doctor, who agreed with the attending after his assessment. The woman put up a fight, scratching the psychiatrist across the forehead, and he had to call the judge and have her involuntarily committed. One policeman had to hold her down while another put handcuffs on her. She cursed at them and kicked them, and they both had beads of sweat on their foreheads by the time they walked her to the door. Lish had watched the psychiatrist sign off on the court papers. "Poses an immediate threat to herself and others," he'd written, and she walked with the policeman and the woman, kicking and screaming, over to President Street to the Institute of Psychiatry, where the doctor took her in a holding area and gave her a shot that knocked her out. Lish could still see the woman's pale, thin legs like toothpicks protruding from the gray gown when the doctor picked her up and carried her to a gurney by the elevator.

She knew the attending wanted to see if she needed to take the same walk to President Street. He wanted to quickly rule out any organic cause and move her out and over to the Institute of Psychiatry.

"You recently had a C-section?"

"Yes." She felt the saliva pooling on her tongue, and she stopped herself from spitting. "About six weeks ago."

"Are you still taking your pain medication?" He looked up from his clipboard after he asked the question.

"No. I ran out maybe ten days ago." She didn't know

when she ran out, but she couldn't remember the last time she took one.

"Have you been drinking during the last twenty-four hours?"

"No." Had she? She didn't think she'd had a drink since the baby was born.

"Do you have diabetes?"

"No."

"A seizure disorder?"

"No." Once a boy, one of her patients, had a seizure in her office. He'd slapped her jaw hard as she and his mother tried to restrain him. Her cheek was black for a week.

The doctor tapped his pencil. "Family illness that might pertain to how you are feeling?"

Family illness? She tried to picture the members of her family—Drew, the children, Nana, Papa, Mama, Rick, Mama's husband, and then her daddy standing on the piazza on Rutledge Avenue, waving to her as she rode her bike over to East Bay Playground the week before he died.

She swallowed. It burned. "No."

"Recent head injury?"

She held her head. "No, but it hurts."

"Tell me about your head."

She blinked and her eyes seemed dry. She put one hand on the top of her head and the other on her throat. Her breasts were sore and hard, and she knew her milk was drying up. She couldn't recall the last time she'd fed the baby.

"I've had a thumping here for weeks." She pointed to the place where there was a groove. Where the two sides of her skull came together. "It hurts worse when I stand up. And even worse when I walk. It seems in synch with my heartbeat. And it's in my throat too."

He nodded. "Okay. We're going to draw blood first. You know how this goes."

"Yes," Lish said. "A quick organic etiology. You want to see if I'm physically sick or just plain crazy." She still had her hand on her head.

The young doctor cleared his throat and looked down at his chart. He scratched the back of his neck and seemed to search for the proper response as if it was written on the clipboard.

"No response necessary," she said. "Send in the nurse."

An hour later, the psychiatrist came in for her mental status examination. It was Sharon Swan. She'd been a year ahead of Drew and Lish in medical school. She was several years older than the other students, had gone back to school later in life, after her kids were in grade school. Lish always wondered how she managed it. She had a great deal of respect for Sharon Swan, and she thought it was mutual. At a cocktail party not six months ago, Sharon had complimented Lish on her recent column about detecting ADHD in young children.

The woman reached out her soft, middle-aged hand. "Hello, Dr. Sutton."

Lish nodded. She couldn't bear to swallow any more so she spit into the bedpan. "Hello," she whispered.

"I'm sorry you aren't feeling well." She took out a pen from the pocket in her coat. "I need to ask you a few standard questions, so bear with me."

"Okay," Lish said.

"What's your name?" The doctor watched her spit before answering.

She wiped her mouth with a tissue from the counter. "Lish Sutton."

"Do you know where you are?"

Lish nodded and held her throat. She saw the doctor studying her fingernails. She removed her hands from her neck and noticed the dried blood and dirt on her fingertips. "The emergency room at the Med U."

"Do you know what today is?"

Lish narrowed her eyebrows and shook her head. She thought for a moment. She remembered taking the kids to their first days of school last week, but she had no idea what today's date was.

She shook her head. "I know it's August."

"Do you know the day of the week?"

She took a guess. "Saturday?"

Dr. Swan's face flickered briefly, just enough that Lish guessed she was wrong.

"Have you had any suicidal thoughts?"

Her head hurt.

"I need relief, Sharon."

"Have you had any thoughts about hurting someone else?"

She thought of the baby and the fear of smothering her. She remembered staring at the new set of kitchen knives from Williams-Sonoma that were in a decorative wooden block on the counter. When Drew left town, she threw them away in a neighbor's garbage can. Did she grab a letter opener today?

Dr. Swan stared at her, and she tried to breathe. She shook her head no even as she felt the burn of the tears in her eyes.

Dr. Swan took a deep breath and slowly nodded her head. She didn't look down at her chart.

Her next question was, "Can you spell the word *world*?"

Lish pictured the felt map of the world in Andrew's room. How he liked to take the penguin out of Antarctica and move it over to Madagascar—the world according to Walt Disney. "W-o-r-l-d."

"Can you spell it backwards?"

"D." Lish's head throbbed. The pounding was more pronounced now.

"W."

She grabbed her skull and shook her head no.

Dr. Swan bit her lip. She gently reached for Lish's shoulder as if to steady her. "I'm going to tell you three words, okay?"

Lish nodded.

"Boat, car, and chair," said the doctor. She took a deep breath. "What three words did I tell you, Dr. Sutton?"

Lish spit again. "Boat-car-chair." She looked up at Dr. Swan. "Are you going to send me to the Institute, Sharon?"

Dr. Swan met her eyes, reached out, and gently squeezed Lish's shoulder. "Let's finish the examination, okay?"

She looked away and then back to Lish. "What were those three words I told you?"

"Boat . . ." Lish grabbed her head. She swallowed. It burned. She grabbed her neck and dug the tips of her fingers into it.

She looked up at Dr. Swan. "I'll go, Sharon. Send me to President Street. I'm not going to put up a fight."

Dr. Swan looked at her. Then she gently patted her back. "Lish, I think it would be the wisest thing to do," she said. "We'll find out what's going on and we'll help you." She tucked a strand of hair behind her ear and looked Lish dead in the eyes. "You're going to be all right. You hear me? And I'll do anything I can to help you."

Dr. Swan consulted with the nurse, who quickly brought Lish a pill containing one milligram of Ativan. She took it, and it hurt all the way down.

Dr. Swan explained her decision to Della. Then the doctor and a security guard walked Lish over to the Institute of Psychiatry, where a nurse with soft, kind eyes met them at the front desk.

Lish was thankful for Dr. Swan and the nurse and the Ativan, which was making her feel light, very light, and remarkably sleepy. She stretched out on the bed in the room where the nurse had led her. The nurse pulled the covers over her. The sounds of the hall faded away. She thought she heard someone in the next room calling out, but it immediately became muffled and even the muffled sound was gone within moments. She was surrounded by darkness, and she closed her eyes. She felt as if she were floating.

Chapter 11

DELLA

Friday, August 29

Della scrubbed the dried lasagna off the plates she'd been soaking all day. She was in the kitchen of 18 Legare Street, where she'd been cleaning clothes and sheets, mopping the floors and scrubbing the surfaces of the bathroom and kitchen. Drew should be home from the airport by now. He'd called her at two in the morning before Dr. Swan sent Lish over to President Street, and when she told him that Lish was in the emergency room, he exhaled deeply and said, "Okay."

He was practically silent when she called him this morning and reported that Lish had been voluntarily admitted to the Institute of Psychiatry. He let out a groan and she said, "Dr. Swan says she's going to be okay. She just needs a few days there . . . a little time to get straight, you know?"

"Hmm," he said faintly.

Now she heard someone fiddling with the lock, and when she went toward the foyer, Drew flung open the door and stood before her, seeming taller than usual in his straight-leg jeans and crisp white oxford. His salt-and-pepper curls seemed to gleam, and his fresh-shaven face had a squeaky-clean glow to it.

"Della, thank you for your help." He gestured subtly toward her car with his elbow as he stepped inside. "It's time you leave."

She wrinkled her brow. "Have you been to see Lish? Tell me what's going on."

He picked at an invisible fleck on his shirt sleeve, then looked down to meet her gaze. "You really care about Lish?"

"What?" she said. "Of course I do."

"Mmmn." He crossed his arms, and she noticed the small black tufts of hair below his knuckles.

He took a cursory survey of the house before staring back at her. "You care about her and yet you drop her off"—he pinched his brow—"a successful physician and mother of the decade, for crying out loud"—he inhaled—"at the emergency room for a *psychological evaluation?*"

He shook his head and now refused to meet her eye. He looked above her at a portrait of Andrew hanging at the bottom of the stairwell. She watched as he gently kicked the door closed before counting off her offenses on his hands. "You threatened her reputation; you allowed her to be prodded and drugged and forced to sleep in a closet of a room next door to a teenage girl who swallowed a medicine cabinet full of pills for the second time in a month." He cupped his chin and narrowed his eyes. "Yep, you really care about her."

Della's stomach lurched. "But Todd advised—"

Drew raked his hair with his right hand and looked at her dead-on now. "I asked *you* to wait until I got home. It was twenty-four hours, and you couldn't do it, could you? You and your old ex in *my* home deciding what is best for *my* wife?"

Della bit her lip. "Drew, come on!" She took a step toward him and met his gaze. "She was not right. The kids were in potential danger. And I thought she might be too. She needed help, and we didn't know what kind."

He quickly leaned down, inches away from her face. "Don't be so dramatic, Della! This is not one of your fictional plot trajectories, all right?" He pointed his index finger toward her. "This is my wife's life. Her reputation. She has never endangered our children. Not for a second, and you *know* that."

"The baby hadn't eaten. She was dehydrated." Della got her footing and spread her hands out before him as if she was carrying a large and fragile bowl. "I don't think you understand." She clenched her thin fists. "Your wife couldn't move. She couldn't get up. She was practically catatonic, and the one time she did move, it was with a sharp object in her hand coming toward me."

She took a deep breath and lowered her voice. "You know I love Lish. All I want is to protect and help her."

He nodded toward the door. "Get out," he said. "Lish doesn't want to see you now or for a while, all right?" His nostrils flared and for the first time Della noticed a small mole beneath his chin. "I can take care of her. Rosetta will be back. Melanie, the doctor who lives in the carriage house, can help. She'll have all the support she needs. Now go."

Della threw down the dishrag, strode through the foyer, and slammed the front door. She felt as though she'd been kicked in the stomach. What an out-of-touch cad. He had no idea. Poor Lish.

As she walked to her car, she saw a shadowy figure in the passenger seat of the Suttons' Volvo. It was Lish, still strapped in, gazing in the opposite direction. Della wanted to run over, knock on the window, and tell Lish she loved her, but she could feel Drew's eyes on her as he stood on the piazza waiting for her to exit.

Now she walked toward the gate, shaking her head.

When Della arrived home, it was dusk. The night was cooler than usual and all of the rickety windows were open. She saw the thin strips of paint peeling off of the sills and wondered if they had lead in them.

As she walked through the foyer, she saw that Peter and the children had painted a mural on the hallway walls. One image was of Burl and Bernice and their newfound mutt, Beauregard. The other was of a bed and three little monkeys jumping on it. In the background there was a mother monkey wagging her finger at them and a Dr. Monkey, much smaller, in the distance, scratching his head as he talked on his cell phone.

In the kitchen Della saw an open, empty Domino's pizza box and the browning skins of some apple slices on paper plates. A half-drunk pitcher of lemonade was on the table, attracting a lone fly.

She found them all in the backyard in between the tool shed and two half-built, headless crustaceans that stood four feet tall. Peter had laid out a blanket, and they were listening to the crickets. No one was in anything matching and Mary Jane's dress was on backward. But they were clean. They had been fed, and they were listening to the crickets.

"Mama!" Cozy shouted when she turned and spotted her. She ran and jumped into her arms, and then Mary Jane and Andrew danced around her, chanting, "Cousin Del, Cousin Del!"

Then Andrew rested his head against her hip and said, "Where's Mama?"

"And Baby Cecilia?" Mary Jane asked, her cheeks flushed from the excitement.

Della rubbed their heads and found her gentlest voice. "Mama's at your home and Baby Cecilia is with Aunt Anne, but I imagine your daddy will be picking you and her up real soon."

Peter rolled on his side, cocked his head on his hand, and looked at Della.

"Cozy, why don't you take Andrew and Mary Jane into the kitchen and let them pick out a Popsicle for dessert?"

"Okay!" she said and they quickly followed her.

Della sat down next to Peter on the blanket, half wanting to collapse into his arms and tell him what her last twenty-four hours had been like, half wanting to keep it to herself, the frightening parts with Lish and her conversation with Todd Jervey over meatball subs in the middle of the night.

He sat up, tapped her sandal with his bare toe.

"How's Lish?"

"Not good." Della suddenly felt the weariness from the night spent at the hospital. For the first time, her eyes were beginning to blur. "She's had some kind of real mental break. A postpartum thing, I think."

She teared up. "Drew just chewed me out for taking her to the emergency room." She rubbed her eyes with the tip of her index fingers as the kids came running down the rotting back steps.

"He wants me to stay out of it. Says I overreacted." Her lower back ached, and she leaned over to stretch it out. When she sat up, Cozy jumped into her lap, and it was as if the very weight of the little girl's body breathed a new kind of life into Della. Holding her daughter was a kind of resuscitation. Something that jump-started her heart and got her blood pumping. *I am someone's mama*, she told herself. *Someone is depending on me. I've got to keep it together.*

Cozy reached up and played with Della's earring, a silver drop with turquoise that dangled just below her ear. "Tell us a Burl and Bernice story, Mama."

"Yeah!" said Andrew, "but make it one about Burl, okay?" He crossed his arm, a miniature version of his disgruntled father with black, curly hair and long, dark eyelashes. "Bernice is a brat."

Cozy rolled her eyes, and Mary Jane watched her older cousin and tried hard to do the same thing but seemed to get dizzy in the process. Della reached out her hand to steady the little girl.

"All right, Andrew," Cozy said, and she wrapped her arms around her mother's neck as if to claim her for her very own. "I guess it can be a Burl story even though it's Bernice's turn."

"Someone give me a line," Della said.

"I've got one," said Peter, rolling down on his back.

"Okay, Daddy." Cozy turned to him, grinning with expectation.

"Burl's Mama Seems Sad, and He Wants to Cheer Her Up."

"Mmm," Cozy tucked a strand of hair behind her mother's ear. "That sounds pretty good."

"Yeah," Mary Jane added. "Tell us why Burl's mama is sad."

After Drew picked the children up, Della tucked Cozy into bed. She had a stack of quizzes on her desk to grade before her first class tomorrow morning, and she had to be at school at 7:30 to take roll. If she got behind now, the whole quarter would spin out of control.

Peter was in the yard, welding a head on one of the crustaceans. She knew he didn't have a commission, so why was he wasting his time and materials? She hoped he'd given more thought to the idea of a new career, but she doubted it.

As she put the pillow over her head, she wondered how she could check on Lish without Drew's disapproving glare in the background. She'd give it a few days and then start with an e-mail to test the waters. As she closed her eyes and tried to feel a thumping in her own head, she wondered what was going on in her cousin's brain. How did it all start, and how could they get it to stop? As the sound of the blowtorch halted, she removed the pillow from her head and suddenly recalled the rest of her conversation with Todd.

"So you never married?" she said after she unloaded on him in a way she hadn't with anyone in a long time.

He shook his head, looked up at the indigo sky and then back at her until their eyes locked.

"I've only been in love once." He bit his lower lip, looked down at his feet and then back to her. "And you pretty well ripped my heart out."

Della tried hard to swallow. They had been engaged for six months. Todd was on his way to residency at the University of Colorado where they had an established program that specialized in his real interest, the revival of electroshock therapy to treat severe depression and bipolar disorder. She was going to go with him to Boulder—until she had her epiphany that she should follow in her mother's footsteps and write. Once she received her acceptance letter from NYU's M.F.A. program, she knew she had to go for it. And that very next summer she met Peter.

"Oh, come on." She brushed him off like she used to do when he got too intense or emotional. "You're a nice, attractive, successful guy. I'm sure you've had to beat off the women with a stick."

His eyes glistened in the thick air. He nodded and wiped his brow. "If you're wondering if I'm over you . . ." He leaned in and gently patted her knee. "I can't say the answer is yes."

Now she wondered, as she did from time to time, if she made the best decision, not to marry Todd Jervey. Did she follow the right career path? Did she marry the right man? All she needed to do was open the door by her bed and see Cozy sleeping soundly, her eyelids fluttering, to know she could never call it a mistake. And yet it was hard. Not at all what she imagined.

Todd would take her back now. She knew that from the look in his eyes, and she wondered, for the good of them all, if she should go.

Chapter 12

LISH

Drew pulled two chairs beneath the loquat tree so they could have some shade. Lish took a seat, and they watched the children jump over the rotating sprinklers while they talked.

Drew shook his head and reached his arm around her. "How are you feeling?"

She cleared her dry throat and swallowed slowly. It didn't burn or throb like it did in the emergency room, but she braced herself just in case. Each time she swallowed, she curled her toes and squeezed her hands into fists. The thumping in her head was significantly dulled. She was barely cognizant of it. It was as if an occasional raindrop hit the top of her head.

"Your cousin and your sister really let you down." He squeezed her shoulder. "Drama queens. None of this would have happened if I'd been here."

Lish's breasts ached. The milk was gone, and an hour ago she had scooped the powdery formula into a bottle that Drew shook hard before feeding to Cecilia. The Ativan that the on-duty psychiatrist at the Institute prescribed made her feel groggy and slightly nauseous. She would taper off of it as soon as she could.

Now Lish felt Drew observing her. He saw her toes curl and her hands ball into fists every few seconds. He wanted her to respond, but all she could manage was a steady nod.

He rubbed her back with the palm of his hand. "You know what we're going to do?"

She turned to him and worked to meet his steady gaze. "Mmm?" she said just above a whisper.

"We're going to have a normal week. Get back in our routine. You know?"

She nodded, and he continued to rub her back in tight circles. She pictured the circles, his hand going around and around between her shoulder blades, and it made her dizzy.

He leaned in and talked in the voice he used to convince her of something. It was a skillful blend of consideration and vim. "We've had a lot on us, honey—the baby coming so early, entertaining the kids all summer, the conference, and the job offer"—he touched his cheek to hers and whispered—"it's gotten us all out of whack. I think each one of us could benefit, and you especially, from getting back in our workaday, school-year routine."

He removed his hand from her back and turned his chair to face her. "Today, we'll take a walk with the kids like we used to do on Sunday afternoons, and tonight I'll pick up a

couple of steaks from Earthfare and put them on the grill."
He tapped her knee with his fingertips.

"When's the last time I've done that?" He leaned back
and shook his head. "Man, it must have been months." He
looked out over the garden and back to her. "Then Monday,
I'll help you get the kids ready and we'll drive them to
school, all right? I'll go to work, Rosetta will stay here and
help you with the baby. Okay?"

She nodded slowly.

"The hospital made an appointment with the doc
Sharon suggested, right?"

She nodded again.

"When is it?"

"Tuesday afternoon." She winced, and he mistook it for
a smile.

"Great." He grinned and patted her knees. "Two days. I
bet you'll be feeling a lot better by then."

Lish braced herself for her swallow. She nodded her
head and tried for an earnest smile.

"Okay?" He furrowed his brow until she looked back at
him. She noticed a pocket of skin at the top of his nose. It
was almost a perfect square.

He leaned even closer. "It's going to be okay, honey.
Things are going so well on so many fronts."

She looked up at the trees and noticed the hazy afternoon
light filtering through the branches as he continued. "We've
got three beautiful, healthy children who have the greatest
mother I've ever known." He paused and touched his index
finger to his lips, then removed it to continue. "Work couldn't

be better. Word from the NIH at the conference is that the R01 grant is going to come through any day now, and the CDC keeps sweetening the pot on their offer." He shook his head vigorously, and she noticed a small stream of sweat rolling down his cheek. "I'd be a fool not to consider it."

CDC. She started to sing the ABC song in her head using CDC over and over.

He licked his lips until they glistened and looked out over the garden. "Maybe I'll be able to convince the center to set up a satellite office for my team here in Charleston." He looked back to her. "But Atlanta wouldn't be so bad, right? For a few years anyway? For a quantum career leap?" When she didn't respond, he looked back out to the garden, setting his eye on the rosebushes that outlined the carriage house. "But maybe we can do our research here. Have our cake and eat it too."

He grinned and took a deep breath. "We're going to get you right in no time, Lish." He tilted his head to the side and gazed at her. She tried to meet his eyes, but it took an effort for her to focus. "We have so much ahead of us, and I want you to enjoy it. Every last second of it."

She instinctively reached up and tore down a leaf like she used to do when she was a kid. The loquat leaf was about the size of a magnolia's, with a slightly lighter green tint, but it was the underside that was unique. It was a pale green and felt just like the outside of a ripe peach, fuzzy and remarkably soft. She stroked her forefinger across the bottom and remembered her daddy sitting with her beneath the tree when she was young. He'd reach up high, tear off a leaf from a long branch, and rub it against his cheek for a moment before handing it to her.

"Wanna feel something good?" he'd say.

And she'd rub it between her finger and thumb and then against her own cheek. It felt just like the outside of the small, gray velvet crèche figurines he had given her the year she was chosen to be Mary's Donkey in the St. Michael's Christmas pageant. She must have been four or five. She had a place in the center of the stage beside Mary and Joseph, and she was able to watch Baby Jesus, who was actually the new baby girl of her next-door neighbors on Rutledge Avenue. She still had the little figures tucked away in one of the Christmas boxes in the attic. It was always one of the first decorations she displayed each season. She usually set them on the breakfast table in the kitchen so Andrew and Mary Jane could play with them. They had reenacted the story with them so many times that the fuzz had rubbed off of the rounded edges of Mary's shoulder and the donkey's pointed ears.

"How does that sound?" Drew pulled her back with his confident voice. She watched him blink several times. "A normal week?"

She nodded and mustered a "Good," though her voice sounded, even to her, as though it was coming from the bottom of a well. She could barely hear it.

Now Mary Jane came racing over and leapt, soaking wet, into her lap. "Hold me, Mama." The little girl collapsed into Lish's sore chest.

Just as Andrew moseyed over, rubbing his long, damp eyelashes, the baby let out a cry from inside the house. Drew consulted his watch. " 'Bout that time."

Lish knew she should rise and put together the bottle, but she felt weary. It seemed to take a great effort to move any muscle in her body. Mary Jane reached up and stroked the back of her hair. "When are you going to play with me, Mommy? We haven't played Candy Land in a long time." Lish closed her eyes. The stroking felt good. The tug on her scalp made her feel awake, but she couldn't seem to think of how to respond to her daughter.

Drew leaned in and took Mary Jane's plump little hand. "Let's go find the water guns in the shed. It can be me and you against your brother."

"Yeah!" Andrew formed a fist and pumped his small tanned arm. "Bring it on!"

Drew peeled Mary Jane away from Lish, though the little girl still reached out for her mother. "Better go feed that hungry baby," he said as Lish curled her toes and swallowed.

Now she slowly stood and walked toward the kitchen, where Rosetta was mopping the floor.

The older woman stepped back when Lish entered. Lish turned to look at her. Rosetta had been avoiding her all day, and she wished she knew why, but she didn't have the nerve or energy to ask.

Rosetta nodded toward a fresh bottle on the counter. "Just made it."

"Thank you," Lish said as the baby continued to wail.

She grabbed the warm bottle and made what felt like a tremendous effort to walk up the stairs to the nursery.

Baby Cecilia kicked and wailed even louder when she caught sight of the bottle. Lish lifted her awkwardly and sat down on the glider and put the bottle in her mouth, forgetting to put on a bib. The baby grabbed the bottle and sucked, and Lish watched the little bubbles form at the bottom end as her infant gulped it down in a matter of minutes.

Lish's swallowing started to burn just slightly for a moment as she held the baby over her shoulder to burp. The thumping on her head was still very distant, but she kept batting her eyelids, expecting it to worsen. The baby belched, then she twisted and turned and fussed again. Lish could see by her bulging diaper that she needed a change.

She placed her on the changing table and opened the drawer underneath where the diapers and wipes were stored. She stared at the wipes for a long time, dazed. The baby was on her back with her dirty diaper open. She cried, kicked, and eventually spit up some of the formula in chunky streams that rolled down her chin and into the folds of skin around her neck.

Lish wasn't sure about what to do next. She curled her toes as she swallowed. *What comes first*, she thought to herself, *pulling the dirty diaper off or opening the clean one and putting it beneath the dirty one?* She feared she would upset the baby more if she did it out of order. She was not sure how long she stood there, her back tightening, staring at her kicking, spitting child.

There were footsteps on the stairs and then Rosetta was

there, striding through the doorway. The woman stepped in front of Lish and finished the job. As Lish turned around to head back to the glider, she saw Drew standing in the doorway, his shirt damp from the water gun fight. He studied her the way she'd seen him study a patient with an unidentified flu or a virus growing in a Petri dish. She sat down; she glided. Her mouth was filling with saliva. It was time to swallow, and she braced herself.

Drew guided Lish through the next couple of days. Though she moved in slow motion, she felt better, especially when the sun hit her face, blinding her momentarily, or when she stood in the shower watching the steam rise up and form beads of moisture along the thick windowpanes in Nana's old bathroom.

The baby smiled at her every time she walked into her room, though this bothered Lish. She didn't deserve a smile from Cecilia. Her heart ached when she saw those rosy lips tilt upward to reveal the pink gums behind them. She tried to smile back and meet her daughter's eyes, but she was ashamed of the kind of mother she had been to her so far.

As for Andrew and Mary Jane, it seemed to Lish that they had never asked so many questions:

"What's for supper?"

"Where's my Triggerhappy Transformer?"

"What are sequins made from, and how do they get to be different colors?"

"How do you get cooties?"

"Can we go to the Piggly Wiggly and buy the Popsicles like Uncle Peter has in his freezer?"

"What are you staring at, Mama?"

"Did you hear me?"

"How come you say, 'Uh-huh,' and you don't know what I said, Mama?"

Rosetta didn't usually take care of the children, but she had been willing to help with the baby. She fed Cecilia every two and a half to three hours and changed her several times a day. She bathed her in the nursery sink in the mornings, and then she laid her on her stomach on the floor of the den and put a shiny silver rattle in front of her.

"Don't want her head to get flat," she told Lish.

Lish knew this was a good idea. She remembered writing a column titled "The Value of Tummy Time" shortly after Mary Jane was twelve weeks old. The column warned against positional plagiocephaly—a condition where the skull flattens if a baby is left on his or her back too long—and it outlined the benefits of tummy time, including trunk stability, limb coordination, and head control, all of which would aid the baby in turning over and crawling as he or she grew.

However, Lish could hardly stand to watch Cecilia on her belly. The child grunted and struggled to lift her head in a way that made Lish cringe in both sorrow and sympathy.

On Tuesday, she stood in the doorway and watched her daughter's pink arms collapse. Her little chin hit the floor, and she did an out-and-out face plant where she breathed into her blanket and made a muffled cry that tore at Lish's gut for whole minutes until Rosetta grabbed Cecilia, rocked her, and stuck the pacifier in her mouth.

Lish described this scene to Dr. Cussler, the psychiatrist, during her first meeting with him. She had driven her car over the new and majestic Cooper River Bridge to Mount Pleasant, where she found his office in a little home in the Old Village.

He had asked her about her medical history and her family history, and now he seemed to be giving her time to talk. He was young, barely thirty by her estimation, and sort of nerdy with a small frame, a pasty white complexion, and a red paisley tie that clashed with a green striped shirt. She noted the wide gold band on his left ring finger and wondered if he had any children. *What kind of mother was his wife?*

He scratched his eyebrow and swooped a swath of his thin mousy brown hair out of his face. She knew he'd read her discharge papers, and she wondered if he thought she was trying to minimize and rationalize her thoughts and actions.

He screwed his long nose up, and for some reason he reminded her of the easily irritated rabbit from the Winnie the Pooh books. "Before we develop our goals and come up with a treatment plan, I want us to do a rating scale."

She swallowed. Her throat didn't burn right now in his office. His office reminded her of a dentist's office. It smelled like new carpet and something more. Whatever it was, she noticed that her nose tingled the way it did when the dentist put the mask over it and turned on the laughing gas. She felt relaxed. She felt like his big green leather chair could swallow her up; she wouldn't mind if it did.

He wiped his shiny, narrow nose and brought his pen back to his yellow legal pad. "All right, Dr. Sutton, on a scale of one to four"—he looked up at her briefly–"with four being the highest"—he looked back down—"I want you to rate your overall outlook on life right now."

She settled even further into the soft padding of the chair. Her legs made a squeaking sound as she leaned back and closed her eyes. "Four."

He scribbled on his pad as though she was telling him something that was essential to the survival of all mankind.

She sensed him looking up, and she opened her eyes but couldn't seem to sit up straight. "Rate your interest in doing your usual daily responsibilities."

She pushed herself up a little. "I'm interested, but I don't have the energy, and I think that's because of the Ativan." She slouched back down. "I'd say a drug-induced two."

"So how would you rate your energy level?"

Didn't she just say that? "The same."

He nodded and wrote some more. Then he intertwined his fingers and narrowed his eyes. She gnawed on the inside of her cheek as if she expected to lose feeling there soon. He said in a hushed tone, "Rate your feelings of helplessness."

She took a deep breath. Honestly, she felt very helpless, but she thought it was the medicine. She bit down so hard on her cheek that she reached up to rub the outside of it.

"We need to do this after I taper off of the anti-anxiety pills."

He nodded. "We will, but let's continue with it today. Right now, rate your feelings of helplessness."

She sucked her teeth and felt the pain pounding in her cheek. "Two and a half."

"Okay. Rate your feelings of hopelessness."

She rolled her head as if she was warming up in her aerobics class. "Two and a half." *Should she say two point five?* She breathed in the newness of the room. What was making her nose tingle? Maybe it was a new coat of paint or the leather of the chair. There was a window behind her and the sun filtered through the half-opened blinds, creating a horizontal pattern of slats of light across the arm of her chair and her lap. She felt relaxed here.

Dr. Cussler cleared his throat. "Have you felt, during this time, that you are a failure somehow?"

She gradually nodded *yes*. The room was very quiet. All she could hear was the hum of the air through the vents.

"Rate your feelings right now about that."

"Three." She closed her eyes. The AC cut off, and his voice seemed louder and clearer.

"Lish," he said. "Have you considered harming yourself?"

She kept her eyes closed. She sat very still. She swallowed and it barely burned. She searched her brain. *Had she?*

She could hear him sniff. He was trying to hold back a sneeze. He rubbed the tip of his nose and said, "On a scale of one to four, rate your thoughts about harming yourself."

He sneezed. "Excuse me."

"Two," she said.

Her lap felt warm, but she was not hot. She thought she could feel her heartbeat in her ears. She opened her mouth, and her ears popped just like they did when she was on an airplane.

Dr. Cussler seemed both miles away and right across the room from her.

She thought she heard him swallow. "One more question." He paused. "Have you had any thoughts about hurting anyone else?"

She felt her eyes moving back and forth beneath her eyelids. She searched her mind. She wanted to be honest. She wouldn't get better unless she was honest. She thought of the knives on the kitchen counter and how nervous they made her the day Drew had left for his conference. How she had thought, *The baby is vulnerable*. How she had watched her infant sleeping in the bouncy seat on the kitchen table. How she had picked up the whole block of knives and walked them over to the neighbor's trash can and threw them in. Did she actually think she would use a knife to harm Cecilia? Or was it just their proximity to the baby that made her uneasy? Should she connect those dots in her mind?

She wanted to weep, but she held it in.

"Rate your thoughts of harming someone else," the voice called from across the room.

She squinted her eyelids. She twisted in the chair. She sat upright and met his stare.

"One."

She felt stronger, somehow, as she started to cross the grand Arthur Ravenel Jr. Bridge that spanned the Cooper River connecting Mount Pleasant to Charleston. As she passed by each of the mighty, slanted cables that held up the longest bridge of its kind in the Western Hemisphere, she noticed the bright afternoon sun filtering through the clouds above her, and when she reached the crest of the bridge she felt as though she was ascending into the rays of light. As though each of the cars, including hers, was on its way to someplace so brilliant and so high it could take your breath away.

Dr. Cussler wanted to see her once a week for the next six weeks. After the rating questions, they came up with a treatment plan. She could taper from three down to two Ativan a day starting this Sunday. He believed this would help with her sluggishness, and he hoped to have her off of them in six weeks. He would keep her on her current 25 milligrams of Zoloft for one more week, then he would raise it to 50 milligrams for four weeks. If all went well, he would raise it to 75 milligrams. By six weeks she would be off the Ativan and on 100 milligrams of Zoloft. He expected her to be back to normal, or close to it, by Thanksgiving.

Chapter 13

ROY

September 6, 2008

On moving day, Ms. B. met Roy and Rose at the front of the rectory with the keys to his new home and a warm loaf of banana bread. It was all he could do to keep Rose from dancing as Ms. B. led them from room to room in the enormous three-story rectory that sat on the corner of Meeting Street and St. Michael's Alley.

"It's okay," Ms. B. said after he told Rose to settle down. "I'd be twirling too if I were her." Ms. B. took Rose's hand and swung it back and forth. "Tell your daddy it's time to celebrate."

Rose smiled at the impeccably dressed older lady in her pale yellow pantsuit and double-strand pearls with a gold hummingbird brooch on the top of her left shoulder. The bird's wings were spread wide, and Roy imagined the creature taking flight, buzzing around his new home in search of a flower.

Before long the moving van arrived, with Mama, Donny, and Chick less than twenty minutes behind it. When Mama stepped one foot onto the piazza, her jaw dropped so low you could see the three fillings on her bottom molars. Then she started asking Ms. B. a gazillion questions.

"How old is this place?"

"It was built in 1785."

"How high are the ceilings?"

"Ten feet."

"On each floor?"

"Yes, I believe so." Ms. B. looked to Roy and smiled as his mama stepped closer, pinched her elbow. "Tell me what else I should know about it, darlin'."

Ms. B. pointed to the piazza entry that led to Meeting Street. "This neoclassical screen door is of particular note." She pointed toward the back where the white clapboard became brick but not like any brick his mama had ever seen. "And so is the line of original brick outbuildings. They are connected to the house now via the butler's pantry, but they used to be a separate building which included the kitchen, laundry, stables, and slave quarters."

"Look, Granny! Horses!" Rose took her grandmother's hand and they ran out onto Meeting Street. Roy chuckled as Mama pinched off the large pink hair doohickey she had clipped to her jean miniskirt. She quickly twisted her long frosted hair and clipped it on the top of her head. Then she waved along with Rose as the carriage driver pointed out the rectory.

"We live here!" Rose hollered, and the group of tourists

smiled and nodded. Mama smoothed out the wrinkles in her jean skirt and nodded. "That's right, folks!"

Ms. B. turned to Roy. "Such enthusiasm!"

He rotated his bum shoulder forward and looked down at her. "You can say that again."

Pretty soon the men got to work unloading boxes and hanging pictures, and Mama sat with Ms. B. in the kitchen looking at swatches of paint for the formal living room.

"I'm fond of this lavender here," Mama said. "How 'bout you, Ms. B.?"

Ms. B. raised her eyebrows. "Well, since this is the gathering spot for many a meeting and even a tea or party, it might be best to go with something neutral."

"Mama?" Roy called over his shoulder as he held up his picture of the Clemson End Zone over the fireplace in the den right off of the kitchen. "We've got eight rooms upstairs. You can pick one just for yourself and paint it any color you like."

"Oh, my!" Mama pointed to the swatches. "Can I keep that lavender one, Ms. B.?"

"Why yes, of course." Ms. B. carefully pulled the swatch out and handed it over to Mama who leaned in and said, "I saw this black-and-white-striped bedspread the other day at Marshall's, and I'm going to buy that thing and fix me up a nice guest room for me and Donny."

"That sounds lovely," said Ms. B.

Then Roy could hear Mama whispering. " 'Course, the truth is, Rose and I are hoping Roy will meet someone down here and get back going on that big family he always wanted." He turned and watched her squeeze Ms. B.'s hand.

"Will you be on the lookout for someone to introduce him to, Ms. B?"

Ms. B. looked back and saw Roy shaking his head in disbelief. "If it pleases Father Summerall, I will keep my eyes open."

"Oh, thank you." Mama clicked her silver nails together. "You're as lovely as Roy said."

By nightfall, he and Rose had placed some plastic lawn furniture on the upstairs piazza, and they feasted with Chick and Mama and Donny on one of the umpteen casseroles Ms. B. had stacked in the freezer. As the sun set over the picturesque rooftops, a flock of pelicans flew right by them at eye level on their way to roost.

"Good gracious, those birds are big, Daddy!" Rose said.

"They are, sugar," he said with a nod. He was seeing everything through her eyes and was not surprised when she climbed into his lap and said, "Don't you feel like this is a dream?"

He pulled her close as Mama looked on grinning. "Maybe so, Rosebud."

When Roy arrived at work the next day, he found a stack of resignation letters on his desk from the staff of St. Michael's, including the assistant rector, the youth minister, the children's education director, the bookkeeper, the organist and choirmaster, the office manager, the sexton, the housekeeper, and the receptionist. (Back at Good Shepherd, it had just been Roy and Skeeter and a whole lot of volunteer parishioners, and he had spent many a day scrubbing toilets and sweeping floors.). He had heard this was the protocol when a new rector took over a church, but he had no intention of getting rid of anyone unless, after getting to know them well, he realized they directly opposed his vision for the place.

He called them all together in his office, took a seat on his desk, and tugged at the collar encircling his wide neck. Then he held up the stack of resignation letters and smiled at this group of well-dressed, bright-eyed strangers, his staff. "I'm not accepting any of these right now." He looked to each of them. "Let's get to know one another. My hope is that we can be a team." He glanced out at the nine a.m. hustle and bustle of Broad Street before pulling out the well-worn Bible Miss Ruby gave him after his confirmation.

"Let's start with a little Scripture and prayer. We can do this every morning if you'd like. And we can pray for each other. You know, let each other know what's going on in our work lives and home lives so we can look after each other."

"Wow," the youth minister said. He was a clean-cut young fellow with the exception of his tattered sandals and the tiny silver dot on the side of his nostril. *Is that an earring?* Roy wondered. The youth minister nodded his head with confidence. "I like what you're saying, Father Roy." He reached out his hand. "By the way, I'm Keith Norris."

"Me too," a woman piped up, her eyes brimming with tears.

Roy leaned toward her. "You're Keith Norris?"

"No." She shook her head and chuckled as she brushed

away a tear. "I'm Trish Dickerson, the office manager, and I like what you said about praying for each other."

Roy put down his Bible gently on his desk. "Well, we can start right now, Trish." He saw a box of Kleenex on a bookshelf and held it out to her. "If there's something you want to share."

She nodded and reached for the box. "I'm just so relieved you're keeping us on." She looked out of the window. "My husband is in real estate, and he hasn't had a sale in almost a year." She looked around the room at the staff, and Roy wondered how well they knew one another. "And my mama broke her hip and needs to move in with us." Trish's shoulders began to shudder as she silently held back her weeping. "And I tell you the truth, she's not the easiest person to live with."

Roy walked over and patted Trish's shoulder. Then he motioned for them all to come together and pray for her on the spot.

When they were finished, she blew her nose and nodded her head. "Thank you," she said as she looked around the room. "Thank you so much."

Then Roy opened his Bible right in the center and read aloud the first full psalm he could find. It was Psalm 121:

I lift up my eyes to the hills—
where does my help come from?
My help comes from the Lord,
the maker of heaven and earth.

He will not let your foot slip—
he who watches over you will not slumber;

> *Indeed, he who watches over Israel*
> *will neither slumber nor sleep.*
>
> *The Lord watches over you—*
> *the Lord is your shade at your right hand;*
> *the sun will not harm you by day,*
> *nor the moon by night.*
>
> *The Lord will keep you from all harm—*
> *he will watch over your life;*
> *The Lord will watch over your coming and going*
> *both now and forevermore.*

Roy could feel a kind of peace taking root in his own heart as he read the words. God was watching over all of them, even him. And when he looked up at this staff he hadn't known yesterday, he saw them as he thought they really were—people longing for mercy and love, and he knew that ministering to them and having them minister to one another was one of the things he was brought here to do.

By the end of the week, he'd met with the vestry, though Heyward Rutledge, the senior warden, was a surprising no-show. Roy tried all the numbers for him listed in the church directory, but the junior warden, Commander Carleton with the eye patch, recommended they proceed without him. Roy made his pitch to start up the Alpha Course in mid-October (which he all but insisted the leadership and the staff should take), and the vestry approved the small budget for this endeavor and seemed willing, if half-heartedly, to participate.

Roy also met with Ms. B. twice that week (at her strong suggestion) to plan his installation, which sounded like a whole lot more hoopla that he was hoping for, with an engraved invitation to all the clergy in the diocese, a trumpeter, a bagpiper, a quarter peal of the church bells, and a reception for three hundred in the Parish Hall.

"Is all this necessary?" he said to Ms. B., who stood in his door asking for the proper names and addresses of the folks from Ellijay he wanted to invite. "I mean, I'm a little uncomfortable with all of the expense, and I don't want too much of a to-do."

Ms. B. clucked. "It's quite necessary, Father Summerall. You're the fifteenth rector who has taken the helm of this church in over two hundred and fifty years, and it's cause for a celebration."

On Friday, Roy walked down to Waterfront Park to write his sermon. He was a little fretful since it was his first one to this congregation, and the Gospel from the lectionary was a spiky one: Matthew 18:15–20, where Christ tells his followers how to treat a brother who sins against them. He could bypass the spikes for this time and head straight to the last verse, where Christ promises believers that if two or more are gathered together in his name, he will be there in the midst of them. That was an uplifting one, and he really wanted to start on a high note. The verse meant Christ would be there at that moment even as Roy preached. But as he started to write the sermon, he kept going back to Matthew 18:18. It was a verse that both haunted and perplexed him as Christ said, "I tell you the truth, whatever you bind on earth will be bound in heaven, and whatever you loose on earth will be loosed in heaven."

As far as Roy could tell, it meant that the stuff we do in the here and now has an eternal ripple. That was pretty frightening if you stopped to think about it. And yet, as he stared at the words, this came to his mind. *What we do here counts. And we often get sidetracked, even with the best of intentions, and before long we are building our lives on a foundation that might not be what we were made for.* He realized as he wrote that this was a perfect invitation to Alpha. He would put forth these questions:

Why am I here? Where did I come from? Where am I going? For anyone who thinks there might be more to life than meets the eye right now, for anyone who has questions about life or God, no matter how simple or even hostile, you need to come have dinner with us in the Parish Hall every week for ten weeks starting on Tuesday, October 19. And bring that friend or neighbor who has these questions too.

The next day was Saturday and he was getting a little antsy about how his first Sunday would unfold. It was just him and Rose in the big, rambling house now. They spent the morning riding bikes around the peninsula, and in the afternoon he put on his old Clemson jersey and she put on the orange cheerleading uniform he bought during his last trip to a game, and they spent the afternoon watching the Tigers pummel The Citadel with a final score of 45-17. Around four, he heard someone ringing up the one-ton tenor bell in the steeple tower, and he remembered that there was a wedding in the church that a priest from Columbia was officiating.

Rose ran out to the piazza and called him. "Daddy, come quick!" When he ambled out, his knees aching too much for a thirty-five-year-old man, he saw her pointing toward the street where the tall, redheaded woman was walking toward the steps that led to the bell tower.

Roy looked at the striking woman he'd spotted the day he came for his interview and then down at Rose who was watching him. "Do you think that's an angel?" the little girl said. "Like Mr. Jackson told us about?"

"Maybe," he said. "But my guess is she's a bell ringer. A really tall one."

Rose cocked her head. "Can we see the bells? You haven't shown me yet."

He looked down at her. She was so eager that she was bouncing on the balls of her feet.

"I tell you what." He gently rubbed her little back. "There's a TV in the narthex where you can watch the bell ringers ringing. We'll head over there and take a quick look at the end of the wedding."

"Yippee!" Rose said. She pulled her plastic chair up to the edge of the second-floor piazza. "Now I'm just gonna sit here and watch."

"Okay," he said. He went and got her some lemonade

and sat beside her as the groomsmen and bridesmaids lined up outside the sanctuary, and then came the lovely young bride on the arm of her father.

"That might be you one day," Roy said.

She smiled and took a deep breath. "Yeah."

As the bells sounded at the end of the ceremony, they ran to the narthex and Roy flipped on the television. The eight ringers were standing in a circle facing one another as they took turns pulling on the long ropes of the pulleys that rung the enormous bells two floors above them. It was the most jubilant sound Roy could imagine, and just as he was about to tell Rose the long story of the bells, the priest from Columbia grabbed his arm and introduced himself.

The priest, a fellow by the name of Mike Dunlap, bent Roy's ear for nearly twenty minutes about national church politics as the last guests filed out and the bells stopped ringing. Just as the priest's wife tugged on his arm, Rose hollered, "Daddy!" She was pointing at the television. "Look!"

Roy peered at the screen and saw the tall, redheaded woman in the empty tower. She was on the resting bench, in her white vestments, weeping.

"How do you get up there?" Rose asked.

"There's the stairs on the other side."

Before he could stop her, Rose bolted toward the steps. He followed her up two flights and around the narrow, winding stairwell to the bell tower, where she pushed open the door to the room before he could grab her little arm.

"What's the matter?" Rose asked as she stood in front of the woman. The afternoon sunlight flooded the room and he could see Rose's shadow, long and narrow against the unfinished hardwood floors, her little pleated cheerleading skirt swaying from side to side like a bell itself.

The woman sat up straight and wiped her bright green eyes with her wrists. She was speechless and she shook her head, her long, wavy hair moving back and forth across her shoulders.

Rose turned quickly to Roy. "I think she is one," she whispered. "I don't even think she speaks this language."

Roy stood behind his child and put both hands on her shoulder as if to steady her.

"We're sorry to barge in on you, ma'am." He reached out his wide hand. "I'm Roy and this is Rose, and we were just—"

"We were watching the TV downstairs." Rose looked the woman head-on as if she was a school-yard friend who had just fallen off of a swing.

The woman furrowed her lovely red eyebrows. "They don't turn that on for weddings."

He took back his hand once he realized she was not reaching out to shake it. He squeezed his daughter's little shoulders. "No. I just turned it on to show Rose. I'm the new rector, and we're still sort of getting to know the place. I'm sorry if we did something we shouldn't have." He wondered if she even believed him. He didn't look like a priest at the moment in his old football jersey (which was getting a little tight) and his well-worn blue jeans.

"Yeah, and we saw you crying on the TV." Rose nodded. "I thought you might be an angel because, well, you're so tall." She leaned slightly toward the woman. "Are you?"

"No." The woman smiled through her tears. "I'm just a bell ringer. One who's having a hard day." She reached out her long, delicate hand. "I'm Anne Brumley."

Instantly he recognized her from childhood. She had grown up with two other girls down the street from his Aunt Elfrieda, and he had seen them walking along the High Battery and down at the East Bay Playground. They were all way too pretty for him or Chick to get the nerve up to ask for a dance.

"My daddy can help you." Rose grabbed Anne's hand and squeezed it. "He's real good at that."

He rubbed the back of his wide neck and smiled.

"Okay," she said more to Rose than to him. She looked up to meet his eye and smiled. "I could use a little guidance."

When they entered the piazza of the rectory, he motioned toward the white wicker chairs Ms. B. had someone deliver yesterday, and she took a seat. She had taken off her vestments, and she was in a lovely dusty-green sundress with the smallest white flowers embroidered around the edge of her skirt.

"I'm going to go get you some iced tea," Rose said. "My granny made it, and it always makes me feel better."

"All right," Anne said. "That sounds wonderful."

She sat back in her chair and twisted her hair into a knot. "She's precious."

"Thanks." Roy shook his head. He had not noticed a

woman in a long time and he could feel his face redden. It wasn't anything puritanical, his unawareness of physical beauty. It was just God's way of binding up his heart since losing Jean Lee, and Roy wondered when God would unwrap it and proclaim it healed.

"Here you go." Rose brought out the tea with a paper towel and an orange coaster with a tiger paw. She turned to Roy. "I'm going to go unpack my Barbies upstairs."

"Okay, Rosebud." He watched Anne take a big sip of tea as Rose's feet padded up the stairs to the second floor. She recrossed her legs and put her hands on her narrow, freckled knee.

Doggone, this woman was pretty. If she needed ongoing counsel or prayer, he was going to have to turn her over to the assistant rector.

He smiled at her, and before he could ask she spoke. "I guess maybe I'm having a crisis of faith." She put the tea down and then picked it up for another sip. "That *is* good," she said.

"Tell me what you mean by crisis?" He prayed, *Lord show me how to help this woman.*

She straightened out her sundress and spoke to the ground. "I thought God spoke to me. A few years ago about something specific." She shook her head and looked up at him. "Anyway, I've been waiting and waiting and nothing has happened."

He nodded.

Anne chuckled. "My cousin and sister don't believe me, I think. Anyway, they encouraged me to move on, and I think that's what I'm going to do." She tilted her head and looked at him. "Only, what if I'm wrong? What if I miss what I was supposed to be waiting for?"

Funny how God worked. He spoke to some people very clearly and then it took a long time to materialize. Then he didn't speak to Roy at all about Charleston and embarking on this new ministry and—*bam*! He was blindsided by it. Tackled before he had a chance to run.

"You know, there are some stories in the Bible about promises that take a long time for our human eyes to see. There's Abraham and Sarah, for one."

"Yeah, I thought about that one," she said. "And Sarah took matters into her own hands and ended up with some trouble."

"Absolutely." He could hear Rose singing upstairs. She always had this little music routine she did with her Barbies. "And there's the forty years in the desert and then Zechariah at the temple . . ."

She bit her lip until it turned white. "Those people were really important, though."

"We're all important, Anne."

She met his eyes, and he didn't look away.

He rotated his bum shoulder and, out of habit, leaned forward. "Look, waiting is hard. Maybe even harder than the surprises."

"But what if I was wrong? What if I didn't hear it right?"

"Well," he said. "I don't think it would be too bad to ask for a little encouragement, do you?"

She took another sip of tea and a strand of wavy hair fell out of her twist. It covered her eye for a moment before she tucked it behind her ear. "Okay."

Then he bowed his head and prayed for her to receive some sort of tangible encouragement.

"Thank you so much." She stood and shook his hand. "And thank Rose for me too."

"I will," he said. "I hope to see you around the church."

Then she walked out of the piazza door onto the street, and he couldn't help but watch her as she walked down Meeting Street, the sun on her back, her pale green dress billowing out.

When a little plastic Barbie shoe fluttered down to his feet, he looked up to the second-floor piazza where Rose was watching too.

"Well, she wasn't an angel, Daddy," she said as the woman rounded the corner where Meeting met Broad, "but she was really nice." Rose licked her little red lips. "And pretty."

He looked up at her and shook his head. She was a little Granny in the making.

She raised her dark eyebrows. "I'm just saying . . ."

"Get on down here," he said. "Let's have supper."

When she came down, she grabbed his hand. "Daddy, I don't think I can eat another casserole."

"I agree," he said. "What do you say we hop on our bikes and find a pizza joint?"

"Hooray!" She made her hands into fists and cheered. "Only cheese on my half—"

"I know, I know," he said.

Chapter 14

DELLA

The bell rang and the seventh graders exited Della's classroom, stepping over a pencil sharpened down to its nub and a couple of used tissues someone had discarded relatively near the trash can. *Nice aim*, Della thought. It was only September, but several of the girls had runny noses and coughs and even fevers. Della went through at least one box of tissues a day as student after student stood at the front of the room by her desk (in the middle of a lecture), blowing their noses, examining the contents of the tissue, then blowing again.

Twelve-year-old girls were good at killing time, and they were still relatively fascinated with their own bodily functions. They giggled when they hiccupped; they studied a mosquito bite on their leg for whole minutes, squeezing it and scratching it until a trip to the nurse's office for a Band-Aid was inevitable; and they winced when their throats hurt and asked to be excused just at the climax of her lecture so they could examine their tonsils in the bathroom mirror from every possible angle until Della had to send a fellow student in to call them back to class.

"No, you may not go to the nurse because the cuticle of your pinky finger is peeling a little," Della told one. She wanted to sound irritated like some of the other teachers who hemmed and hawed and rolled their eyes in an exaggerated manner, but she couldn't. She honestly loved her students, and after years of teaching on and off in the public and private schools around the lowcountry, she remained in awe of how distinct, and sensitive, and full of life each one was, from their gait to their yawn to their sense of humor to whatever quick glance or whispered word from a peer caused their lips to suddenly quiver and their eyes to fill with tears.

She had sixty of them this year, and when she first stared at their names on her roster and looked out at the seemingly homogenous group during the first day of school, she thought, *How will I ever learn their names?* But within the week, each of them said or did something that stuck out in her mind as if to say, "Don't you know? There is no one quite like me, Mrs. Limehouse."

And Della understood how true this was, and before the end of the second Monday of the school year, she knew their names automatically and could spot them from behind several yards down the hall as they squealed and giggled and shuffled along in the same plaid uniforms with the same haircuts and the same hundred-dollar backpacks and tennis shoes.

Right now they were reading *A Raisin in the Sun* as a class.

It was a great American play about an African-American family eking out a life in the south side of Chicago during the 1950s. It was inspired by Langston Hughes' famous poem "Harlem," where he considered through a series of metaphors what happened to dreams that were forever put off.

The majority of Della's students were quite privileged, and they chuckled as they read their assigned parts. There was a somewhat dated African-American slang that Della had to interpret, and this tripped the students up during the first act. But eventually they were captivated by the story and settled into it without letting a foreign word or idiom break their stride.

Today they were reading the first scene in Act II, where Walter, the protagonist, home from an afternoon spent at the local bar, stood on the kitchen table and pretended he was an African warrior. The girls were in hysterics by the time he made up an African war cry and shouted, "Ocomogysiay," with his sister Beneatha egging him on.

Della had read this play a dozen times at least, but this year it penetrated her heart in a whole new way. Peter hadn't had a commission in months now, and two-thirds of her paycheck went to pay their mortgage. He'd had a toothache that he couldn't afford to go to the dentist to check out. (Neither one of them had been to a dentist in a decade.) And they'd had a rat infestation that they'd had to deal with themselves by setting up traps with peanut butter on a sticky, white square.

Della religiously checked the traps each morning ever since she'd found three baby rats curled up like backward c's on the pad beneath the kitchen sink just as Cozy came in to ask for breakfast. She'd slammed the door and ordered Cozy back to her bedroom to put on her shoes while she ran into the backyard and tossed them in the big green trash can. Now every time Della passed the outside garbage container, she pictured those miniature rodents—their small, rigid feet, their shut eyes, their pink ears pinned back on the sides of their little heads.

Last week after Peter looked at the stack of month-old water and electric and credit card bills on the kitchen table, he picked up the phone and called Old South, the carriage company he worked for during college, and he immediately took the same job he had fifteen years ago—giving carriage tours (for minimum wage and the hope of a few decent tips) up and down the peninsula dressed in a polyester Confederate uniform costume in the blistering heat.

In the play, when Walter's disillusioned wife, Ruth, said to her mother-in-law, "Yes, life can be a barrel of disappointments, sometimes," Della nodded her head and knew that it would likely be years before her students understood what Ruth meant.

These girls were blessed, immeasurably so. At the least, their lives were extremely comfortable. They had loving parents, refrigerators full of fresh produce and organic meat, luxury SUVs with leather seats, nannies and housekeepers to keep their mothers sane, vacations that required airline tickets and even passports from time to time, and simplest yet best of all—soft, clean beds in their very own rooms where they could lay their heads at night and dream of something nice like a picnic at the beach or a Wii under the

Christmas tree or a purebred puppy wagging his tail at the sight of them.

Their lives were the very ones Walter fantasized about. The ones that were so far out of reach, it was making him crazy. Of course, they couldn't see this. How could they? They might never see it if they stayed on the trajectory their parents had in mind for them: attractive, straight-toothed, and educated young woman lands spot at very decent if not above-average college, meets attractive, straight-toothed young man from similar background, begets another generation of a privileged life, and so on.

Della looked out of her window and spotted the first-grade class walking to the lunchroom, and there in the middle of the pack was Cozy holding another little girl's hand. The girl leaned toward her and made a remark that caused Cozy to laugh and pull away for a moment without releasing the hand. She turned back and smiled at her friend, and they began to swing their arms together until their teacher stopped the group and instructed them to line up single file before they went in to eat.

Now Della knew she must call Todd Jervey. She'd made her decision, and it was time to move forward. In the teacher's lounge, she dialed the number of his pager, and a few minutes later he called back during her planning period. "Della?"

"Yeah." She cleared her throat.

"What's going on?"

"Well . . ." Her voice sounded unusually high-pitched

and unfamiliar to her. "I was wondering if you'd like to meet me for lunch sometime this week."

He paused. She thought she could hear him breathing. He chuckled nervously. "Sure, I can get away for a little while tomorrow or maybe Wednesday, if that works for you."

"Tomorrow," she said. "Blend at noon?"

"Yeah." He paused a second time. "I look forward to it."

She met him outside of the restaurant the next day. He was in his white coat with his name and title inscribed in royal blue thread across the upper left side. He'd shaved off his beard, and he looked younger and a lot like the fiancé she left one July morning after buying a one-way flight to LaGuardia airport.

He held open the door for her and they took a seat at a small table on the back of the piazza. Her favorite black sleeveless dress with the thick, red patent-leather belt had a rip under the arm, so she'd settled for a short brown-and-blue floral skirt missing a button and a brown silk top that still passed for professional despite its significantly scooped neck.

"So." He fiddled with the brass edge of the menu. She crossed her legs and flashed a smile. If she needed dental work, it was well concealed. Thank goodness Nana sprung for braces when she was a teenager and stayed after her about brushing and flossing until the day she left for college. "How's Lish holding up?"

"I don't know for sure." For some reason she couldn't recall what he had just asked. She took a gulp of her iced tea. While it was nearly October, the heat index was still 100 degrees. She regretted wearing the Spanx Lish handed down to her last year, though it did suck it all in. She didn't yet have the midsection rolls that a lot of her friends had acquired, but she had this overall gravity thing going on that was really depressing. Her breasts seemed to droop in a way they never had before, like heavy raindrops dripping down from the roof gutter, and her rear end sort of sagged down, overlaying the back of her upper thighs. Aging was sad, Della had thought as she stood on top of her bed that morning, studying herself in front of their bureau mirror while Peter poured Cozy a bowl of the Food Lion-brand Cheerios.

Now Todd repositioned the salt-and-pepper shakers as he waited for her response. "Della?" he said. "How's Lish?"

Della snapped back. "Oh, sorry." She blushed and let out a guffaw. "Um, she's sent me a few vague e-mails about focusing on her family and getting better." She brushed away a fly that had just landed on the edge of the table. "I guess that doesn't involve me. Or so her husband is convincing her, I'm sure." She blushed and flipped her hair. "Drew was *furious* about us sending her to the hospital that night."

Todd shook his head in disbelief. "I don't see what other choice we had."

"I don't either," Della said. "I think Drew sees what Drew wants to see, you know?"

Todd nodded knowingly, then lifted the white cloth

napkin and patted the beads of perspiration on his fair, freckled forehead.

Della repositioned herself in her chair and corrected her
posture. "So how's the new job?" She lifted her chin and read
the title beneath his name. "Chair of the Department of
Psychiatry. That sounds like a pretty big deal." She watched
him remove his tortoiseshell glasses and clean them with the
tip of his tie. "Is it an administrative drag or do you get to do
the research you love?"

He chuckled as the waiter delivered their salads. He'd
ordered the Atlantic salmon on mixed greens, and she'd
ordered the pan-seared tuna served over tangled lettuce,
topped with roasted asparagus and kalamata olives.

"Well, the deal I struck is that I continue with the
research." He took a bite. "I've got a great administrative
assistant who seems, so far anyway, like she can help me keep
the paper-pushing to a minimum."

Della's eyes narrowed. She noted nothing else around but
him. Not the clink of the other diners as they cut and stabbed
their food or the hum of the cars whizzing by. She leaned in.
"Tell me about the research." She knew he'd received some
kind of award for a study he conducted during his fellowship
at Johns Hopkins a few years back and that Lish and Drew
had called him the shock doc because of his interest in electroshock therapy. "Are you working with electricity?"

He wiped his mouth, looked up, and raised his eyebrows.
She knew it had suddenly dawned on him that she'd been
keeping up with him. He smiled. "Sort of. But we think we're
on to a less invasive method." He placed his napkin back in

his lap and began to talk with his hands. "There's a local neurologist I'm working with who came up with the idea for what's called transcranial magnetic stimulation."

She tried to stop the wrinkles from forming on her forehead. *What did he just say? Focus.* "You mean using magnets instead?"

"Exactly." He took a sip of his iced coffee. "ECT causes seizures which sort of set the reset button on the brain, but the seizures can be harmful to the patients and there are all sorts of negative side effects." He counted them off with his damp fingers. "Significant memory loss, a reaction to the anesthesia, stuff like that."

"Hmm," she said. "And there's a stigma, right? I mean, who doesn't visualize *One Flew Over the Cuckoo's Nest* when you say electroshock treatment?"

He chuckled and took a hearty bite of his greens. "Right."

"So this one is gentler?" She gazed at him until he glanced up, wiped his mouth, and locked eyes with her.

"Much more so." He paused to take her in. She tried to subtly correct her posture and push her shoulders back. He looked her up and down through his round lenses with a kind of warm familiarity. She suspected he wondered at this moment *why* she'd asked him to lunch.

"How?"

He grinned at her and lifted his hand to his head. He enjoyed talking about his work. "We use strong electromagnets to bypass the skull with a magnetic field." He tilted his head and stared into her blue eyes. Then his cheeks turned pink, and he looked down at his plate.

This was easy and familiar. She had hoped it would be, and it was. She nodded for him to continue.

"Then we put a weak electrical current on the brain. It works by reenergizing the brain's left prefrontal cortex, where nerve cells in patients with serious depression become sluggish and don't fire off like they should."

"Mmm," she said. "Noninvasive is the key."

He nodded. "We're preparing a trial that we'll run in a few weeks in hopes that we can prove that depressed patients receiving four weeks of daily, thirty-minute TMS sessions will improve."

"Wow. That's fascinating." And it was, if she stopped to think about it. There were a lot of things Della wished she could reset. She watched Todd's Adam's apple bob up and down as he sipped his iced coffee.

She thought he was onto her; he seemed nervous. She patted his knee and let her hand linger for a moment before he looked up.

"Can we do this again, Todd?" She grinned.

He returned her gaze. "Really?"

She nodded. "Yeah. It's so good to see you."

Yep, she was working it. She admitted it, and he likely did too. Todd was insightful, no denying that, but as she suspected, he seemed willing to go along.

This was what was best, she thought as she walked briskly down Doughty and crossed over Rutledge Avenue. She'd have a class full of students in less than five minutes, but thankfully, they would spend the period reading the play.

As she watched a well-heeled mother walking her daughter through the gates after some kind of trip or doctor's appointment, she nodded her head. Yes, she was going to get the life that she wanted for Cozy, and Peter would be free to pursue his art. They would all be taken care of. Like her students and their easy existences. Like Lish and her family.

Why should she feel ashamed? In fact, perhaps this was the way most women think. They just never actually talked about it. Maybe that very woman, signing her daughter in at the front desk, was at one time this calculated and brazen. Maybe it was only Della who was finally cluing in to how this whole thing worked.

She remembered some of the girls from her high school days who were hell-bent on finding a well-off man in college. The ones who sat in the senior hut the day before graduation and proclaimed their goal: "To get hitched to a great guy, of course."

She had scoffed at them. Even her favorite friend, Hilah Roberts, who had a shockingly tight-fisted father compared to the others, all but stated that she was out to marry a wealthy man. She found him at law school, and now she was living high on the hog in Atlanta with four kids and a live-in nanny from China who had been teaching her children Mandarin from birth. Hilah loved her husband, yes, but she made sure he fit the bill. It was a decision she'd made long before she ever laid eyes on him.

It was so obvious, Della thought as cars flew by her down Rutledge Avenue. Had she been an idiot not to see it? The

irony was not lost on her. She considered herself an intellec-
tual, and yet she'd missed this most rudimentary of objectives
for a woman who was not independently wealthy. It was like
when she learned about what sex actually was at the age of
ten. She'd been racking her brain trying to figure out what it
meant to "do it" after she heard some boys talking about it
outside the bathroom at one of the East Bay Playground
dances. *Well, I'll be doggone*, she'd said to herself when she
consulted a book titled *Human Sexuality* in the public library.
She'd sat down on the floor between the shelves and studied
the black-and-white illustration. *Of course, that fits inside
there. Duh! How could I not have seen that coming?*

Getting together with Todd was not a stretch. She had
been engaged to him before, right? She had every right to
hit the reset button on her life, didn't she? Todd would love
Cozy and provide for them both. And she could have more
children whom he would adore. Doctors, especially research
ones, weren't rolling in it, of course, but they made enough
of a living to go to the dentist, to educate children in a safe,
clean, cool environment, and to give their wives the opportunity to raise those children and to even consider pursuing
some of their own dreams beyond the bliss of domesticity.

It made Della dizzy to think of money as happiness, to
think of money as freedom, to think of money as life, as
Walter so shamelessly proclaimed to his mama in *A Raisin in
the Sun*. Yes, Della was calculating. And her old self might
argue that she was shallow. But she would tell that young girl
to sit down and bite her idealistic tongue. She was a mother.
Her child needed some security. Mothers were the fiercest,

most ferocious beasts in the animal kingdom, were they not? It was time to trade in her lofty (and unfeasible, she now knew) principles for the good of the whole.

Now, as she punched in the code of the wrought-iron gates of The Pinckney School, she heard the *click-clack* of a horse-drawn carriage bustling down a street in the distance and wondered if it was Peter, sweating like a pig in polyester with a gaggle of middle-aged women from the Midwest gawking at him and laughing at his well-timed jokes.

On campus, the seventh-grade girls were chasing one another during the last couple of minutes of recess. And the first graders were out and about, too, running cross country around campus as part of their PE period.

Cozy waved to Della as she bolted toward the gate. Just when Della thought she would whiz on by to keep her time low, the little girl stopped and held open her arms, and Della embraced her as the PE teacher smiled from the other side of the campus lawn.

During last period, Della's third-section class got all the way through Act II, Scene 2 of *Raisin*. When the money from Walter's father's life insurance came in, and his mama allowed him to be in charge of it, he immediately entrusted it to his business partners in hopes that they would open up a liquor store and make their fortunes together.

That evening, he came home jubilant and painted a picture to his young son, Travis, of the beautiful future they would soon share. This picture included a lovely home with a gardener, his wife Ruth in pearls, and best of all, Travis as a teenager filling out applications to the top colleges in the country.

The scene took place on the common room couch, which doubled as Travis's bed in the small ghetto apartment. At the end of the scene, Walter tells his wide-eyed son that he can grow up to be anything he wants to be. At this Travis leaps into his father's arms and Walter, with a voice that is both elated and hysterical, lifts his son up high and promises him the world as the lights black out.

And this afternoon Della was the one who reached for the last tissue from the box on her desk as she tried to keep her shoulders from shuddering for the two minutes before the dismissal bell rang.

Then one of her students, Meredith on the second row in the far left corner, asked, "Mrs. Limehouse? Are you okay?"

Chapter 15

LISH

October 5, 2008

The last few weeks had been easier than Lish expected them to be. She'd seen Dr. Cussler three more times, and her energy level had markedly increased as she gradually tapered from three down to one Ativan pill a day. Despite a faint nausea from time to time, she'd experienced no ill side effects from the Zoloft, and Dr. Cussler had continued to steadily increase the dose.

Now she took the children to and from school without Drew's help, and she cared for the baby on her own at night, though it still took her longer than usual to find the strength to pull herself out of bed when she heard Cecilia's cries.

More than a month of Saturdays had come and gone, and she wondered how Anne and Della were doing. She'd received voice messages and e-mails from them both, and she often wondered how Anne was fairing at her training program in

England, but she hadn't had the energy to send more than a one-word reply to either of them. "Fry one fish at a time," Drew told her when she asked him if she should call them back. "And right now you've got to focus on your immediate family."

Lish hoped she would have the strength to invite Della and her family to a Thanksgiving dinner at her home. This was one of the goals she'd secretly set for herself now that it was mid-October, and she was feeling so much better. By then she could show her cousin that she'd made a full recovery, and maybe the two of them could go to England to visit Anne before her upcoming move.

Drew had accepted the position at the Centers for Disease Control, and his start date was the first of December. Lish would finish up the school year with the children and her treatment with Dr. Cussler, and the plan was for her to have the house rented and the children moved by the first of May. That way, she could enroll Andrew and Mary Jane in a school for the last few weeks of the academic year, and they would hopefully make a few friends who they could get together with over the summer.

Of course, Lish was sad to be leaving her home, but she knew she should support Drew who couldn't be more excited about the opportunity. He was even able to bring the majority of his MUSC research team with him, including Rob, Melanie, and the two other fellows who had helped create the rotavirus vaccine. The fellows were all thrilled about the chance to work on the new flu vaccine team that Drew would oversee. All of the research showed that a pandemic was likely in the next five years, and Drew might very well play a role in saving a large number of lives through his work.

On Friday, though it was a week before planned, Lish decided to cut the Ativan and move down to a half milligram per day. She had agreed to resume writing her newspaper column and needed as much energy as possible to complete the first article she'd written in months. She knew what she wanted to write about—the health benefits of formula if you are unable to nurse. She was going to critique the brands and cover the bottle sterilization process as well as the general feeding schedule for newborns. Also, she was planning a birthday party for Andrew at Jump-Castle-Kingdom, and she wanted to be able to print and mail out the invitations within the week.

On Saturday, her second day on the half milligram of Ativan, she felt an energy like she hadn't felt since before the baby was born. She even sent Rosetta home early and ordered Drew's favorite dinner from Cru Catering—beef Wellington, roasted asparagus, and a cinnamon crème brûlée. Then she drove to the Wine Shop with all three children and purchased an eighty-dollar bottle of a Cotes du Rhone, his favorite.

Drew raised his eyebrows when he saw the dining room table set with linen place mats and silver and crystal.

"What's all this?" He put his hands on his hips, causing his pale blue scrubs to pucker.

Mary Jane came scampering up in her Cinderella night-gown. "Mama made you a romantic dinner, Daddy."

He lifted her up and rocked her back and forth as he looked at Lish, who had managed to take a shower, put on makeup, and iron a floral sundress with spaghetti straps that she'd worn before she was pregnant.

"So she did," he said. "And doesn't she look nice?"

Mary Jane pulled back, looked at her mama and then back to her daddy. She nodded yes and said, "Very."

❧

The next week started off strong for Lish as she sent in her article, mailed the birthday invitations, and managed to make a haircut appointment, but by Friday she felt a little jumpy and her throat began to burn like before.

She continued to have more energy, but something else was happening too. Every time she went to make a bottle for Cecilia, she saw microorganisms growing inside the bottom of the bottle, inching their way up toward the nipple. On Wednesday, the day Rosetta had the afternoon off, Lish refused to expose the baby to the awful germs, and Cecilia went hungry for hours until Drew came home, heard the child wailing, and said, "What the heck is going on with the baby, Lish?"

"There are microorganisms in the bottle," she said.

"You couldn't see them with the naked eye, even if there were," he said. He rolled his eyes before stomping into the kitchen and holding up a bottle up to the light. "See," he said. "Nothing's there."

Andrew raced in from the back garden with his fingers in his ears and quickly grabbed a juice box out of the refrigerator. He turned to his father. "The baby's been crying *all* afternoon. I can't stand the sound, Daddy, so I'm going back outside, okay?"

After Drew made a bottle and fed the baby, who went to sleep almost instantly after sucking twelve ounces down, he came out on the piazza where Lish was rocking in a chair.

He leaned against the railing. "Don't go back down this road, Lish." She watched him set his jaw and look out over their garden. She wondered if he was noticing the last pink blooms on the crepe myrtles along the far edge of the wrought-iron fence. He waved to a neighbor who was walking his dog, then turned back to her.

"You've been doing really well, honey. You've got to get a grip, okay?"

She nodded as if she was in slow motion and swallowed. It burned like strep throat or the time she had her tonsils out. "I'm okay. I think I'm just tired."

He sent her to bed at six o'clock and ordered a pizza for the kids.

❧

Friday, on the way to taking the children to school, Lish's car hit a bump in the road on Meeting Street and she was seized by the fear that she had run over someone. She pictured the basket weaver who sat at the corner of Meeting and John Street, tying the pine needles and sweetgrass into knots that she shaped into exquisite bowls and baskets. Lish was sure she had run over the woman. She could hardly breathe by the time the teacher's aide opened the car door for Andrew and Mary Jane and cheerfully escorted them into the building.

Immediately, Lish drove back to the spot and circled it four times, searching for the body of a thin and elderly black woman. She pulled over, got out, and walked back and forth around the block, examining the sidewalk, looking for traces of blood. She found nothing and circled again and again in her car. Where was the body? Had the woman been carted off to the emergency room?

Andrew and Mary Jane were the last in line to be picked up that day. Lish had spent the entire morning driving around and around the corner of Meeting and John Streets. She had been only three blocks from school, but she was over a half hour late picking up her children. Her eyelids were blinking incessantly, and her throat was dry and sore.

One of the teachers, a young girl right out of the early education program at the College of Charleston, walked with Lish and the children to the car. "Are you all right, Dr. Sutton?"

Lish's throat was too dry to answer. She nodded.

"Mommy," Mary Jane said. She was holding up a large piece of construction paper and talking, but Lish couldn't make out her words.

The aide paused for a moment before gently closing the door. Lish looked at the paper and Mary Jane's proud smile.

She couldn't find the words to comment, so she turned back around. With a jerking motion, she put the car in drive and rolled slowly out of the school parking lot.

Rosetta told Lish she wanted to work through the weekend. "Get yourself some rest, Miss Lish," she said, and she walked her up the stairs to her bedroom. Lish almost called Dr. Cussler once or twice on Saturday morning when her throat felt particularly hot and she didn't want to swallow, but she felt better after she drank some cool water and took a long, hot shower before crawling back into bed.

Despite their good intentions, the Suttons hadn't made it to church since Baby Cecilia's birth. They were scheduled to have her christened in November, and Drew said it would be pretty bad if he showed up just for the baptism and then left town.

So on Sunday, Rosetta laid out a beige suit for Lish and a pair of black, sling-back pumps. Drew rubbed her back in the early morning and said, "Let's go to church, all right?" Rosetta brought in a tray with a poached egg on toast and bacon, and Lish sat up, took a bite, and then set it aside. It hurt to swallow. She would call Dr. Cussler on Monday. She didn't want to go back on the Ativan, but she couldn't stand this either.

As she stood in front of the full-length mirror in her closet, attempting to zip up her skirt, Drew came up behind her in his charcoal gray suit and bow tie, rubbed her arms, and said, "You look great, Lish."

Rosetta dressed the children in matching green corduroy outfits and put Cecilia in a pale green dress with little pink sheep smocked across the neckline. She made a warm bottle and put it in the diaper bag along with Cecilia's pacifier and the little blanket with satin edges she seemed to be favoring.

They walked the four blocks to church, a handsome family in their pressed garments and their clean faces and their powdered and perfumed bodies. Drew pushed the stroller as Lish walked between Andrew and Mary Jane. The little girl reached up to hold her hand, and Lish took the hand lightly and began to swing it slightly. But as the historic church bells pealed from the stately steeple of St. Michael's Church, Lish became completely focused on avoiding the sidewalk cracks or the round black circles of dried gum that were splattered across the well-worn sidewalk.

In church Lish couldn't get comfortable. The enclosed wooden pew was hard, and it made her spine ache as she leaned back into it. The children were in their own worship service and the baby was in the nursery. Drew was seated to her right, looking away from her toward the altar and the pulpit whose large, ornate wooden roof seemed precariously perched on two columns. For a moment, Lish feared it would topple over and crush the new rector's head when he took his place in its center and looked out over the congregation as the organist played the last stanza of "A Mighty Fortress is Our God."

It felt like a strong hand was on Lish's throat, pressing mightily down on her vocal cords. She couldn't sing. She made a fist and rubbed her knuckles against the velvet cushion when the spit pooled in her throat and she had to swallow. She wanted to stop this. She'd been doing so much better. How in the world could this have come down on her again? If the hand pressed any tighter, she might choke.

After the young rector, who seemed familiar somehow, read the Bible and began his sermon, she grasped her throat as if to yank the hand off of it, and Drew glanced over and patted her knee. She abruptly bent forward, hiding herself in the high walls of the pews. She didn't want to embarrass him, but she had to get this hand off of her throat.

Drew faked a cough and leaned in. "You okay?" he whispered as the priest moved into the first point of his sermon.

She nodded. She didn't want to disappoint him. She was not going to backtrack now. She sat up and tried to concentrate on the priest's words. He was talking about Abraham's faith. How Isaac asked him where the animal was that they were going to sacrifice as he carried the sticks on his back for the altar they were to build at the top of the mountain.

Before she heard Abraham's response, the thumping started again on her head. She hadn't felt it in months and it was like a small hammer, pounding with force in the very center of the top of her head.

She could hardly breathe; she couldn't swallow. *No!* she thought to herself. She squirmed in her seat. Drew noted her in his peripheral vision. She moved back and forth, then she grasped the top of her head. The pounding worsened. Her throat burned. *No! No! No!* she whispered. Someone in the pew in front of her turned to look back.

The fire in her throat was throbbing in her head now. Drew turned to her. He reached out to squeeze her knee, to steady her, but she pushed his hand away. Then she stood and shrieked like she had been shot, and she felt like she had. "No! No!" she screamed and all eyes were on her, including the priest perched high above her in the top-heavy pulpit.

Drew stood up and put his arm around her, but she pushed him off and continued to scream. An internist in a pew several rows back came forward and the priest made his way down the pulpit stairs and across the aisle to her.

Drew squeezed her shoulders with force. "Lish. Come on. Lish, stop."

She shook her head. She spit. She couldn't swallow any more. She couldn't stand it. As two more physicians from the congregation moved toward them, Drew restrained her from the back, picked her up, and carried her screaming down the aisle and out of the building onto the busy corner of Meeting and Broad Street where she collapsed in a heap at the foot of one of the grand white columns as the shadows of the figures attempting to help rose above her.

Someone was asking Drew questions. Someone was praying with their hands open toward her. She heard Drew tell someone to get the children, and then she spit and shut her eyes until she was lifted and carried toward a car that drove her home with Drew pinning her arms to her sides the whole way.

In her bedroom, he poured an Ativan out of her medicine bottle. She put it on her tongue and he watched her until she swallowed. Then he pulled back the covers and stuffed her under them. Rosetta kept an eye on Lish as Drew paged Dr. Cussler, and she agreed to spend the night and look after the kids once a friend from church brought them home. Lish heard all of this from the bed where her head, heavy as an anvil, rested against a thick goose-down pillow. She knew it wouldn't be long before the medicine would calm her as she entered its thick, heavy haze. She lifted her hand to touch her head. She rubbed the spot where the pounding was becoming duller, and she wondered why she was being tortured so.

Hold on, she said to herself. It will be gone by the second pill.

That night, after Drew forced the second Ativan down her, she stumbled out to the piazza where she crouched beside the rocking chair and took in the fresh air. She could hear Drew check on the children who were all asleep, with Rosetta in the guest bed in Cecilia's nursery. Then she watched him walk quietly outside and over to the carriage house, where he discreetly rapped on the door.

"Hello there, doctor." Melanie stepped to the side and closed the door after he slipped in.

The young woman forgot to close the blinds, and Lish could see Drew taking a sip from Melanie's glass of wine and then a bite of her pasta. The young woman rubbed his back in wide strokes, then massaged his neck. Drew let his head drop so she could get to that spot in the center where he usually had a knot.

"Ahh," Lish imagined him saying. "That's the place." Then Drew glanced over his shoulder, noticed the opened blinds, and turned back to shut them tight.

"Daddy?" Rose tried to twirl the spaghetti casserole with her fork into her wide spoon as they sat at the long antique table in the rectory dining room. The table had belonged to the original owner of the home, a local judge, who had left it as a housewarming gift for the first rector when St. Michael's purchased it toward the end of the eighteenth century.

"You hear me, Daddy?" the little girl said. Roy reached out and patted her hand. "I'm sorry, Rosebud." His mind was on the woman who had collapsed in church that morning. He had found her address in the directory and walked over to see about her, but the husband met him at the front door and said she was sleeping.

Roy had seen a lot of things during his few short years as a priest, but he'd never heard the kind of suffering expressed in that woman's shriek. It was as if she were choking or burning from the inside out, and he had felt helpless, which both angered and terrified him.

He rotated his shoulder and smiled at his child. "I'm all ears. Go ahead."

"Did a lady start screaming in church today?" Rose had a worried look on her face. She glanced at the twisted noodles on her fork and put them down. "I think you better cut up the pasta for me. That's what Granny does."

"Okay." He reached over with a knife and fork. "And to answer your question, yes, a lady did scream in church today. In fact, that's what I was just thinking about."

"I saw her." Rose stared at him with wide eyes. "When the teacher was walking us over from children's chapel. I saw a man carrying her and then I heard some folks talking about it at the coffee hour." She looked down at her cut pasta and took a bite. "Why do you think she did that?"

"I don't know," Roy said. "I tried to go over to her house and see her when you were on your play date, but she was resting."

"Mmm." Rose took a sip of milk and wiped the little mustache off of her face. "I wonder what's wrong with her."

"Me too," he said.

Roy's installation was scheduled for that Thursday, October 9th. The Parish Hall was remarkably hectic that week with Ms. B. and her team polishing silver, ironing linens, cooking and baking, and arranging the flowers.

More than four hundred people had responded positively

to the invitation, and she decided to double her order of wine and coffee-ice-cream punch and crab cakes and shrimp-salad finger sandwiches from Miss Hamby's.

There was a pang in Roy's heart as he stood at the window of his office looking down on Broad Street at the worker bees who hurried in and out of the ornate wrought-iron gates of his church, carrying tables and china and blocks of oasis and baskets of greenery clipped from their gardens.

He felt the Lord led him to St. Michael's, though the part about actually being here still unnerved him. And there was something else. He sensed a heaviness as he looked out at the faces of the people who walked up and down Broad Street— the worker bees and the businessmen, attorneys, real estate agents, and tour guides.

He didn't know much about the financial world. He made sure to keep his life real simple where money was concerned. He only owned one credit card, which he paid off every month, and he'd bought his used truck outright and paid off his student loans right after he graduated, thanks to his little inheritance from his father. As for his homes, they had been owned through the church ever since he took his first job, and he didn't know what it was like to have a mortgage or be upside down in one. But he understood enough to know that the economy was nosediving, and the people around him, in their designer clothes and luxury cars, must be suffering.

He thought back to the woman in church last Sunday. Her terrifying shriek had instantly brought to mind the dream he'd had of the city South of Broad with the dark, rectangular windows and the people still as stones. Back in Ellijay, folks wore their troubles on their coat sleeves. You could see it in their gait, in their well-worn clothes, in their sagging jowls. And they rarely hesitated in opening up and telling all, in hopes someone would lend them a hand. Everybody knew everyone else's business anyhow, so it was silly to pretend like all was well when it wasn't. But in downtown Charleston, people's mental and emotional states were difficult to discern. Fear and suffering could easily be masked with a fine hairdo, a tailored suit, and a stiff, white-toothed smile, and he worried that he might not be able to put his finger on the very needs of the flock the Lord had called him to shepherd.

Of course, what they needed was the love of Christ. And the joyful expectation of an eternity with him. That was always the answer for everyone, no matter what their circumstances. But how to find the door that leads to someone's heart? The search always started with identifying someone's longings and needs, and at the moment, this remained a mystery to him.

His first sermon with the Alpha promotion was met with very little response. Only two people outside of the vestry and staff had signed up for the program that started next week, and Roy was feeling discouraged about it.

He often envisioned the tall and beautiful woman in the bell tower. Anne Brumley. He had thought about her more than once since she sat on his piazza sipping tea. With a little research, he'd found out that the bell ringers practiced every Thursday evening at five, and somehow he always found himself walking toward the corner of Meeting and Broad around that time, but he hadn't seen her yet. She was one of the few people he'd met thus far who didn't hide her faith or what was truly on her heart. This gave him hope, somehow. He prayed he might cross paths with her again.

He called the home of the Doctors Sutton each day that week, but he always got the answering machine. On the afternoon of his installation, while his mama took Rose to pick up the dress Ms. B. had picked out for her at a children's boutique on King Street, Roy walked on over to Legare Street again and knocked on the door.

A woman who introduced herself as the housekeeper answered, but he could see the woman from church, Dr. Lish Sutton, sitting in a chair in a drawing room just beyond the foyer, and he could hear a baby crying somewhere else in the house.

"I was hoping to check in on Dr. Sutton. To see how she's feeling."

The woman looked at his clerical collar and then over to Dr. Sutton. "She's not all the way awake right now."

The baby's cry grew into a wail that echoed through the two-story foyer. The housekeeper looked up to the stairs and back to him. Then she called over her shoulder. "Miss Lish, the preacher's here to see you. I'm going to let him in and go feed the baby."

The woman sitting in the chair looked toward the foyer. She was squinting her eyes as though she were trying to see him from a long distance away.

The housekeeper shook her head in what seemed to be

exasperation. "Come on in, Father," she said. "I don't see how it could hurt." She walked to the kitchen, grabbed a bottle, and made her way up the stairs as the baby wailed on.

Roy ambled carefully into the sitting room and kept a good distance from the woman. He didn't want to startle her.

"Dr. Sutton, I'm Roy Summerall, the new rector at St. Michael's." He reached out his hand, but she didn't move to shake it, so he put it gently down at his side. He tried to meet her eyes. "I just came by to see about you."

The woman continued to stare at him through an invisible haze. He figured she was on some kind of medication. There must be something mental going on, and he didn't want to press her or upset her.

"May I pray with you?" he asked.

She looked down and nodded her head slowly.

"Thank you," he said. He didn't want to lay hands on her like he usually did with someone who was ill, so he stood right where he was, lifted out his hands, and uttered, "Come, Holy Spirit. Be present in this home. Take care of Dr. Sutton and her family. Heal any ailment that exists. Flood her heart with your love."

As he uttered the words, he watched her almost go limp for a moment, and he was afraid she might fall forward out of her chair. He stepped closer so he could catch her if need be. But in a few moments, she sat back up and squinted at him again.

Before long, the housekeeper came downstairs with a red-cheeked baby girl who gave him a wide, gummy smile. His heart did a flip. Oh, he wanted another baby. Was there anything like having one? When the child reached for him, the housekeeper said, "You can hold her." He took her in his arms as the woman went over to Dr. Sutton with a glass of water and a pill.

When the baby started to fuss, the housekeeper said, "See if she'll burp." And she put a cloth on his shoulder and he patted the child's back as he walked back and forth in the foyer admiring all of the family photos.

Suddenly he saw a picture of three little girls, arm in arm on a bench at The Battery and he recognized the redhead at once. It was Anne Brumley who had spent her summers in this home. Then he scanned the other pictures on the wall and found a recent image of Anne, her long wavy hair draped across her shoulders with a big smile and her arm around Dr. Sutton and another woman.

Then he heard, in the distance, the tenor bell being rung up in preparation for the two forty-five-minute peals that would both precede and follow his installation.

He prayed a blessing over the child, then walked into the kitchen where the housekeeper was pulling a roast out of the oven. "I've got a service soon. Mind if I give her back to you?"

"Yes, sir." She opened her arms.

He looked toward the living room and back again. "I hope you all will call on me if I can help in any way."

The housekeeper nodded. "I'll let Mr. Drew know you came by."

"Thank you," he said. He kissed the baby on the forehead and said good-bye to Dr. Sutton, who seemed to have fallen asleep upright in the chair, though her eyes weren't completely closed.

The installation was glorious. The bishop, dressed in his long, heavy robe and high hat and shepherd's crook, gave a stirring homily about the mystery of grace, and the church presented Roy with a variety of symbolic gifts for his ministry, including an antique key, a silver chalice, a miniature bell attached to a pulley, and a King James Bible that had been handed down by each of the preceding rectors dating back to 1751.

Roy's mama was all dressed up for the ceremony in a purple lacy cocktail dress from the Myrtle Beach Outlet Mall, and Rose looked like an angel herself in a pale pink dress with puffy sleeves and a wide sash, which Ms. B. informed him was made of something called raw silk. And Ms. B. had pulled Rose's hair back in a bun, into which she had tucked some pink rosebuds. Roy felt a lump in his throat when he saw those roses in her shiny black hair.

Even Chick wore a coat and tie for the occasion. He and Nikki and the kids had made the trip, and his boys looked terribly uncomfortable in the clip-on ties and polyester oxford shirts their granny had bought them at the Marshall's in Darlington.

Skeeter and Candy Mills were there, too, their faces and hair all fixed up, sporting the jewelry they only wore at Christmas and Easter time. They both gave him a warm embrace. And Candy presented Ms. B. with some bright orange cupcakes from the Piggly Wiggly with candy corn on top. The elderly lady graciously accepted the contribution and immediately moved them from their plastic container to an ornate silver tray. She put them front and center on the sweets table alongside the petits fours and lemon squares and slices of hummingbird cake.

Roy stood in a receiving line for over an hour with Rose by his side and Mama nearby in case the little girl grew weary of shaking hands. She didn't. She wanted to know everyone's name, and he was surprised how she looked each person in the eye, smiled a genuine smile, and answered their rote questions about her age and grade.

The bishop was the last in line, and he embraced Roy hard and said, "This is good, son. Very good."

"I sure hope so," Roy said.

The bishop grabbed the young priest's bum right shoulder and looked him in the eye. He pounded the staff once on the linoleum floor and nodded hard. Then he turned around and headed for the beef tenderloin at the end of the table.

Roy could hear the bells as the ringers continued to change ring from the steeple for a good hour after the installation, and when they finally came down to the parish hall to partake of the festivities, he looked around for the beautiful redhead, but she was nowhere to be seen.

After the last guest left, his mama took Rose home to bed and then Roy helped Samuel, the sexton, break down the tables. When the last chair was stacked, he shook Samuel's hand, then walked into the kitchen where Ms. B. and her team were putting all the leftovers in plastic containers and pulled her aside.

"Ms. B., do you know Anne Brumley?"

The lady raised her trim eyebrows and smiled. "Yes, I do." She clamped down the top of a container full of cheese straws. "She's a lovely lady. A bit tall, but that wouldn't bother someone as secure in their skin as you."

He felt his cheeks redden. "I didn't mean . . ."

The blush gave him away. Ms. B. cocked her head and stacked the container on top of a box of finger sandwiches. "Well, that might be good because Anne Brumley is in England."

"What?"

"She did an exchange program through a bell ringer association, and she's over there for some time, I believe."

"Oh," he said. He tried not to look too disappointed. He washed his hands and started loading two silver trays full of lemon squares into plastic containers.

After he helped Ms. B. and the worker bees clean the dishes (in spite of their passionate pleas that he not clean up after his own party), he ambled home and found Mama and Rose asleep on her Barbie bed and Donny sawing logs on the sofa in the den with ESPN replaying the NASCAR Talladega race. (Tony Stewart had won after Regan Smith was penalized for his pass.)

When Roy climbed into bed, he looked out of his window at the steeple and the bell tower. It was a clear night and a nearly full moon was hanging beyond the steeple, and he imagined it illuminating the choppy water of the harbor just two blocks away.

It had been a beautiful occasion. So much work on his behalf. He felt both thankful and unworthy. Yet despite Ms.

B.'s tireless efforts and the bishop's stalwart support and the presence of his close-knit family filling up his big house with the sound of their snoozes and snores, he felt alone in this world. Alone like he did in those dark days after he had laid Jean Lee's body into the earth. Alone like John the Baptist must have felt after Herod had imprisoned him. Roy remembered when John sent word to Christ, saying, "Are you really the One? Or should we expect another?" It was tough to trust in God's plan for your life when the black void of loneliness engulfed you. When you longed for someone to reach out and hold you, to rest her head against your wide chest and relax in a moment of solace and contentment. Roy braced himself for the awful self-pity that usually followed moments like this. In an effort to stave it off, he put his head in his hands and prayed, "Comfort me. Comfort me, Lord Jesus."

A few days later, he found a note in his box and recognized Ms. B.'s writing. It simply read:

Miss Anne Brumley
c/o The Central Council of Church Bell Ringers
35 A High Street
Andover, Hampshire County
SP10 1LJ United Kingdom
abrumley@gmail.com

For a few days he kept the little piece of paper tucked in his Bible. He wondered what to do. Should he write? Or e-mail? Should he contact her at all? He prayed, but he did not receive any sort of confirmation, so he didn't do a thing.

Alpha started the following week and it was just the staff and the vestry minus Heyward, who had been missing in action for everything except a brief appearance at the installation. Even one of the people who had signed up after his first sermon dropped away, citing a work conflict. The first session was titled "Who is God?" and Nicky Gumbel went to work answering this question on the video screen as Roy and Ms. B. served up fresh-baked flounder with grits and sliced tomatoes to the participants.

Ms. B. seemed discouraged as well that night. When they were washing dishes, she said, "Roy, I think you ought to include a description of Alpha in your next sermon and see if we can get more people for next week. I can think of a good hundred people that need to be here."

He took the Pyrex dish she handed him and began to dry it. "I sense that too."

"Of course you do." She dipped a pair of salad tongs into the soapy water and he watched three bubbles fly up into the air and thought of Rose.

His right shoulder ached and he rubbed it for a moment. "You know, I worry sometimes, Ms. B. That I don't understand these folks too well. I'm country come to town. We both know that. But I think I'm supposed to be here—"

"I know you are." She handed him the tongs.

"Well, how do you think I can reach these folks? I mean, what makes them tick?"

She turned for a moment and faced him head-on. "Why don't you ask them?"

Roy blinked hard and wondered how to go about that. The thought occurred to him—the Advent prayers. He had once attended a church in seminary where the priest prayed for every member and their specific needs during Advent. Why couldn't he do that? He would pass out the cards over the next few Sundays and ask folks to put their specific requests down.

"Wow." He smiled at Ms. B. who had already piled three trays beside him by the time he came to. "You sure are a wise woman."

"Lady." She winked at him and her twinkly gray eyes smiled.

"Yes, ma'am," he said. "Don't ever stop correcting me."

The following week when Roy picked Rose up from school, she dissolved into tears in the back seat of his truck before the teacher had even closed the door.

"What's wrong, baby?" She had been adjusting to her new life so beautifully. She'd made friends at school and church and had so many invitations to parties and play dates that he could hardly keep up.

He pulled over just beyond the pickup line. Then he got out and moved to the back seat beside her, where he took her in his arms. "What in the world is wrong, Rosebud?" He rubbed her bony little back. "Tell me, now."

He noticed a bright yellow piece of paper that she had crumbled in her hand. She opened it up for him to see. It read:

Margaret is turning seven
Hooray! Hoorah! Yippee!
And she'd like you to come
To a Mother-Daughter tea!
Wear your fancy dress
And bring your Mom along.
We'll provide the white gloves
And tea cakes and song.

October 22, 2008
4 pm
124 Tradd Street
RSVP to Margaret's Mom at 224-6741

When he finished reading the invitation, he looked over to Rose, who was staring at him with a kind of righteous fury in her eyes.

"Oh, honey," he said. "It'll be okay. We could ask Granny to come down for this, or I bet Ms. B. would be downright delighted to take you."

She bit her lip and her round chin puckered as the tears came again.

"I don't want Granny or Ms. B!"

He pulled a strand of dark hair out of her eyes. "I could take you then. Wouldn't that be neat?"

"No!" She looked out through the back window as one smiling, well-dressed mother after another picked up a child from the carpool line.

Then she turned back to him. "I want a mother!"

Roy fell back against the seat.

She pounded him on his arm. Hard. "I wish you would find one. And so does Granny."

He leaned his head back against the headrest. He could feel her staring him down.

"I've been praying about this, sweetie."

"I'm tired of you praying, Daddy." She sat up until he looked at her. "I want you to do something about it!"

He furrowed his thick dark eyebrows and pulled her close to him.

"Please, Daddy!" She relaxed into his arms and whispered. "Please try. I didn't know Mama, except through what you've told me. But I know she'd want me to have a mother."

He pulled back and kissed the top of her head. "You're right," he whispered. "She would."

"So you'll try?" She wouldn't let him out of her gaze.

He took a deep breath and swallowed. He nodded, and she unfolded the crumpled paper.

"If you'll really try, then let's ask Ms. B. to take me to this." She handed him the invite. " 'Cause I know it doesn't happen that fast."

That night, Roy got out his paper and pen and wrote Anne Brumley a good old-fashioned letter.

Dear Miss Brumley,

I hope this finds you well. Rose and I kept hoping we would cross paths with you again, but I recently learned that you are in England for an extended period of time. How long?

I hope you are enjoying your exchange program. It must be exciting to study with the experts in the field. I often imagine what it might be like to work for Nicky Gumbel or Billy Graham or C.S. Lewis (if he were still alive). Those are my heroes.

Anyway, I hope you don't mind me writing to you. The truth is, I've been thinking about you ever since we met. This may be unmannerly and forward, but I want you to know I'm a widower. I have been for almost six years now, and my daughter and I both feel as though we are missing a vital member of our family. Kind of like a three-legged stool without the second leg. I haven't been on a date since my wife died, but I think it might be time.

If you're at all interested in getting to know me in that regard, write back and we can begin a dialogue. If you're not, please don't feel bad. And don't feel strange about coming back to St. Michael's after your exchange program.

I'm trusting God in this, and I know he'll bring the right person at the right time for me and for you if you so desire.

Sincerely,

Roy Summerall

That Sunday, he gave a heartfelt sermon based on the passage from Matthew 6:25–33 about how the Lord clothes the lilies of the field and feeds the birds of the air, so be certain in these uncertain times that he will take care of you. How much more valuable are you than the birds and lilies? Much more. He had the ushers hand out little pieces of paper with "Prayer Requests" written on top, and he asked everyone to put down one request from their heart. (They could sign their name, but they didn't have to.) And he would pray for each member of the congregation. Then he concluded with a second invitation to Alpha the following Tuesday.

Two days later, forty-three new people showed up at the church for the program! Ms. B. quickly pulled casseroles out of the freezer and sent some members of her hospitality committee down to the Harris Teeter to get some salad makings and bread, and she served a delicious hodgepodge supper that included lasagna, chicken Divan, egg-and-sausage casserole, and a garden salad.

"It was a loaves-and-fishes miracle!" she said to Roy after he walked the last surprise participant to their car. "The freezer just kept producing Pyrex dishes with frozen meals. I had no idea we had so many in there!"

Two weeks later he received a letter with unfamiliar handwriting and a stamp of Queen Elizabeth on the front.

He tucked it in his Bible, and after he got Rose down that night, he unsealed it.

Dear Mr. Summerall,

Thank you for your letter. It was a true surprise, and I must admit—a delightful one. Yes, I am learning a great deal here. I am committed to a six-month exchange program where I'll ring many of the oldest bells around the country with changing ringers who are masters and even composers of this rare ministry and art form. Last week I rang a two-ton tenor bell in a church in Bath! It nearly lifted me off the floor on the first hand stroke. Like the change ringers in Charleston, it is a warm, friendly, and eclectic group, and I am quite at home here. (I spent several months in London when I was in college, and I very much enjoy the people and the culture, from the charming accents to the time set aside for tea and scones every afternoon!)

As for your request, I must answer, yes; I would be interested in getting to know you better. I am single, and I have never been married. If we're going to be perfectly honest, I might as well say it has been a longstanding, fervent prayer of mine to meet someone. It may not be what God has in store for my life, but I am willing to take another step down this road if you are. I'll look forward to hearing from you.

Sincerely,

Anne Brumley (Please call me by my first name from now on. Also, in the interest of time, I am happy to receive e-mails as well. I'm at abrumley@gmail.com)

Doggone if his heart didn't skip a beat when he read and reread the letter! After the third time, he immediately thanked God and sat down at his computer where he spent the next hour typing Anne Brumley an e-mail, telling her whatever popped in his mind about him, his family, and his ministry. It was ten paragraphs by the time he pressed Send. He hoped she would write back soon.

Chapter 17

DELLA

November 25, 2008

"Where's Mr. Pickles, Mama?" Cozy asked. She was eagerly packing her overnight bag with her favorite pajamas and her toothbrush and her stuffed lobster that reminded her of one of her daddy's sculptures.

Cozy was becoming a good reader, and she couldn't wait to show her grandfather. She was only going for three nights, but she'd packed four of *The Magic Tree House* books she checked out at the library and one of the *Frog and Toad* books that she had read ten times over the last twenty-four hours.

It was the Tuesday before Thanksgiving and tomorrow Della would drive Cozy halfway to the upstate, where she'd meet her Pop Pop and her step-grandmother, who simply liked to be called Sue, and they'd head on back to Pop Pop's house at the foot of the Blue Ridge Mountains where they'd build a fire and roast marshmallows right in the living room.

Della came in with Mr. Pickles, the well-worn blanket Cozy had slept with since she was an infant. Over the last couple of years, Della had patched up two of the blanket's rips with Nana's old sewing machine. One of the patches looked like Pac Man or the main character of Shel Silverstein's story *The Missing Piece*. The other one looked like a pickle—a rectangle with two rounded edges at the top left side of the blanket.

"Do you think you're getting a little old for Mr. Pickles?" Della tossed the blanket to Cozy, who embraced it, found the pickle-shaped spot, and rubbed it against her cheek.

"Never!"

Della had reservations about sending Cozy to her dad's for the holiday. She'd had some tough run-ins with her stepmother growing up, but Sue seemed to have mellowed over the years, and Della's daddy, a gentle (if not timid) soul, was absolutely crazy about Cozy. This would be the second year Cozy had begged to let her go. Last year Della agreed, because she had been desperate to have a little time to meet her book deadline. And it all went well. This year, she planned to meet Todd Jervey at The Woodlands, a five-star inn tucked away in the forest outside of Summerville where they would consummate what had started with a lunch date at Blend a few months ago. Peter would be working double shifts at the carriage company. This was a busy tourism week in Charleston, and Della had told him she'd received a scholarship to a writer's retreat where she could finish the final chapters of her novel, which was due December 1st.

"Okay," he'd said last week when she spelled out the plan. "After work on Thanksgiving, I guess I'll drive over to see my parents in McClellanville." He shook his head and looked at Cozy. "Man, what a lonely holiday."

His words had bothered Cozy so much that on Sunday she set the table with her parents' wedding china and begged Della to cook a turkey breast. Thankfully, Della found one on special at the Piggly Wiggly, and she baked it and made some rice and gravy, and they ate when Peter came home around eight that evening.

"See, Daddy," Cozy had said. "We're just having our dinner early. That's all."

Lish's Thanksgiving invitation to Della's family had been retracted a couple of weeks ago. After a parent at school told Della what had happened in church, Della went by 18 Legare the very next afternoon to see about her cousin. Just as she was pulling up, Drew intercepted her in the driveway and nearly kept her out.

"Della," he said. "I know you mean well, but Lish needs some time to herself right now. She's making strides every day, and the more rest she has, the better."

"I haven't seen her in almost two months." Della crossed her thin arms and looked him fiercely in the eye. "She's my family, Drew. Can't I lay eyes on her?"

Just then Mary Jane and Andrew had come barreling

out of the house. They'd run up to Della and squeezed her tight. She had lifted both of them up in her arms and spun them around.

"Where's Cozy?" Andrew said. He peered behind her toward her old car.

"She's on a play date with one of her classmates." She brushed a thick dark curl out of Andrew's eye. "I have to pick her up in a little while. I just came by to check in on your mama." She bent down and rested her hands on her knees so that she was eye to eye with her nephew. "How's she doing?"

Andrew shrugged. "She's fine." Drew came up behind him and grabbed his shoulder.

Mary Jane tugged at Della's hand. "Did you know we're moving, Cousin Del?"

"No," she said, looking back to Drew.

Mary Jane grinned, happy to be the one to divulge the big news. "Yes, we're moving to Atlanta, Georgia . . . right, Daddy?"

Della squinted her eyes. She knew Lish didn't want to move. She tried not to sound devastated. "When?"

Just then she heard the screech of the big oak door. Lish walked out slowly with a half smile on her face. "Hi, Della," she said before clutching the rail and moving slowly down the steps, one pale bare foot at a time.

Della went to her cousin and embraced her. Her hair smelled like something sweet and clean, like a ripe apple, and her face was made up even though she was still in her night-gown. "I'm glad to see you."

Della pulled back and searched her cousin's eyes. They

seemed more dull than usual, or maybe it was serene. She couldn't quite place the look.

"Come in," Lish said. "Have some tea."

The house was immaculate except for a small corner of the room where Andrew was building something narrow and tall with a zillion little Lego pieces. The air smelled of roasting chicken and Febreze and that old musty house stench.

Lish wore a subdued smile as she watched the children play with the Legos. Mary Jane was trying to feed one of the small black blocks to her Madame Alexander doll, the one dressed up like Little Red Riding Hood, while Andrew added another layer to his tower.

Within minutes Rosetta brought Della a cup of hot tea on a tray with a bowl full of sugar and a pitcher of cream. Drew sat down on the ottoman opposite them and showed Della the article in *The Atlanta Journal-Constitution* about his MUSC research team moving to the CDC.

Della studied Lish, who maintained her dull smile and nodded her head. She turned to Della for a moment. "Isn't it exciting?" she said.

Della took a sip of tea. It was hot, and she winced. "Yes." She put the teacup back in its delicate saucer. "And very unexpected."

Lish raised her eyebrows as the baby began to cry somewhere upstairs. "We'll be back in a few years. Right, Drew?"

He laced his hands together and nodded. "Yep. We just couldn't pass this opportunity up."

Della watched Rosetta carry a bottle upstairs. She repositioned herself on the couch and addressed Lish. "When will you go?"

"I have to be there December first," Drew said. He reached for the article and put it on the bookshelf. "Lish and the kids will come in the spring."

Della looked at Lish, who now seemed weary as she studied her fingers with her eyes half open. She tilted her head slowly to the side as if what Drew said was something she needed to ponder in order to accomplish. She swallowed hard and looked at him. "That's right."

They sat there and made small talk for twenty minutes or so before Della stood and said, "Well, I've got to pick Cozy up. Will you walk me to my car, Lish?"

Drew cleared his throat, and Lish slowly stood and followed Della to the car.

When they made it down the stairs and out into the driveway, Della turned to her, squeezed her hand, and said, "Are you really okay?"

Lish nodded. Her eyes seemed clouded. Like an invisible film was over them. She looked beyond Della at something in the street. "It's taken longer than I thought, but I'm getting there."

Then she turned back to Della with the faintest glint in her eye. "These pills make me feel sluggish. That's the tough part." She nodded as if she was listening to a reassuring voice in her mind. "But I'll get to taper off of them soon."

Della hugged Lish and put her lips to her ear. "You get in touch with me if you need anything, okay?" She squeezed her even tighter. "I'm here for you like always."

Lish pulled back carefully, but she held onto Della's arms as if she needed them for balance. Then she looked down at her bare feet. "I don't think I can manage Thanksgiving this year." She looked back up to Della. "Would it be too awful if I took back the invitation?"

Della chuckled. "No, of course not. Don't give it a second thought." She patted her cousin's arm and waited for her to say more. They stood this way for several minutes, with Lish steadying herself by holding on tight to Della's arms. When Drew walked out on the piazza and started to pace, Della leaned in again and kissed Lish's cheek. "We'll talk more soon."

Then she let go of her arms, climbed in her old car, and drove out of the driveway wondering how she could see Lish again, in private. She would wait until Drew moved in a few weeks. Then she'd be able to get the full scoop and assess her cousin's condition.

When she turned onto Meeting Street and spotted a bell ringer in vestments heading into St. Michael's for practice, she was overcome by a sense of grief. She missed Anne (though Della was the very one who had pushed her to go), and now Lish was leaving in a few short months. There would be no more Saturday get-togethers with their tight-knit threesome, no more walks along the beach, no more Nana's house or the loquat tree to remember their shared childhood. Her cousins were her best friends. They kept her on track. They were like sisters and mothers all rolled into one, and now they both seemed very far way. It was a sad and awful realization (their absence in her daily life), and it would take a long time for her to get over this painful change.

That was three weeks ago, and Della had e-mailed and called Lish every few days with no response. (She was counting down the days until Drew took off so she could have a real conversation with her.) Truth was, she had enough on her plate right now. She was ready to seal this deal with Todd and get her life on a new path.

She worried about Peter, but she knew this was best for him. He loathed driving the carriages, and she saw on his bureau the other day a schedule for an electrical engineering course he had signed up for at Trident Technical College. And his father, a big, lovable salty dog from McClellanville, had invited him to work with him on the shrimp boat next summer.

"I'm open," Della had heard Peter say. "We've got to find a way to bring in more income, Dad."

An incident last week reaffirmed Della's decision to solidify her new relationship with Todd. It had to do with a school field trip they had to tell Cozy they couldn't afford. The Pinckney School's science teacher was coordinating an optional (but strongly encouraged) "Sea Turtle Camp" at Kiawah Island during the first weekend in December. It involved spending two nights at the swanky beach-front inn, a tour of the sea turtle hospital, and a private viewing of a release of a fully rehabilitated sea turtle into the ocean.

Nearly all of Cozy's classmates had signed up. It cost

$550 and there was no way they could swing it. Della dreaded having to tell her daughter. She had tried to find a way to make it work, but Peter said, "We can't, Della. We can hardly make the mortgage payment this month. Let me talk to her."

Della stood in the doorway of Cozy's room as Peter walked over to where the little girl was on her belly on her bed reading *Merry Christmas, Amelia Bedelia*.

"Sweetheart." Peter took a seat on her bed.

She looked up at him and smiled. "Hi, Daddy."

"Mama and I need to talk to you about something."

She sat up, put the "I can read now!" bookmark the school librarian had given her in the center of the book and placed it on her pillow.

"Okay." She rubbed her eyes.

"It's about the turtle camp."

"Oh, yeah," she said. Her eyes widened. "Miss Jackson is organizing it. Most of my class has already signed up."

He stroked his broad chin, then reached out to hold her hand. "The thing is, Cozy, we're not going to be able to send you this year."

The little girl looked to Della, who had said, "We'll see," when she brought home the brochure in her homework folder a month ago.

She looked down at her book and rubbed her fingers over the plastic shield the library slides on all of their hardcovers. Then she nodded. "Okay."

Peter swallowed, tilted his head, and examined her. He peered out of her window into the dark street and squinted his eyes.

"Hey, but I've got an idea." He looked to Della and winked as Cozy lifted her head.

"What?" the little girl said.

"You remember Daddy's old johnboat?"

"The one in the shed?" She started to bounce gently on the bed.

"Yeah." He patted her knee. "That's the one."

She nodded and wrinkled her brow. "It's got a hole in it."

"Yeah, but I think I can patch it up with a little fancy metal work." He put his forehead next to hers. "What do you say I take the day off next Saturday, and you and me and your mama take a boat ride over to Capers Island? We'll do a little fishing and look for porpoises. Heck, maybe we'll see a sea turtle on our way."

She lifted her little eyebrows, smiled, and looked at Della.

"Yeah!" she said. She turned to him. "Can we pack a picnic?"

"Sure we can." He grinned and turned to his wife. He swept his hand across his forehead as if to say *Whew* as Cozy stood up and started jumping on the bed.

"Can we bring some fried chicken, Daddy?"

"Yep." He stood on the little bed and bounced with her. "And some chips and soda!"

"Grape soda?" She grabbed his hands, and they jumped together in time.

"Any flavor you want," he said.

She squeezed his waist. "That sounds great, Daddy!"

Della smiled. How easy it was to persuade her little girl at age six. But it might not be so good for her the Monday after the turtle camp when all the girls talked about their experiences and watched the slide show in the lower school courtyard. And it certainly wouldn't be this easy as Cozy grew up and continued to go to play dates in magnificent homes where housekeepers, cooks, and full-time nannies brought in as much in a week as either she or Peter. It wouldn't be near as easy then.

As Della and Cozy drove to the halfway spot just south of Columbia on Interstate 26, Cozy drew on her sketch pad with her colored pencils while Della worried about the "check engine" light that lit up on her dashboard as soon as they hit the highway. Before she had a chance to fret too much, Cozy said, "How about a Binklemeyer story?" Della nodded as the engine icon faded in and out. They told a long and winding Burl and Bernice Binklemeyer story that started with the line "Burl and Bernice Visit Their Crazy Uncle on His Farm in Illinois."

It began with a flight to Chicago that Bernice nearly missed because she refused to board the connecting flight after she discovered that her lucky marble had disappeared from the little zipper pocket on the inside of her carry-on bag.

She'd had it when they ate lunch at Chick-Fil-A in the airport food court, and she didn't want to leave Charlotte International until she found it. Cozy's eyes widened from the back seat when Della described how Burl had to grab Bernice by the back of her sweatshirt and drag her onto the airplane, kicking and screaming.

Then Cozy squealed with joy when the flight attendant helped Bernice double-check her carry-on bag only to discover that there was a small hole in the little zipper pocket and the marble was actually sitting on top of Bernice's carefully folded purple-and-pink-striped underwear.

"That was a close one!" Cozy said as they puttered down the highway. The engine of the old Honda rumbled when it exceeded sixty miles an hour, and Della had had to tell the story at such a loud volume that her throat now ached.

She looked in the rearview mirror at her daughter and smiled. She thought of her own father driving her down the very same highway to meet Nana. How she could hardly sit still on the trip and how when she saw her Nana's white Cadillac parked at the edge of the filling station, her heart would beat wildly inside the little cage of her chest, and she knew that for the next several days she would be held and sung to and walked around the High Battery as the soft, thick harbor air lifted her thin golden hair off of her cheeks.

Della's childhood had been a sad and frustrating one, with the exception of her time with Nana in Charleston. From an early age, she'd had a vision of what a family was supposed to be, and she knew that hers wasn't it. Every time her mama had come to see her, she thought she could persuade her to stay. Secretly, she had hoped her mama would be sorry and her daddy would be, too, and that they might somehow come together and form the kind of family Della read about in her favorite childhood books—the Browns from the Paddington series, the Ingalls from *Little House on the Prairie*, the Quimbys from the Ramona books, and the Johansens from *Number the Stars*.

Now as she pulled off the exit, she watched Cozy scanning the parking lot of the McDonald's until she spotted her Pop Pop and Sue sitting in their burgundy Toyota Prius. Pop Pop started to wave and Sue let out a tight grin as Della's old Honda came rumbling to a stop.

"Let me out! Let me out!" Cozy called, and as soon as Della opened the door, Cozy bounded into her Pop Pop's arms. "I can read now!" she said. "I brought four books, and I can read them all to you while we roast marshmallows."

He held her tight and rocked her back and forth. "That sounds great, pumpkin."

Sue gave Della the once-over, then looked at the old car. "That thing is a wonder, isn't it? Who'd have thought it would still be running after twenty years?"

"Hi, Sue," Della said. She squinted her eyes and noted her stepmother's ever-widening midsection paunch. "You look great."

Sue cocked her head and crossed her arms. Just before she sent a sharp comment back, Cozy leapt into her arms and she softened a little. She returned Cozy's embrace, then let her gently down before straightening out her pressed oxford blouse.

Della's daddy kissed her on her forehead. "How are you doing, sweetie?"

He didn't ask her about her writing. It was a subject they steered clear of around Sue, who was still angry about Della's first book, a coming-of-age novel featuring a grumpy step-mother as one of the primary antagonists. Even Della had to admit (only to herself, of course) that the character did bear a striking resemblance.

"I'm all right." She tousled Cozy's hair. "I'm going to miss this little girl, though. We're never apart for three whole nights, are we?"

Cozy flapped her away. "Oh, Mama, we were last year, remember?"

Della smiled. She tapped her finger on her chin as if to look back in time. "I guess you're right." She leaned over and kissed her daughter on the forehead. "We were, and I survived, somehow."

Cozy giggled and hugged her mama.

"Well, we'll see you Saturday?" her father said. "Same place, same time?" He took Cozy by the hand, and she dragged him toward the car.

"Yeah," Della said. She handed Sue the suitcase and Mr. Pickles and the stuffed lobster.

"Be a good girl," she called to Cozy, who was already being buckled into the back seat of her Pop Pop's car.

"Have you heard of The Magic Tree House series?" she heard her daughter ask.

When Della got home, she packed her own overnight bag, including a black silk dress she'd had since college and a faux silk nightie she bought at Target last week. Tonight she would clean the house and wash the linens, and then in the morning she'd head to the library where she'd pound out the last chapter of her book before meeting Todd at The Woodlands in the afternoon.

She was at the point where she had no idea if her book was any good or not. Her chapters were getting longer as she had to tie up so many loose ends, and she didn't even get to some of the places she'd hoped to go after the murder—the courtroom, the prison, the congressional floor where they would introduce new legislation regarding stalking and law enforcement-to-victim notification before a stalker was released from prison. The story had a lot of potential, but she just couldn't flesh it all out and make her deadline. It looked like it would end with the inevitable murder in the last chapter—a pretty morose conclusion, even by her standards.

When Peter came home in his Confederate uniform, his walkie talkie still clipped on the outside of his right pocket, he asked, "Coz get off all right?"

"Yeah," she said. He examined her suitcase in the hall. "And where are you off to?"

Didn't she tell him this? She took a deep breath. "A writing retreat, remember? I'm going to finish the book there."

He nodded. "We can afford that?"

"It's free." Her voice was flat, even spiteful. She didn't like how she talked to him, but it was hard for her to stop herself. "I applied and was accepted, remember?" She raised her eyebrow, turned back to the bathroom, and poured the Food Lion version of Comet into the rusting toilet bowl.

He took off his cap and tossed it on the kitchen table.

"I'm beat." He pulled a wad of cash out of his pocket and deposited it beside his cap. "Take what you need for your trip."

Then he grabbed a beer and headed out to the back steps, where he surveyed the backyard and shed. He'd been patching up the johnboat for days now. He walked over to it, lifted the tarp off of the rust hole, and lit his blowtorch.

As she scrubbed the grime off of the old toilet bowl, she thought back to her conversation with Todd a few weeks ago.

"Are you sure about this?" he'd said. They were at Kudu Coffee House, looking at the room choices of The Woodlands online. They had only managed to see each other for small chunks of time since they'd reconnected. Both of their schedules were crowded. They'd managed a lunch break here and a walk around the Med U. there, but that was it. This would be the first time they would be alone together for several hours at a time, not to mention a whole night.

He had turned to her. She knew he wasn't asking about the accommodations. He was asking about their going away together. It was a big step. One you couldn't take back.

She had felt as if she was on autopilot. The decision had been made months ago, and there was no need to rethink it again. Her child was in need, her biological clock was ticking, and she and Peter were barely scraping by. She gently tapped his foot with her own, studied the rim of his glasses before looking him in the eye. "Very," she had said. He had leaned forward and discreetly squeezed her knee one quick time.

As she finished her last chapter, she didn't have the sense of relief she usually had at the close of a novel. The book didn't feel right in so many ways, but she had no time (not to mention any idea) of how to change it. She headed out of the library parking lot, into the Honda, and out to The Woodlands. Todd, who was on his way back from a group home in rural Georgia where he was conducting one of his research studies, would meet her there.

As she drove down I-26 and then through Summerville, she thought of the last time she'd made a trip out to The Woodlands. It was the weekend that Todd proposed to her more than a decade ago. They'd had dinner at the award-winning restaurant in the inn and then on a walk through the back gardens, he'd gotten down on his knee and opened a small, black velvet box containing a large sapphire flanked by two diamonds set in platinum.

She had felt like an actress in a play that day. She had gasped, cupped her hand around her mouth, and presented her left hand just like she had seen so many other women do in movies and television shows and even in a few cheesy beach reads she'd succumbed to during her teenage summers.

"Yes," she'd said, and as he slid the ring on her finger, a bee stung her ankle. "Ouch!" She jumped back and reached toward her sandal. She'd mistaken the sting for a bad omen. Looking back now, she chuckled at her immaturity. It was just a bee sting. Why did she have to analyze everything so much?

Of course, she would never say that she regretted marrying Peter. Too much good had come out of their union. And they had given it their all; it just wasn't enough. They had tried to make it, and the world seemed stacked against them. It was that simple.

Now as she drove slowly down the winding roads and then the dirt path that cut through the pine trees toward the inn, she spotted Todd's car—the sporty BMW convertible at the edge of The Woodlands' circular driveway. There was a space right next to him, and she pulled into it and cut off the engine.

She glanced up at the grand house and was surprised to see him, his back turned to her. He was perched on the railing of the upstairs porch of the suite they had picked out together. He was looking out over the back garden as he pinched the crystal stem of a full glass of red wine.

Now she examined him, his tall, thin frame repositioning itself on the railing, his strawberry blondish/gray hair and his freckled neck with the crisscross of wrinkles from age and sun exposure now forming across it. He adjusted his posture as if his mother has just scolded him and breathed slowly in and out. Then he brought the glass of wine to his lips.

Della's palms were sweaty and her heart was beating fast. She watched a young couple come out of the front door hand in hand and noticed a churning in the pit of her stomach. The couple slid into their sleek car and drove off.

Now Della examined her dank palms and rubbed them on the side of her blue jean skirt. Was she nervous? Guilty? Fearful? *Yes*, she thought. *All of the above.* It was like the moment before she and her cousins dared one another to jump off of the highest limb of the loquat tree in Nana's backyard. Something in her said, *Don't think, just do it*, and she knew this was what she should do now. *Don't think, just put one foot in front of the other and walk up to that suite, and in no time you'll land on the soft ground of Nana's garden without a scratch.*

She reached into her back seat and pulled out her suitcase. Below it, she noticed a crumpled piece of paper from Cozy's sketch pad. She reached for it, opened it up, and took in what her daughter had drawn on the way to meet her grandfather.

It was a picture of Cozy and Peter and Della in the patched-up johnboat, holding hands, with a sea turtle and several small fish swimming in the water beneath the boat. There were clouds, a couple of pelicans, and a bright yellow heart directly above the boat with rays of light surrounding it as if the heart was the sun. On the back of the picture she had written, "Famly bote tip by Cozy Limehouse."

Della looked at the words and then back at the picture. In it, she had a brick-red smile shaped like a crescent moon that took up most of her face. And so did Peter. This was how Cozy saw her parents, or how she wanted to see them anyway. And there was Cozy herself, right in between her mom and dad with a pink round O for a mouth and a bubble above her that read, "Look! A trtle!"

Della didn't know how long she stared at the wide smiles on her face and Peter's, her heart racing, her palms sweating.

Suddenly she felt a gentle squeeze on her shoulder and then a light peck at her neck. She turned around and looked up at Todd. She folded the picture over.

"You okay?" He smiled gently down on her.

"No." She shook her head. She tucked the paper in the outside pocket of her suitcase and looked up to him. "I can't do this, Todd."

He studied her face for whole seconds. Then he squinted his eyes and let out a muffled groan, and she knew that he fully comprehended what she was saying. "Not again, Della."

"I'm sorry," she said. "I've had this thing all wrong." She leaned back against the car and crossed her arms. "This isn't what I want, and it's not what's best for my family. Or for you, for that matter."

He took a step back and bit his lip. Whole minutes passed as he kicked at the gravel between their cars. When he looked up, he said, "I don't like it." He inhaled and exhaled deeply. "But I can't fully understand what it's like to be in your shoes."

She blew a loose strand of hair out of her eyes, rubbed her sweaty palms together. "It wasn't right the first time, and it's not right this time." She took a deep breath. "It will happen for you, Todd. I know it will." He crossed his arms and shrugged his shoulders. "Maybe."

Then she slipped back into the Honda, smirking at the squeaky sound it made when she sat down. She quickly put the car in reverse and puttered out of the gravelly driveway, leaving dust and her old beau and the five-star inn behind.

It didn't take long for her to find a parking place on the outskirts of the downtown market just off Hassell Street. She jumped out of the car and raced over the cobblestones with just her keys in her hand until she reached the center of the market, where she immediately spotted Peter sitting in an empty carriage in front of the basket weavers, waiting for his turn to load up.

He didn't notice Della coming up behind his carriage as he lifted the cap off of his head and wiped his sweaty brow with his forearm. He looked around and nodded at the passers-by. Then he leaned forward to straighten the reins.

"Welcome aboard," he said without turning around as he reached out his hand.

She put her hand in his and let him pull her up onto the carriage, where she took her seat beside him as he slowly turned around.

"Hey." He scratched his chin. "What are you doing here?"

She seized his strong, wide, calloused hands and looked into his dark eyes as the carriage in front of him loaded up and pulled out into North Market Street.

"I haven't been gypped." She felt the lump in her throat rising. "I haven't been gypped at all, Peter." She tried to hold back the tears. "But *you* have."

He watched the wetness form in her eyes.

She swallowed. "I've gypped you countless times, and you know it." She wiped her cheek with the heel of her hand. "I don't deserve you, but I honestly want to make this work. And I can start by treating you the way you deserve to be

Love, Charleston

treated." She leaned back and took a deep breath. "I hope you'll let me make it up to you, Peter."

A half grin formed across his face. Then his eyes softened, and he pulled her close with all of his might. She squeezed his broad chest and rested her head in the nook of his neck. He smelled like Peter—a combination of metal, perspiration, and sunscreen. It was the smell of her husband. The man she loved. The man she had married and promised to honor.

She pulled back and looked into his eyes. "Thank you."

He reached up and rubbed her cheek with his warm hand. "It's been tough on you, Della. I know it's been tough. But we're going to get through this rough spot. We're going to make it, and we're going to add to our brood and do the best we can for them. I promise."

He pulled her to him. "Stick with me, okay? Trust me."

She cherished the feel of him in her arms. She nodded into his chest. "I will."

He lifted up her face and kissed her until some older gentleman ambling by tapped the side of the carriage and said, "Take that gal for her own private tour."

"Great idea, sir," Peter said. He lifted the reins of his horse and pulled out, heading into North Market and turning left on Church Street.

Della stood up beside him, and he put his arm tightly around her hips. Then he took a right onto Cumberland and a left onto Meeting Street and guided the horse by The Wells Gallery, where they had met for the first time, and then up Queen Street and down King to the High Battery where he had leaned in to kiss her the very next night after watching the reflection of the moonlight on the harbor. They took a left on East Bay Street and another left on Broad and drove right by St. Michael's Episcopal Church at the center of the city, where they'd exchanged their vows on a temperate October afternoon more than nine years ago as the old bells pealed and the sun blazed a reddish pink before setting behind the steeples and slanted chimneys and slate rooftops of the Holy City they loved.

Chapter 18

December 12, 2008

Lish and Drew had had a friend in residency who took his life just two months after he was married. He had been folding laundry and left a note to his wife on top of the dryer that simply read, "Don't go in the basement." When she came home from work, the dryer was still warm and their towels were neatly folded on the kitchen table. She had taken one look at the note and then cautiously made her way down the basement, where she found him hanging from a rafter with a noose around his neck.

Lish couldn't say she'd thought anything through. But on the Friday after Drew moved to Atlanta, she dropped the children off at school, parked her car at the foot of the new Cooper River Bridge, and walked steadily toward the top. It was mid-morning and there were usually dozens of people jogging across the bridge's pedestrian path this time of day. But it was a gray and foggy day with a light rain spitting on

Lish's face, and she didn't see any pedestrians ahead. She was not in any kind of sport attire. Just jeans, an MUSC sweatshirt, and some dark green rain boots. There was no note. No phone call. Just the unbearable thumping in her head that had returned now that she'd lowered her Ativan dose again.

Suddenly a lone cyclist came her way. He was in a helmet and a spandex body suit with his biking shoes clipped to his pedals. She noted the flash of him out of her peripheral vision and the hiss of his wheels on the wet walkway beside her.

Her eyes were on the crest of the bridge, which stood at an impressive 575 feet high, and she was steadily making her way toward it. One foot in front of the other and soon she'd have gone half a mile toward the top as the trucks and station wagons and school buses whizzed by on the other side of the pedestrian walkway, creating a brisk wind and a steady rumble that could be felt beneath her feet as she stepped forward.

When she arrived at the crest, she didn't hesitate. She simply turned and reached toward the top of the tall metal railing where she gripped the wet edge and pulled herself up. The railing was slick and it was hard for her to keep her footing, but after a couple of tries she managed to reach the top. She leaned over the railing in a pike position and just as she swung her right leg over the side, something clutched her left ankle and yanked her firmly down to the ground, where her whole left side hit the wet concrete with a painfully hard thwack.

She came to in the back of an ambulance barreling down the bridge toward the city. She was sitting up on a gurney with her hands behind her back. She ached when she tried to move them and realized that she was handcuffed. On her left a police officer watched her every move, and on her right a paramedic reached out to steady the bandage across the side of her head. As she turned toward him, her skull ached. It pounded all over instead of just at the top. She tasted the metal tang of blood in her mouth and wondered in all earnestness, *What am I doing here?*

She couldn't account for this day. She didn't remember waking up, dressing the children, dropping them off at school. She had no idea that she had walked to the top of the bridge and climbed halfway over the rail before a security guard who was driving to Wal-Mart to work the day shift jerked his car into Park, jumped over the walkway, and pulled her down.

When they arrived at MUSC, the paramedics wheeled her into the emergency room where a young resident stitched up the left side of her head. She opened her eyes for a moment, but all she could see was the latex glove on the doctor's hand as he sewed the skin above her left temple back together.

She didn't know how long she lay in the dark room with the curtain drawn. She heard the static and muffled voices from the walkie talkies of the police officers and paramedics, and she heard a wail from time to time from a baby in the waiting room.

All she could do was breathe in and out. It was the only thing she was capable of, and she felt it might be that way indefinitely.

When the curtain was drawn back she made out the silhouette of Dr. Sharon Swan, who walked slowly toward her bedside.

Lish found her voice before the questions began. It was gravelly, but she managed to form the words. "Yes, I know where I am, Sharon." She swallowed and a pain shot through the left side of her body. "But I don't know why I'm here."

Lish tugged at the handcuffs. A pain shot up her left shoulder. She looked up at the hazy image of her old classmate and whispered, "Do you?"

Dr. Swan gave her a sympathetic nod and then turned to say something to the police officer who immediately unlocked the handcuffs.

Lish massaged her aching wrists. She couldn't yet see the red ring the handcuffs had formed around them, but she could feel it. "Why am I here?" she said.

Dr. Swan gently took Lish's hands and leaned in. "Lish, you tried to jump off the Cooper River Bridge this morning."

Her heart pounded; she could feel it in her throat and her ears. She vaguely recalled walking up the bridge in the rain, but that was all. Now her teeth chattered, and as they did the left side of her jaw pounded with pain.

She tried to find her voice again. "Don't tell Drew. Please don't tell Drew." She swallowed. "I need Dr. Cussler. And I need my sister, Anne, or my cousin Della."

Dr. Swan spoke clearly into Lish's right ear. "I have to admit you to the Institute, Lish. If you comply right off, I don't have to call the judge." She paused and exhaled deeply. "If you don't, I've got to get a court order."

Dr. Swan held a clipboard in front of Lish's face. "Will you sign the admittance papers?"

Lish's hands were swollen. She was not sure she could control them, but she managed to reach up, grasp the pen chained to the board, and sign wherever Dr. Swan pointed.

Then the doctor and the police officer helped her off of the gurney and into a wheelchair, where they walked her over to President Street.

A young nurse met them at the glass doors. She took the handles of the wheelchair and slowly rolled Lish onto the elevator and up to the psych ward. Once they were in a hospital room, she helped her onto the bed and out of her clothes. Then she draped Lish in a paper gown with no strings or buttons that she could use against herself.

Next she handed her a pill—an antipsychotic, Lish was sure. Before she asked which one, the nurse introduced her to an attendant who would sit and watch her until his shift was over.

"Can I have the phone?" Lish said after swallowing her pill.

The attendant reached for it. "I'd be happy to dial for you," he said.

Lish took a deep breath and nodded. Then she called out Della's number at school.

Chapter 19

DELLA

At the hospital, Della called her husband and filled him in on what had happened. "Lish wants you and me to drive up to Atlanta and tell Drew in person."

"Okay." Peter exhaled. "Let me tell Joe I need the rest of the day off."

Next Della called Anne in England and had to leave her a message about what was going on. Then she drove over to 18 Legare to see if Rosetta could stay the night with the kids. When she arrived, she found the older woman brooding on the porch swing of the front piazza with Baby Cecilia asleep in the bouncy seat next to her.

"This is my last day, Miss Della." Rosetta stood slowly before placing her hands firmly on her hips. "I told them both in October that I've got a new job come the first of the year." She sucked her teeth. "But I'm not sure neither of them heard me."

Rosetta leaned toward Della. "Now I was going to work one more week, but today I've missed my bus *and* my doctor's appointment, and I'm not happy." She gently pointed her finger toward the bus stop. "It took me three months to get in to see that orthopedist, and I'll have to wait three *more* months thanks to Miss Lish." The woman reached down and picked up her brown velvet hat that was resting on the top of the rocking chair. Then she placed it squarely on her head and whispered in Della's ear, "Something's not right with her. And I can't bear this burden any longer."

"I'm so sorry, Rosetta." Della wasn't sure what to say. She knew she should persuade Rosetta to stay, but she clearly saw that the woman was worn out and fed up. "She's sick, you know. I'm not sure what it is, but it's serious."

Rosetta nodded and pointed to her head. "I do. It's something up here," she whispered again. "But Mr. Drew doesn't. Or he doesn't want to, anyway."

As the city bus pulled up at the corner, Rosetta adjusted her hat. "The school called and said the preacher volunteered to bring them home. I said okay, so they should be here soon." She turned toward the steps and then back to Della. "I pray they get things straightened out around here, but I can't be the one to do it."

Della reached out to give Rosetta a hug. "I understand, Rosetta. Thank you for all you've done. I'm sure no one will ever know how much."

Rosetta nodded. "Tell Miss Lish to mail me a check, all right?"

"Okay."

The older woman reached down and squeezed the baby's round foot. "God bless you, sweet girl." Then she hobbled down the steps toward her bus.

As Della watched Rosetta ride off in one of the front window seats of the big green bus, she spotted a young, barrel-chested man on the sidewalk in a dark suit and a collar, and she wondered which church he belonged to.

The children ran through the gate and toward Della where they both jumped into her arms. She hugged them back, and then Mary Jane pulled away and said, "Mama didn't pick us up today. We were the last ones on the playground, and they called Daddy's old office and nobody came." She pointed to the priest and a pretty little black-headed girl beside him. "Rose's daddy brought us home."

Della looked up at the priest and nodded. Anne had told her a few weeks ago that the priest at St. Michael's had been writing to her and that he had a little girl named Rose. Della said to the children, "I'm sorry you had to wait." She reached out and clasped both of their shoulders. "Your mama wasn't feeling well, kids. But she's going to be okay, in time."

Andrew stepped back and threw a rock he must have been holding all along. It hit the front steps and bounced down into the grass. Della came up behind him and leaned down toward his cheek. She kissed it. "I'm going to help y'all until she gets better. Don't worry, baby."

Then she smiled at the little girl named Rose and back to her niece and nephew and said, "Y'all take Rose in the house, and I'll fix you something sweet after I have a word with her father, okay?"

Andrew's eyes lit up. "Can we have a Popsicle?"

"Sure." Della patted his back. "Get you and the girls a Popsicle and eat it in the backyard."

"All right!" the little boy said. He ran toward the kitchen with Mary Jane and Rose scurrying behind him.

Della looked at the man. He had warm brown eyes with long dark lashes, and he looked a little uncomfortable in his suit and collar. Kind of like a weight lifter in a tuxedo one size too small.

"I'm Della Limehouse." She shook his hand. "Have you been corresponding with my cousin Anne?"

He smiled and nodded. "That's me. Roy Summerall. Call me Roy."

She put her hands on her hips and shook her head. "Well, I can't believe it. Maybe Anne heard right after all."

"I'm sorry?" He had a confused look on his face.

She shook her head and waved him off. "Nothing, nothing. It's been a tough day, and I'm a little fuzzy right now."

"I hope everything is okay with Dr. Sutton," he said.

She looked up at him and though she had her frustrations with God, she sensed something in this man. Something larger and more pure than the life around her. And she knew it was safe to confide in him. "She tried to jump off the Cooper River Bridge this morning."

Roy leaned against the piazza railing as if to steady his large frame. He groaned.

"A security guard on his way to work pulled over and

yanked her down before she got all the way over." Della bit her lip hard as the children giggled and carried on in the backyard. "Maybe there is a God, Roy Summerall."

Roy took a deep breath and regained his composure. He looked down to meet her eye. "There is, Della." He tugged at his collar. "What can I do to help?"

"Well, can you stay with these four children this afternoon while my husband and I go to Atlanta and tell Drew what's going on?"

"I'd be happy to," he said. "There's nothing I can't push back on the schedule for the next day or so."

"Thank you." Della felt a lump in her throat. She swallowed hard and said, "I'll get the bottles and some food ready. Come on in." As she held open the door, he insisted that she go first. And she turned back and said, "Oh, and call Anne, will you?"

"Okay." He pulled out his cell phone and hit the button for his contacts. "She gave me her number last week, but I've been too nervous to call her. The e-mail has been going so well."

Della nodded and couldn't help but smile. "Call her and tell her to come home, Roy."

When Della and Peter arrived in Atlanta, it didn't take them long to find the address of the Courtyard Marriott where the CDC was putting Drew up.

Della saw his Volvo sedan parked in front of one of the efficiency suites, so she and Peter walked up and knocked on the door.

"Room service. Hot dog!" they heard Drew's voice call from behind the door. When he opened it, he was in a thin white towel wrapped loosely around his waist. He looked at them, his unshaven jaw dropping slowly, as though they both had three heads.

"What?" a female voice called from the bathroom. The shower stopped and the voice called, "Can you bring me my hair brush, babe?" When he didn't respond, the bathroom door flew open, revealing a young woman draped in a towel. The wet tips of her long blonde hair dripped on the tile floor causing a little pool of water to form at her bare feet.

Della, still in the doorway, crossed her arms and narrowed her eyes at Drew. "This is not so sublime," she said.

The woman—Melanie from the carriage house—looked up, shrieked, and quickly closed herself back in the bathroom.

Drew raked the top of his salt-and-pepper curls with both of his hands. "What are you all doing here?"

Della cocked her head and stepped inside. She was grinding her teeth so hard that her head ached. "Well, we're not having as much fun as you."

Drew clenched his hands and leaned toward Della, who was balling her own little hands into tight fists. But before Drew realized what had hit him, Peter pinned him against the adjacent wall with force. A framed print of Stone Mountain just to the right of the two men fell to the carpeted floor.

"Watch yourself," Peter whispered sternly to Drew. Peter stood a head taller than Drew, his muscles taut, and ready to throw a serious punch if need be.

Della exhaled for the first time since she stepped into the

room. Her temples were throbbing, and she felt her heart catch in her throat. *Thank God for Peter*, she thought. *Thank Roy Summerall's God*. She didn't deserve her husband, but she was overwhelmed by how much she cherished him—a man who understood right from wrong instinctively, a man who would protect her from the dangers of this world—including her own hot head and her likeliness to mishandle a just rage.

When Peter released him, Drew pushed him back. Then he quickly grabbed his towel which was coming untied. He pulled it tight around his waist.

"What are you two doing here?"

Della stepped in front of Drew, took a deep breath, and tried not to grind her teeth too hard. "Your wife is in trouble, and we came to tell you."

He wiped his nose with his forearm. "What do you mean?"

Della narrowed her eyes. "She tried to jump off the Cooper River Bridge today."

Drew looked away from them. His eyes were on the closed bathroom door, moving back and forth as a shadow crossed the threshold. He pulled at his hair and looked down at his bare feet.

"*Why?*" he shouted. "Why is she doing this!"

Della grabbed his arm firmly. "She's not *doing* this, you idiot." She pressed her fingernails into his skin, but she stopped herself from puncturing him good like every cell in her body wanted her to. "I'm no physician, but even I understand that." She shook his arm until he looked at her. "She's sick, Drew. She's contracted a disease, like cancer, only it's in her brain, and she needs serious help to get better."

He bit his lip. Something plastic toppled to the tile floor in the bathroom.

Della let go of his arm and met his gaze again. "You need to come home right away and take care of her."

"This can't be happening," he said, looking away and toward the window. Outside a bright yellow truck with a Domino's Pizza sign was pulling into a nearby space. "Not right now. We're just getting started. There's a weird flu in Mexico, and we're in charge of working with labs around the world to create a vaccine."

"It is happening," Peter said. His voice was deep and full, and it jolted Drew into looking at him. "It may not be convenient, but it's happening right now. And your wife needs you to man up."

Della nodded. She felt like she and Peter were of one mind and heart. Like they were in the same skin. It was an intimacy she treasured in this moment, and she vowed never to take it for granted. Then she and her husband walked toward the door before she turned back. "She's on President Street. If I were you, I'd get there tonight."

Drew took a seat on the unmade bed and looked back at them. He was still clutching his towel. When he nodded, Peter closed the door. Then he and Della drove back down the highway home.

Chapter 20

ROY

Roy drove to the Charleston airport the next afternoon to pick up Anne. His mama had come in to take care of Rose so he could help with whatever Anne and her family might need.

Since they had been corresponding, he'd had this whole plan of how they would meet face-to-face again, and it involved a dozen red roses and a nice night out on the town at one of the fancy restaurants on East Bay Street.

But she was coming home to help take care of a very sick sister, and he'd have to put those plans on hold. However, he did get the roses. Roses were never ill-timed, and he stood by the security check point clutching the waxy paper in which they were wrapped as the passengers on the flight from Charlotte walked down the narrow hallway toward him.

He spotted Anne right away. Her height, her narrow shoulders, her long, wavy red hair. She was just as he had remembered, and he could see her smiling as she walked toward him, pulling her suitcase along behind her.

She stopped a foot from him, and he clutched the roses tighter. Then he jumped back when he realized a thorn had pricked his index finger.

"It's so good to see you." He nodded and sucked his finger for a moment. "Let me take your bag."

Then he handed her the roses and she smelled them and rested them in the crook of her arm. "Thank you."

He wanted to hug her for a lot of different reasons. They had exchanged dozens of letters over the last six weeks, but this was only the second time they had been face-to-face in their adult lives. What was the protocol for this sort of thing?

"I want to hug you," he blurted out as she looked up from her bouquet.

"I wish you would," she said, and he released her bag, grabbed the roses and set them carefully on top, then opened his arms wide and stepped forward and embraced her long, delicate frame.

Did she feel good? Oh, man! She smelled like honey and she felt like life itself. He breathed in as her hair tickled his nose, and he stepped back and smiled. "Wow."

She blushed and looked down at the ground for a moment, then back up at him and nodded with an unhindered grin.

They stood like this for whole moments until a security guard came over, pointed to the bag, and said, "Does this belong to one of you?"

"Oh, yes," Roy said. He could feel the beads of perspiration forming on his head. He grabbed the bag and the bouquet and pointed toward the door. "I know you're eager to see your sister."

"I am," she said, and she walked beside him toward the electric doors. "But I was eager to see you, too, and I have a feeling you're going to be the joyful part of this trip."

It was strange to feel sad for someone whose loved one was suffering and yet feel so happy at the same time to be in their presence.

"I pray that there will be joy in all the parts of this trip," he said.

She looked at him as they stepped out into the balmy December afternoon. He watched her take in the familiar smell of low tide and salt air. "It's good to be home," she said.

When Roy pulled back into the St. Michael's parking lot late that afternoon, his bookkeeper, Gretchen, was standing by the commander with a worried look on her face.

"Y'all okay?" Roy said as he ambled toward them.

"No," the commander said. "Gretchen just brought to my attention that none of the cash from last week's offering was deposited into the account."

Roy shook his head. "Who is the vestry member in charge this month?"

The commander narrowed his eyes. "Heyward."

Roy uttered a prayer for Heyward. He nodded toward the office building. "Let me try to get him on the phone, all right? I'm sure there's an explanation. Y'all go on home and I'll call you tonight if I find something out."

They didn't make a move toward their cars, but he turned away and headed toward the Broad Street building. Roy had been concerned about Heyward ever since he moved to Charleston, and he wanted to reach out to him and find out if something was wrong.

Heyward picked up his cell phone the third time Roy dialed it. "Hello?"

"Heyward," Roy said. "Do you think you could come over to the church office this evening and meet with me?"

He heard him slowly exhale on the other end of the phone. "Now's not a good time, Roy. Maybe sometime next week?"

"Heyward, the bookkeeper is concerned because the offering from last week has not yet been deposited. Do you know anything about that?"

There was a long pause.

"Heyward?"

"I'm on my way down there," the man said before he hung up the phone.

An hour later Heyward showed up. His bow tie was untied and his boyish face looked worn and ashen.

Roy pointed to the couch in his office. "Let's talk," he said.

Heyward took a seat and buried his hands in his head. "I'm broke. I haven't made any money in six months, and the bank is getting ready to foreclose on my home."

"I'm so sorry," Roy said. "What can I do to help?"

Heyward blew air out of his clenched teeth. "I borrowed the cash from the offertory so I could buy my kids something for Christmas." He looked up at Roy. "My wife said she'd leave me if there was nothing under the tree for the kids."

Heyward bit his lip. "I can't believe I did it, Roy. Took from my church. I've been waiting on a check from a client who owes me money. He assured me he'd pay me this week, and I was going to pay back the church account last Monday, the day after I took the cash, but my client won't answer my calls and now I'm in a heap of trouble. The commander will want to press charges. I guess I can't blame him."

"How much was it?" Roy sat back in his chair and rubbed his aching shoulder.

"Almost a thousand."

Roy turned to his computer, logged on to his personal account at Bank of America, and transferred $2,000 from his savings to his checking account. Then he wrote Heyward a check for $2,000. "Cash this and put $1,000 in the church account. Use the rest for whatever you need."

Heyward looked up and wrinkled his brow. "No, Roy. I know how much you make, and I don't know if or when I can pay you back."

"I'm your priest," Roy said. "You have to do what I say, right?" He leaned in. "Take the money, then ask your wife to come in with you for some marital counseling. I want to meet and pray with the two of you on a regular basis."

The man nodded and exhaled deeply. "Okay."

"God's got you," Roy said. "Even when things look the bleakest. Especially then."

As Heyward stood to shake Roy's hand, the commander

knocked on the glass pane of the door. "Do I need to call the authorities?" he said in his gruff voice.

"No," Roy said. "It's all taken care of. Now go home like I asked you to and be at peace."

The man scowled at Heyward and turned and headed down the steps, then Roy walked Heyward to his car and watched him pull out onto Meeting Street.

When Roy looked up at the picturesque steeple trimmed in garland for the Advent season, he thought of the couple lying still in the dream he had last summer. Could it have been Heyward and his wife? He didn't know the answer to that question, but he did know that whoever the couple represented, the Lord had a plan to breathe life into their stone-like bodies.

Chapter 21

LISH

On the Monday before Christmas, Lish was released from the Institute of Psychiatry. As she sat in the lobby, watching the nurses walk up and down the hallway with little cups of medication, she thought of the bits and pieces of conversations she'd had with Drew and Della and Anne and Dr. Cussler since she'd been in the hospital.

Because Drew had to be in Atlanta until Christmas, Della and Anne were in charge of the safety plan. Lish knew she would be watched around the clock for the first several weeks, and once she felt strong enough, they would allow her to be alone for short periods of time.

Drew had come back twice to visit her. All she could remember of those visits were his eyes, jumpy and bloodshot, and him squeezing her hand saying, "I need you to pull it together, sweetheart."

❧

She had sat quietly on her bed, kneading her sheets one afternoon as Drew explained to Dr. Cussler the enormous and highly stressful task ahead of him at the CDC. A rare flu had been recently identified in a Mexican village, and it could turn into a pandemic. It was up to his team to assess the virus and help create a vaccine.

"Lish's sister and cousin will be on site to take care of her through Christmas," he had told Dr. Cussler, who seemed nervous in front of Drew. Lish had noticed Dr. Cussler tapping the wrong side of his pen on his khaki pants, and she could see the little black lines forming across his thigh, but she couldn't find the words to tell him. "Then I want Lish to be able to move with our kids to Atlanta as soon as possible."

Dr. Cussler had gently poked the ball point of the pen into his leg and seemed to work up his courage. "I strongly advise against a move within the next twelve months." The psychiatrist turned to Lish, and she knew he expected her to weigh in. She had rubbed the edge of the sheet and did not respond.

"Look," Drew said. "Let us get through Christmas, then we'll see how she's doing." He stepped toward Dr. Cussler, who stepped back as if he wanted ample space between them.

Dr. Cussler cleared his throat, lifted his chin toward Drew, and shook his head. "With all due respect, Dr. Sutton, it could be a mistake to rush a recovery."

❧

Lish felt a light tap on her shoulder. She looked to her side and saw Anne and Della standing beside her, smiling tentatively. They took turns hugging her and then they each grabbed an elbow and gently lifted her up.

The Abilify, an antipsychotic medicine she'd been on since she arrived, made her dizzy, and they knew she liked to get up very slowly and feel her feet firmly under her before she took a step.

"We're so happy to see you," Della said. Lish noticed that Della had put lipstick on, and she was wearing the oval-shaped turquoise earrings Lish had bought her during a trip she took with Drew to Mexico several years ago.

Anne grinned and rubbed her sister's arm. "Ready to go home?" Lish turned to her sister, who looked better than ever. She held her shoulders back as if she was proud of her height, and her crimson hair glistened even beneath the stark fluorescent light of the Institute of Psychiatry. Lish didn't know the details, but she understood that Anne was dating the new priest at St. Michael's. Roy Summerall, a boy they had known as children. One of Elfrieda Summerall's nephews. She thought of Anne's revelation in the bell tower a few years ago. Maybe she had heard the voice of God after all.

"Yes." Lish turned toward the elevator. "I'm ready." She swallowed and waited for the burn, but it didn't follow. The Abilify had short-circuited the chemicals in her brain, and whatever made it hard for her to swallow was gone now. Sometimes she still felt the thump on the top of her head. It was very faint and usually came upon her when she'd over-done it or when she took a long, hot shower, but it usually subsided after a deep nap or a good night's sleep.

"Maybe it's just the memory of the thump . . ." Dr. Cussler suggested during their session a few days ago. He had been rubbing the heels of his hands together like he did sometimes when he was thinking hard.

She had nodded. "It could be."

Now as they drove up to 18 Legare Street, Lish grinned and pointed to the door, where Anne had made a beautiful wreath out of dozens of big waxy magnolia leaves from the tree in Mrs. Emerson's front yard. It was just like the ones Nana used to make. And someone had strung fresh garland along the piazza rails, and she could see through the big thick windows that there was a grand, brightly lit Christmas tree whose top must surely reach the high ceiling.

Della reached over to the passenger seat and rubbed her back. "Like it?"

Lish smiled and slowly blinked.

As she stepped out of the car, one foot finding the ground and positioning itself and then the next, the children scurried out with a long white banner that said, "Welcome Home, Mama." There was a red-and-green wreath on the banner made out of their handprints.

When Andrew and Mary Jane spotted their mother stepping slowly out of the car, they let go of the banner and ran to her. Andrew gently hugged her, and Mary Jane stood up on her tippy-toes, reached up her arms, and said, "Uhh, uhh." Lish didn't think she could lift her. She was still groggy and the pills made her lose her balance from time to time. Instead, she squatted down and took her daughter in her arms. She tried not to weep too hard when she felt the little girl's soft, full cheek against her own. She squeezed her tight and then rubbed her smooth dark hair, which smelled like baby shampoo and Frasier fir needles and maple syrup. Lish could stay this way for hours. She had missed her children, and she yearned to make up for the lost time.

When Mary Jane pulled back, she grabbed Lish's face and said, "I've been waiting for you, Mama."

"Me too," said Andrew. Lish reached out her arm, and the little boy fell into it so hard that they all three plunked down on the ground. She hugged them both as tight as she could. She wanted to tell them how much she loved them, but the words were hard to find and string together. Both Andrew and Mary Jane pulled back and looked at her as if they were expecting her to say something.

"She's happy to be home," Della said as Cozy came over and leaned against her own mother. Mary Jane rested her head against her mother's chest and said, "We're happy to have her."

Then Anne helped to lift Lish up and Della came to the other side, and they walked her slowly up the stairs and into the house while Peter ran down the steps and picked both Mary Jane and Andrew up in his strong arms. He whispered to them, "Remember what we talked about, guys?" They nodded. "It's going to take a little while for your mama to get used to being home. She's getting well, but she's not all the way well."

"I remember," Andrew said, his arms crossed.

Peter kissed his forehead. "That's my man." Then he spun them around until they were both giggling and holding out their arms to feel the rush of cool air.

They had two quiet nights where they set their routine. Anne slept with Lish one night and then Della the next. Whoever was not with Lish took care of the baby, who still needed a bottle and a diaper change around four a.m.

Peter and Cozy entertained the children and Lish tried to meet her goals for the day: to get up by nine a.m., to take a shower, to get dressed, to eat a meal or two, to have a conversation with her children and watch them play in the garden for an hour or so.

On Christmas morning, Lish stood in her shower and stared into space for several minutes before she heard Anne's voice. "You're going to be okay," Anne said. Then Lish stepped slowly out of the shower and let her sister wrap a towel around her and pull her close. "It's slow going right now," Anne whispered. "But it won't be this way forever."

Lish's eyes filled with tears and she nodded her head. "Some Christmas, huh?" She wiped her cheek. "Is Drew here yet?"

"No." Anne squeezed her damp hair with the towel. "I'm sure he's on his way."

By noon on Christmas day, Drew pulled into the driveway in his new car, a big black Range Rover. The children ran out to greet him, and he opened the trunk and pulled out his extravagant gifts—a life-size, battery-operated Groovy Girl jeep for Mary Jane that she could drive around the yard, and a three-wheeled motorcycle of the same ilk for Andrew.

"Awesome!" Andrew shouted. He called Cozy over, and they all took turns circling the loquat tree and the rosebushes and the swimming pool over and over until Mary Jane fell out of the driver's seat on a sharp turn by the carriage house and scraped her shoulder on a stepping stone.

Drew had little to say to the adults. Della and Anne tried giving him as much space as possible. They pretended to be busy cooking the turkey and the dressing, and Peter spent most of the afternoon unpacking the toys that were so thoroughly wired into their packaging that he said he needed his blowtorch to extract them.

After a hectic lunch where Baby Cecilia fussed and Andrew popped Cozy so hard on the back with a spoon that she cried, the kids settled themselves in front of the Rudolph movie and the adults cleaned up—everyone but Lish and Drew, who walked slowly up to the third-floor piazza for a talk. Lish tried to keep her voice low in hopes that Drew would follow suit. She was counting on the hum of the dishwasher and the shrieks of the snow monster on the television to keep the others from hearing their conversation.

Drew didn't follow suit, and Lish imagined Della and Anne raising their eyebrows from two floors below as his voice rose and fell while he rationalized away his distance and detachment. Lish, too weary and weak to respond, listened and nodded and looked toward the carriage house where she had the faintest memory of watching Melanie rub Drew's back. She wondered if it was all a bad dream.

After the children were put to bed, Lish walked Drew down the stairs, where he shook Peter's hand and nodded to Della and Anne. "I've got to get back to Atlanta," he said.

Della rolled her eyes and opened her mouth to speak. But Peter quickly grabbed her arm, and she kept quiet.

"Let me walk you out," Peter said to Drew. The two men were out in the driveway for nearly thirty minutes. Lish knew Peter was trying to talk Drew into staying, but he wouldn't succeed. Then the rumble of Drew's huge motor sounded, and the bright beams of his headlights exposed a marsh rat in the garden. He pulled right out of the driveway and Lish could hear him, from their bedroom, as he pressed the gas and powered down the south end of Legare Street in his tall, dark cage of a car.

That night, as Lish sat in front of her vanity mirror examining her sagging jowls, Anne and Della came up together. "Time to get ready for bed." Anne handed Lish a pill and a glass of water.

"He's gone," Lish said as she swallowed the little white tablet that made her dizzy and dull. She scanned their bedroom before viewing herself in the mirror again. "He doesn't want this . . . anymore."

"What do you mean?" Anne stood behind Lish. Three worry lines formed across the thin blue vein in the center of Anne's forehead.

Lish turned slowly around to face them. "I know Drew." She stood up and walked slowly to her bed, where she sat down and sucked her teeth. Then she rubbed the center of her head. *It's not the thump, just the memory of it*, she said to herself. "He wants a . . . new life."

Della crossed her arms. "Now *that's* insane."

Lish chuckled and shrugged her shoulder. Her voice was strong, but she parceled her words out one or two at a time, and it seemed like seconds before the next one followed. "There's probably . . . someone else. I don't . . . know." She placed her hand on the bed and looked up to Anne and Della. "But . . . this has gotten . . . too messy . . . for him. I know . . . Drew. He . . . wants out."

Anne breathed deeply, and she shook her head in disbelief. "How could he ever walk away from you and the children? That's just—" She cleared her throat. "Unconscionable."

Lish leaned back on the mound of pillows at the head of her bed and pulled the covers up to her neck. "It can all . . . come unraveled . . . so quickly, can't it?"

"It can't be someone else." Anne sat down beside her and took her hand.

Della was silent. She stood to hang up Lish's cream wool pants, and when she turned back, her eyes met Lish's. They locked for several seconds as Anne looked back and forth between the two women. Lish could tell that Della knew something, but whatever it was, it didn't need to be said. The reality was that while Drew's leaving wasn't right, it could certainly be what was happening. It could be exactly what Lish suspected.

Lish watched Della as she laid down next to her and gently sighed.

It was disconcerting when Della was quiet. Like a summer night without the hum of the crickets. Della took Lish's other hand and squeezed it. And they stayed this way for several minutes before Lish said, "Good night, y'all."

Chapter 22

Roy

January 21, 2009

Roy had a spring in his step. It was a spring he hadn't had in a long, long time. Though it was January, the most depressing month of the year for some, he couldn't help but grin at any passerby as he stood under the church portico just before the weekday midday prayer service, inviting folks off the street to come in for prayer and a fifteen-minute respite.

Sometimes folks took him up on the offer. Quite often a tourist had the time to spare, and occasionally a lawyer or some other business person in a tailored suit would come on in and take a place in one of the box pews as a lay reader read the Scripture passage.

Anne was there most every day with Baby Cecilia bouncing on her knee. The baby girl had grown quite fond of him, and after the service he loved to carry her in his arms down Meeting Street to wherever Anne felt like having lunch.

Every other night, Anne was off the babysitting duty, and he would make sure they found some time to get together. If it was Alpha or vestry meeting night, she'd come by the house afterward and play Candy Land or Hi-Ho-Cheerio with him and Rose, and Roy thought Rose enjoyed it even more than him—if that were possible.

One Friday night after Rose said she wanted to go up to her room and play with her Barbies, Roy found himself next to Anne on the couch, just looking at her and smiling. They had very few moments when they were alone, and perhaps this was good. It was all he could do not to take her in his arms and profess his love for her, but he wanted to make sure they proceeded at a pace that was right with her and with God.

"I'm not going back to England," she said.

He wasn't sure how to respond. He knew the reason she had come home was to see about her sister, and Lish still needed a lot of help. But he was hoping that another one of the reasons that she wasn't going back was him.

She sighed her lovely sigh and tucked her hair behind her delicate shoulders. "My sister needs me."

"Yes, she does," he said. His heart was pounding so hard, he could feel it in his ears. "And so does someone else."

She met his brown eyes, and he pointed to his chest and then upstairs to the sound of Rose pitter-pattering in her room just above their heads.

Anne took another deep breath. He couldn't help himself. He wanted to know where she stood when it came to him.

"Anne, even if your sister had made a full recovery by now, I would have asked you not to go back."

He squeezed her hand. Her long, thin bones reminded him of the graceful herons he saw wading in the salt marsh. He pulled his hand away, not wanting to be too forward.

She blushed and then looked up to him. "Roy," she said. "If you would have asked me to stay, I would have said yes."

His heart seemed to pound even stronger in his chest, and his throat tightened. A few weeks ago he would have thought he was coming down with something, but he was familiar enough with the feeling by now to know just what it was. He was afraid to call it by its name just yet. But it filled his heart with an indescribable joy. He knew Anne was a gift from the Lord, and he said, *Thank you, Thank you* to his Maker as he leaned in to kiss her on the lips for the very first time.

"Yippee!" a voice called from the grand stairway. He looked over his shoulder to see the tail of Rose's fuzzy purple bathrobe as she ran quickly back up the stairs. Had she been watching all along?

"She's excited about where this might be going," he said.

Anne settled into the couch and took his heavy hand in hers. "She's not the only one."

Sometimes it's hard to focus when you're in love. But Roy had prayed for the Lord to continue to show him how to minister to his new flock. He asked them to fill out another prayer request card so he could pray for their specific needs during

Lent. This go-round, everyone seemed more comfortable, and he received over 150 cards. This time folks were more honest too. It wasn't just "Pray for my Great Aunt So-and-So who is sick" kind of stuff. They wrote the things they were struggling with themselves: financial hardship, marriage problems, depression, chronic lust, envy, regret over a decision, unresolved conflict with a family member or old friend. Real-life stuff. But what struck him was the struggle that every fourth or fifth card seemed to name: anxiety. One-third of his flock had anxious thoughts or felt overwhelmed. Why? The needs of the Church of the Good Shepherd had been much more concrete and simpler to solve. But this anxiety—where did it come from? Nearly half the people who came and sat in his office were struggling with some form of fear or fretfulness. He started to pray for the troubled hearts and minds of each member of his congregation. He took the directory out and prayed for a page full of church members each day.

Then he asked some prayer ministers from a church he knew in Jacksonville to come over and lead a Saturday of healing prayer in February that focused on the verse "You will keep him in perfect peace, whose mind is stayed on You, because he trusts in You" (Isaiah 26:3). Over one hundred people signed up.

Chapter 23

DELLA

One remarkably mild Saturday afternoon at the end of January, Della and Lish were watching the kids kick a soccer ball in the garden when an unfamiliar car pulled up and a young man stepped out with a certified letter that he asked Lish to sign.

Della helped Lish stand and steady herself by holding the rocking chair with her fingertips. Lish slowly nodded at the man and carefully signed the letter with his thick silver pen. Then she sat down and carefully broke the seal as the man backed out. Della watched her eyes move back and forth as she took in the words.

Then Lish handed the letter to Della, who read it quickly to herself as the children screamed with delight as the ball made its way into their makeshift goal, a cast net draped over two camellia bushes. Drew was filing for a separation. He admitted that he had committed adultery. He would provide for Lish and the kids. He would give them whatever they needed. He wanted to end their marriage as soon as possible.

"Lish." Della took her cousin's hand and squeezed it tight. She watched as Lish brought a teacup up to her lips, sipped, and swallowed before scooting back in her chair.

Then Lish settled the cup back in its saucer, placed it on the rail, and reached over to pat Della's arm as if she was the one who needed reassuring: "No . . . surprise."

"Mama!" Andrew called. "Look at this lizard we just found!" He lumbered up the piazza stairs, with his sister on his heels, and opened his hand to reveal a bright green lizard with a red, bloated throat. Mary Jane squealed as the lizard promptly leapt out and onto the old floorboards, darting between their feet. They all watched with wide eyes as the creature scurried off the side of the porch and onto a limb of the tea rose bush.

"Wow," Lish said unhurriedly. She forced a smile and nodded her head. "That's something."

One afternoon in February as Della was checking her e-mail during a planning period at school, she received a letter from the editor at her publishing house. She'd been waiting for him to respond to her novel for three months now. It had never taken this long.

Now she stared at the three-paragraph response to her three-hundred-page novel with disbelief. She read the heart of the letter several times:

While the writing is strong and the story, at times, is quite riveting, the ending fails on many levels. It doesn't ring true somehow. It's abrupt and incomplete. And it leaves the reader feeling both baffled and cheated. Yes, the murder is inevitable, but is that all there is to the story? I'm not sure why you chose to end it here, Della. What was your thinking?

As it stands now, the novel is unpublishable, and we simply can't accept it. In my mind, you have two options: 1. To rewrite the last third of the manuscript, contemplating what makes an ending that is both complete and resonant. 2. Take nine months and write something new.

Let me know what you want to do as soon as possible.

"Ugh." She leaned over her desk and rested her forehead on the heel of her hand. She didn't know whether to scream or cry. It was not too easy to write a novel when you taught six sections of middle school English every day, and you were caring for your cousin and her children every other night. And she needed that advance money something awful. Her old Honda had died two weeks ago on her way over to Legare Street, and she and Peter had picked out a used pickup on the lot at Marsden's Mitsubishi that they were going to buy as soon as the money came in.

"Bye-bye best seller," she said to herself as the students filed into her classroom, laughing and throwing a crumpled ball of notebook paper back and forth. She had tried to create a kind of commercial novel, a page-turner, and her editor had out-and-out rejected it. That hadn't happened to her in years.

❧

She walked home in a daze with Cozy's hand in hers. The girl was chatting a mile a minute about a scuffle that occurred on the playground between two fourth-grade girls who were fighting over a swing. Her teacher had had to come between them and order them both to the lower school principal's office.

When they rounded the corner toward their crumbling, plum-colored duplex, Della saw Peter in the driveway putting a license plate on the truck they'd been eyeing.

Cozy ran ahead. "Daddy! Daddy!" He hugged her tight, and then he threw her high up in the air, her thin arms and legs spread and slightly bent at the joints as if she was a marionette or a sky diver in mid-fall.

"You bought the truck?" Della said. Her right hand was firmly on her hip, and she was trying to keep her composure.

He turned to her and grinned. "Remember the two shrimp I took out to that new art gallery on Kiawah Island a few weeks ago?"

"Yeah." She vaguely recalled him loading the sculptures in his father's truck early one morning.

He mimicked her by cocking his hip and slapping his hand on it. "They sold late yesterday to a couple from New York." He leaned forward and put his nose against hers.

"Turns out this couple is pretty well-to-do, and they've asked me to sculpt three turtles for a home they have in Maine."

Then he straightened up and pulled a wad of cash out of his pocket. "I cashed the check, bought the truck, and I've got a dental appointment for Friday afternoon."

"You're kidding, right?" Della breathed deeply and let her hand fall to her side.

Peter shook his head as if to say no. "And there will be enough left over to put a few thousand bucks in the bank." He stuffed the cash back in his pocket, reached over and patted her backside. "How about them apples?"

She swung her arms around his hips and rested her head against his chest as Cozy jumped up and down chanting, "Take us for a ride!"

"In a minute," Peter said as he pecked the top of Della's head. "So how was your day?"

She pulled back and looked up at him. "Not nearly as good as yours."

"You can tell me all about it over dinner at Rue de Jean."

"Rue?" she said. It was her favorite restaurant, but they hadn't been able to afford a meal out in months.

"Yep." He reached out and pulled Cozy into the center of their embrace. "Anne agreed to watch this little monkey along with the rest of the gang tonight." He rubbed the little girl's head with his knuckles, then leaned down and cupped his hand around her ear to whisper, "I'm taking Mama on a date."

"All right!" Cozy looked up at her mother and flashed a knowing grin. "Can I help you get dressed up, Mama?"

"You better." Della rubbed the child's cheek with the back of her hand.

❧

That night after a bowl of the curry mussels, the duck special, and a choice glass of champagne, Peter and Della rode over in their newly purchased truck to 18 Legare to pick up Cozy, who they hoped was sound asleep in the lower bunk of Andrew's bed.

Lish was waiting for them on the piazza. She was rocking slowly back and forth in the dark in a flannel nightgown with two thick wool blankets draped around her shoulders.

"Hi."

Della jumped back, and Peter steadied her. She made out the figure of her cousin and said, "Sorry, Lish. You scared me."

Della hadn't seen her cousin in more than forty-eight hours, and it seemed like a long time now that she spent every other night at her home.

Lish looked up to them both. "How was . . . your date?" She tried to focus, to meet their eyes; Della knew it was hard for her this time of night, and she was not surprised when Lish looked away.

"Really nice." Peter leaned against the railing. "We were overdue for one of those."

"I'll say," Della chuckled.

They watched Lish for a moment as she grasped the edge of the chair and began to rock. They heard the heavy breathing of two late-night joggers, and in the distance the honk of a car horn.

Lish turned back to them. "Can I talk"—she swallowed with effort—"to you both?"

"Sure." Della took a seat next to Lish, and Peter leaned forward, giving Lish his full attention. "What's up?" he said.

Lish adjusted her posture. She examined the veins snaking their way across the tops of her hands and said, "I want y'all . . . to move in." She nodded across the garden. "To the carriage house."

Della looked to Peter, who crossed his arms and waited for more.

Lish's blue eyes glistened in the darkness. She licked her chapped lips and turned to Della. "I won't charge you . . . any rent." She wrung her hands. "Maybe you could . . . sell your place . . . or rent it out."

Then she peered up at the half moon hanging in the clear winter sky above them. "I . . . need you." She shook off a chill. "I need . . . your help."

Della cleared her throat. The thought hadn't crossed her mind, but she knew what Lish was trying to say. She might not get well this year or next year or the next after that. And they couldn't go on this way, spending every other night over here, living out of suitcases and Food Lion grocery store bags. Plus, Anne was in love for the first time ever, and she needed more time with Roy to see where things were leading.

Della reached out and took hold of Lish's shoulder. Her eyes were on Peter. "Let us talk about it, okay?"

Lish waited for a moment before she slowly nodded her head twice. "Okay." She stood and turned toward the grand front door. "Thank . . . you."

‿≈⁓

That night on their back porch, Peter patted his knee, and Della took a seat on it.

He squeezed her tight. "What do you think about your cousin's proposal?"

Della rested her head against his and looked up at the same half moon. "I don't know."

Ever since they drove away from 18 Legare, she'd been trying to decode a hidden message or another layer behind her cousin's request. She stared at the half face of the man on the moon. "I think she's trying to tell us she's not sure if she's going to get well." She sighed. "And that terrifies me."

He rubbed her back and pulled her even closer. "I think she was just asking for our help." He kissed her forehead. "Nothing more and nothing less."

"Maybe." Della sat up and turned back to him. "She's asking for help—indefinitely, I guess."

"Don't think of it like that." He rubbed her thin arms with his wide hands. "None of us can predict what's going to happen from one day to the next, you know?"

They both watched a thin layer of mist move across the moon. She felt his lips on her ear as he said, "I'm up for it if you are."

❧

Two weeks later, Della and Peter got an offer on their half of the duplex. It was practically a miracle; nothing was selling on the peninsula as the economy continued to tank. But the parents of two college kids who had bought the upstairs unit a few years ago, when their twins enrolled at the College of Charleston, spotted the For Sale By Owner sign one Saturday morning, knocked on the door, and said: "We're interested."

"That's fantastic," Della had said as she stepped to the side and invited them in for coffee.

By the next week, they'd signed a contract, and by the end of March, Della and Peter and Cozy packed their little life into cardboard boxes and hauled it all over to the charming old two-bedroom carriage house behind the grand home at 18 Legare.

Chapter 24

In April, Dr. Cussler called a meeting with Della and Anne. He was not pleased with how slowly Lish still seemed to be moving—both mentally and physically. She walked like an old lady, hunched over and wobbly, and her energy level remained remarkably low. As for the depression, it had a strong hold on her. Three consecutive months of a high dose of Zoloft should be making a significant difference by this point, but wasn't. She was not the Lish they'd always known and loved—that much Della knew for certain. There were few flickers of the real her, and they were all concerned.

"There's a research project at MUSC," Dr. Cussler said. "It's new and fairly unconventional. But I think Lish could benefit from it."

"Tell us about it." Anne leaned forward on his big leather sofa. Her long legs squeaked against it.

Dr. Cussler raised his eyebrows and leaned in to meet them both from his chair opposite them. "It's called transcranial magnetic stimulation."

"I've heard of it." Della tapped her foot; then she nudged Anne on the knee. "Todd told me about it." She looked to Dr. Cussler. "It's like electroshock, but gentler, right?"

He nodded. "Precisely." He touched his fingertips to his head. "It uses a powerful electromagnet to bypass the skull with a magnetic field, and then the procedure is to induce weak electrical currents in the brain."

"Ugh." Anne rubbed her temples. "Does it hurt?"

"No." Dr. Cussler shook his head emphatically. "That's the beauty of it. It requires no anesthesia, unlike electroshock therapy, so it doesn't induce seizures or the side effects that come with them, like memory loss, headaches, and so forth."

The young doctor set his yellow legal pad on his knobby knee and looked back and forth between them. "This could jump-start the sluggish nerve cells that are maintaining Lish's severe depression." He shook his head. "Unfortunately, she hasn't responded to the antidepressants in the way I hoped she would by now. I think this is worth a try."

Della rubbed her knees. "Me too."

"How do you feel about it?" Della asked Lish that afternoon as they walked at a snail's pace down Meeting Street on their daily stroll with Baby Cecilia.

"I'm . . . scared." Lish talked like a record in slow motion and looked down at her feet; she put one foot in front of the other. "But maybe . . ." She stepped and stepped again. "It will help."

Della noticed the petals of a dogwood tree, fluttering down onto the sidewalk. She heard the *clip-clop* of a horse pulling a carriage down Broad Street and the *brush brush* of the custodian sweeping the entrance into St. Michael's Church. As she watched the old city, still alive and thriving, she pictured Lish as a ten-year-old, running down this block in her tea-length dress on the way to dancing school at South Carolina Society Hall. She envisioned her turning, looking back, and pulling her arm toward her shoulder, gesturing for Della to hurry up.

Now Della nodded as Baby Cecilia started to protest. She was probably irritated by how slowly they were moving. Della looked at her cousin, who seemed oblivious to the protest and to the evocative streets and the beautiful spring blooming all around them. She just watched her feet, one foot in front of the other. One foot in front of the other was all she could manage. Lish reminded Della of Papa in the afternoons, unable to face the world.

This is the hardest part, Della thought. *Having someone right beside you who is no longer really there. It's like you've lost someone and yet—there they are—breathing, walking, and every once in a while talking. But the personality and the voice and the vitality behind the voice are gone. How did Nana stand it?*

"Hey, you two!" a voice called from the cemetery. Della turned to see Roy bounding down the slate path toward the street. He was in purple shorts and a bright orange polo shirt. The unfortunate colors of Clemson University. (Anne would have to convince him to go with either purple or orange from now on, Della thought.)

He reached out to shake their hands, then he smiled at Baby Cecilia, who had settled down now that she saw his bright face. "I've been thinking about you all. Why don't you come on up to my office and let's catch up?"

Lish straightened up and turned to him. "Okay," she said. "Maybe . . . you can help us." She took a deep breath. "We're trying . . . to make a decision."

He nodded and smiled. "Absolutely." He gestured toward the Broad Street building where Della and her cousins had attended Sunday school and confirmation classes year after year when they were kids.

"There's nothing I'd rather do than catch up and pray for you." He turned to Della and patted her shoulder. "That's what it's all about, right?"

Della parked the stroller in the cemetery and lifted the baby out of her seat. They walked down the slate path toward the building and up a flight of stairs, where they found his office. It was a beautiful corner room, looking out over Broad Street. As Della stared at the bookshelves and the icons and the painted crosses from Honduras and Ecuador, she remembered the stained-glass one hanging in Nana's kitchen when she was a child. There were words above it—some sort of Scripture—but she couldn't recall them.

Della bounced Baby Cecilia on her knee as Lish slowly told Roy about the TMS treatment. (Anne had taken off for a bell ringing retreat in Richmond just after the meeting at Dr. Cussler's.)

Roy listened with soft eyes and a palpable empathy, and then he scooted his leather chair over toward the couch where they were sitting and took their hands in his. As he prayed for guidance, Della felt a kind of warmth radiating from his palms. She opened her eyes slightly, and as he closed with a heartfelt petition for Lish's complete recovery, she pictured the hands of a twelve-year-old boy, wrapping his shirt around Lish's bloody shin and then lifting her up into the paper basket on the front of his bike. Della could almost feel the hot air lifting up the strands of her hair as she chased behind the bike while he pedaled Lish home with remarkable speed.

When Roy said *Amen*, Della turned to watch Lish look up and attempt a smile. "I'm going . . . to do it," she said.

He nodded assuringly and took her hand again. "I think you should."

When they stood Della said, "What happened to your wife?" She knew from Anne that he was a widower, but she had not heard the particulars.

Roy turned back and met Della's gaze. "She passed away a couple of months after we had Rose."

Della couldn't help but put her hand over her mouth. "I'm so sorry."

He put one hand on his hip and shook his head. His eyes were warm, and he took the time to look at both of them. "She had a cancerous spot on her tongue, and we didn't discover it until she was six months pregnant."

Lish let out a sympathetic moan.

"It was tragic." He took a deep breath. "There's no other way to describe it." He gradually put his hands palm up and bit his lower lip. "But God's mercy somehow carried us through each day." He raised his eyebrows. "And the honest truth is, he still does." Looking back out the window, he added, "It's funny. Rose told me last night after Anne read her a bedtime story that she's never been happier. And I have to say I agree."

Suddenly Della remembered the words on the cross hanging in Nana's kitchen window. She never consciously memorized them, but the words came right to her mind. *"In all their affliction He was afflicted, and the Angel of His Presence saved them"* (Isaiah 63:9).

She felt a burning in her throat, and she wanted to both laugh and cry. Did she have that many bones to pick with God after all? Or did she have him to thank for all that was good in her life?

❧

"So I'll call Dr. Cussler when we get home," Della said as they took a right turn off of Meeting onto Lamboll Street.

"All right." Lish swallowed and clenched her fists. "Thank you."

She's not completely gone, Della said to herself as she watched her cousin walk one laborious step at a time back toward her home as the birds twittered and the scent of the wisteria blossoms permeated the air with a syrupy sweetness. *At least the most essential part of her isn't, anyway.*

Della looked through a hole in a crumbling brick wall and watched a blue jay dunk its head in a cracked birdbath. *Only Lish would endure this whole thing without throwing a pity party or asking, time and time again in an outraged tone, why?*

Two weeks later, Della drove Lish over to MUSC for her first treatment. She would receive four weeks of the daily forty-minute TMS sessions, and then Dr. Cussler and the neurologist would examine her to see if there'd been a significant change.

Anne met them in the neurology unit, and within moments Lish followed Todd Jervey, Dr. Cussler, and Dr. Rand, the neurologist, beyond the thick swinging doors and into the research ward.

Della and Anne stood still for whole minutes as if paralyzed as they listened to the steady drone of the machine on the other side of the wall. Della had conducted her fair share of online research about the effect of putting electricity on the brain. Back around the turn of the century, doctors in Italy noticed that their depressed patients with epilepsy actually improved after a seizure, and since then, they'd sought all sorts of ways to reboot the mind with a jolt.

Eventually, Anne took a seat and Della started to pace. She pointed to the stack of papers in her seat. "I should be grading," she said. "But I can't sit still."

Anne fingered a stack of magazines and pulled out a

Newsweek and started to read the lead story, "Obama's First One Hundred Days" as Della's flats slapped the tile floor. "You're making me nervous."

"Sorry." Della sat down next to Anne and squeezed her wrist the way she used to when they were girls. "Man, I hope this works."

"Me too." Anne leaned her head on Della's shoulder. "I miss her."

Della put her face in her hands and let out a muffled, "I know." She rubbed her eyes. "I want her back." She looked at Anne head on. "All the way back."

Anne nodded her head in agreement. They had not said this to one another and it hurt to admit it. How far away the Lish they knew and loved seemed. Anne squeezed Della's wrist back.

Lish came out leaning on Dr. Cussler's arm. She was bleary-eyed and appeared even more exhausted than before she went in.

"There's a . . . tapping . . . in my head," she said to no one in particular. It was as if she was talking to the wall or the stack of magazines by Anne's chair.

"She needs to rest," Dr. Cussler said. Anne rushed over and took her by the arm.

"I'll pull the car around." Della fished in her pocketbook for her keys as she scurried down the hall toward the parking garage.

When they arrived home, Peter and Della walked Lish

up the stairs, one step at a time, to her room, and they didn't hear a peep out of her for the rest of the night.

During the next two weeks, Della and Anne took turns driving Lish to the late afternoon TMS sessions. Each time Lish came out seeming wearier than before, her arms limp and her shoulders hunched over. By the fourteenth session she could hardly lift her feet. She shuffled them now, like an old man. She didn't have the energy to lift them up.

"The treatment seems to be wearing her down," Della told Dr. Cussler, who called for a report on a day he couldn't be there. "She is worse than before."

He met Della and Anne at the hospital the next day and saw what they saw—an aged person, hunched over and shuffling, barely able to walk or string a few words into a sentence.

"I'm calling a meeting with the researchers," he said. He blinked several times and pulled at his little chin. "The last thing I want is to put her in a worse state than before."

The following week, Dr. Cussler discussed his concerns with the three research physicians before Monday's session. Then he met Della, Anne, and Lish in the waiting room at the usual appointment time and ushered them into a conference room.

"Dr. Jervey and Dr. Rand think we should keep going," said Dr. Cussler. He looked to Lish, who was hunched over in a plastic chair, her back like an arc or a question mark. She reminded Della of their Great Aunt Bess, who had osteoporosis so bad that she spent the last decade of her life staring at her toes. "But I'm not sure."

He patted Lish's shoulder, and Della watched her slowly look up. Lish could barely meet his gaze, and after she tried she let her head flop back down. He gently touched her hand. "I don't want this to set you further back."

Lish slowly lifted her head once more to look him head-on. Her eyelids were still half closed as if they were weighted with lead, but she could make out his eyes. Just as Della was about to say, "Let's stop," Lish said, "Keep . . . going." Then she dropped her head again.

Della gnawed at the inside of her cheek, and she tapped her foot so strongly that the whole room seemed to be pulsing until Anne reached over and patted her leg.

"Are you sure?" Della pleaded.

Lish nodded in slow motion.

"Okay." Dr. Cussler scratched the top of his head as if he was nervous. "We'll proceed for another week, and then we'll meet again."

On the thirty-third session, on a late May afternoon, Lish slowly shuffled in with her eyes half closed as Della graded a pile of essays and Anne read the newspaper from front to back. Della was used to the steady drone by now, and it almost had a calming effect on her as she waited.

Anne had read two months' worth of all the magazines in the entire waiting room, so after she discarded the paper, she turned to a stack of brochures at the front desk and read them each twice. The first one was about headaches, the second was about depression, and the third was about the swine flu.

So much had changed in a year, Della thought as she lifted her head from her essays and stared at the back of the swine flu brochure. They practically all lived at 18 Legare taking care of Lish and her brood. Drew was gone. Lish was gone in a way too. But Della and Peter had never been tighter, and Anne was finally in love.

Baby Cecilia was about to turn one, and she was pulling up on the tables and putting everything in sight in her mouth. She only wanted Peter to hold her when he was around, and he made a fuss over her, kissing her and patting her in a way that filled Della's heart with a kind of joy and hope.

Lish's children were doing as well as they could despite the fact that their father rarely came to see them and their mother was here in body but not so much in spirit. Andrew could read the level two books, and Mary Jane just wanted to play dress-up with Cozy, who humored her most evenings by doing just about anything she wanted her to do.

This might be the way it is for years, Della thought to herself. She hadn't said this to Anne or even to Peter, but she had thought it for weeks now as the TMS wore them all down. Surely they had all thought it.

It is what it is, Nana used to say. And then Della thought of what the wise matriarch said to her one day when she didn't catch a second piece of candy from the Christmas parade. *You get what you get and don't throw a fit.* Words to live by, Della thought. She could feel her grandmother's love all around them still like a sturdy wall, a sturdy wall she leaned on quite often.

There were only four more treatments to go. Then what? *Don't ask that*, Della said to herself. *Just don't even wonder.*

Della was on her thirty-seventh essay comparing and contrasting *Number the Stars* by Lois Lowry to *Suzy and Leah* by Jane Yolen when she looked up to find Lish gazing back with her eyes a little wider and a look in them that seemed more alive somehow and remarkably familiar. It was the look of her cousin—the real one—and she watched as Lish blinked twice, held the front of her head, and said, "I feel a little better . . . this time."

Anne rushed over to her as Della stood and studied her frame. Then Lish reached out as if she wanted to take both of their hands. Within moments, Della was on the other side of her, squeezing her warm, fleshy fingers. She narrowed her eyes. "You look better," she said tentatively.

"I agree." Anne nodded.

Lish smiled slowly. "Maybe," she said. "Maybe something's . . . happening."

Chapter 25

ROY

The time came when Roy couldn't wait any longer. By mid-May, the spring in his step had turned into an out-and-out jump. One day, Ms. B. took him aside and said, "Shall we go look at some rings?"

"I want to," he said. "I just don't want it to be too fast for her."

"Look," Ms. B. said. She narrowed her little gray eyes. "I've known Anne Brumley all her life, and she's one of the finest young ladies in this city. I've known you a little while, but I have a real good feeling about you." She winked. "It's not too fast."

That night he had a sit-down with Rose about the matter. He took her out on the second-floor piazza with two glasses of milk and a plate full of Oreo cookies.

She was onto him immediately. "Why all the treats, Daddy?"

"Well," he said as they took a seat on the plastic lawn furniture at the edge of the piazza. "We need to talk about something."

"Okay," she said. She leaned forward in her chair and grabbed a cookie, which she dunked in the milk.

"Remember that day you got that invitation to the mother-daughter tea party, and you told me that you wanted me to meet someone?"

She nodded. "And you have."

"Yes, I have." He rolled his shoulder forward, then patted her knee. "I want to know . . . I guess I want to see how you feel about the idea of me asking Anne to marry me."

Rose's eyes grew wide and she nodded her head yes.

He held up his hand to slow her down. "Now, there's no guarantee that she's gonna say yes, Rosebud. I can't know anything for sure. We haven't known each other that long, so I don't want you to get your hopes up too high."

She went from nodding to bouncing in her chair. "Okay, but can't I be a little excited? I'm not sure if I can help it!"

"Of course you can." He looked out over the rooftops and then back to her as she rose and fell on the seat of her chair. "So you like the idea of it? You'd like it if she said yes and came and made her home here with us?"

"Daddy." Rose gave an exasperated sigh. "You *know* I do. I've wanted this a lot longer than you have."

"Maybe she's the one." He felt his throat tighten. He

wanted to protect his precious child, but he couldn't help but share in her excitement.

She crinkled her head. "Who else would there be?"

"All right then." He rubbed his calloused palms together. "Since I have your blessing, I'm going to do it."

Rose dunked her cookie in the milk a second time, took a soggy bite, and smiled a chocolate smile. "I knew it would happen," she said.

The next week, Ms. B. took him down to look at rings at Croghan's on King Street. They were awfully expensive but beautiful, and he settled on a single solitaire set in platinum that he thought would be just right for her. Ms. B. approved, and late in the afternoon on the last Tuesday in May, he grabbed Anne's hand after their usual lunch date and said, "Let's go to the top of the steeple. I heard you can see the Spoleto sculpture on top of the Exchange Building from there."

"Okay," she said and she led the way up the several flights of winding stairs to the utmost balcony at the tip-top of the 186-foot steeple. Once they were there, she looked down Broad Street toward the exhibit, and when she turned back around, he was down on his knees holding a little blue velvet box in his hands.

She cupped her freckled cheeks and her face turned bright red, and when she broke into a smile, he opened up the box and said, "Anne Brumley. Every good and perfect gift is from above. And I believe that you are a gift to me. I hope you will say yes and be my beloved partner on this earth for the rest of our days. Will you?"

She took a deep breath and reached down and took his strong, thick hands in hers. She pulled him up and looked him right in his eyes. "There is nothing I would love more."

"Whoo hoo!" he called. Then he took her in his arms, as her soft, sweet-smelling hair blanketed his face. They stood this way for a long time until he remembered the plan and stomped his foot four times on the balcony. It was the signal he had given to Ms. B., who had coordinated the bell ringers to ring a whole peal if she said yes, and the poor lady had been waiting on a rickety staircase for nearly a half hour before she got the sign.

Then as the rounds began and the steeple swayed the way it did when the bells were calling out to the city, he took the ring out of the box, slipped it on Anne's delicate finger, and embraced her beneath the beautiful arches as Rose and Mama looked on from the rectory window and clapped.

As he held his future wife in his arms, Roy looked down at the picturesque old city and then out to the harbor, where the sails of the boats twittered like moths on the water as the sun lit up the surface with little chips of light. He chuckled at how reluctant he had been to move to Charleston. God's plans were always better than ours. And he could feel a sermon forming in his mind about how we might miss the blessing if we don't acknowledge our shortsightedness, trust in his grace, and make ourselves downright pliable.

As the bells reverberated, filling the air with the sound of God's glory, Roy knew the Almighty had given him a gift he never thought he could have again. Roy loved the city, he had to admit it now, and the city, to his great surprise, loved him back. He had a new home, a very happy little girl, and a partner he could lean on until the end of their fleeting days of this earthly life.

Chapter 26

DELLA

June 7, 2009

The TMS seemed to be the answer. Lish regained her strength little by little as the treatments continued, and by late May she was spending several nights by herself with the children. Della and Peter were right across the garden, and she called them whenever she needed help. But she hadn't called much lately.

At long last Anne was planning the wedding she always told Della she'd have, and as for Peter, he couldn't make crustaceans fast enough for the second-home owners with deep pockets out on Kiawah Island. His shrimp and turtles were all the rage, and the president of the College of Charleston had recently received an "English professor shrimp" as a gift from a wealthy alum. It was a shrimp with a goatee and horn-rimmed glasses reading Dante's *Inferno*. The president was so impressed that he asked Peter to teach a metal-sculpting class for Maymester and apply for a visiting instructor position in the Studio Art Department. And Peter loved what he was doing—sculpting and working with young people. It couldn't be a better fit.

One Sunday afternoon in June when the loquats had ripened and were falling off the trees, Della picked up the ringing phone with Lish's number flashing on the caller ID. She looked out the window and saw Lish, with the receiver to her ear, waving at her from the upstairs piazza.

"Wanna harvest some Japanese plums?" Lish pointed to the tree behind the big house.

"Yeah," Della said. "You bet we do."

Lish rubbed Mary Jane's head as Andrew flew an airplane around them. Then she looked Della in the eye across the yard and spoke into the receiver. "I'll call Anne and gather some buckets. Y'all meet us beneath the tree in half an hour."

"Yippee!" Cozy said from the den as Della told her the plan. The little girl was playing pick-up-sticks with Peter, and she held up her fistful of colorful wooden sticks. "Let's call it a game, Dad, okay?"

"No way." He pointed to his meager pile. "Give me one more turn."

"Oh, all right," she said.

When Cozy heard the rumble of Roy's truck and then the call of Mary Jane and Andrew who flew out of the back door of the main house, she abandoned the game and ran out to see everyone. Within minutes, the kids climbed up the tree, spread out in all directions, and snapped the loquats off of the limbs.

"Slow down!" Peter called as the kids tossed the fruit to the ground. He grabbed one of Nana's old metal buckets and held it beneath the center of the tree as the little orange plums rained down.

Then Roy stepped down from the porch with Baby Cecilia in his arms. She preferred the men—both Roy and Peter. But today she squiggled out and wanted to get down on the grass and stand up for herself.

Della stepped back to watch this scene. The kids in the trees, the Japanese plums falling, and then this—Lish squatting down and reaching her hands out to the baby, who reached back with a smile, saying, "Ma, ma, ma!" as Roy led her over to her mother.

Della laughed and brought her hands to her cheeks. The sun was on her face, and she looked up to Cozy, who plunked down on a limb near the center of the tree and began to peel back the skin and take a sweet bite.

Della thought about her editor's rejection of her murder manuscript and how she had decided to scrap the whole thing and start a new book, with Lish's blessing, about a young mother who battled a severe postpartum depression. As she contemplated the importance of endings, like she had so many times since her editor's response, she wondered what actually constituted not only a full and resonant ending but a happy one. She knew happy didn't mean perfect. It didn't mean all the loose ends tied up in a tight, tidy bow like the end of a fairy tale. (Does anyone actually believe that Cinderella and the prince never gained weight or uttered a harsh word to one another?) That wasn't real life, and she wanted her work to mirror reality. She suspected her readers wanted that too. Yet the ending had to have more than just a snapshot of our concrete existence. It needed that intangible something that buoyed us all this side of heaven. That feeling Della only could describe as hope. That undeniable mixture of joy and expectation that superseded the mess known as "real life."

Is this a happy ending? Della asked herself as she watched her daughter suck the meat of the loquat and reach for another. And then she turned to see Lish, who took Cecilia in her arms and kissed her cheek and neck before rocking her back and forth. Della watched her cousin's hands. They seemed sturdy and capable as they took hold of the toddler, as if to confirm through the sense of touch what every child longed to hear from their parent: "Yes, my little one. I am here for you."

Della took a deep breath as Lish lifted Cecilia up into the sky, the sun filtering through her plump little toes.

Yes, Della thought as Anne nudged her elbow and handed her a loquat. *This is.*

Acknowledgments

I would like to thank my sisters, Peggy J. McKinney and Libby J. Johnson, for planting the seed for this story as well as my friend, The Very Reverend R. Peet Dickinson, for earnestly answering my questions regarding the calling and life of a priest. Thanks also to my rector and good shepherd, The Reverend Al Zadig Jr., who gave me his blessing to set the book at St. Michael's in Charleston. And to his predecessor, The Reverend Rick Belser, who along with Al and Peet, is responsible for much of my spiritual growth. Also, I am grateful to C.J. Cantwell and the St. Michael's bell ringers, who literally showed me the ropes while allowing me to observe their glorious craft and ministry.

I am tremendously indebted to my brother-in-law, Dr. James McKinney, and my friend, Dr. Michael Smith. Their advice and knowledge as psychiatrists played an invaluable role in forming Lish's story line.

As usual, I owe a great deal of thanks to my editor, Ami McConnell, whose critique reshaped the foundation of the story, and to my agent, Claudia Cross, for her steadfast support. Also, I am grateful to Rachelle Gardner, a remarkably

shrewd and gifted line editor, and my dear friend and publi-
cist, Marjory Wentworth, who eagerly pounds the pavement
on behalf of the story like no one else I know.

Also, I want to thank the women in my life, who continu-
ally lift me and the stories up in prayer—Meredith Myers,
Jenny Dickinson, Amy Smith, Jeannie Lyles, Swain Marion,
Lisa Hughes, Susie Morrison, Dee Goehring, Elizabeth Zadig,
Karen Turner, Elisabeth Hunter, Suzanne Livengood, and
Avery Smith. I adore you.

Most of all, I want to thank my dear husband, Dr.
Edward B. Hart Jr., who babysat, edited raw chapters, lovingly reminded me of my deadlines, and cheered me on day
in and day out while somehow managing to keep a busy
work and creative life of his own in full swing. I love you.

Reading Group Guide

1. Why doesn't Roy want to move to Charleston? How does his view of Charleston society, particularly the parishioners of St. Michael's Episcopal Church, change over the course of the story?

2. Describe Roy's faith and his approach to ministering to his new flock. What makes his ministry effective?

3. The children play a crucial role in the three narratives of this story. How do both Rose and Cozy shed a new and hopeful light on the struggles of their parents?

4. When did you suspect that Drew's commitment to Lish was tenuous? Why didn't he stay and help her through her post-partum depression?

5. Do you think there are prejudices and misunderstandings about mental illness in our society? Discuss the story's treatment of Lish's post-partum depression. How do her loved ones react to her condition? How important is their reaction to her recovery?

6. Della's desire to provide for her daughter nearly justifies her potential infidelity. How has she come to view financial means as the ultimate source of both security

and happiness? What is the danger in cultivating this kind of view?

7. What type of spouse is Peter? How do his actions prove his commitment to Della and their family?

8. This novel takes a close look at marriage. What are the typical conflicts and challenges husbands and wives face today? Are they any different than the struggles of previous generations? What does this novel say about the importance (and the deep-seated joy) of sticking together?

9. Della grapples with what makes a story ending both full and resonant. Is the ending to *Love, Charleston* a happy one? Why or why not?

10. By the end of the novel, Roy admits that God's plans are better than our own. How can we (in Roy's words) "acknowledge our short-sightedness, trust in His grace, and make ourselves downright pliable"?

A Note from the Author

Dear Friend,

One theme which inevitably surfaces in each of my stories is the power of female friendships, and *Love, Charleston* is no exception. As one of three daughters raised in a Christian home, I was born into women's ministry, and I wholeheartedly believe that our sisters in Christ play a crucial role in building us up, allowing us opportunities to give and receive grace, and providing a good laugh when the tensions in life build.

Since we are fearfully and wonderfully made, it is no surprise that science backs this notion up. A recent landmark study from UCLA showed that female friendships counter stress. That is, when women get together the wonderful "bonding" hormone, oxytocin, is released which buffers the typical "fight or flight" response and produces an overall calming effect. And the famed Nurses' Health Study form Harvard Medical School found that the "more friends women had, the less likely they were to develop physical impairments as they aged, and the more likely they were to be leading a joyful life."

All this to say, I don't think it is a stretch to argue that attending a Women of Faith Conference will surely benefit any woman's spiritual, mental and physical well-being. You won't regret setting aside the time to come together with your fellow sisters for worship, teaching, laughter, fellowship, and if the science is on target, a little oxytocin too!

Warmest Regards,
Beth Webb Hart

About the Author

Beth Webb Hart is the critically acclaimed author of *The Wedding Machine*. After having studied under Madeline L'Engle and Brett Lott in New York City, she moved to her hometown in Charleston, South Carolina, with her husband, composer Edward Hart, to raise their family.

Author photo: Amey M. Warder.

Seaside Letters

Other Novels by Denise Hunter

THE BIG SKY ROMANCE SERIES

A Cowboy's Touch

THE NANTUCKET LOVE STORIES

The Convenient Groom

Seaside Letters

Driftwood Lane

Surrender Bay

Sweetwater Gap

Sweetpea: Betrayal flips a switch you didn't know existed. Suddenly you're on guard. No one is above suspicion, no one is as honest as they seem, and it's all because of this basic truth: You're too afraid to risk it all again.

$\mathcal{O}ne$

Sabrina Kincaid heard the jingle of the café's glass door opening and glanced at the clock above the workstation: 7:12 on the dot.

She grabbed the fresh pot, turned toward the tables crowding the Cobblestone Café, then headed straight to his table—might as well get it over with—table seven, a two-topper near the front.

He would be seated against the beadboard wall, facing the kitchen, unfortunately. He would be wearing a blue "Cap'n Tucker's Water Taxi" cap, a light-colored T-shirt, and a crooked grin. She would offer him coffee, he would accept, then he would spread open *The Inquirer and Mirror* and take thirty minutes on all twelve articles while she waited on other customers, her bony knees knocking together like bamboo wind chimes.

"Evan," Gordon called from the kitchen. "Table twelve needs to be bussed."

Evan's blond ponytail flipped over his shoulder as he turned and wiped his hands on his stained brown apron. "Right, dude."

Sabrina stopped a foot from the scarred maple table, avoiding eye contact, looking only at the fat rim of the ivory mug as he slid it toward her.

How many words had they exchanged in the year he'd been coming to the café? One hundred? Two hundred? Couldn't be much more than that.

As always her expression was free of emotion, though a powerful hurricane brewed inside. It was a skill she'd learned early, perfected well, and if that had earned her the title of Ice Princess, so be it.

"Morning, Sabrina." Tucker's deep voice was raspy. And, as usual, he cleared his throat after the greeting.

Was she the first person he spoke to each morning? The thought made her hand tremble. A stream of hot coffee flowed over the cup's rim and onto Tucker's thumb. He jerked his hand back.

Idiot! Her first spill in months and it had to be Tucker. And with hot coffee.

"I'm sorry. Let me fetch a towel." She turned toward the kitchen, heat flooding her face.

He stopped her with his other hand. "I'm fine." He wiped his thumb on a napkin and held it out. "See?"

Sabrina made the mistake of meeting his eyes. Oh, yes. She saw, all right. Under the brim of his cap, his blue eyes contrasted with his summer-brown skin. One strand of dark hair curled like a backward *C*, nearly tangling with his eyelashes. He disliked his curly hair, but hated going to the barber so much that he procrastinated until it was an unruly mop. He wore contacts because he was nearsighted and because glasses would blur under the sprays of water as he guided his boat.

He was still looking at her.

She was still looking at him.

Look away. Say something. "Anything else?"

"A smile?" Tucker's own grin lifted the tiny scar near the corner of his mouth—a souvenir from the time his twin sister dared him to jump from his second-story bedroom window when he was nine.

But Sabrina wasn't supposed to know about that. She pulled at the tip of her ponytail with her empty hand.

"Give it up, McCabe." Behind her, Oliver Franklin's voice was a lifeline. "Top me off, Sabrina?"

She turned, grateful for the distraction, and filled his cup. The sand-colored coffee darkened to caramel as she poured, the rich smell of the brew drifting upward on wings of steam.

"Not feeling particularly *efficacious* this morning?" Oliver tilted his round head, his hairline receding another inch as he hiked his bushy gray brows. He gripped the mug with fat hands calloused from garden tools.

"I'm as efficient as always, just a bit clumsy today." Sabrina took his egg-streaked plate and stacked a smaller plate on top.

"Dagnabit, Sabrina," he said as she walked away. "Is there a word you don't know?"

She deposited the plates into Evan's tub, set the pot on the warmer, and loaded a tray with table five's food. Was Tucker watching her? She always felt like he was, which was ludicrous. Still, it made her stand a little straighter, smile a little more—at other customers. He was good for her tips.

You're just some server he toys with. Nothing else.

When she turned with the loaded tray, her eyes pulled toward him. *Don't look. Just walk.* Look at the sun streaming through the glass front. Look at the family at table four, the toddler, crouched in the wooden high chair, letting loose a wail that could be heard clear down at the wharf. Sabrina pulled a packet of crackers from her apron pocket and slipped it to the mom as she passed.

When she reached table five, she served the food, then tucked the tray under her arm. "Anything else?"

"Tabasco sauce?" the mother asked. "Oh, and he needs a refill of juice." She handed Sabrina her son's cup. The overhead lights sparkled off a huge diamond.

"Be right back." She had to pass Tucker's table on the way.

He turned as she passed, his sandaled foot sliding into her path as he shifted into the aisle. "Sabrina. I know you're busy, but I was wondering if we could chat a minute."

The request stopped her cold. Sabrina didn't chat with customers. Char chatted with customers, even the rich ones. Evan chatted with customers too. But not Sabrina, and certainly not with Tucker. It broke her unspoken line between customer and server, and that line was the only thing separating her from disaster. "I—I have too many tables."

"Miss, some decaf, please?" An elderly tourist, seated at the table behind Oliver's, corroborated her excuse.

"Of course." Sabrina went to fill the cup with juice, grabbed a bottle of Tabasco and the decaf pot. What could Tucker want? As far as he knew, she was only a server at the café.

Maybe he knows.

But he couldn't. She'd been so careful.

Yeah, so careful she'd lost her heart to the man.

I have not lost my heart. He's just a friend. A dear friend who would be lost forever with one little slip of the tongue. The relationship was hanging by a thread and she knew it.

Sabrina dropped off the two items for the family, then poured the decaf. She'd no sooner turned the carafe upright when Tucker stopped her again. His cup was empty. "I'll be right back with the regular," she said, even though she knew it wasn't coffee he wanted. It was a feeble stall that would buy her thirty seconds.

She stopped on the way to the coffee station and took the orders of a middle-aged couple, buying herself a few more minutes. Maybe if she took too long, Tucker would leave.

Sabrina put the order on the wheel and reviewed the lunch special with Gordon. She filled glasses with orange juice and ice water, set them on a tray, and delivered them to the table. In her peripheral vision, she saw Tucker waiting, his arms folded across the newspaper, rooted like a hundred-year-old oak tree. He wasn't going anywhere.

Reluctantly, she retrieved the coffeepot and returned to his table, filling his cup carefully.

"How about after work?" he asked, picking up the conversation as if it were only seconds later.

What did he want? Maybe he wanted to ask her out. The thought filled her, expanding her lungs like an inflated balloon. Then she felt the prick of jealousy. *Pop.*

She nearly rolled her eyes at the irony. "I have to be somewhere."

Behind her, Oliver chuckled, and Tucker shot him a look. He gave the brim of his hat a sharp tug.

Sabrina walked away. Her second job had flexible hours, but he didn't know that. Besides, Renny was expecting her. She had to find the perfect poison, and that would take a while.

The bell at the kitchen window dinged.

She was at the coffee station before she realized Tucker had followed her. His large frame made her feel small and cornered. He'd never gone farther than his table, and the fact that he did so today confirmed her suspicion that he wanted something more than idle conversation. And he wasn't giving up.

The rubber heels of her shoes brushed the wall behind her, and she straightened, meeting his gaze.

"Just a few minutes, all I'm asking."

His nearness sucked the moisture from her mouth and the thoughts from her head. She smoothed her thick hair toward her low ponytail. *Say something. Anything.*

"All right," she blurted. *Anything but that.*

His mouth relaxed, and the relief in his blue eyes made something twist in the pit of her stomach. "Thank you. I won't take much of your time. I'll meet you out front if it's all right with you? There's a bench down the way . . ."

She nodded, all at once relieved and disappointed they were meeting someplace so public. *What is wrong with you?*

His lips quivered at the corners, and the faint lines around his eyes relaxed. He touched his fingers to the brim of his hat and retreated.

"What was that all about?" Char was a veteran waitress at the diner. Though not as efficient as Sabrina, her affability scored points with the regulars. "He finally making his move?" Her blonde hair had kinked into poodle curls, forecasting the day's weather.

Sabrina turned and put two slices of bread in the toaster. "Don't be ridiculous."

The kitchen bell dinged twice.

"Char, you want to stop your gabbing and come get this food before it turns to rubber?" Gordon called through the window, wiping the back of his hand across his fat jowls.

"Don't say I didn't tell you so." Char winked a wide green eye, the mascara-thickened lashes fluttering.

Sabrina watched her walk away, wondering if Char was right, hoping she was, then hoping she wasn't. She gave her head a sharp shake. She had five hours and four minutes to get her act together, and suddenly that didn't seem like nearly enough time.

I could really use some help here, God. Can you hear me?

But no, why would he? There's been nothing but silence on that front in months.

⌒)(⌒

Sabrina threw her apron in the laundry bin and pulled her bag from the cubby in the break room. At least, Gordon *called* it a break room. It was more of a large closet with a table, two chairs, and enough wattage to light up Main Street at midnight.

The five hours since Tucker left had dragged by. She told herself she was dreading the meeting, but if that were the case, time would've raced, wouldn't it?

She slid the purse onto her shoulder and met her own gaze in the black-speckled mirror Char had perched on a shelf. Bending her knees so she could see her face, Sabrina pulled the rubber band, loosening the ponytail, and freeing her brown hair. She raked her fingers through it, wishing for smooth, glossy strands like her cousins', but her fingers worked fruitlessly.

Giving up on her hair, she rubbed at a fleck of mystery food that clung to her temple. Maybe she should splash water on her face. She stood back and surveyed her reflection. Her brown eyes gazed back, her best feature, framed with dark lashes thick enough to make Char jealous.

What could Tucker want with her? Her respiration quickened at the thought of him. What if he knew? What if she'd slipped and said something that would ruin everything?

Char's words tweaked at the corners of her mind. *"He's finally making his move . . ."*

Oh, for Pete's sake. He is not making his move. Sabrina grabbed the rubber band from her pocket and gathered her hair. *He owns a company. Maybe he's hosting some event and wants you to serve.*

"Better not keep him waiting." Char's voice sounded from the doorway.

Her eyes tilted coyly, and Sabrina felt heat flooding her face at being caught primping in the mirror like some pathetic adolescent. How many times had she found Jaylee and Arielle artfully applying makeup in front of their mirrors? Of course, it had paid off for her cousins.

"Oh, no, you don't." Char reached behind Sabrina and freed her hair.

"What are you doing?"

"Wear it down. Why do you always wear this infernal ponytail?"

Sabrina shifted as Char fluffed her hair. "We work in the restaurant industry."

"If I had hair like yours . . ." Char leaned back. "There. Much better. No street clothes, huh? Well, I guess your uniform will have to do. At least you have nice legs. Now, go, before he thinks you chickened out."

She squeezed past Char.

"Good luck, honey."

Luck. She'd need it if she hoped to hold it together. She exited the café, blinking against May's bright sunlight. Her feet navigated the bumpy brick sidewalk, and she fell in step behind a cluster of tourists. If only she could squeeze into the middle and sneak past Tucker.

The bench was only three stores from the diner and, over the bobbing heads, she saw Tucker sitting there, elbows propped on his knees, staring across the street. There was no backing out now.

When she approached the bench, he stood. The group of tourists deserted her, leaving them alone on the sidewalk. In the distance, the ferry horn sounded, announcing its arrival at the wharf.

"Hi. Thanks for meeting me." He gestured toward the bench.

She lowered herself onto the wooden seat and set her bag in her lap. "You're welcome." *Act normal. This is nothing out of the ordinary. You are a server and he is your customer. Nothing more.*

"I know you have another job to get to, so I'll make this quick."

Quick would be good. Merciful. She gripped the leather handles of her purse and pulled it into her stomach.

"I was hoping to hire you for a project."

A curious mixture of relief and disappointment flooded Sabrina. She told herself it was relief that tightened her stomach. *Now it's just a matter of listening to his proposal and saying no. I can say no, then go home.* She envisioned the cozy loft above Renny's garage as if she could beam herself there. She pictured her favorite quilt spread across the bed, the built-in shelves brimming with novels, the antique desk in the corner where her computer awaited her.

Focus, Sabrina.

"Go on." Sabrina crossed her legs. A pedestrian passed with a golden retriever on a pink leash, and she shifted to make room. The movement left her facing Tucker. He had one elbow propped on the back of the bench, his hand curling dangerously close to her shoulder.

"Well, the idea came to me when Renny Hannigan contacted me about a trip to Tuckernuck Island. We started talking about her stories, and she told me you're the mastermind behind the mysteries she writes—"

Sabrina shook her head. "I just do a little research for her."

"You're being modest. Renny told me about the twists you come up with. She raved that the stories are unsolvable because you find fresh angles and innovative ways to confuse the reader."

If Sabrina were that good, Renny's stories would be published by now. It wasn't lack of writing skill that kept her from publication. But what did her work for Renny have to do with Tucker?

"The things Renny said about you, combined with what I already know, made me think you were the perfect person for this project."

"I already have two jobs. Between the diner and my research for Renny . . ." Her words petered out as he held up his hand.

"I know you're busy right now, but Renny said in another couple weeks you'd be finished with the book she's writing now, and that she'd need several weeks of editing time before she'd need your help again with her next story."

Renny. Sabrina clenched her teeth together. Why'd the woman have to go and tell Tucker that? Maybe she should close the door on this conversation before it went any further.

"I don't think—I was looking forward to the time off when I finished the research. I think it would be best if—"

"Just hear me out, okay? If you don't want to do it, that's fine."

His hand spread across his thigh. He had big hands with long fingers that tapered down to squared-off fingertips. He liked working with them. He carved wooden animals in his spare time and gave them as gifts to his family. He'd once wanted to give her a seagull he'd carved, but she'd refused the gift.

"Sabrina?"

She cleared her throat and watched a family of four squeeze into a taxi across the street, the brother and sister fighting over the middle seat. "I'm listening." *Please just say what you have to say and let me go home where my heart rate can return to normal.*

"Well, as I was saying, I have this project I need help with."

His voice was so deep it seemed to rumble through her body. *Practice saying no. It's not my cup of tea. I don't have time, but thank you for the offer.*

"It's kind of embarrassing, but here goes."

Now he had her attention.

"There's this girl—this woman, I mean."

Sabrina thought her heart was already in her toes, but it didn't quite hit the tips until then. She reached for the end of her ponytail but found her hair loose.

"I have feelings for her and—" He pulled off his cap and raked his hands through his curls. "Well, the sad fact is, I don't know where she is."

Sabrina looked at him. She couldn't help it. "What?" A missing person? He wanted help finding his missing girlfriend? But he didn't have a girlfriend, did he? A seed of pure jealousy, something she'd thought she'd banished from her life long ago, sprang up, twisting, leaving that familiar ache in its path.

"I'm bungling this, aren't I? Let me start at the beginning and maybe I can explain this better. There's this woman I've been exchanging letters with. Email. We've been communicating online for about a year."

Oh.

"We've gotten pretty friendly. Actually, she's an amazing woman."

He looked off into the distance, and Sabrina was relieved to have his eyes anywhere but on her. *This is not happening.*

"I want to meet her in person. I know it sounds clichéd and corny, but I have feelings for her."

He looked at her, and she swore he could see right into her. She clutched the leather purse straps until her short nails dug into the flesh of her palm.

"Yeah, I know. You're wondering how I could fall for someone I've never met, but this is different. It's not like we set out to date online; it just happened. And you're probably wondering why we don't just meet up and live happily ever after."

Sabrina tried to speak, but her voice had jumped off two exits ago.

"I'd like nothing more, but the problem is, she won't meet in person. I don't know why, but it doesn't matter. I need to find her."

"Find her?"

His eyes bore into hers. "I need your help."

"I can't."

"You're the perfect person for the job. I need someone who can string together clues. I have hundreds of letters filled with information, but she's been careful not to write anything overt about her location. I need someone smart and intuitive. Someone like you."

"I'm not the right person."

"Renny thinks you'd be perfect."

Renny. She'd wring the woman's neck! Sabrina needed another tactic. Anything. "This woman—obviously she doesn't want to be found. Maybe you should leave things alone and continue the relationship as it is."

"I want to be with her."

"Maybe—" Could she be so cruel? She pressed her spine to the bench. Desperate needs called for desperate measures. "Maybe she doesn't want to be with you. Maybe she's—I don't know—married or something."

"She's not married."

"How can you know?"

"She's not. I *know.*"

Sabrina wet her lips. Brushed at a mustard spot on her uniform. "There has to be some reason she won't meet you."

He lowered his voice. "I'm sure there is. I think she's afraid of taking the next step or something, but I don't think she'll tell me until I find her."

She gulped. *God? What do I say? How do I get out of this?*

She could almost hear the crickets chirping.

Once again, she was on her own.

But she couldn't say yes. She just couldn't. But if she said no, he'd find someone else to help, and then what?

That would be ten times worse. If someone else helped him—if someone else sifted through the letters and figured out the truth—then he'd discover that the person he's trying to find is . . . *her.*

Harbormaster: No matter where you are or how long it takes until we can be together, I'll keep searching for you.

Two

Tucker pulled his eyes from Sabrina's, and it wasn't easy. He'd never seen her hair all flowy around her shoulders. He made himself watch a tour van pass slowly, stop for a bicyclist, then continue toward the First Congregational Church.

He pulled his arm from the splintered bench back and clasped his hands between his knees.

"If she doesn't want to be found," Sabrina's voice quivered, "maybe she has a good reason. Maybe you'll only be hurt or disappointed if you find her."

He wanted to look at her; he wanted to grasp her shoulders between his hands and tell her that could never be true. *Tone it down, buddy. You'll scare her away.*

He sucked in a deep breath, letting the salty air permeate his lungs before he released it on a steady exhale. He wished he could jump inside her head and know what she was thinking. Was she thinking about telling him the truth right now? Was she wishing she'd never started the email relationship to begin with? She clutched her bag to her body like a shield, and he could almost feel the waves of fear rolling off her.

He had to back her into a corner, but the thought of it was killing him. Maybe he should forget it. Maybe he should drop the whole thing. The whole relationship felt so precarious. As if one little breeze would send it crashing to the ground.

Then he remembered his daily trip to the café, sitting at his table pretending to read the paper, pretending they were strangers. How long could he continue with the charade? And the hours sitting at the computer, reading her letters, wishing for more . . .

No. He'd made his decision, and he was going through with it.

He leaned back against the bench. "I'm going to find her, regardless of any disappointment or hurt it might bring. I can't go on like this. I think you're the best person for the job, but if you're not interested—I'll find someone else."

There. He'd done it. He could feel the realization sinking into Sabrina. The realization that if she didn't help him, someone else would. It was a cheap trick, but for his plan to work, she had to say yes.

Maybe she'd just admit who she was right now. *Come on, Sabrina, say it.*

"You seem determined." Her words wobbled pitifully.

I am such a jerk.

But it was for her own good. She was so beautiful, inside and out. He'd never known anyone so unaware of it. It was as if she still saw herself as the girl with acne and a gapped smile. Time and braces had fixed the external, but the inside was permanently damaged. She wore invisible armor that let no one through. Only in her letters was she transparent. Only when she was hiding behind a computer. If only he could get that to translate over to real life. And he would. If only he could accomplish Step One.

"I'm going to find her. It's not a matter of if, only when."

"Have you looked through the emails yourself? Surely if she'd left clues, you would've seen them."

"I'm not much of a between-the-lines person. I'm not even a computer person, except for this one email relationship. I use the thing for my business, but that's it."

"What's her name?"

As if you don't know. "She goes by Sweetpea."

"You don't know her name?"

He nearly said he had her photo, but it wasn't hers, was it? Instead, he met her almond-shaped eyes and spent a couple seconds just floating there in the sea of chocolate. "I know I care about her. I know she's special. And I know I'm going to find her." *You want to be found, don't you, Sabrina? Deep down? What are you afraid of?*

She looked so rigid, her chin set, her mouth drawn into a flat line. But behind that tough mask, there was tender flesh, a warm heart, a vulnerable soul. If only she would agree, he could set his plan in motion. Maybe if she spent time with him, he could gain her trust.

But she trusts Harbormaster, and she still doesn't want to meet him, doesn't want the relationship to progress. He'd been through this a million times.

He set his cap back on his head, feeling suddenly weary. Had he thought it was going to be easy? "You can mull it over if you like.

I want to find someone by the end of the week, though, so if you could let me know if I need to look elsewhere—"

"No, I'll do it." Her chin tilted up stubbornly. She knew she'd been trapped.

His stomach did a funny flop at the thought of having her in his home, where he'd spent hours writing her, reading her letters, thinking about her. It was just a matter of time now. Surely, once they had time alone together, he could penetrate that wall she kept around her heart. Surely he could get her to admit who she was when he had all the right tools in place.

"I can start in two weeks, when I finish Renny's manuscript."

There was one more matter to discuss, but he felt a smile breaking out on his face and couldn't stop it. "That'll be fine. Your hours would be flexible, but evenings are best for me, if that works for you."

She rubbed her neck, and her charm bracelet slid down her wrist, making a soft jingling sound. "Evenings . . ." Confusion etched lines across her forehead. "Aren't you going to print off the emails for me?"

He was glad he'd thought this through. "I wouldn't feel right about that. I feel bad enough letting someone else read her personal thoughts, much less have printed copies floating around."

"I'd be exceedingly vigilant—"

"I know you would. I just don't feel right about it. I hope you understand."

She didn't understand at all, but that didn't matter so long as she agreed. He could see her wavering. He drove the last nail home. "If you'd rather I find someone else . . ."

"No. That won't be a problem." She scooted to the edge of the bench and stood, hanging her bag on her shoulder.

He stood with her. "Great, then. Two weeks." He extended a hand, and she returned his firm handshake before walking away. "But I'll see you at the café before that," he called to her stiffened back.

He watched her go, her long legs swallowing the distance. Operation Sweetpea was under way, and the future suddenly looked brighter than the sunlight glinting off Nantucket Harbor at noon.

Sweetpea: If I thought planning a wedding was time consuming, it was only because I'd never had to cancel one in six days.

Three

Sabrina stopped pedaling and coasted, taking a breather. She wished she'd stayed in bed for the day. How had she let herself be persuaded to spend hours alone with Tucker? Didn't she know how difficult the task would be? How could she maintain her composure, keep her focus with him nearby? She must be plumb crazy.

It wasn't as if I had a choice. He was prepared to hire someone else if she said no. She couldn't allow that, could she?

At least now she could control the outcome. She could read the emails, pretend to give her best effort, then tell him it was an impossible task. She could even manufacture red herrings to sidetrack him, just like in Renny's books.

But you'll be alone with him for hours . . .

Despite the warm air, the thought sent a shiver down her arms. The relationship had seemed so simple in the beginning, just a friend she traded quips with. She liked the way he valued her opinions and the way he was only a mouse click away. He listened without judging, a rarity in her experience. Her feelings had evolved slowly, and by the time she knew they'd gone too far, she was helpless to stop them.

She signaled left and made the turn onto Renny's lane. And now she would somehow have to hide them. It was difficult enough facing him at the café, pretending he was a stranger. How would she conceal her feelings when they were alone in close quarters? And she must conceal them. Tucker might think he wanted Sweetpea, but that was only because he didn't know who she was.

Sabrina followed the gravel lane toward Renny's two-story oceanfront home. The shaker shingles, previously a pale blue, had faded to gray under the relentless erosion of wind and sand. Lining the front walk, Renny's flower garden was a riot of pink, yellow, and white. A prolific vine of some kind clung to the front entryway, climbing the white columns and creeping onto the small roof that shaded the patio. Many of the islanders hired men like Oliver for landscaping, but Renny managed her own garden and had affectionately named it *Gan Eden*, Hebrew for Garden of Eden. The Hebrew language was another of Renny's interests.

Sabrina parked her bike in front of the garage that housed her loft apartment. She sifted through the mailbox for her mail, then climbed the wooden stairs along the west side of the house that led to her private entry.

A tall oak rose above the roofline, and her eyes searched the length of the closest limb until they came to a nest a robin had built that spring. Cradled in the nook of two intersecting branches, the nest was tilted to the side precariously. Each day Sabrina expected to find the nest gone, blown to the ground by a harbor breeze, but it still hung there.

Cool air and the remnants of Pine-Sol greeted her as she entered and set the mail on the desk, moving quickly, eager to see if Tucker had written before he left that morning.

Would he admit he was trying to locate her, or would he keep it a secret? She sat at the desk and opened her email. They had a predictable pattern. He wrote in the morning after she left for work, and in the afternoon she'd reply. Then when he returned in the evening, messages flew back and forth, mostly short quips about nothing in particular.

Her inbox appeared, and Sabrina scanned the few emails, her heart bailing when she saw nothing from Harbormaster. She browsed the four emails. Two were junk mail, one was a shipping notice from Amazon, and the other was from her cousin Jaylee. The sight of Jaylee's name jolted her from complacency. Of their own volition, her eyes scanned the subject:

IMPORTANT PLEASE READ.

Sabrina highlighted the email and gave the Delete button a hard tap. The message vanished in a split second. Instead of satisfaction, the action left her with a vague sense of unease. What could Jaylee want? Hadn't her cousin taken more than enough? For a moment she was tempted to retrieve the message, then decided it wasn't worth the feelings it would arouse.

But the emotions appeared at the door of her heart anyway,

like unwelcome guests. Jealousy, Bitterness, and their close friend, Aching Pain.

No. She would not entertain the feelings today. *I choose not to.* Willfully, she pushed the thoughts to the back of her mind for another day and closed the email program.

Normally, she looked forward to this time of day. Returning to her little loft with its efficient layout and familiar furnishings, anticipating a message from Tucker. Here she could be alone to read and think and escape.

Today, though, offered her none of the above. Her mind whirled like a window fan. She needed to finish Renny's research, but instead she started a kettle of tea and wandered past the kitchen table to the window overlooking the ocean.

Clouds had gathered, obscuring the sun, muting the daylight. On the water, a blue, triangular sail dotted the horizon. She wondered about the people inhabiting the boat. Were they a vacationing family? A wealthy retired couple killing time? A married man seeking peace and solitude from a nagging wife and a gaggle of boisterous kids?

Other than the ferry that had brought her to Nantucket, Sabrina had never stepped foot on a boat. It seemed peculiar when she was surrounded by water.

She let the curtain fall into place, then went to change into shorts and a crew neck T-shirt. The weather was mild today. Maybe later she'd go for a jog.

When the kettle whistled, she made a cup of tea before settling into her computer chair. Renny needed a poison for her story—

something that would leave no trace in a blood test—and she needed it by tomorrow.

Sabrina made it as far as opening her internet program before her restless mind took her hostage.

Spying the stack of mail, she sorted through it, tossing the junk into the can by the desk and slipping the bills into the cubby above her. When she saw the last envelope, she stopped.

Her name and address were slanted across the front of the delicate pink parchment envelope. She would recognize the neat script anywhere, even if not for the return address in the upper left-hand corner. Dread coated her tongue, sticking it to the roof of her mouth.

She wished she could delete the envelope as easily as she'd deleted the email, because the temptation to open it was overwhelming. Three-dimensional letters were apparently more difficult to resist.

Succumbing to curiosity, she turned the envelope and slid her index finger under the flap. The pink scalloped card slid out easily. Sabrina read the printed script: *Mr. and Mrs. Everett Daniels and Mr. and Mrs. Lloyd Tanner invite you to share in the joy of the marriage uniting their children, Jaylee Daniels and Jared Tanner, on Saturday, the twenty-second of August, at five thirty in the evening.*

Sabrina's eyes returned to Jared's name and rested there. The card trembled in her hand. How had it come this far without her knowing? Where was the warning, the announcement of the engagement, for heaven's sake?

Then she remembered the emails from Aunt Bev she'd deleted. She remembered the voice mails from Jaylee and Arielle she'd never returned.

She hadn't regretted the distance she'd put between herself and the relatives who'd raised her after her dad . . . died. They'd hurt her. It was natural that she'd want space between them, natural that she'd avoid them.

Still, this was a harsh way to find out. It was cruel to pop a wedding invitation into her mailbox with no warning. They should've tried harder. She looked at the date again. Less than three months away.

This shouldn't be happening. How could life be so inequitable?

What does it matter now? I don't love him anymore.

But she had. She'd loved him so much.

But that was over a year ago. She'd moved on. She'd learned from the experience. She was no longer a naive young woman waiting to have her heart trampled. She was savvier now. A well-protected fortress.

She walked to the trash basket and dropped the invitation. At the motion, her bracelet slid down her wrist, drawing her eye to it. She pulled her hand closer and found the dangling heart pendant. Her thumb ran over the familiar surface.

The old emotions welled up, stuffing her lungs with something thick and stifling. She wrapped her hand around her wrist, bracelet and all, as if she could contain the thoughts as easily.

She longed to throw on her tennis shoes now and run until she was out of steam. Run until she was too tired to think, too tired to feel. But she'd promised Renny an answer on the poison, and it might take all evening. So instead, she sank down into her chair. But still her thoughts rebelled.

Somewhere out there, Jaylee and Jared were choosing place settings and planning a honeymoon. Her aunt and uncle would spare no expense. Where was the event? Sabrina couldn't remember. Did she even want to?

She did. She wanted to know the truth, every last painful drop of it, because it wasn't the truth that hurt so badly, but the secrets that preceded it.

Harbormaster: My sister needs a miracle. But I'm not worried. I trust God to work it out. How about you, Sweetpea . . . do you trust God?

Sweetpea: God and me are kind of on the outs right now.

Four

Sabrina pedaled down Tucker's lane, parallel to the harbor. The cottages along Nantucket's wharf resembled enlarged birdhouses perched on pilings at the water's edge. Their front yards were the ocean, dotted with small, bobbing boats. In the winter these homes, mostly vacant, suffered relentless wind and bitter cold sprays of salt-laden water, but in the summer they drew hefty rental fees from tourists.

The day before, Tucker had jotted his address on a thin café napkin and asked her to arrive around six. His eyes had a boyish light behind them. Hope, she realized, feeling the pierce of guilt.

It was cruel to ignite a fire of hope when she planned to smother every last ember. She had stuffed her hands in her khaki pockets and squeezed the napkin into a tight ball.

She'd weighed her options a hundred times since he'd approached her two weeks earlier. There was no alternative. She would suck it up, and complete the task as quickly as possible.

She would read the emails as though detached from the people writing them. She would list harmless details, making sure they in no way offered any hope of pinpointing Sweetpea's location. That was her plan, and she was sticking to it. Once it was over, she and Harbormaster would continue their relationship as it was before. The relationship was too important to risk losing.

She arrived at Tucker's cottage and parked her bike. It was one of the smaller homes on the water, not much more than a dollhouse, but even these ran over a million. Tucker's house would fit into her loft twice over, but you couldn't argue with the charm of a harbor house. Weathered shaker shingles clothed the building, and its two front windows, like square eyes, flanked the Craftsman-style door at the top of a stoop. A potted plant was the home's only exterior adornment, and it looked as if it had been forgotten long ago.

Sabrina knocked, then tucked a loose strand of hair behind her ear. Her heart, beating up into her throat, seemed to have escaped her rib cage, and she wished she could tuck it in place so easily. Darkness hovered behind the windows. Maybe he wasn't home.

Don't get your hopes up. Of course he's home. He asked you to be here at six. Sabrina checked her watch. One minute before the hour. Well, she could hope, couldn't she? Maybe he'd let her work in peace. Maybe once she was acclimated to his computer, she could come directly after work. He'd be gone, and she could work alone. Maybe this wouldn't be so difficult after all.

The door opened, and Tucker's frame filled the doorway. He

wore a black T-shirt and faded jeans from which his bare feet poked. Sabrina forced her eyes to his face as he opened the door wider.

"Right on time." His cap was missing, and his loose curls were damp, as if he'd recently showered.

Sabrina's tongue felt stapled to the roof of her mouth. She smiled benignly as she squeezed past, catching a faint whiff of his woodsy cologne. The familiar scent drew her.

She held her breath until she was a safe distance away, then forced her eyes around the living room's dim interior. A lone lamp lit the space, its inverted cone of light splaying upward, highlighting a sparse, clay-colored wall. A sofa, two chairs, and a TV hogged the space. A line of carved marine animals perched on the low mantel.

"The office is back that way." He pointed to a short hall beyond the living room. "Can I get you something to drink? I have soda, juice, coffee . . ."

"No, thank you."

She followed him down the hall, her sandals clicking on the wood floor behind his padding feet. She wondered if she should've removed her shoes, but they were clean and, judging by the dust ball in the corner, Tucker wasn't exactly fastidious.

"Here we are. This is my office, slash computer room, slash junk room."

Everything in the room faded in the wake of the harbor view. Evening light flooded the space through a large bay window, tinting the room golden pink.

"Nice view." Strange that he'd never mentioned it in his letters. If she had such a view, she was certain she'd find it distracting. Then again, when she wrote Tucker, she was focused on him alone.

"I had the bay window installed after I bought the place. It's supposed to be a spare bedroom, but it makes a nice office."

Her eyes left the harbor to travel the small space. An oak desk anchored a large rug and faced a pale blue wall. In one corner, a louvered door covered what she assumed was a closet, and stacks of boxes lined the wall opposite the desk.

Tucker had pulled another chair to the desk and gestured toward it. Sabrina set down her bag and sank into the seat as Tucker settled behind the computer, inches away.

She focused on the screen, a fifteen-inch Dell. Several icons covered a photo of Nantucket's harbor. She'd just identified Tucker in the picture before he opened his email program.

"We've been writing about a year, so there are lots of messages to wade through. Most are just quick back-and-forth stuff, but some are longer. I've reread them, trying to figure things out, but like I said, that's not my thing."

Sabrina watched him navigate the screen, going to the oldest letters. Something strange filled her at the sight of her email address in his inbox. As he scrolled, she saw there were few messages from anyone else.

"Her email address is right here." He pointed to the screen. "Sweetpea."

At least her screen name revealed nothing. She folded her hands in her lap.

"Are you always this quiet?"

She should be asking questions, not acting as if she already knew the answers. Even if she did. "I'm just observing."

"They say it's the quiet ones you have to watch out for."

"Who's 'they'?"

His eyes flickered away from the screen long enough to give her a grin. "I don't know, but they must know what they're talking about, because everyone quotes them."

The line was so like the tone of his emails, she nearly smiled, but caught it in time.

Questions. She needed to ask questions. "What kind of factual data do you have on your friend? Perhaps you can make a list of everything you know about her."

"Sure. Here, switch chairs and you can start reading."

His arm brushed hers as they passed, and the hairs on her forearm stood on end, drawn toward him as if he were a magnet. She settled into the leather chair and opened the first message.

He'd initially addressed her on Nantucket Chat, a community for those interested in Nantucket. The group was talking about the controversial offshore wind turbine program, a community hot-button issue, and after several days, Tucker emailed her privately.

"I wonder if she grows peas," he said now, jokingly.

"Sweet peas are flowers, not a vegetable."

"Oh. See, that's why I need your help."

She rolled her eyes. "You don't know her occupation, then?"

He pulled a pen and paper from a drawer in the desk and hunched over the corner, way too close. His knee was a fraction of an inch from hers. What if she shifted? What would it hurt to touch him? He'd assume it was an accident if he noticed at all. She wanted to touch him so badly her palms began sweating. If only she could erase the past. If only this could be a normal relationship.

Get a grip, Sabrina. Focus. Read the letter.

"I wish I did. Like I said, she's been careful. On the chat site where I met her, her screen name was SweetpeaKS. Maybe those are her initials or something."

His words were a sharp smack across the face, waking her from her careless daze. He couldn't know, could he? Of course he couldn't. She'd sent Arielle's picture, not her own. She didn't think he'd remember that screen name. It had been over a year ago.

Say something quick. Before he realizes those are your initials backward. "Maybe the KS is for Kansas."

The tip of his pen paused over the paper, and his head tilted sideways as he studied her. "Could be."

Relax. He doesn't know anything. Sabrina got caught in his eyes, sinking in the blue pools. How could a cool color feel so warm? Silver flecks splintered out from the center like shiny threads.

"It could stand for anything, I guess," he said softly.

She pulled her attention to the screen where it belonged. *For heaven's sake, you have got to focus.*

Pretend you're at the café. Why was it easier there? Because she was on her feet and busy? Because when things grew difficult, she could retreat? Because they weren't alone?

Tucker returned to his list, shifting until his knee grazed her thigh.

Because there was no actual touching involved? His body heat permeated the material of her khakis, warming her skin. She should move. She should shift, or cross her legs, or casually lean away. But the contact with him felt so good. So temptingly wonderful.

She didn't want to move away. What could it hurt anyway?

Sabrina crossed her legs and leaned forward, breaking contact for her own sanity. Now she could focus. She opened the next letter and scanned it. They were still discussing the wind farm. Nothing extraneous here.

She waded through several more letters, noting that two or three days separated their messages at this point.

"Just keep going," Tucker said. "I know there's little information in the early emails, but it gets better." He bowed his head over his list again. "Much better," he mumbled, or at least she thought he did.

She read three more, her thoughts going back all those months. She'd never reread the early letters. It had begun harmlessly, a casual exchange of information and ideas. It was in this email, three weeks into their correspondence, that he'd gotten personal:

> You know a lot about the wind farm project. Are you from Nantucket? Or are you a summer person? I live near the harbor.

She remembered freezing at the question, recognizing it as a potential turning point. If she told him yes, would she open a can of worms? He seemed kind, but she wasn't ready for a relationship or even a friendship. Her bad track record had sworn her off men months ago.

But it wasn't really a relationship. She didn't know him, he didn't know her. It was just words on a screen. What could it hurt? And yet, now that she knew for sure he was here on Nantucket . . . the proximity was frightening. If he knew she lived here, would he want to meet? That question sealed the deal.

No to both, she'd answered, and technically she wasn't, though she lived here now.

"What do you think?" Tucker interrupted her thoughts.

Sabrina wasn't sure what he meant. "She seems nice."

His eyes teased her. "I'm not asking for a character reference. Have you found anything interesting yet?"

Her face warmed. "Oh." She curled her fingers on the keyboard. "No, I'm just getting to the good stuff."

"Maybe this will help." He handed her the list. "That's all I can think of right offhand. I'm going to get a soda. Can I get you one?"

"No, thank you."

When he left the room, she scanned the list.

Loves to read mysteries

Works until two or three in the afternoon—the service industry, I think??

Lives alone

Allergic to cats and peanuts

Reads poetry—partial to Longfellow

Likes to clean

Favorite foods: pasta, dark chocolate, cupcakes, drinks iced tea

Hates corn

Never married—no kids

Has an extended family—two cousins, aunt and uncle, where??

The list continued, covering both sides of the paper. She felt increasingly exposed with each item. He knew a lot about her. And the list didn't even include the personal experiences she'd shared, only the bland facts. Although no one detail was particularly telling, the summation was like a fingerprint, surely unique to her alone.

The revelation frightened her. What if she said or did something to reveal herself? She'd have to be extremely vigilant.

She scanned the list again and noted an oddity. For all the factual information on the list, there was not one description of her appearance.

Harbormaster: My mom encouraged me to follow in her footsteps and become an attorney. I wasted three years of higher learning pursuing that goal until I finally realized I wasn't trying to become a lawyer at all. I was trying to gain my mother's approval.

Five

Tucker pulled open the refrigerator door and considered the drink options. Pepsi, milk, orange juice, and an old can of root beer that was probably flat. He'd already finished two sodas today, but milk or juice didn't appeal. He wasn't even thirsty.

He ran his hand through his hair. The real problem was Sabrina was in his house, in his office, fifteen paces away, and nothing was different. She was no more than a stranger, yet she was so much more.

He shut the fridge door. She was this close. *This close.* His leg had been pressed to hers, and okay, he'd manufactured the event, but still. He knew it hadn't meant anything. From her perspective the contact was accidental, probably even unnoticed. But for an instant he'd let himself believe it was significant. He imagined that she initiated the contact. He wouldn't delve into all the reasons why that was so pathetic. But it didn't matter anyway.

She'd pulled away, and that pretty much busted his imaginary bubble.

This was hard. Harder than he'd expected. He'd decided not to put Operation Sweetpea into full swing just yet. Let her settle in first, get comfortable. Allow her to know him a little. He hadn't realized that having her here would be so torturous.

What was holding her back? He knew she'd been hurt by her ex-fiancé. Hurt badly enough to cause rifts in her family and a chasm between her and God. Was she afraid of relationships? Or was it something more? Something she hadn't mentioned at all?

He remembered the first time he'd seen her. He stopped at the café on a Monday morning and took a seat near Oliver. A new server entered the dining room, a full tray balanced on one hand. She unloaded the tray with quick, efficient movements. She was tall, and her long limbs were fluid, graceful. She moved like a dancer.

Char appeared, filling his coffee mug. "Good morning, Tucker. How are you this morning, hon?"

"Fine, thanks."

Char moved on, and Tucker found himself watching the new server. There was something about her. He tried to figure out what. She had dark hair, pulled tightly into a ponytail and secured with a white band. She reached for it now and then, playing with the frayed end. Delicate eyebrows arched over a pair of almond-shaped brown eyes. She was a natural beauty. Her face, unadorned by makeup, would be perfect for a Dove soap ad. She was completely unaffected, as if she didn't know there were a couple male customers checking her out.

"Fancy the new gal, do you?"

Oliver's voice interrupted his thoughts. Tucker tore his eyes from the retreating server and sipped his coffee. "Where's she from?"

Oliver shrugged. "Don't know. Why don't you ask her?"

Tucker watched the new employee prepare a fresh pot of coffee like someone who'd done it a hundred times. He imagined himself starting a conversation with her, then realized what was different about the woman. For all her grace, her shoulders were too rigid, her back too straight. Her eyes engaged no one. She was all business.

He wasn't afraid of a challenge. "Might do that," Tucker replied.

"She don't look real friendly." Oliver smoothed his sparse hair.

A few minutes later, the new server stopped and refilled his coffee.

"You must be new around here." Tucker gave a smile that usually warmed up a woman pretty well.

"I am." The server turned her back, filling Oliver's cup.

"Where are you from?" Tucker asked.

She set the pot down and pulled out her tablet. "The mainland. Char's on break. Can I get you anything?"

She was a tough cookie; it didn't take a genius to see that. The all-business-don't-get-too-close sort. He cleared his throat. "I usually just have coffee."

She nodded once and went to take a family's order.

Oliver snickered. "That went real well."

The same scene had replayed itself many times over, some more humiliating than others. But eventually, he'd figured a way around her defenses. Even if it hadn't been ideal.

Now, he heard the faint tapping of Sabrina's fingers on the keyboard, and drew a breath. They'd come so far since then. He knew her so well, and loved what he knew. Loved how she toyed with her hair when she felt insecure, loved how openly she communicated with him, loved how honest she was about herself. He even loved her wry sense of humor. If only he could get that to translate outside of cyberspace.

Why was he in the kitchen, obsessing over the problem, when she was in the next room? He needed to loosen her up, get her accustomed to him so she'd let down her guard. He needed to focus on his plan, which began with that list he'd just made her.

When he reentered the office, Sabrina didn't look up from the screen. She'd jotted her own notes on his list. The screen displayed a letter she'd written a few weeks into their relationship. She was moving too quickly. If she continued at this pace, she'd be done in two weeks.

"Find anything?" He settled in the chair beside her.

"Nothing conclusive. Just jotting a few notes."

A strand of hair had slipped loose from her ponytail and fell over the curve of her cheek while she leaned forward, intent on her notes. It was easy to forget how delicate her features were. Her hands-off approach made most people avoid her, and that's probably how she liked it. But she had so much to offer under that hardened shell.

Her words from a message replayed in his mind. She'd written it after telling him about her ex-fiancé.

I guess you never know another person entirely. The parts you do know are formed by that person's words and actions. The parts you don't know you fill in with wishful thinking, which you eventually convince yourself is fact. When you're not looking, this nugget of illusion will come back to smash you over the head.

They were the sad words of a disillusioned soul. He'd turned them over and over in his head that night.

Now, Tucker watched her press her lips together, returning her attention to the screen. His eyes roamed her face—her long, dark lashes, her perfectly shaped nose, her stubborn chin—and determination twisted strong and hard in his gut. *No matter how hard this is on me, Sabrina Kincaid, I'm going to prove to you that love doesn't have to hurt.*

The picture. Ask about the picture. Sabrina pinched the bridge of her nose. It was the obvious question: Do you have a picture of her?

So simple, yet she'd avoided asking. Could she bear hearing Tucker fawn over Arielle's beauty?

Tucker appeared for the third time. For heaven's sake, was he going to stare over her shoulder every minute? She closed the email she'd been staring at blindly and opened the next one.

"How's it going?" He sat beside her.

Just peachy. "Are you going to ask that every five minutes?"

"Will it make you work harder?"

"It will make me irritable."

"Is that why your eyes are shooting sparks?"

She leveled a stare at him.

"All right, all right, I'll be quiet." Chastened, he leaned back in his chair, going nowhere.

Sabrina sighed and returned her attention to the screen. She couldn't focus with him staring a hole through her head. Heat gathered at the base of her skull and climbed to her ears. Was it hot in here?

She should ask about the picture. Just get it over with. It can't be worse than this.

She wetted her lips. "You haven't said anything about what she looks like. Surely you've exchanged photos." She pretended to read the next email, then realized Tucker was taking too much time in answering.

When she looked at him, he wore a strange expression, but when he blinked it was gone. He leaned over and took the mouse, brushing her hand.

Sabrina jerked back, then covered her overreaction by tucking a strand of hair behind her ear.

"I'll have to find the email that had the photo attached." He leaned toward the screen, his shoulder touching hers. "I think it's the only one with an attachment, so it shouldn't be hard."

She was only aware of the three square inches where their shoulders touched. If she turned toward him, it would take no more than a tip of her head to plant a kiss on his jawline. Her breaths became shallow, and she made a concerted effort to regulate them. *Breathe. In. Out.*

Oh, this was ridiculous. What was taking him so long?

She reached for the mouse. "I'll find it."

"Here it is." He clicked on an email, finally settling back in his seat.

Arielle smiled in the photo taken on Florida's gulf coast. She'd been walking toward the ocean, and it looked as if someone had called her name. The photo was from the waist up, shot from behind, taken as she'd turned to face the camera. Her long, blonde hair was spinning. Her blue eyes were sparkling brighter than the ocean in the background. But it was her trademark wide smile, the one that had won her numerous beauty pageants, that stole the show.

Sabrina wasn't jealous of Arielle. She loved her and was proud of her achievements. But knowing Tucker was gawking at her beautiful cousin twisted her insides painfully. She wanted to close the photo, but that would seem strange when she'd just asked to see it.

Instead she cleared her throat and pried the words off her tongue. "She's beautiful."

Her heart beat unnaturally fast waiting for his concurrence. She steeled herself against the inevitable sting.

"She's a beautiful person."

It was an odd response. Not what your typical man would say, but then Tucker wasn't your typical man. He was still staring at the screen. At least, she thought he was. She wasn't about to check.

Say something. "It's not a close-up. And her face is kind of shadowed. Is this the only one you have?"

"Yeah."

It was odd that he hadn't printed the photo. She'd expected an eight-by-ten glossy framed, matted, and placed on his nightstand or desk. Maybe even a wallet photo so he could show her off to his buddies.

"I'm not sure how much it'll help," she said. "Unless we can narrow the search down to a small town where everyone knows everyone."

"She's on the beach obviously." He gestured to the screen.

"You don't have any idea where she lives?"

"She was on Nantucket Chat when we met. I know she's been here at some point."

Better if he thought she lived elsewhere. Somewhere far, far away.

"We'd recognize her if she lived here."

Sabrina could feel his gaze on her. "You'd think."

"There's only ten thousand residents."

"But there are four or five times that in the summer. And this photo was taken at a beach."

Shoot. "True." She searched the photo for something that might sidetrack him. "There's a shadow falling on the sand beside her."

"A big tree, I think."

"That rules out Nantucket." Not that big trees didn't grow on the island, but none that big near the shoreline.

"Yeah, I guess you're right." He seemed reluctant to agree.

Sabrina searched the photo for more clues. "The waves look pretty small."

"That rules out the east and west coasts."

"Well, that narrows it down to a mere five states," she said.

"Better than fifty."

"Unless it's a vacation photo."

"Boy, sunshine, you're just full of positive thoughts."

"Just trying to be realistic." She closed the photo. "I should probably start reading these letters." She opened the next one and read the first sentence five times before she could focus enough to comprehend it. Was he going to sit there watching her read? It would take her months at this rate.

He picked up a pencil and tapped it on the desk, the sharpened end ticking against the wood surface.

She read the second sentence again. *Focus, Sabrina. For heaven's sake, you could have read the whole email twice by now.*

The tapping continued, pulling her attention from her task.

Finally she turned to him, sighing hard.

His brows disappeared under a dark, wavy tendril. "Oh, sorry. Am I distracting you?"

You think? If only she could read the emails in her apartment. She could get this done much quicker. "Are you sure you can't print them off? Or you could forward them to me. I wouldn't be in your way every night, and I promise I'd be careful with them."

He stood, shaking his head. "I wouldn't feel right about it. I feel bad enough just letting you read them."

If only he knew.

Sweetpea: My nickname in elementary school was Money Mouth. That's what happens when the class bully finds out a quarter will fit into the gap between your teeth. Braces only fix the exterior. Inside, I'm still the wallflower watching her cousins dance.

Six

Three days later, Sabrina gathered the thick stack of manuscript pages and checked the digital clock. It was one o'clock, late by her own standards, but Renny would be up working. The woman swore creativity flowed after midnight, and maybe it did, because the story Sabrina just finished reading was stellar.

She slid into sandals and walked down the stairs. A cool breeze ruffled the leaves above her and raised gooseflesh on her arms. When she reached Renny's kitchen door, she knocked.

"Sabrina, good heavens, what are you doing up?" Renny's gray hair protruded in all directions, an indication the woman had been using her scalp massager again. *"It stimulates the creative neurons,"* Renny had told her when Sabrina caught her at the computer, rubbing her head with the thing. It looked like a silver squid had latched on and wasn't letting loose.

"I couldn't go to sleep, and it's all your fault." Sabrina held up the manuscript.

Renny opened the door wider, letting Sabrina pass. "You liked it?"

"I couldn't put it down. Honestly, I started reading it today and couldn't go to bed until I finished. The writing is crisp, the characters are compelling, and the plot was woven together so tightly . . . Renny, if this one doesn't sell, those publishers are just incompetent. Your agent will be so pleased."

"Oh, thank God. I'm so relieved you liked it. The plot you helped me with is fresh and unique, I know that." A light behind Renny's eyes dimmed. "But the writing—it's not as good as I wanted it to be."

Sometimes Sabrina wanted to shake her. "The writing is superb."

Renny sank into an oak chair and stared through the window into the dark night. She didn't believe Sabrina. Anyone could see that. She wore her black and gray Hawaiian shirt, a sure sign her mood was down.

Renny twisted her diamond-studded wedding set around her wrinkled finger.

"You said that about the last one too."

"Because it's true."

Renny picked up the scalp massager and tapped its legs on the table. "I think the characters need more fleshing out. Especially Drew. That male point of view gets me every time."

"Every character was beautifully drawn."

"I don't know. It lacks . . . *chai*!"

"Chai? Like the tea?"

"Life! It lacks life."

Renny's late husband had done a job on her confidence. He'd been gone for three years, long before Sabrina had arrived, but she didn't have to know the man to see the effects he'd had on Renny.

"It lacks nothing. I have a good feeling about this one," Sabrina said.

"Well." Renny's gaze flickered to the hutch along the wall, then out the window. "Well, it's all in God's hands anyway, right?"

Sabrina needed to turn in if she was going to be lucid for work in the morning. Yet one look at Renny's drawn cheeks and ruffled hair and she sank into the heavy chair opposite the woman.

"How's your next story coming?"

She let out a Darth Vader sigh. "It's not. I have nothing at all, and I've been praying about it all week."

"Maybe we can brainstorm tomorrow."

"You're working for the McCabe boy after the café. Honey, you don't have time for that."

"I'll make time, Renny. Besides, it's fun."

"Well, you're a genius at it, there's no doubt. Maybe I should just sign your name to these stories and be done with it." She gave a weak laugh.

"I couldn't write my way out of a paper bag. Has your agent heard from any publishers on *Danger in the Night*?" The quality of Renny's writing had taken a huge leap in her last story about a Nantucket family's murder.

Renny set down the massager and yawned. "No, no word. Heavens, I don't think the ideas are going to flow tonight. Tell me how things are going for you. Work? Have you heard from your family?"

"Work's fine." She thought of the wedding invitation, a part of her shriveling at the thought.

"And your family?"

"I got a wedding invitation in the mail. Jared and Jaylee's."

Renny sucked in a breath. "No!" Her brows creased into a V between her shiny eyes. Righteous indignation.

"Afraid so."

She laid her hand over Sabrina's. "Oh, *amita,* I'm so sorry. God will give you peace on this. I know it."

Sometimes Renny's faith felt like enough for both of them. This was not one of those times. Still, it did comfort her when Renny called her "friend" that way. "Thanks, Renny."

"Will you go? I could go with you."

"No, I—I'm not going. But thanks for the offer."

"Well, if you change your mind, you have only to let me know and I'll be packing my suitcase."

After Sabrina left, her thoughts went back to Renny's manuscript. She wondered if it would take a sale for Renny to believe in her work. If so, there was no need to worry, because Sabrina knew great writing, and Renny's recent stories were nothing short of that.

Tucker sipped the coffee Sabrina had poured, then spread out *The Inquirer and Mirror* and pretended to read. She was posting an order for two men in suits and neckties. They chatted quietly over a thin stack of papers, sipping their coffee between notations. It seemed a little early for business, but hey, better them than him. He relished the idea of a day spent on the open sea instead of chained to some desk.

Glancing around the café, he caught two high school boys ogling Sabrina all the way to the kitchen. One of them met his eyes, and Tucker stared until the kid looked away. *Aren't you a little young for her, pal?* They couldn't be more than eighteen and Sabrina was twenty-four. No, he reminded himself, she was twenty-five today. He'd thought she'd request the night off, but she hadn't.

He remembered his own twenty-fifth birthday. He'd gone home to New York for Thanksgiving break, and his family had thrown a surprise dinner party for him and his twin sister at Le Bernardin, complete with friends from high school and college.

He wanted to do something special for Sabrina, but an email greeting would have to suffice. Maybe he could make tonight special.

If only she would open up to him, even as a friend. She was so guarded. When she'd first come to the island, he'd tried for months to get to know her.

He'd begun to wonder if Oliver's sole reason for coming to the café wasn't to watch the show.

"Don't you have anything better to do than eavesdrop on my conversations?" he'd asked more than once.

"Last I checked, it took two to have a conversation."

Being publicly rejected on a regular basis wasn't much fun. Still, there was something about Sabrina. He sensed a vulnerability in her that drew him. Watching her reminded him of a quote he'd once heard: *"The people with the highest walls have the softest hearts."* Watching Sabrina, he suspected it was true. He wanted to know for sure. He wanted to know her, if only she'd let him in.

He'd never been so interested in someone who, apparently, didn't return the favor. Was it her thinly disguised vulnerability that drew him, or something else? He reflected on that often and came to the conclusion that it was those unguarded moments that captured him. She presented a disinterested front, but there were moments when she didn't think anyone was looking that he caught an unvarnished glimpse of the real Sabrina.

One evening after she'd first started working at the café, he'd seen her resting on a bench at Jetties Beach. The sun was low in the sky, and the beach crowd was gone for the day. It was just Sabrina, watching the sunset. She had a little smile on her face and was so caught up in the view she didn't notice him, only twenty feet away. He wanted to stroll over and say hi. But she looked so peaceful, and though he hadn't known her long, he knew the instant she saw him, her guard would go up. He didn't want to spoil her relaxing evening.

So he continued to try and spark conversations at the café. Just when he was about to give up, he'd catch a glimpse of her chatting with Char or coming off break and see her unmasked. He was determined to find out who she really was, why she kept such a distance between herself and others.

The first time he'd asked her out, he'd been more nervous than ever before. Of course, he didn't normally ask out a woman who'd given him no encouragement. He dismissed his failed attempts at conversation. She was busy during breakfast, and he got to thinking that if he came at a slower time, she might be more receptive.

So on a chilly fall day during slow season, he showed up after the lunch hour and took a seat at his regular table. He saw the surprise on Sabrina's face before she could mask it.

He opened the menu and surveyed the lunch selection. The thought of food made his stomach turn.

"Coffee?" she asked.

He flipped his mug over and gave her what he hoped was a charming smile. "Sure." He thought she might comment about his unscheduled appearance, but she didn't.

Instead she pulled out her order pad and poised a pen over it. "What can I get you?"

Now, there was a loaded question. He considered whether to order or just say what he'd come for. His heart drummed wildly in the pause.

Her brows lifted ever so slightly.

He closed his menu. "Actually, to be honest, I didn't come here to eat."

She hardly missed a beat. "Just coffee then?"

"No," he said quickly before she could skedaddle away. "No, I—" He sat up straight in his chair as if the boost would raise his confidence. "I wanted to ask if you'd like to go out for coffee sometime. Or dinner. My friend works at DeMarco and could probably even get us in—"

"I can't," she said. "I'm sorry." She scooted off toward the coffee station while he gathered what was left of his pride. Not even a reason, just *"I'm sorry."* Was she dating someone? Wouldn't she have said so if she were? He never saw her with anyone else, and neither had anyone else, because he'd asked around. No, he didn't think she was taken. And that only made the rejection worse.

But he'd survived it and had even gotten up the courage to ask again. With the same results.

It was only when he'd overheard a conversation between Sabrina and Char that the idea had formed. It was a slow, rainy morning, and they were rolling silverware in napkins at a table behind him, close enough for eavesdropping. Char was telling Sabrina about Nantucket Chat, a place where people from all over the country posted messages on a variety of topics. Some posters were residents, others just people who'd visited and fallen in love with Nantucket's charms. Tucker had logged on a few times to see what people were saying about local politics or preservation of the island's ecology.

"That's a good idea," Char was saying. "You should write that on Nantucket Chat. I think a lot of people would be interested. It's free to join. Just log in and post it in the Nantucket Ecology discussion forum."

"I might do that," Sabrina said.

Tucker watched the forum for two days, waiting for a new name to appear. When it did, it was SweetpeaKS, and he recognized Sabrina's idea. He'd posted a couple comments himself, then emailed her privately to discuss her idea. The rest had been history.

A kid two tables over let out a piercing cry, drawing his attention from the past. The baby pounded his fists on the table, demanding more Cheerios from his mom, who was busy with two other kids. Several feet away, Char stopped Sabrina, two coffeepots grasped in her bony hands. "Hey, Sabrina, I had this family thing come up last minute and need to leave early. You think you could stay over a few hours?"

Sabrina pulled her order pad and pen from her apron pocket. "Sure, no problem."

She went to take an order from an elderly couple three tables away. Char must not know it was Sabrina's birthday. In fact, he hadn't heard anyone mention it. Between her hours at the café and working on his project, she wouldn't have a spare minute today. Maybe Sabrina needed the money.

He recalled their email conversation the evening before.

It's almost your day, he'd written.

Got big plans?

Are you kidding? she'd replied.

It's my twenty-fifth birthday.

Don't have too much fun without me, birthday girl.

It sounded at the time like she had something fun planned, but now he realized she'd never answered his question. She did that sometimes—changed the subject.

"Warm you up?" Sabrina's voice interrupted his thoughts.

He realized his paper blocked the mug, and moved it. Color bloomed on her cheeks as she realized her words' double meaning. His lips twitched with the urge to comment, but he stopped himself. "Thanks."

Oliver sank into the chair at his usual table. Sabrina turned over his mug and filled it. "Good morning."

"Morning, Sabrina." Oliver folded his sausagelike fingers on the table, leaning back. "You know, I'm feeling rather *edacious* this morning."

She set down the coffee and poised her pen over her tablet. "Great, then can I get you something more than coffee?"

Oliver pursed his lips, and Tucker smothered a grin as the man reluctantly ordered rye toast. Poor rascal. He tried so hard.

Tucker checked his watch. He had to gas up his boat before they opened. When Sabrina returned with the toast, she set his tab on the table.

He reached for his wallet. "See you tonight around six?"

She nodded once, no eye contact. Tucker watched her gather dishes a few tables away, her motions efficient and fluid.

"No way." Oliver glanced back and forth between them, gray brows crouching low over his eyes.

Tucker pulled out three bills and set them by the saltshaker.

Oliver lowered his voice. "You did not get a date with the Ice Princess."

Tucker stood, pocketing his wallet, taking one last peek at Sabrina as she put an order on the wheel.

"Is she going out with you, McCabe?"

Tucker pushed in his chair and adjusted his hat as he walked away.

"McCabe?"

A smile tickled Tucker's lips as he exited the café.

Harbormaster: My twin sister called tonight. What a mess. Her jerk of a husband cheated on her and now they're separated. If I see him again, I'm afraid what I might do to him. He deserves it for what he's putting Tracey through.

Seven

A large, teal envelope was waiting in Sabrina's mailbox when she arrived home. She hurriedly tore it open and skipped the card's flowery greeting. Her aunt had signed for both of them. *Love, Uncle Everett and Aunt Bev.*

She held the card a moment, then dropped it in the wastebasket and checked her email. Nothing. She reread the email Tucker sent early that morning.

Happy 25th birthday! I hope you have a great day. I'm thinking about you.

After she showered and dressed in modest shorts and a clean blouse, she gathered her hair into a ponytail and headed for Tucker's. Her palms sweated against the handlebars, turning sticky. Would she ever relax in Tucker's presence? Being with him was painful. Bad enough serving him at the café, but there was something intimate about being in his home. And the man would not leave her alone. If he didn't stay in the office, he peeked in every few minutes. She was constantly tense, waiting for him to materialize.

She wiped one damp palm at a time on her beige shorts. *You have got to relax. As far as he's concerned, he's only your employer. Do your job and forget about the relationship.*

It was the relationship that prevented her from relaxing. *It's not a relationship. It's just a—a correspondence.*

A daily, intimate correspondence.

He doesn't even know my name.

He knows who you are deep inside.

Sabrina's stomach tightened as she clutched the handlebars. It was true. Tucker did know her, better than anyone ever had.

Except Jared.

A pool of panic welled up in her. Had she made a terrible mistake in corresponding with Tucker? She'd thought the anonymity provided safety, but then, she'd thought Jared was safe, and she'd been wrong about that. How was she to know he'd hurt her when she'd met him under such noble circumstances?

It had been the second semester of her sophomore year at college when she met Jared. After high school she left Macon to study literature at Miami University in the quaint town of Oxford, Ohio. Putting distance between herself and her family had been both frightening and liberating. Without her beautiful and charming Southern cousins at her side, a seedling of confidence began to sprout.

One night she walked from her last class to her car, unlocked it, and slid inside, closing the door against the bitter-cold wind. She had twenty-three minutes to be at Bruno's, where she would serve pizza to a rowdy weekend college crowd until closing.

Vapor plumed in front of her face as she slid the key into the ignition, and she turned it, eager to get some heat going.

But nothing happened at the motion. Nothing except a clicking sound. *No, no, no.* She turned the key again, and the same noise greeted her. A dead battery, she was sure, but she had no cables. She glanced around the darkened parking lot through windows that had begun to fog with her breath. There was no one in sight. Besides, she wondered how many college students carried battery cables in their cars.

She could call her roommate, but by the time Zoe arrived, Sabrina would be late. She'd have to walk to Bruno's and worry about her car later. She grabbed her backpack and exited the car, locking it and hoping it wouldn't be towed in the dead of night.

The hum of an approaching engine startled her. It was a dark pickup truck, and the man behind the wheel was a stranger. But that wasn't unusual, given the size of the campus.

"Need help?" He'd rolled down his window and leaned out, the corner of his elbow poking from the vehicle. He had short, dark hair, but shadows masked his facial features.

Sabrina was suddenly aware of how alone she was in the massive parking lot. She clutched the keys in her palm, searching for her car key in case she needed to unlock the vehicle quickly. Just last month she'd overheard students discussing the latest sexual assault that had occurred at the victim's off-campus home.

"No." She hitched the bag higher on her shoulder, hoping he'd leave. "Thanks for asking though." Her words should've dismissed him.

He looked out his front window, then back to her. "Can I call someone for you?"

"No, thanks." She made her voice sound confident. Should she walk toward town or get in her car and lock the door? Maybe she should call Zoe and be late for work.

But the last person who'd been late for work had been fired. Bruno had no tolerance for irresponsible college students. He'd only hired her because of her shining references from her former bosses back in Macon.

"It sounded like a dead battery. If you have jumper cables, I can give you a jump."

"I don't have any."

"Shoot, I don't either. Listen, it's not safe to walk around at night, especially a pretty girl like you. If you don't have anyone to pick you up, I can give you a ride."

As if jumping in a car with a stranger was safer. "No, thanks, I'm fine." She turned in the opposite direction and began walking toward Main Street. Her legs wobbled as she navigated the maze of cars, huddled against the wind.

She was relieved when she reached the sidewalk, but the short distance to Main Street seemed to stretch out forever.

When she heard the hum of an engine approaching from behind, her legs pumped faster. Was the man returning? He seemed friendly, but she supposed that had been the rape victim's last thought before the guy violated her.

Her longer stride was no match for the vehicle. The truck pulled along the curb and kept pace with her.

The man rolled down the passenger window and called through it, "Hey, why don't you just let me give you a ride? It's too cold out there. You're shivering."

"I'm fine. I'm almost where I'm going."

"Have it your way." His voice had changed, and the kindness peeled off his face like a mask. He put the truck in park, and he reached for his handle.

Fear clawed at Sabrina's spine. She broke into a run. She heard footsteps behind her, rubber soles grinding on the pebbled cement. Then she ran into something hard.

Run! You've got to move!

But the hard thing she'd run into steadied her. The man released her and stepped around her. "Everything okay here?"

The truck driver stopped in his tracks ten feet away. His hard face slackened as he sized up the man in front of her and found himself on the short end. He stepped back. "No trouble, dude. Just trying to help the girl."

The new man looked over his shoulder. "You all right?"

Sabrina swallowed, her breath still caught like a bubble in her throat. She nodded.

"I've got it from here," he said. "Why don't you get back in your truck and call it a night?"

The truck driver's jaw twitched as he clamped it down, staring at her. Sabrina's gaze fell to his tennis shoes as she prayed he'd leave. He seemed to stand there forever before he returned to his truck. It roared away loudly.

The other man moved from her side, walking away, and she wondered where he was going. Then he stooped and picked up something. Her purse. She hadn't even realized she'd dropped it.

"Thanks," she said as he handed it to her, meaning the word in more ways than one.

"Are you sure you're okay?"

Her hands shook as she set her purse on her shoulder, and she wasn't sure if it was the cold or the belated terror kicking in.

"I'm fine," she said, feeling oddly safe for someone who'd nearly been attacked. Jared had walked her to Bruno's that night and had eaten there two nights later. Because of how they'd met, she'd thought of him as her knight. Thought it was safe to love him. It had been three years before she realized the foolishness of her thinking.

Sabrina shook the memories from her mind as she turned into Tucker's drive.

"Hey, neighbor!" She followed the sound of the voice to the porch next to Tucker's house. A blond guy leaned on the railing, smiling widely.

"Uh, hi. I don't live here, actually."

"Renting?"

"I'm just working here for a few weeks."

Blondie ambled down the porch steps and onto the lawn barefooted. "My friends and I rented this place for the month."

Sabrina slid off the bike and set the kickstand. "Hope you have a nice visit." She smiled in a dismissive way. She had enough on her mind with Tucker.

"Maybe I'll see you around."

"Maybe." She stepped onto Tucker's porch and rapped, conscious that Blondie was still standing on his lawn, watching her. *Keep your head in the game. Be professional. Do the job, and don't let it become personal.*

Tucker opened the door and ushered her inside. "Hey there." His voice was chipper, his smile engaging. There were tiny lines beside his mouth that made him look a little older than his twenty-nine years. And that little scar by his mouth . . .

Look away, you ninny.

"Something to drink? Iced tea?"

"No, thank you." She went straight to the office and settled behind his desk. He stood in the doorway. She could feel him staring into her back. "I'll go ahead and get started."

She'd hoped the words would dismiss him, but the quiet behind her made her think he hadn't gone anywhere, and the way the hairs on her neck stood on end made her sure of it. She opened the email program, then the folder where the messages were stored.

Go away. She couldn't think with him standing there.

She started where she'd left off, opening the letter and reading it. The messages became short and quippy, and she remembered it was a time they'd both been at their computers, exchanging emails for a couple hours.

She heard a shuffle in the doorway and felt that Tucker had left. Finally, she could concentrate. It took almost an hour to read one evening's messages. Opening each email for only a sentence or two was tedious and time-consuming. At some point she heard the phone ring, followed by Tucker's friendly greeting, then the sliding of the patio door as he continued his conversation outside.

Turning her attention back to her work, Sabrina saw that she'd finally reached the last emails sent that night. She remembered it well. She had opened it expecting another short quip, and had gotten the shock of her life instead.

This is me, he'd written.

Pasted into the email was a photo. Her breath caught and hung in her throat, choking her. The photo was from a distance, but she would've known Tucker McCabe anywhere.

It can't be. She stared at the photo, taken beside a boat. No, it was definitely him. The blue cap, the dark curls, the T-shirt with his company's logo. Tucker McCabe whom she waited on every morning at the café. How could it be? What were the chances?

What do I do? He was sitting at his computer, waiting for her reply. Did he—oh, for heaven's sake, no—did he expect her to send a photo of herself? *I can't do it.*

Sure, it was easy for him. He had nothing to hide with his dark good looks and muscular physique. What would he think when he discovered who he'd befriended? That it was the Ice Princess from the café? The plain, gawky one with a ponytail and sharp tongue? He'd want nothing more to do with Sweetpea, that's what. And maybe that was best, because a real relationship was not going to happen.

Her pulse began to pound at her temples.

I have to write back. What do I say? She cupped her forehead in her palms. Maybe if she didn't reply, he'd think she'd gone to bed. But that would be rude after he'd sent his photo. And they always said goodnight before they signed off for the night.

Another email appeared.

Hello?

She had to respond. She put her fingers on the keyboard.

I'm here.

She sent the message and waited. Finally a reply appeared.

Am I that ugly?

She closed her eyes, then forced her fingers onto the keys again. What to say? She bit her lip.

Of course not.

She hit Send.
A few seconds later another email appeared.

I'd love to see who I'm spending all these hours with. I want to picture you. ☺

She'd known it was coming. What should she do? If she sent her photo, he'd know who she was. It would be the end of their relationship, one way or another. At the very least, mornings at the café would become awkward. What if he wasn't repelled by the fact that Sabrina was Sweetpea? What if he wanted to start dating or something?

An email appeared in her inbox.

Are you there? Are you downloading a photo or fretting over it? I don't care what you look like (in case you're wondering).

Sabrina choked on a laugh. But of course he cared. He was a man, wasn't he? She'd learned early that a woman's looks were her currency, and Sabrina had been bankrupt from the beginning. If she hadn't known it before she'd moved in with her cousins, she'd learned it afterward. Arielle and Jaylee had no idea how lucky they were to be born with—

The picture. Arielle had sent a photo of herself the week before. Maybe she could send it . . .

That's not right, Sabrina.

But what did it matter?

She couldn't let him know who she was, so what did it matter if he thought she was beautiful? He probably already did.

She opened her cousin's last email, copied the photo, then pasted it into a reply to Tucker. She stared at the picture. Even at the beach, Arielle's face was artfully made up, her lips cherry red. The photo resembled a CoverGirl ad. Dread sank like a weight in her stomach. Before she could reconsider, she sent the photo.

Her fingers tapped on the desk while she waited. Had she done the right thing? *It's not as if you have a choice. He can't know who you are. What could it hurt if he thinks you're beautiful?*

It's not as if they were going to meet. Well, they *had* met, but it's not as if Tucker would discover her identity. And if he had to imagine her, why not picture a beautiful woman? If she'd refused to send a photo, he might assume she was homely. And what if he decided to discontinue their relationship? She couldn't bear the thought of returning to the lonely life she'd had before their email relationship. She couldn't lose him.

She shook her head, trying to connect the visual image of Tucker with the mental image of Harbormaster. He was the one who listened so carefully, who took her ideas and thoughts seriously, who never judged her regardless of what she said.

What was taking him so long to reply?

He was probably on his knees, thanking his lucky stars that she was so gorgeous.

The weight in Sabrina's stomach sank lower. She opened the email with his photo. She couldn't believe it was Tucker.

But he doesn't know it's you. Thank God for that.

A reply appeared in her inbox. She rushed to open it.

Thanks for the photo. You don't know how much I enjoy our chats.

Sabrina reread his words. He hadn't mentioned her appearance. She'd expected a compliment at least. It wasn't the first time Tucker surprised her, and it probably wouldn't be the last.

A knock at the front door snagged her attention. She closed out the email. So much for remaining detached. This was harder than she'd thought it was going to be. She opened a new one and began reading. *Stay detached,* she told herself. *You do not know these people. They are characters, like the ones in Renny's—*

Another knock sounded. She listened for Tucker's footsteps but instead heard the deep rumble of his voice from the deck outside. Still on the phone.

Sabrina went to the door and opened it. Blondie stood on the stoop, hands pocketed in his Hawaiian-print swim trunks. "Sorry to bother you—uh, didn't catch your name before."

"Sabrina."

She was rewarded with a bright smile. "I'm Cody. My friends and I are grilling steaks, and we forgot to get steak sauce. You wouldn't happen to have any?" He winced like he hated to ask.

She turned and saw Tucker sitting in the deck chair, his feet propped on the railing, the phone tucked against his shoulder. Surely he wouldn't mind. "Come on in. I'll check."

After riffling through the contents, she found a bottle of A1 Steak Sauce corralled in the fridge door behind a bulk-sized bottle of ketchup. She grabbed the sauce and took it to Cody. He was leaning against the door frame when she returned.

She handed him the bottle.

"Great, thanks," he said but didn't budge. Instead he asked her a few questions about the local beaches. After they covered that topic, he straightened. "Say, we made plenty of food. You want to come over for dinner?"

"She's working."

Sabrina turned at the sound of Tucker's voice. She hadn't heard him enter. His arms crossed his chest, and his jaw was set in a way she'd never seen.

Sabrina turned back to Cody. "He's right. But thanks for the invite."

"Maybe another time." His eyes swung to Tucker's, his smile smug. "Thanks for the steak sauce."

Sabrina shut the door, feeling like she was in trouble. "He'll bring it back."

Tucker pursed his lips, and she wondered what he was thinking. It was only steak sauce, for crying out loud.

"You were on the phone."

Shadows danced over his face as his jaw clenched and loosened. He turned toward the patio door.

Okay then. "I'll get back to work." She was almost to the hall when his voice stopped her.

"It's her birthday today," he said.

It took a moment for his words to register. "What?"

"Her twenty-fifth birthday. And all I can do is send a stinking email greeting."

Maybe that's why he was all moody. Then anxiety kicked in. Did he know it was *her* birthday? There was nothing to give her away. No card, no present, no bouquet of flowers delivered to the restaurant. She looked into his eyes. She wanted to soothe away his sadness. She wanted to lay her palm against his cheek and tell him it was okay. She wanted to—

She turned away.

"I need to find her." His tone was sobering. "I want to be with her."

His words filled a hollow spot inside her. Sure he wanted to be with her, she reminded herself. Because he thought she looked like Arielle. *Because he doesn't know who you are and what you did.*

Sabrina cleared her throat. "I'm working on that."

She could hear the water lapping the sides of the pier outside. The ferry horn sounded in the distance.

"Let's get out of here," he said.

She glanced at him, then looked away, resisting the pull of those eyes. "What?"

He stood. "Let's go for a ride in my boat."

"I'm working."

"You've read a lot of messages already. You've got notes. Bring them along, and we can toss ideas around."

Panic welled in her, rushing her words. "It's getting late."

"There's plenty of light. Come on, you're not afraid of a little water, are you?"

"Of course not."

"Then come on." He approached and reached for her hand, tugging. The contact felt good, his hand warm and strong around hers.

"All right, all right," she snapped, pulling her hand away. She turned toward the door.

"Don't forget your list." His eye held a sparkle of humor, but he blinked away the expression before she could fathom its meaning.

Sweetpea: My aunt entered me in a beauty pageant after I came to live with them. I felt like a fraud with layers of caked-on makeup and hair goop. After overhearing other contestants laughing behind my back, I purposely bungled the interview to assure I wouldn't final. Not that I would have anyway. My aunt never again entered me in a pageant.

Eight

They were miles from shore by the time Tucker cut the engine. She'd expected they'd take his large passenger boat, but instead he'd led her down the steps of his deck, where a smaller craft was roped to a piling. A much smaller craft. Instead of being spread out on a fifty-foot boat, they were side by side on pedestal seats. Miles from land. Miles from the nearest person. Alone took on new meaning.

A seagull flew overhead, its piercing cry echoing the panic building inside Sabrina.

Tucker swiveled his seat around. His cap removed, his curls were wind tousled. Wondering what the wind had done to her own hair, she smoothed it back toward her nape, feeling all the strands that had escaped the rubber band.

He looked more relaxed than he had earlier, his lips slack, almost grinning. He loved the ocean. He'd once said he never felt better than when he was on the water. He'd said even on his worst day at work, he never regretted giving up a career in law.

Watching him now, she believed it. He looked at peace with the world, his eyes closed, his head leaning against the headrest.

"So," he said without opening his eyes, "have you come up with anything that might help me locate her?"

Sabrina took the list from her bag. It had been tricky pulling details from the letters. She'd chosen facts that might mislead him and omitted details that pointed to her.

"I think she might be from the South," Sabrina said.

He opened one eye, peeking at her sideways. "What makes you say that?"

"She mentioned Piggly Wiggly once. She doesn't say she goes there, but she uses it in a metaphor."

He shrugged. "Could be. But everyone's heard of Piggly Wiggly, haven't they?"

"It wouldn't be the first thing to come to mind if she didn't live near one."

"She doesn't have a Southern accent."

Sabrina smirked. "You've never talked to her."

"It would come through in email, don't you think? 'Y'all' and 'bless your heart' and all that," he said with a country twang.

"No stereotypes there."

He grinned. "What else have you got?"

She perused her list. "Some of the same things on your list. Her allergies, the poetry, the food preferences."

"What about her ex-fiancé?"

She crossed her legs, tucking her feet under the chair. "What about him?"

"They met at college. Maybe if we can figure out which one, we could go from there."

"She mentioned being a literature major," Sabrina admitted reluctantly.

"What was Jared's major?"

Hearing Jared's name on his lips distracted her, and she opened her mouth, the words *political science* on her tongue. Then she realized she'd never revealed that. "I don't think she said."

"Hmmm." Quiet settled around them, filling the space between them.

He probably thought she wasn't earning her pay. She studied the list again. "If you combine the clues of her major and the fact that she seems to spend a lot of time at the computer, maybe she works in a library. Or maybe she's a journalist," Sabrina added, remembering her old ambitions.

"If only I knew her name."

Sabrina had been careful about that. She'd never revealed her initials, other than her original screen name on Nantucket Chat and, even then, they were backward. But he didn't know those were initials.

"Are there any Piggly Wigglys near the Gulf Coast?" she asked.

"Why?"

She jotted a note on the paper. "The photo taken at the beach. She's been careful about the details she's given, so I think we'll need to combine facts and draw conclusions."

He tipped his head back, and the setting sun cast a golden glow over his skin. His dark eyelashes brushed the top of his cheeks. She studied the Cupid's bow of his upper lip. She wondered how he'd react if she dipped her finger into the arch.

"Listen to that."

She startled, as if he'd caught her staring, but his eyes were still closed. "What?" she asked, then slowly became aware of the sounds around them. The gurgle of water lapping the sides of the boat, the cry of a distant seagull, the sound of the wind cutting across the water.

"I never get tired of this. I want to bring her out here," he said. "I want to share this with her."

The air smelled of salt. The taste of it coated her lips. The gentle rock of the boat lulled her. What would it be like if he knew she was Sweetpea? If he knew she was with him right now? Would he pull her close and kiss the salt from her lips? Would he hold her tenderly and tell her he loved her?

He opened his eyes, trapping her under his gaze.

Sabrina fought the ache in her chest. She had to say something. Something to break the spell he wove around her. "I'm sure she'd love it."

Something flickered in his eyes. She wanted to know what that emotion was, but to find out, she'd have to stare, and staring was dangerous. Staring sucked her in and held her captive. Staring made her careless. She looked away.

"Do you think there's any hope?" he asked.

Sabrina clenched her fist in her lap. Guilt pricked her conscience. How could she reassure him when she planned to fail? She let his question drift away on the wind. There was nothing she could say because he hoped for the impossible, and she knew how he felt. Hope was the fuel of life, and she'd been running on empty a long time.

Sweetpea: My cousins had a big white fluffy cat when I came to live with them. I sneezed ferociously for two weeks before my aunt and uncle finally got rid of Roxy. My cousins didn't speak to me for days.

$\mathcal{N}ine$

"How's the schedule looking, Dorothy?" Tucker asked. The sixty-two-year-old woman was his part-time office employee. Her thinning gray hair was short, and she wore large-framed glasses that only helped minimally with her sight. Still, she was efficient and dependable. Even if she did have to sit six inches from the computer screen.

"Pretty full for the next week or so, especially with Nate being out for a couple days. You'll be run ragged."

"I'll survive." He sat at his desk to review the repairs estimate on one of his boats. Three grand. He sighed. Nothing he could do about that.

"Hey, boss." Nate poked his head in the door. Tucker had hired him three years earlier when the business outgrew one driver.

"How'd the Parkers enjoy their trip to the Vineyard?" Tucker asked.

"They had a blast. I have a family I'm taking around the island now."

Tucker checked his watch. Sabrina would be at his place in thirty minutes, and he needed a shower.

"You didn't forget about my two days off this week for my mom's surprise party, did you?"

"It's on the schedule," Dorothy said.

"It won't be a problem." Tucker stood and gathered the papers. Maybe he should get another estimate on the repairs. Three grand seemed steep.

Tucker put his cap on.

"Uh, I was wondering something." Nate shifted his bulky frame in the doorway, looking like a sheepish schoolboy.

"Beth had arrangements for Nickels while we were gone," he continued. "But they had a family emergency and can't keep him now. We, uh, were wondering if one of you might take him in for a couple days." He looked between Dorothy and Tucker.

The silver cat was notorious in the office, though Dorothy and Tucker had never seen the feline. Nickels had come into the marriage with Beth, and he and Nate had a love/hate relationship. Heavy on the hate.

Tucker wasn't fond of cats, and they weren't crazy about him either.

"I'm gone all day," he said. "I know Beth wouldn't want her baby orphaned."

"Count me out." Dorothy filed a thin stack of papers, leaning so close to the tabbed files she could've licked them. "I'm allergic to cats."

Nate turned pleading eyes on Tucker.

He envisioned his favorite recliner becoming a scratching post, litter strewn across his carpet, and that brought another thought: the smell.

"Just this once?" Nate scrunched up his eyebrows.

"Aw, come on. Can't Beth ask one of her friends?"

"She already tried. You're my last resort, man."

Dorothy smiled innocently, eyes widening behind her thick glasses. She blinked slowly. "You're his last resort."

Tucker glared at her, wishing he was the one with a cat allergy. *Very convenient, Dorothy.*

He remembered Sabrina's email from months ago. Something about her cousins having a cat that made her sneeze incessantly. There was his excuse. With Sabrina coming over, he couldn't have a cat around making her sneeze, making her eyes redden and her nose—

Or could he?

He wasn't supposed to know who Sabrina was. Wasn't supposed to know she had a cat allergy. What would happen if he suddenly had a cat? She wouldn't be able to hide her allergic reaction. Maybe it would flush her out of hiding. It had been a week since she'd started coming over. She was settled in, and maybe this was just the thing to get his plan started. Maybe—

"Just think about it?" Nate continued. "I promised Beth I'd find somebody, and she's gonna kill me if I come home—"

"I'll do it," Tucker said firmly.

Nate's chin tilted away while he stared suspiciously at Tucker from the corner of his narrowed eyes. "You will?"

"You will?" Dorothy's fingers stopped on the files, and she looked at him, doubt written all over her pale, wrinkled face. "You hate cats."

"Hate is a strong word," Tucker said.

"You hate cats," Dorothy repeated.

Tucker pulled his hat down firmly on his head. "What are friends for?"

He left the office and began the short walk home. *Sabrina, you'd better enjoy the dander-free air tonight, because when you come over tomorrow, no more Mr. Nice Guy.*

───

Sabrina tapped on Tucker's door.

"Come on in," Tucker called from somewhere in the house.

She turned the knob and entered. The house smelled like a mixture of Tucker's woodsy cologne and the remnants of his supper—something Italian, she thought, detecting the tang of onion and garlic.

Tucker rounded the corner from the kitchen. "Want some leftover spaghetti? I made plenty."

"No, thank you." She took a step toward the office, but stopped abruptly when a cat slinked from behind the chair and blocked her path. She pulled in a silent breath.

It stopped and stared up at her, its long, silver tail fanning the air gracefully like a fluffy flag, its back arched high. The cat rubbed against her bare leg.

"You got a cat?" She tried to tame the panic in her voice.

"Just temporarily." He scooped up the feline and cradled it.

"Nickels is going to be my houseguest for a couple days, aren't you, buddy?" The cat struggled for release, and Tucker set him down.

She opened her mouth to inform him of her allergy, then snapped it shut. He knew Sweetpea had cat allergies. She couldn't let him know she did too. It would be one more detail that linked them, one more piece of this two-sided puzzle. *You'll have to avoid that cat and hope for the best.*

How long would it take her allergies to kick in? The cat was new to the home, so the dander levels would be low. And he usually kept the office door closed . . . maybe the cat hadn't been in there.

"Nate from work asked me to take him while he and his wife are out of town."

"That was kind of you." She walked down the hall, her heart sinking at the open office door.

"I'm not much of a cat person, but Nate's a good friend, and he was in a bind."

She knew he had a distinct dislike of cats. When he was little, he'd rescued a stray cat from its high perch on a tree limb and had been rewarded with a scratch on his shoulder deep enough to require stitches.

Tucker followed her into the office. Nickels came along too. He jumped on her chair and sniffed the keyboard.

She had to get the cat out of there.

"Good day at the café?" Tucker propped his hands on his hips. He wore a white T-shirt that set off his tan, and a pair of frayed jeans that looked as if they'd been washed a hundred times.

"It was fine." Sabrina set her bag on the desk and looked at

Nickels, wondering how she could get him off the chair without touching him.

"Well, I'll let you get to work. I put your check on the desk." Tucker left, leaving a wake of yummy-smelling cologne behind. A moment later she heard him in the kitchen, washing dishes. Her paycheck sat beside the computer, a reminder of her deceit.

Never mind the money. She had bigger problems.

She glared at Nickels. She needed a decoy. She looked around for a toy to lure him away. Nothing but computer cords and boxes. Her eyes fell on the blind cord dangling against the window. Well, that would at least get him off the chair. Maybe.

She walked to the window and jiggled the cord. "Here, kitty, kitty," she whispered. Nickels roosted on the chair's edge, yellow eyes half-closed, looking like a king on his throne.

She jiggled the cord again, and the plastic weights bobbed up and down, knocking together. "Come here, Nickels!" she said quietly.

The cat seemed insulted by her attempt to lure him with something as juvenile as a cord. *All right, then, mister, have it your way.* Sabrina took hold of the chair's back and tipped it forward until the cat leapt off. He turned and stared her down.

"It's not as if you gave me a choice."

From the other room, she heard the patio door slide open. Nickels's ears twitched, then he slinked out of the room.

Finally. Sabrina closed the door, making sure it caught so Nickels couldn't wander back in. Already she felt itchy—or was it her imagination? Like this wasn't difficult enough without adding a cat to the mix. She sat on the chair, hoping there was a minimal amount of dander in the area.

She opened the email program, noticing the check beside her

hand. How was she going to take his money? What she was doing was no better than stealing.

What kind of person was she?

She couldn't keep it. Bad enough that she was wasting his time, getting his hopes up; she was not taking his money too.

She opened the next message. She could do something else with the money. Something Tucker would approve of. She could donate it to some cause or charity or even to his church. She remembered his first messages on Nantucket Chat about the island's ecology. He was passionate about protecting it. Maybe she could donate the money to Nantucket Soundkeeper. It wasn't ideal, but at least his money would be used for a cause he believed in.

She spent the next thirty minutes reading letters and jotting notes. She'd once written that she was going into the city, saying it facetiously at first because Nantucket Town was a far cry from the city, but she left the phrase in the email, thinking it would throw him off track.

She jotted down a note that Sweetpea must live near a big city. Of course, that still left it wide open. She needed to make this mission seem futile; otherwise, after she failed, he'd hire someone else.

She rubbed her eyes and opened the next email—the one where she'd told him about Jared. She'd vacillated about whether or not to tell him. In the end, she'd decided it couldn't hurt when he didn't know who she was. She read the end of the letter where she'd summarized her thoughts.

I know Jared and my cousin didn't set out to hurt me. Things are never that simple. People make their bad choices with a side of justification and a side of entitlement, never considering the pain their overindulgence might cause. Even if they had carefully considered the ramifications, they couldn't possibly have imagined what deep damage their selfishness would inflict.

"She has a way with words." Tucker's voice startled her.

She hadn't heard him enter the room. He stood beside her, too close. She felt his hand pressing on the chair's back near her shoulder.

"Almost poetic, don't you think?" he asked.

Sabrina cleared her throat. "She did say she enjoys poetry."

Something rubbed against her leg under the desk, and she remembered the cat. She sneezed, hard and sudden.

"Bless you," Tucker said.

Her nose started to run. She sniffed.

"Tissue?"

The cat curled around her leg. "I'm fine."

Her eyes started itching. She rubbed casually. She had to get that thing out of there.

"Turn up anything new?"

Sabrina nudged the cat with her foot.

"A few things." She handed him her list, hoping he'd take it and leave, cat and all.

Instead he sat in the chair beside her. *Great*.

"The city, huh?"

She sniffed again. A sneeze was coming. She could feel it. She breathed through her mouth, hoping to squelch it. "She mentioned going to the city," she said between silent gulps of air.

"She didn't say which one."

"True." Under the guise of shifting her legs, Sabrina knocked Nickels away from her feet.

"Do you know how many cities there are? And who says she even lives near it? I don't remember her mentioning it other than the one time."

She tried to blink away the itch in her eyes. Were they turning bloodshot? She needed to blow her nose.

She was surprised she was reacting so severely to a cat that had been in the house less than twenty-four hours. She turned away from Tucker to discreetly wipe her nose and saw something she hadn't noticed before.

A cat bed. Just then Nickels slinked toward the round sheep-skin-covered bed.

Oh, great. This is Nickels's bedroom. That explained why she was having such a—

"Uh-CHOOOO!" The sneeze sneaked up on her. She glanced at Tucker.

His brows hiked upward. "Bless you."

She had to get out of there. It would only get worse. "Goodness. I must be coming down with something." *Like allergies. Or insanity.*

"Can I get you anything? Tylenol? Orange juice?"

Beside the desk, Nickels curled into a ball and closed his eyes.

Another sneeze was building at the back of her nose. Her throat felt scratchy, and any minute her eyelids were going to swell.

Tucker was going to figure it out if she didn't get out of there. Quickly. "No, I—I think I need to go home and rest." She stood, grabbing her bag.

"Oh." His voice rang with disappointment. "Are you sure?"

She felt terrible, but what could she do? "I'll be fine by Monday." *Presuming that infernal hairball is gone.* The pressure at the back of her nose was building. *Get out of here, Sabrina.*

"Hope you feel better." Tucker stood as she walked toward the office door.

The sneeze was coming. *Breathe through your mouth.* She'd reached the hallway when she heard his voice again.

"Don't forget your check."

She returned and snapped the paper from his hand as the sneeze ripped through her, louder than the last one. She couldn't cover her mouth in time. "Sorry." She turned and rushed toward the door.

"Take care of yourself," Tucker called, but by then, she was out the door.

⌒⌒

Tucker watched Sabrina pedal away on her bike until she rounded the corner and headed toward Main Street. He slapped the wooden door frame with his palm. *Way to go, McCabe.*

Not only had he succeeded in causing Sabrina pain and misery, but his plan to force her out of hiding had totally backfired. He'd accomplished nothing except chasing her away. He shook his head. *Brilliant.*

He turned into the house and shut the door. He'd been so close. It had been on the tip of his tongue after the second sneeze. *Maybe you're allergic to cats.* It would've been so easy, such a reasonable remark. It might've been the nudge she needed to admit who she was.

Maybe that one sentence would've helped. If only he'd been able to say it. He nearly *had*.

But then he'd seen the look on her face. The fear scrolled between her eyebrows, glazing her eyes. She had the look of a trapped animal, and he couldn't do it. Words she'd written months ago surfaced in his mind, words about people inflicting harm on others without thought to the ramifications. Maybe using the cat against her was a small thing when weighed against the actions of Jared and her cousin, but the fact that he was capable of this small infraction against her shook him, shamed him.

Nickels entered the living room and stared at him, eyes half-closed, and Tucker could have sworn they were full of reproach.

"What are you looking at?"

The cat lifted his pointy chin and exited as quietly as he'd appeared.

Tucker made his way toward the office. He had a bed to move and a room to vacuum.

Harbormaster: Growing up, I thought my sister and I would always be together. After all, we'd been in the womb together, shared everything all our lives. We grew up and went our separate ways, though we remain close. And one day I know I'll be married and my wife will be everything to me—even closer than a twin sister.

Ten

The next week Tucker was relieved that he'd successfully removed the cat dander. Sabrina didn't sneeze once all week.

That was the good news. The bad news was his plan wasn't progressing as quickly as he'd like, and he was running out of time. Sabrina was working through the emails all too fast. Maybe if they did something together. Something that didn't involve computers and lists. Something that would force her from her comfort zone and put them face-to-face.

But he'd already taken her out on his boat, and what had come of that? Nothing.

It was time to raise the stakes. He wandered into his office and sat where Sabrina had been an hour earlier. He picked up the tablet with her notes. She was careful, including only innocuous details that were so broad as to be useless, or things he'd already listed.

Can't whistle

Takes a daily walk

Likes her steak well-done

Reads mysteries

Has an aversion to bees

He smiled at that one. Sabrina had been stung on the eyelid when she was five and had been terrified of bees since.

Imagine a chicken flapping her wings and running in circles, and you have an accurate picture of me in the presence of a bee. Not rational, I know, but I can't seem to help it. I once spilled a glass of fruit punch all over my cousin's favorite pashmina scarf in my hysteria.

He opened the email program and checked his inbox. It was empty. She wasn't writing as often as she had before she'd started working for him. But then, she had less time. He missed her. How could he miss someone who sat right next to him? Because the Sabrina he loved was honest and vulnerable, but the Sabrina who worked for him wasn't sharing that part of herself yet. He missed that intimacy.

He opened a blank email and started a letter. Right now he didn't want to trick her or corner her, he didn't want to manipulate her. He just wanted to talk with her.

I miss you, Sweetpea. Work's been hectic, but you must be busy too.

I took in a friend's cat last week. Yeah, I know, I'm a glutton for punishment. The thing did not like me. I have several scratches to prove it.

Read any good books lately? I got another novel at the library, but couldn't make it past page twenty. You can't say I didn't try. I'll leave the fiction to you and stick with the newspaper.

Tucker paused, his fingers hovering over the keyboard. He wanted to say so much more. *I miss you. Even when you're here, I miss you. Why won't you open yourself to the possibility of us? Every time you're near me, I want to touch you. But if I did that, I'd scare you away. You're like a doe in a field, so beautiful and proud and strong. But at the slightest hint of danger, off you go. What are you so afraid of?*

Tucker scowled at his thoughts. He couldn't say any of that. He'd nearly scared her off for good when he'd mentioned meeting in the first place, and he wasn't going to risk losing his only contact with her after she finished this job. Or rather, failed at finishing this job. He knew that was the plan, and it frustrated him, but that's what he deserved for backing her into a corner.

Did I do the wrong thing, God?

It was too late for that question, wasn't it? But it was never too late to ask for help. He whispered a quick prayer, then sent the email.

He wondered if she was home. Maybe she'd get his message and reply. It had been a while since their last exchange.

The house was quiet except for the hum of the dishwasher. He'd offered Sabrina a slice of the roast he'd slow-cooked that day, but she'd turned it down as always. He wondered if he could convince Sabrina to stay for dinner after she finished. He could cook while she worked, maybe grill a couple steaks on the deck, serve her the corn he knew she wouldn't eat, couldn't eat, ever since she'd gotten sick on it in the seventh grade.

He fantasized about sharing a candlelit meal on the water with a salted breeze ruffling her hair. Sure, she wore it scraped back in that ponytail, but it was his fantasy; he could imagine her hair down if he wanted.

If only they could have a normal date. The kind where he picked her up and took her someplace quiet, where she could let down her guard and let him in a little. But he couldn't ask Sabrina out. She knew he was in love with Sweetpea, and he wasn't supposed to know she and Sabrina were one and the same. How would it look to her if he put the moves on her?

Well, you've got yourself a quandary, don't you?

The computer chimed as a message appeared in his inbox. Sabrina.

I can't believe you took in a cat. That's above and beyond.

I haven't had time to read lately, but am hoping to get back into a good book soon. I still think you need to keep trying until you find what you like. There's a genre for everyone. I haven't given up on you. ☺

I got a wedding invitation from Jared and my cousin.

That was the end of her message. His thoughts spun like a whirlpool. How had the news affected her? Was she still pining for Jared? She hadn't seemed upset at the café or at his house.

He replied, hoping she hadn't left.

I'm sorry. When?

Less than a minute later, her response arrived.

About a month ago. :-/

A month ago? He'd wanted to know when the wedding was, but she must mean it had been a month since she'd received the invitation. And she was just now telling him? It must've hurt if she hadn't told him sooner. And if it hurt, maybe she still loved Jared. Tucker was hurt now too. Hurt that she still had feelings for Jared and that she hadn't confided in him sooner. He poised his hands over the keyboard and typed.

When's the wedding? I really am sorry. ☹

At least she was telling him now. What did she need from him? He wished he could do more than type a few words of encouragement. He wanted to hunt Jared down and beat him to a pulp, but that's probably not what she needed from him. He wished that he could at least wrap his arms around her and tell her he loved her, that Jared didn't deserve her anyway.

Another email arrived.

Twenty-second of August.

He typed a response,

Are you doing okay? Want to talk about it?

A few moments later another message arrived.

No, thanks. I'm coping. Just wanted to tell you.

'Cause I could beat him up, if you want, he replied, then sat back, waiting for her response. It arrived seconds later.

<g> Good to know. I'll let you know if I need to call in my manpower.

Tucker grinned. He wondered if her family had given her any warning. But she didn't want to talk about it, so he refrained from asking. Instead, he asked the obvious question.

Are you going?

He pushed Send.
Before he could lean back, she replied,

Going where? :-P

He smiled.

To the wedding, goofball.

No.

When the sinking sensation hit his gut, he realized he'd been hoping she'd go. To avoid the wedding meant she was still angry with her cousin. And if she was angry with her cousin, she still had feelings for Jared, didn't she?

Coward. Just ask.

Before he could stop himself, he typed the words.

Do you still love him?

After he hit Send, regrets of all sizes and shapes crowded into the room. What if she did? She still wore that infernal bracelet, and he was sure it was a gift from Jared. Why would she still wear it if she was over him? He considered writing back. *Never mind*, he'd say. But before he could act on the thought, another message appeared. Maybe he should delete it without reading.

Who was he kidding? He wanted to know. Needed to know. He felt sick as he opened the email.

Why do you ask?

Well, duh. Wasn't it obvious he had feelings for her? Maybe he'd never come out and said he loved her—she might think it was weird or pathetic.

Why didn't you answer my question?

He tapped his fingers on the keys, waiting. It had been over a year since she'd seen Jared. Could you love someone that long from a distance? Could you even be certain of your feelings?

A new message arrived.

My aunt and uncle seem to have given up on reaching me. Part of me is relieved, but I admit the victory feels a little hollow.

She was changing the subject. Not a good sign. He replied,

Maybe they haven't given up. They're probably distracted by the wedding.

He hated the loneliness her words implied. She knew he was there for her, didn't she? A message appeared.

Maybe.
And no, I don't love Jared.

Relief filled him. If she didn't love Jared, there was room in her heart for him, wasn't there? Feeling renewed, he changed the subject to current news events, secure in the knowledge that, while her heart may not fully belong to him, it didn't belong to someone else either.

Sweetpea: I got the name Sweetpea from my mom. I don't remember much about her, but she was always working in our garden. I can still hear the soothing sound of her voice as she whispered "Goodnight, Sweetpea" from my bedroom door.

Eleven

A week later Sabrina was grabbing her bag from the kitchen counter when she noticed the blinking light. Checking the time, she decided she could spare an extra minute before leaving for Tucker's. Char had been queasy when Sabrina left the café. Maybe Gordon needed her to finish Char's shift. Truth was, she'd welcome the opportunity to avoid Tucker.

The stress was eating her alive. Sitting there, pretending to work, desperate to escape before she did something stupid, like grabbing the man and kissing him full on the mouth. One of these days, her facade was going crack wide open and she'd find herself chin deep in a pit of humiliation.

She pushed the machine's button and listened.

"Hey, Sabrina! It's Arielle. I left a message last week, but you didn't return my call. A-hem! But my feelings aren't hurt. Really. Not hurt at all.

Anyway, call me back, okay? For real this time. I'll keep pestering you until you do. You know I will . . . Bye!"

Sabrina deleted the message and headed out the door. She wouldn't return this message either. And yes, her cousin would continue leaving messages and sending emails. Sabrina knew what Arielle wanted, and her cousin wasn't getting it.

She pushed up the kickstand, hopped on her bike, and began pedaling down the lane. The incident with Jared and Jaylee had drawn a line between Sabrina and her family. And Arielle stood on the line, trying to pull everyone to the middle. Arielle had always been the mediator, but never had her job been so impossible. Maybe that skill served her well in class, but they weren't three-year-olds fighting over a canister of red Play-Doh. Sometimes there was no good resolution.

When she reached town, she stopped to let pedestrians cross. Town was packed when the summer people arrived. She couldn't fathom having a vacation home and six free weeks to spend at it. If she did, she would put up a hammock on her back porch and read all day. But the summer people seemed to prefer sunning at the beach, spending money in the boutiques, and being waited on in the restaurants. Sabrina would rather learn to cook her own gourmet food. But what was the point when she was only feeding one?

Two black Labs were leashed to the bench outside the Even Keel Cafe, and a little girl stopped to pet them. Her parents nudged her along; then her dad swooped her into his arms, and the girl wrapped herself around him. The mom laughed at something the girl said. They looked like the all-American family.

Had she ever had that? Her mom had died of ovarian cancer when Sabrina was five. All she had of her mother were a few foggy memories and a handful of photos. Her dad had seemed like a ghost in the house after her mom died, and then he was gone too.

A horn blared, and she saw that the pedestrians had cleared. She pressed on the pedal and accelerated through town, passing the quaint shops and milling tourists, the wheels of her bike bumping along the cobblestone streets.

When she arrived at Tucker's house, Cody was sitting on his porch, reading a book.

"Hey, Sabrina."

"Hi, Cody." She stopped by Tucker's stoop, swung her leg around, then set the kickstand with the toe of her tennis shoe.

"Invitation for dinner's still good. We're grilling chicken fajitas, and my buddy Ron is making his famous homemade salsa."

Tucker was at the door, on the stoop really, glaring in Cody's general direction. "She's working tonight."

Sabrina tossed Cody a smile of consolation, though by the cocky look he was giving Tucker, he didn't need it. "Guess I'm on the clock," she said.

Tucker followed her to the office. The house didn't smell like supper as it often did, but maybe he'd been in a hurry and had grabbed takeout. Instead of savory scents, she relished the familiar woodsy fragrance of his cologne.

"You should be nicer to the tourists," she said. "It's good for the island economy."

"What am I, the welcome committee?"

Sabrina shrugged, then, settled at the desk, checked her notepad to see where she'd left off.

"How far along are you in terms of the emails?" Tucker asked from the doorway.

She opened the program and compared the date of the one she'd last read with the date of their first letters. "About five months from the time you began writing."

The tablet with her notes was open on the desk, so she started with the next email, hoping Tucker would leave.

"I was thinking we could have another brainstorming session. I have some steaks that I need to cook. How about I grill and we can have dinner while we chat? We can eat out by the water."

A working supper. It was on the tip of her tongue to say she'd already eaten. But she'd been in a rush after staying a few extra minutes to help Evan bus tables and hadn't had time. The last thing she wanted was to sit face-to-face with Tucker. She'd rather be next door with Cody and company.

That's not true, and you know it.

Truth be told, Tucker was just tempting. To know him so well and pretend as if she didn't . . . to care so much and pretend as if she didn't. It was too hard. She needed to get through these letters faster.

"Sabrina?"

If he wanted to use the time to brainstorm, who was she to argue? He was paying for her time.

"That's fine." She could do this. She'd done it on the boat; she could manage supper alone with him. All alone, on the tiny, secluded square of his deck.

"Great. How do you like your steak?"

She started to say well-done. But she'd put that on the Sweetpea list a few weeks ago. Plenty of people liked their steaks well-done, but the fewer similarities between her and Sweetpea, the better.

"Medium well," she said, grimacing on the inside. The thought of pink meat nauseated her.

"Give me half an hour?"

"Sure."

With that, he was gone, allowing Sabrina to work. Now she had a supper and an uncooked steak to endure. She wondered how she was going to control herself and her wayward thoughts through a romantic supper for two.

Shaking the thought, she delved into the next batch of messages. They were full of banal tidbits, so she noted the details on the sheet. How could she sidetrack him later? Sweetpea had made few comments regarding her residence, but now Sabrina had no way of misleading him.

She settled back in the chair and opened the next email. She remembered receiving the original message, and her heart tripped at the memory. They'd been exchanging emails late one night about mundane things, joking around, and then he'd sent this message:

Do you ever think about meeting in person?

She'd frozen in response to the words. What should she say? She had to answer. He was waiting.

Not really, she typed, and sent the message. Would he press her further? What would she say if he asked more about where she lived?

Why not?

Fear curled inside her, thick and hot. Her fingers poked at the keys.

What's with the twenty questions?

Her mouth was as dry as the sand at Jetties Beach. She didn't have to wait long for his reply.

I really want to meet you.

And there it was. Tossed out like a water bomb from a second-story window, and just as unrescindable.

Suddenly their correspondence didn't seem safe at all. It felt immediate and threatening. Like waking from a dream to find it was real after all. Her heart knocking against her rib cage, she'd closed the message, closed the program.

The next morning a message had been waiting in her inbox.

I'm sorry if I overstepped a boundary. Let's forget I said that, okay?

He changed the topic, telling her about a customer who'd been terrified of the water. Sabrina had been relieved at his change of heart, and he hadn't mentioned meeting again until months later.

"Dinner's ready." Tucker leaned against the door frame, arms crossed, as if he'd been there a while. She'd been so absorbed in the emails, she hadn't heard him. So much for remaining detached.

Shaking the remnants of trepidation, Sabrina followed Tucker down the hall and out the sliding door. Three stairs led down to a water-level porch where a plank deck nestled against the back of his house. A wooden railing was the only barrier between them and the boat–dotted harbor.

He gestured toward the round wicker table, set for two. A terracotta pot with a cluster of purple pansies graced its center.

"I hope you like iced tea," he said after they were seated.

"That's fine." A steaming baked potato accompanied the steak. And beside it, corn. Her stomach turned. She retrieved her fork and knife and cut into the steak, then felt like a heel when he bowed his head in prayer.

"I think I may have overcooked your steak," he said when he finished praying. "The timer for the potatoes went off, and I got distracted."

The steak was brown throughout. "It's perfect." Thank God for distractions. What was she going to do about the corn? Everyone liked corn. Everyone except her. It only took her right back to seventh-grade gym class, where she'd vomited her lunch on her favorite Nikes in front of everyone.

"So, tell me about yourself." Tucker stabbed his meat. "You work at the café, do some editing and research for Renny Hannigan. What else is there to know about the mysterious Sabrina Kincaid?"

She took her time chewing the meat, then sipped her tea. "There's no mystery. I grew up in the South and went away to college. I visited Nantucket on my—vacation—and decided to stay. I guess you could say the beauty of the island lured me."

In truth, it had been weeks before she'd come out from her

depression enough to notice the beauty. Slowly, she'd noticed the sweet scent of hydrangea, the rugged, scraggly brush, the beauty of the marina. Initially her only reason for staying was she hadn't wanted to return to Macon. The island felt isolated from the rest of the world, an incubator, and she'd been in sore need of the respite.

He was waiting for her to continue.

"I saw a Help Wanted sign in the window of the café for a server and got the job." She wondered if he thought that was a lame job for someone with a college degree. But he'd quit law school to follow a less lucrative passion.

"I'd intended it to be temporary until I found something more fitting with my degree, but the tips were good, and then I found Renny. My work with her is fulfilling, and it could turn into full-time eventually." She regretted mentioning her degree and hoped he wouldn't inquire further. "Either way, I've enjoyed working with her and have even considered getting into editing someday." See, she had ambitions.

"Tell me about your work with Renny. We attend the same church, but I didn't know she was an author."

"She has an agent, but she's not published yet." Sabrina eyed Tucker. "I thought we were going to brainstorm."

"Are you in a hurry?"

She shrugged, then wiped her mouth. "It's your dime."

"That's right, it is. About Renny . . ."

His eyes twinkled. Why was he curious about her boring life? For a man so rushed to find his lady friend, he was sure taking his time.

"I struck up a conversation with Renny at the café when she was reading a book I'd recently read. We started talking about plots and characters; then she invited me for supper to pick my brain about her work in progress. When my ideas worked for her, she asked if I'd be interested in exchanging room and board for help on her stories."

"But she's not published?"

Sabrina shook her head. "She should be though. She just finished her ninth manuscript, and it's superb. Frankly, I'm shocked her work hasn't been picked up yet."

"She told me you have of way of inventing complicated plots and twists."

Sabrina salted her potato and stirred. "I read a lot. I guess it becomes intuitive after a while." *Change the subject before he asks what you read.* She didn't want to lie, and he knew Sweetpea read mysteries.

"You have a beautiful home." The sun, low in the sky, glowed behind a swath of pink clouds. Somewhere nearby, a boat knocked against the rubber sides of a pier.

"Thanks."

They ate in silence a few minutes. She should ask about him, but couldn't bring herself to inquire about things she already knew. Besides, the sooner they got on with this, the sooner she could leave.

She finished her potato and began poking at the corn. She had to get rid of it. Her stomach gurgled in response to the thought.

She drained the last of her iced tea. "Could I bother you for another glass?"

"Glad to."

When he was out of view, she scraped the corn into the water.

Great. Corn floats. She helped it toward shore with her hand and was in her seat before Tucker returned.

"Thanks." Now that the corn was gone, she could focus on laying the groundwork for the inevitable conclusion that Sweetpea was unfindable.

"I have to say," she started, "most of Sweetpea's clues are vague."

A bee hovered around the porch railing behind Tucker. Sabrina tensed. *Go away, bee.*

"She's been careful not to reveal important details," he said.

The bee passed the railing and entered the porch, flying toward the table. *No, no, no. Go away.* Sabrina set down her fork, keeping a close watch. It flew over Tucker's shoulder and headed toward her.

She pressed her spine against the wicker back, barely breathing. Everything in her wanted to jump up and run into the house.

It's just a bee. It's. Just. A. Bee.

"I keep thinking there must be something there, though," he said. "With so many messages, surely there are enough clues to get us close."

The insect stopped over the pansies, hovering. It caught Tucker's eye. He moved his hand off the table as if to shoo it away, then reached for the saltshaker instead.

Don't panic. It's not going to hurt you. It's just investigating the flowers. She should say something. Her mind couldn't seem to formulate a thought. The bee nearly settled on one of the petals, then moved on to the next.

She glanced at Tucker. He was studying her, one eyebrow higher than the other. *Say something.* "Maybe I'll find something as I get through the rest of the letters."

The bee hovered higher, seemingly bored with the flowers. It flew toward her. She held her breath as it floated in front of her. A red shirt! She'd worn a red shirt. *I'm not a flower, stupid bee!*

"Are you okay?"

Breathe, Sabrina! The bee closed in. She could hear the buzz of its wings. She grabbed her napkin from the table and swatted it away, trying to appear calm despite the fact that her insides were as volatile as a shaken can of coke.

Tucker reached out and waved his hand until the bee retreated. It flew over the railing and around the corner.

"Don't like bees?"

She wasn't hiding it as well as she'd thought. "Not so much."

She reached for her fork. She was trembling, for heaven's sake. She darted a glance toward the corner to ensure the bee wasn't returning for the giant red flower.

"You were saying?" Tucker said.

Sabrina had no idea what she'd been saying. She sucked in a cleansing breath. Where was she?

Oh, yes, that it was time to lay some groundwork. She sipped her tea. "I just read the message where you asked about meeting her."

Tucker's eyes fell, his lashes hooding his blue eyes.

What was he thinking? Was he reliving the moment when she'd ignored his question? How long had he waited that night for her reply? How had he felt when he realized she didn't want to meet? If only she could've explained.

"Why did you ask her?" The question escaped before she could stop it.

"When you really connect with someone, it's a rare and valuable thing. I'd come to care about her." He gave a half grin. "It might seem crazy that I feel so strongly about a woman I met online, but it's not. It's real."

The passion in his eyes mesmerized her. "Why do you care so much about her?"

"Why do you ask?"

She froze for a second, then took a sip of tea and picked up her fork. Was she wrong for keeping him at a distance?

What if? What if she let it happen? What if she told him she was Sweetpea and let the cards fall where they may? She looked at the familiar planes of his face and wondered what it would be like if she had the privilege of running her hand along his jaw, of kissing his eyelids closed, of tucking her face in the crook of his neck, and breathing in the scent of his skin.

What would it be like to come home to him, his smell, his touch, rather than a skimpy email?

She set her fork down and laid her napkin on her plate. She wasn't Arielle, with long, blonde hair and stunning good looks. She was Sabrina, plain and awkward. *Imagine what he'd think if you told him who you are. Imagine the disappointment. The confusion.* And that was just for starters. Eventually he'd find out what she'd done and the relationship would be set on a course for disaster.

She couldn't tell him. To do so would risk everything. She swallowed against the ache in her throat. "It's obvious she doesn't want to meet," she said as gently as she could.

"I've never been one to give up easily."

He was downright stubborn about some things. "What did she say the next time you asked?" The words escaped before she realized her mistake. How could she know he'd mentioned it again? "I'm assuming you asked more than once."

"She insisted she wanted to keep the relationship the way it was. She said it worked for her that way."

"But it doesn't work for you." *What are you doing, Sabrina?*

He pushed back his plate and folded his arms on the table. "I want more."

Her eyes locked on his. She couldn't pull them away if she tried. And truth be told, she didn't want to try. He was looking at her as if . . . as if he *wanted* to look at her.

You're misreading the signal.

He was looking at her like Jared had when he walked her to her apartment at college. When the night was over, but he didn't want it to be. Tucker was looking at her the way Jared had right before his lips found hers.

Ridiculous! Tucker had feelings for Sweetpea, not her. So they were one and the same—he didn't know that. He couldn't be making eyes at her when he thought he had feelings for someone else.

Could he?

"Why do you think she doesn't want to meet?" Vulnerability weighted his eyes.

What could she say that wouldn't hurt him? "Maybe, for whatever reason, she's comfortable with the status quo. Maybe she can't risk losing what she has for the mere possibility of something more."

"Isn't it worth the risk?"

"Not to her, maybe." She was getting perilously close to the cliff's edge. She tore her gaze away, twisted the watch on her wrist. "Or there could be some other reason. Who knows?"

"You think she's married, don't you?"

Sabrina looked up, surprised. "What? No."

"'Cause she's not."

"I never said she was."

"What, then? Locked in someone's attic? In a women's penitentiary? What possible reason could she have for not meeting?"

"I doubt her reasons are so concrete. People are motivated by numerous things, many of them internal and intangible. We could sit here and speculate all day and still not come close. In the end, what does it matter?"

"It matters to me."

"Why? What if you find her and she didn't want to be found? What if she's not who you think she is? How would that affect your relationship? What if it changed everything? What if it ruined what you have now?"

He took that in, staring over her shoulder. The sun had disappeared and the sky had darkened as if someone had twisted a dimmer switch. "It won't."

"You can't know that."

He looked at her, his eyes glittering. "It's a risk I'm willing to take."

"Well." Sabrina clasped her hands tightly in her lap. "Maybe she's not."

Sweetpea: There's nothing like running to pound out your frustrations. After the episode with Jaylee and Jared, I was fit for a marathon.

Twelve

Sabrina's feet pounded the vacant cobblestone street. In the distance, dawn's fingers curled around the horizon, nudging the sky awake with shades of midnight blue and periwinkle.

She liked this time of day, before the island awakened, before the chatter of birds roused the tourists. This time of day she could be alone with her thoughts and enjoy the quiet island sounds that were swallowed by the daytime bustle. The whisper of sea oats brushing together, the sound of the leaves shimmying in the wind.

When the street opened to the wharf, she turned and made her way toward Brant Point Lighthouse and Jetties Beach, where her calves would get a good workout on the sand. Her breath came in shallow puffs, and she welcomed the salt-laden breeze that blew in off the harbor.

Her thoughts turned to the message Arielle had left on her voice mail the day before. How many phone calls would Sabrina have to ignore before her cousin would give it up? Maybe after the wedding, things would settle down and everyone would go back to their lives and leave her alone.

She turned onto Easton Street, realizing her feet had carried her to the route she tried to avoid. She picked up her pace; the sooner she passed it, the better. The White Elephant stood to her right, the hotel's lights still glowing in the early morning hours. But she didn't look. Wouldn't look.

Her lungs protested the sprint, but she kept on. Sweat trickled down her neck and between her shoulder blades. She pushed herself harder, lengthening her stride until she was past the property. Only then did she slow her pace, letting her speed taper to a walk as she neared the end of the road where the beach met the pavement. Her lungs worked to keep pace with her pounding heart. She drew her wrist across her forehead, across her eyes, trying to wipe away the sweat, the thoughts. But still the memory came. The memory of the night that had started it all. Had started a cataclysmic chain of events that changed her life forever.

The restaurant had been slow, and her boss let her go home halfway through her shift. "You've been working so many hours, kiddo. Besides, I'm sure you have last-minute wedding things to do."

Sabrina was grateful. She'd been unprepared for the hundreds of details involved in planning a wedding, and even though Aunt Bev had helped, Sabrina wanted everything to be perfect. She smiled, checking the date on her watch as she drove home. Six more days. She considered stopping at Jared's apartment, but she needed to decide on seating arrangements for the rehearsal dinner, wrap the wedding party gifts, and start packing for their honeymoon. Neither of them had been to Nantucket, but she'd heard it was the perfect honeymoon destination. Quiet and quaint, slow paced. She and Jared could rest after the hectic months leading up to the wedding. She needed to remind him to confirm their reservations.

She pulled into her apartment's drive. Jaylee was home, no doubt resting after a long day studying for her bar exam. Sabrina had been helping her between the hours at the restaurant and the wedding preparations.

She grabbed the bag from the passenger seat. She'd finally found something blue and wanted to show Jaylee. She found the silver pendant earrings with tiny light-blue stones in a small boutique that afternoon, and they were perfect.

The parking lot light buzzed overhead and cast a faint yellow tint on the graveled lot. On the second floor of the building, her apartment was dark behind the thin sheers. She entered the building, dashed up the carpeted stairs, then fished for her keys in her bag. The smell of garlic and onion filled the hallway, and she knew Mr. Figliono had fixed a big batch of lasagna again.

She shifted the bag to her other hand and unlocked the door, stepping through it and closing it behind her. Country music blared from the speakers, a male voice crooning about lost love.

Already Sabrina was considering the rehearsal dinner and wondering what she would do about Aunt Linda and Aunt Cathy. They didn't get along and, in fact, had not spoken since Christmas two years prior when Aunt Cathy bought presents after agreeing on no gift exchange. Words had flown, loud ones. A door had slammed; then tires had peeled from the drive, leaving a roomful of awkward silence.

It hadn't been the first family argument between them, Aunt

Bev had said. Sabrina couldn't imagine anything significant enough to divide two sisters.

Since that Christmas, holidays had been comprised of one aunt or the other, but not both under the same roof, and certainly not in the same room. Sabrina wondered how she could arrange them in a room with a U-shaped table. Maybe one or the other wouldn't show, but they'd both agreed to come.

She set her bag on the foyer table and kicked off her shoes, setting them out of the way. Her middle toe poked through a hole. Time for new socks. One more thing for her to-do list. It could wait until after the wedding. She would only need sandals on their honeymoon.

She rounded the corner where the hall opened to the small living room, her hand reaching for the light switch. But a noise, a groan, sounded over the country crooning. Through the sheers, the parking lot light shed a yellow glow over the space. Two people embraced on the couch. A man was half on top of Jaylee. Sabrina wondered if she should grab a blunt object or call 911. As her eyes adjusted, she realized her cousin was stroking the back of his head, not fighting him off.

Jaylee didn't have a boyfriend, and she didn't sleep around. Sabrina felt like a Peeping Tom standing there, watching. She stepped backward, wondering where she could go.

Her foot connected with the tall metal pail holding a cluster of artificial sunflowers. It scraped backward on the wood floor and clanged against the wall, an awkward percussion over the slow country verse. Jaylee and the man jumped apart.

Sabrina felt her face warming the instant before she saw his face.

In the dark, his features were obscured. It was his silhouette against the pale wall behind him. It was the way he hunched slightly, the way he cleared his throat.

Her fingers felt for the light switch on the wall and stumbled across the protrusion. She flipped it up.

Jared blinked against the glaring overhead light.

Jaylee jumped to her feet. "Sabrina!" She straightened her shirt. The top two buttons of her favorite pink blouse were undone.

Sabrina looked at Jared. His hand covered half his face, his elbow protruding outward.

Jaylee took a step toward her, reaching out.

Sabrina moved away. "Don't touch me." Her voice was a deep snarl.

Jared stood, looking at her, uncertain. "I'm sorry. I'm so sorry, Sabrina."

Sorry? She looked at the two of them. Their expressions, a mixture of shock, horror, and guilt, might have inspired laughter if the lump of pain in her throat hadn't choked it out.

"We didn't mean for it to happen," Jared was saying.

"We were going to tell you," Jaylee said.

How long had this been going on? "After the wedding?" She turned on Jared. "We're getting married in six days! _Six. Days._" How could he do this to her? How could he sit—no, _lie_—with her cousin on her couch? The couch she'd bought and paid for with her own money.

"We didn't mean for it to happen—didn't mean for you to find out like this," Jaylee said.

"How did you mean for me to find out? And when? Why are

you doing this?" Sabrina turned, disinclined to see them standing together like a—like a couple. Jaylee and Jared weren't the couple. Sabrina and Jared were. They were engaged.

"I'm sorry." Jared's voice sounded from behind her, close. The picture on the wall blurred in front of her. It was just like high school. Just like when Ethan Sterling had pretended to like her only to get invited to her house so he could be near Jaylee. Just like when David Ellenburg had befriended her only to pick her brain about Arielle. Just like all those times. Only worse. Much worse.

Jared's apology felt impossibly inadequate. How did an apology rectify the damage her heart suffered? How did an apology justify the pain they'd caused?

Was it only physical? Jaylee was so beautiful. She'd won most of the pageants she'd entered for a reason. Had she been too much for Jared to resist? Could Sabrina bring herself to forgive him?

"I'll leave you two alone," Jaylee was saying. She slid past Sabrina and slipped out the door. She didn't want to think about her cousin right now. One betrayal at a time.

The music died midsentence. Jared must've turned it off. The quiet was alarming, because now she could hear her heart thudding in her head, hear Jared's ragged rasps. Was he winded from the make-out session or from the distress of Sabrina's appearance?

"Come and sit down."

"I don't want to sit down." If he was going to beg her forgiveness, he could do it with her standing, face-to-face. She turned around and met his gaze.

He looked at the floor. "We need to talk."

"You think?" Was this the kind of man Jared was? The kind who was seduced by a pretty face? It was so contrary to her previous convictions it made her head spin. She couldn't have been more surprised if she'd arrived home to find her apartment upside down.

"We didn't mean for it to happen."

We. It was a couple word. But they weren't a couple. Sabrina and Jared were a couple. If she said it enough, it would be true.

"I should've told you. I'm sorry you found out like this."

A weight hung heavily in her middle, sagging downward, dragging her with it. She fought to keep her legs under her. "Should've told me what?" She nearly put her hands over her ears. Instead she steeled herself for his answer.

"It's over, Sabrina."

What was over? He and Jaylee? It was a quick, cold-feet thing, right? One last escapade before he settled down.

"What's—" She cleared her throat. "What's over?"

He looked at her now, but she wished he hadn't. His eyes were laden with guilt and pity. "Us."

She looked deeply into his familiar green eyes. There was nothing familiar about them now. She'd never seen this expression. Never wanted to see it again.

"We're getting married in six days." They had two hundred and forty-six RSVPs, two thousand dollars in flowers, and a three-thousand-dollar dress to prove it.

"I'm in love with Jaylee."

Each word was a nail in her heart. Everything in the room stopped. Everything in the world came to a screeching halt. Everything but the pain.

"What?" *You need to hear it again for torture's sake?*

"We didn't mean for it to happen."

"So you keep saying!" She ran her hand over her face. It was wet. She pushed at his chest with the palm of her hand. "How long?" she demanded.

He looked away, color blooming in his cheeks.

She shoved him again. "How long?"

His eyes glazed over. Good. She was glad he was hurting too. He deserved to hurt.

"I thought it would go away," he said.

"How long?" She needed to know the truth. All of it.

"A few months."

Her mind went back to the week before, when they'd gone to the beach for the day. To the week before that, when they'd shopped for a dress for the rehearsal dinner. To the time they'd gone bowling and laughed when she'd gotten five gutter balls in a row. All the memories from the past few months filed through her mind. All of them lies.

And now she'd lost Jared? Lost him to her cousin? The betrayal bit hard. It was too much. Too overwhelming to bear all at once. "Get out."

"Sabrina." He reached for her.

She flinched away. "Get out!" Her breath came hard and fast.

He stood, unmoving, hunched, for a moment. Then he walked away, toward the door. She heard the soft click of the latch settling into place.

The next six days had been a blur of pain, humiliation, and darkness. She'd cried out to God in bed at night, begging for mercy, begging for answers. Why had He let this happen? Why, when she'd been on the brink of finding her own happily ever after? But her questions went unanswered.

Aunt Bev had made most of the wedding cancellations. Jaylee had made herself scarce, going to stay with her parents.

Now, a seagull called, landing a few paces away in the sand. A wave washed up, and the gull scurried up the beach. The sky was filling with golden light. She had to get home for a shower.

Sabrina quickened her pace, falling into a swift jog. But she wondered if she'd ever run fast enough to escape the memories that haunted her.

Sweetpea: I don't like surprises. I know a lot of people say that, but I really mean it. I do not like surprises.

Thirteen

A week later Sabrina was halfway up the stairs to her apartment before she saw the woman blocking her door.

"Surprise!" Arielle spread her arms wide.

Her cousin wore white shorts that set off her tan, and her long hair was captured in a sleek ponytail.

"Arielle." Sabrina walked up the steps, taking in her cousin's floral suitcase, which looked large enough for a wardrobe or two.

Arielle embraced her, rubbing Sabrina's back. "Oh, it is so good to see you, cuz."

Sabrina had missed the Southern accent. "This is a surprise." An understatement.

A sudden thought sent a shiver of panic up her spine. What if Tucker saw Arielle? He would think she was Sweetpea. How long was Arielle staying? Sabrina had to keep her away from Tucker.

Arielle leaned back, propping both fists on her slim hips. "Well, it wouldn't have been if you'd returned my calls."

"Sorry about that." Sabrina unlocked the door and flipped on the lamp. "Come in."

Arielle rolled her suitcase over the threshold and shut the door. "Nice setup you got here, right on the beach. I met Mrs. Hannigan, but she didn't feel right letting me in without your knowledge, and I didn't want to call you—wanted it to be a surprise . . ." She struck a ta-da pose.

"Well, it certainly is." Sabrina set down her bag and offered her cousin a drink.

"How's your summer break going?" Sabrina asked after they were seated in the tiny living area.

"It's half over already. I miss those little rug rats." Arielle was born to teach preschool.

"You'll be back to school before you know it." A silence gathered between them. There was a white elephant in the room, and Sabrina was doing her best to ignore it.

"I guess you got the wedding invitation," Arielle said.

So much for denial. "Of course." Sabrina stood under the guise of turning on another lamp. "I'm not going, Arielle, so you can save your speech."

Arielle started to speak, but Sabrina put her hand up, palm out.

"I know you mean well, but I've made up my mind. I'm glad you've come for a visit, but let's be clear about this up front: I'm not going to the wedding."

"We don't have to talk about it today."

"Or tomorrow or the next day. Because it's futile."

Arielle studied Sabrina's face. Seeming to recognize her resolution, she turned and surveyed the room, running her hand along the back of the couch.

Sabrina perused the room with a fresh eye. She hadn't done much to the place since she'd moved in. It looked barren and void of personality.

"Did you pick the wall color?"

Sabrina had never liked the dark green, but hadn't cared enough to paint it. "It was that way when I moved in."

"Depressing, don't you think?" She peeked in the dining room. "I like the wood floors. Maybe I can help you with furniture placement while I'm here. The room lacks harmony. We'll have you feeling better before you know it."

"I feel fine."

"Aren't you going to ask about the family?"

"How's the family?"

"You don't have to be sarcastic." Arielle's smile softened her words. She squirmed on the sofa, clearly bothered. She seemed to shake the notion and continued, "Mom is wrapped up in the Miss Georgia Teen pageant. She's on the board again. Dad's traveling a lot still, but seems pretty happy with his work." She paused, as if wondering if it was safe to bring up Jaylee. "And, well, you pretty much know the rest. I'm moving up to the four-year-olds next year, so I'll have the same kiddos I had this year."

What Sabrina really needed to know was how long Arielle was staying. She was glad to see her cousin. She just didn't want Tucker to see her. Sabrina checked her watch. She was due at Tucker's in a couple hours.

"Am I keeping you from something? I don't want to rearrange a thing while I'm here—except maybe your furniture. I did just drop in, after all." Her jaw relaxed slightly, her lip dropping. "It is okay that I'm here, isn't it?"

Even with the pouty frown, Arielle was adorable. Sabrina wondered if she had any idea how lucky she was. "Of course it's okay." She'd missed Arielle. Hadn't known how much until she'd seen her in front of the door. "I do have a part-time evening job though, so I won't be home much. How long can you stay?"

Please not long, she thought, then felt guilty.

Arielle shrugged her tanned shoulders. "I'm free as a bird for another month. I booked a flight back in about four weeks—I hope that's okay."

A whole month? Sabrina pasted a smile on her face. How would she keep Arielle out of town that long? Nantucket wasn't that big, and she didn't want to consider what would happen if Tucker recognized her.

Sweetpea: I'm a little bit stubborn.

Harbormaster: No kidding.

Fourteen

Sabrina didn't notice when the rain began. Her eyes glued to Tucker's computer screen, she'd been absorbed in the messages that had flown between them several months ago. Focused on her new plan.

Only when a clap of thunder pealed did she glance out the office's bay window and see the sheets of rain pouring into the harbor.

Ordinarily, she loved a good downpour, loved the smell of rain, the sound of it on the roof. But today she'd ridden her bike to Tucker's, and the rain didn't look like it was letting up anytime soon.

Deciding to call it an evening, Sabrina shut down the program and gathered her things. When she entered the living room, Tucker was in the corner, carving a piece of wood that didn't yet resemble anything. He smiled as she entered the room, lowering his tool.

"I'm finished for the night," she said. "Can I use your phone?" If she could call a cab before Tucker offered her a ride, she wouldn't risk him seeing Arielle. Why hadn't she brought her cell phone?

"Something wrong?"

A crack of thunder sounded in the distance. "I need to call a cab." *Don't offer. Please don't offer.* She picked up the phone, then realized she'd have to look up the number. The phone book sat on the table under the phone.

He set down the block of wood. "I'll give you a lift."

She flipped open the yellow pages. "No, don't worry about it." While she waited for the cab, she could initiate her plan.

He stood. "Really, I don't mind."

There were too many cab companies to choose from. She picked one and dialed. "It's okay." She imagined him pulling up to her apartment at the same time Arielle arrived home. The thought sent a shiver of dread through her.

He took the phone from her and turned it off.

Why'd he have to be so persistent? She glared at him. "Why'd you do that?"

"It's pouring rain. Every tourist in town is calling for a cab, and you'll have a two-hour wait." He grabbed his keys from the table, then turned, giving her a look she couldn't decipher. "Unless you want to hang around for a couple more hours."

The thought was more tempting than he'd ever know. What choice did she have now?

Huffing, Sabrina headed toward the door. Anyway, what were the chances he'd see Arielle? It was pouring rain. She was probably taking a warm bath by now, or snuggled on the couch, watching the latest chick flick.

As soon as Tucker packed her bike in the trunk and backed the car from the drive, the rain let up. Naturally.

"How far are you with the letters?" he asked.

She'd just come to the one where she'd confided about her dad's death. He was the only person other than Jared whom she'd told. But she didn't want to talk about that. "Lots of back-and-forth stuff."

"She's fun to dialogue with." Sabrina could hear the smile in his voice. "Has a great sense of humor, don't you think?"

No one had ever told her that before. But then, she didn't let loose around just anyone. "You think?"

He propped one hand on the console between them, inches from her thigh. "She has a sarcastic streak a mile wide. A dry sense of humor."

Sabrina shifted away. "I suppose." The wipers arched across the windshield.

"She's witty and intelligent, has a great vocabulary . . ."

He was hitting too close to home. "I didn't notice." Her throat was dry as dirt.

He grinned, stealing her breath with that crooked smile. "That's because you have a great vocabulary."

In town there were tourists clustered under awnings, waiting for the rain to stop.

Tucker braked as a man and woman darted across the road. The man slung his arm around the woman, and they laughed as they ducked through the rain. Sabrina wondered if the couple was as happy as they seemed.

She remembered how it felt to be wrapped in a man's arms. To feel secure and loved. She missed that.

"I contacted the host of Nantucket Chat," Tucker said. "Did I mention that?"

"What for?"

Tucker accelerated through the crosswalk. "He knows the identity of all the members. When you sign up to participate, you have to give your name and contact information."

Why hadn't she thought of that? "What did he say?"

"He said the information is confidential."

She started breathing again. "That's too bad."

"I haven't given up yet. You still have a few months of messages to wade through, and there's always the chance she'll change her mind, right?"

She folded her arms around her stomach. "Actually, I think I may have found some significant details."

"Really?"

"The clues are spread apart, but I think she might be from Ohio."

"Really?"

Why was her heart beating so fast? "She mentions being a Reds fan, and she said something about the Cincinnati airport being in Kentucky. Most people wouldn't know that, right? And she mentions a pretzel festival. I looked it up online, and there's one in Germantown, Ohio, every September."

"There are probably pretzel festivals in other states."

"Maybe, but like I said, it's the cumulative factor. The Reds, the airport, the festival. There are other tidbits that go along with the Ohio theory, too, and nothing to contradict it so far." Of course, Ohio was plenty big, and there weren't enough clues to pin down a particular city. When she was finished, he'd see they were at a dead end.

"There's the beach photo," he said.

She was ready for that one. "It may have been a lake. The waves were small. It could be Lake Erie or any number of lakes. It could also have been taken while she was on vacation."

He pulled into her drive. "I guess you're right."

"So we should definitely focus on Ohio. Maybe I can pin it down to a city as I read further." Sabrina looked at her apartment window. The blinds were up, but the living room was dark except for the faint glow of the TV. *Stay away from the window, Arielle.*

The gravel popped under the tires as Tucker pulled the car to a stop and put it in Park. She reached for the handle. The sooner she got him out of there, the better.

"Wait." He set his hand on her forearm.

She turned and faced him. His palm was warm on her wrist, the heat of it sizzling a path up her arm. She waited for him to say something, afraid and eager at the same time.

"Thanks for what you're doing. I appreciate your help and your confidentiality."

"No problem." She glanced at her apartment. So far, so good. The rain was merely a drizzle now.

He was still holding her arm. She wondered what he'd do if she turned her hand over and twined her fingers through his. She itched to do it. Would he return the touch? She longed to be connected to him. Letters only allowed so much intimacy. She missed the personal contact. The touching. The security of an embrace. Would it be so awful to take the risk and see what happened?

But even as the thought formed, a memory rose, unbidden. A foreign touch, the smell of alcohol, the chill of a cold sheet.

Sabrina knotted her hand into a fist.

Tucker's hand slid down to hers, and he squeezed her closed fist. "You okay?"

She nodded, finding her voice. "Just tired." She glanced up at the window. A light came on. She looked at Tucker, but he was studying her hand. Thank God he hadn't seen.

"You always wear this." His fingers found the *S* charm on her bracelet.

The bracelet had once been a symbol of love. Now it was a reminder of loss. A tangible warning that some risks weren't worth the cost.

Sabrina pulled her hand away. "It was a gift." She pressed her lips together. She needed to get out of there before she said too much. Before she ruined what progress she'd made tonight. She reached for the handle and opened the door.

"I'll get your bike."

She followed him around to the back of the car, and he set the bike at her feet.

"Well, regardless of how this turns out, I've enjoyed getting to know you."

He was sounding as if this project was winding down. He must be buying her Ohio theory. "There goes my mysterious air."

"Oh, you got plenty of mystery left, don't you worry."

"Who's worried?" She reached for the bike's handles.

He laughed, deep and throaty. "Goodnight, Mystery Woman."

"Goodnight," she called, wheeling the bike toward the garage. Even as she scurried through the drizzle, she couldn't stop the smile that formed on her lips.

Tucker pulled from the drive, still smiling. So she hadn't admitted who she was . . . But she was still coming over every night.

Ohio. He shook his head. Well, at least he was spending time with her. She was opening up a little. Okay, so it was a minute amount, but it was something. Ten more years and she'd be an open book.

He breathed a laugh. He had time. He still had a few tricks up his sleeve, and she had four months of letters to wade through. Plus, the list of messages was getting longer every day as they continued to write. In fact, he'd write her when he got home. After all, the more they wrote, the longer she'd be around.

Harbormaster: After my sister's accident, I took her to physical therapy for months and tried to distract her from the pain. Once I got really stupid and stuck a Tic Tac up my nose. An ER tech had to remove it. Good news: It did get a laugh from my sister. What's the stupidest thing you've ever done?

Sweetpea: Go on my honeymoon alone.

Fifteen

"I'm going for a jog," Sabrina called to Arielle the next evening.

"Run a mile for me." Arielle changed the channel to a house-flipping program and settled into the sofa.

Sabrina trotted down the steps and walked down the lane at a brisk pace, warming her muscles. She couldn't stay home tonight. The emails she'd read earlier brought back too much, and it would drive her crazy to sit around dwelling on it.

When she reached the street, she turned toward town and settled into a slow jog. She felt guilty leaving Arielle home alone, but she needed to run tonight like she needed oxygen.

The heat of the day hadn't yet given way to the evening coolness, and the warm air burned her lungs as it came and went. When she reached town, she set a punishing pace, turning down Pleasant Street, hoping to avoid the worst of the traffic.

Daylight was fading, and the summer people were exiting rented homes, clicking down sidewalks in their heels toward their supper reservations. She navigated around such a couple as she crossed Main Street. The woman wore a filmy ivory dress, and the man matched her in his linen suit. They looked like they belonged in a Nantucket ad.

Sabrina hitched her sleeves up her shoulders, thankful for the breeze that whispered across her skin, even if it was warm. She wondered what Tucker was doing right now. Was he on his deck, enjoying the same breeze? Enjoying the way the evening light danced on the surface of the water?

She couldn't get out of there fast enough tonight. It had been disturbing to read that email, the message that had sealed her fate. The message that ensured Sabrina and Tucker could never be more than online friends. Even now, it replayed in her mind, words committed to heart, not by will, but by sheer repetition.

Tracey called today. She wasn't this despondent even after her accident, and I feel helpless to do anything about it. She's divorcing Sebastian.

Her mind flashed back to the first time she'd read the email, her heart skipping in response to the memory. It was the first time he'd mentioned his brother-in-law's name. The first time she'd realized that the terrible mistake she'd made had consequences that reached further than she imagined.

Her thoughts washed back farther in time to the night she'd arrived on Nantucket. To the night she'd met Sebastian.

She'd never felt more alone than she had upon entering the cavernous honeymoon suite at the White Elephant. The room featured a giant bed with puffy pillows, a fireplace, and an ocean view. On the table by the door, a bottle of champagne chilled in a bucket. Everything about the suite said "romance."

Her suitcase hit the floor with a thud, and she sank into the first chair she reached. She should've called ahead and told the hotel she was alone. Even with her aunt's help, there'd been so many things to do in the six days since she'd found Jaylee and Jared. Cancellations, phone calls, gifts to return. She hadn't realized how drained she was, how utterly empty, until this moment, sitting in the darkness in her honeymoon suite.

The amount of money her aunt and uncle had lost was mind-boggling. Sabrina tried not to feel guilty. It was Jaylee and Jared's fault, not hers. Both of them had tried repeatedly to contact her, but after one phone call with Jared, she was done with them both. What could they say to change things now?

Sabrina curled in the recliner, tucking her feet under her. The big bed loomed across the room. The big, empty bed. She and Jared were supposed to be here together. They should be celebrating the beginning of their life together, yet here she was. Alone. How could everything have changed so drastically in a week?

She wanted to curl up in that bed, draw the covers over her, and never come out. She shed her shoes and crawled under the covers, clothes and all. It wasn't quite dark out, she hadn't washed her face, hadn't brushed her teeth, but she didn't care.

Maybe she could spend the next seven days under the blankets. She could hang up a Do Not Disturb sign and disconnect the phone.

But regardless of how she spent the coming week, eventually it would end. And then what? She'd have to return to Macon and face them again. Her family, her friends. Jaylee. Jared.

Sabrina pulled the duvet over her head. She hadn't felt so alone since her father killed himself. Like it was yesterday, she could see his lifeless body on his bedroom floor the way she'd found it after school that day. She'd been nine then, in the third grade. She'd thought he was playing a game.

If her aunt and uncle hadn't taken her in, she would've spent the remainder of her childhood in a foster home. They'd made her feel like a sister and daughter. But the past week had shown her clearly who their daughter was. Blood was thicker than water, and Jaylee had more of their blood than Sabrina did.

She turned over and stared at the lit face of the clock. Were Jared and Jaylee together right now? Were they lying together in each other's arms? Were they glad she was gone so they could be together without having to hide their feelings?

The betrayal had carved an aching hollow spot in the middle of her stomach. She was tired of the ache. Tired of the pain. She wanted it to go away. But the truth was, the betrayal was only now hitting her fully. The busyness of wedding cancellations, she realized, had distracted her. And while all she'd wanted the last six days was to escape, she hadn't realized that being here, that being idle for seven days, would allow her full exposure to the pain.

Why did she lose everyone she loved? Her mom, her dad, now

Jared. Was she unlovable? Was there something about her that was so terribly flawed? Even God seemed so far away.

The ache grew, spreading, swelling, devouring her. Is this how her dad had felt before he killed himself? Had he suffered some heartbreak or had her mother's death been too hard to recover from? Still, he'd had Sabrina. Why hadn't that been enough?

You're not enough, Sabrina. You weren't enough for your dad, and you weren't enough for Jared.

Maybe thoughts such as these had driven her dad to that ultimate act of selfishness. Maybe she wasn't so very different from him. Maybe things like suicide were hereditary.

She rolled over and clutched her hands to her chest, feeling the bracelet Jared had given her all those months ago. It had been Valentine's Day and the bracelet had only held a single heart. Every special occasion after that, he'd given her another charm. A pearl birthstone pendant for her birthday, a key charm for their anniversary, a book charm, an *S* charm, and a ring for when they got engaged. Sabrina wrapped her hand around the bracelet, holding it close to her skin as if by grasping it she could keep a tiny piece of her life with Jared.

She closed her eyes against the throbbing ache. She was so tired. Tired of thinking, tired of hurting, tired of breathing. *Don't think. Don't think about anything except the sound of the water outside. The sound of it lapping the shoreline.*

Eventually she fell asleep, but when she awoke, she wished for sleep again, for oblivion. She spent the next day in her room, telling the maids she didn't need her room serviced. She ordered food only when her gnawing stomach became unbearable, took a long bath, watched TV without seeing it. When the phone rang, she disconnected it.

The next day, when the maids came to the door, she went outside and walked down the beach, listening to the lonely cries of seagulls and the shushing of water lapping the shoreline. When the maids finished, she was relieved to return to the cocoon of her room. The maids had replaced the tepid water in the champagne bucket with fresh ice.

Day three was a duplication of day two. The loneliness was getting to her, and the realization that she'd lost not only her fiancé, but her best friend and family, was weighing hard on her. She missed feeling wanted, feeling needed. She missed feeling normal. She'd never felt so unwanted. Not even in high school when she hadn't exactly shone like a star next to her beautiful cousins. Not even in the beauty pageant her Aunt Bev had entered her in.

Near the end of the week, when evening arrived, she felt suffocated by loneliness. The air in the room seemed thick and impossible to pull into her lungs. Two more days and she would face Jared and Jaylee. She didn't want to go home, dreaded the thought. Visions of her dad lying on the floor haunted her.

Her eyes fell on the champagne still nestled in the bucket. She picked up the bottle and went to work. The cork popped off. She poured the liquid into a fluted glass and made a toast.

"To life alone. May I never be so stupid as to love again." She drained the first glass. Then, feeling somewhat better, Sabrina poured another.

She wondered why she hadn't drunk the champagne earlier. To

think she'd suffered needlessly when a reprieve had been nearby all along.

This was better than lying around depressed. Better than contemplating the similarities between herself and her dad. She wasn't like him. Would never do something so horridly selfish and destructive.

Again, that vision of him on the floor, his denim-clad legs crumpled, his oval glasses askew on his ashen face.

She sprang to her feet.

She needed to leave this depressing place. Go someplace fun and lively. She'd stared at these four walls too long.

The only dress she'd brought slipped easily over her head. The waist hung loosely, so she tightened the belt, then went to run a brush through her hair. By the time she was ready, she almost looked like she fit in with the elite summer crowd.

The Nantucket air was mild at night, a warm breeze blowing in off the harbor. She walked toward town, her sandals clicking on the sidewalk. Main Street was lively. People on their way to supper, dressed in fine linen and suit jackets. There were a lot of couples, she noticed suddenly.

She looked around, from the cars on the cobblestone streets to the tourists milling on the sidewalks. She didn't see anyone alone. Only her. And where was she going to go? Supper reservations were necessary here, especially on a weekend, and she couldn't see herself dining in some exclusive restaurant anyway, certainly not alone.

Music and chatter poured from a doorway as she neared it. A shingled sign beside the canopied entrance read "Cap'n Tully's Tavern." She wouldn't feel out of place there. The sound of laughter pulled her inside. She could count on one hand the times she'd entered a bar. Her feet crunched over peanut shells as she made her way to a darkened corner and took an empty table, a low one with two stools.

The effects of the champagne were wearing off, and the idea of losing herself again held some appeal. She took in her surroundings. A pool table crowded the opposite corner, surrounded by four college-aged men. A few singles sat at the bar, nursing drinks, but even in here, there were couples. She felt like a wallflower, stuffed into the corner of the room, invisible, wilting.

I used to be half of a couple, she reminded herself. What a fool she'd been to think it might last forever. She'd never had Jared, not really. She wondered again what was inherently wrong with her. There had to be something.

Enough, Sabrina. These thoughts were only digging her deeper into the hole of despondency. Keep going and she would end up at the very bottom, where her dad had no doubt landed just before he took his life.

She was not like that. She was not.

When a young male server stopped at her table, she ordered a snakebite. She'd never had one, but there was no time like the present. Now that she'd found her drug of choice, why not take the shortcut to oblivion? It was better than sitting around, writhing in her pain. At least she was *doing* something. It felt good to have a little control back.

She tapped her stubby nails on the tabletop. They'd been long only a week ago. She'd taken exquisite care of them in the two months before the big day, and they'd been longer than ever. She'd had an appointment for a manicure the day before the wedding—another cancellation she'd made. But the six days of stress had taken their toll, and now the edges were short and ragged. She must have gnawed on them, though she didn't remember doing so.

A few minutes later, her shot and a wedge of lemon arrived. *Okay, here we go.* She licked the webbing between her thumb and index finger, salted it, then licked it again. Before the taste faded, she downed the tequila and bit into the lemon wedge. The sourness of the lemon puckered her lips, and she gave a shudder.

Jared's words from that night rang in her head. "*I'm in love with Jaylee. We didn't mean for it to happen. It's over, Sabrina.*"

"*It's over, Sabrina.*"

Were there sadder words in the English language? "*It's over.*" He didn't want her, was rejecting her, discarding her like yesterday's newspaper.

Stop it.

Sabrina ordered a second snakebite, and when it arrived a few minutes later, she repeated the process. She was starting to feel it.

Jared's words were fading like a dream sequence, and a warm, fuzzy feeling was taking their place.

Her gaze collided with a man across the room. He had dark, neatly trimmed hair, and a loosened tie. He was staring at her, or at least she thought he was. She was sitting in a corner, so there was no one behind her. But the room was dim, and maybe she was mistaken. A second glance proved her suspicions. He was at a high table, his hand wrapped around a fancy goblet. His lips turned up at the corners, and she realized she'd been staring.

Sabrina pushed the empty shot glasses past the flickering candle to the table's edge. Across the room, the bartender slid a full mug across the bar to a woman with short blonde hair and a long, ballerina neck. The bartender was flirting with her, smiling. He said something, and she tossed her head back and laughed.

Sabrina was feeling better. Almost giddy. She should've come here days ago instead of locking herself in that depressing suite.

The server approached, blocking her view. He set another snakebite on her table. "From the gentleman over there." He gestured to the corner, where Tie Man dipped his head and raised his goblet in a mock toast.

The server left, and Sabrina lifted her own glass toward Tie Man before she salted her skin and downed the shot. He hadn't taken his eyes off her. His white shirt almost glowed in the dimness of the room. He was broad shouldered and handsome. And he was interested in her.

The sudden knowledge flattered her, emboldened her. She stood. Her legs felt light, as if they were filled with helium, as she approached him. He watched her every step of the way, and when she stopped at his table, his eyes swept down her body to her bare knees, then back up again.

"Thanks for the drink," she said.

"Have a seat." He pushed out the empty chair.

Her body felt weightless as she sank into it. Her thoughts were pleasantly fuzzy. She leaned her elbow on the table and propped her chin in her palm. "I like your tie." It was red with white dots that played tricks with her eyes if she stared at it.

"I like your eyes."

She smiled coyly. "These old things?"

"They're like warm caramel in this candlelight."

Warm caramel. She liked the thought. She liked this man. He was handsome in a Wall Street kind of way, though his loosened tie made her think he was ready to kick back and relax.

"What's a pretty girl like you doing all alone tonight?"

She laughed, though she wasn't sure why. "Looking for company, what else?" It made sense suddenly, why she'd left the hotel, why she'd wandered toward town. It was company she sought. And it looked like she'd found it.

"What's your name?" he asked.

"Sabrina."

"Sabrina." He seemed to taste her name on his tongue. "Sexy."

He made her feel good. Or maybe it was the tequila. He took a drink from his goblet and it left his lower lip wet.

"What should I call you?" Sabrina reached across the table and drew her thumb across his lip.

He let out a quiet curse. "Whatever you want."

She laughed, tossed her hair aside. The movement made her dizzy. "Come on, I told you mine." She tugged his tie, enjoying the flirtation, feeling less like a wallflower and more like Ballerina Neck at the bar.

He smiled lazily. "Sebastian."

He looked like a Sebastian. "Well, Sebastian. What's your story? What do you do for a living?"

He grazed his index finger along the curve of her palm. "Do you really want to know?"

The way he looked at her with those mesmerizing gray eyes made her even dizzier. She realized she didn't care who he was or what he did. "Not really," she replied. His touch was warm and pleasant, making her tingle. He wanted her. The thought empowered her. Made her heady with excitement.

"Why don't we go someplace quiet?" The meaning in his eyes was clear, and suddenly Sabrina wanted that more than she wanted her next breath.

"Lead the way," she said.

He fished his wallet from his pocket and set two crisp bills on the table, hardly taking his eyes from her.

He pulled out her chair, and her head swam as she rose to her feet.

"Okay?" he asked.

She smiled. "Oh, yeah." She followed him through the maze of people and into the cool night.

"I'm parked around back."

She reached for his hand, but he ushered her in front of him, looking around. She drew in a deep breath of tangy sea air, letting it fill her lungs, then blew it out through her mouth. The gravel crunched under her sandals when they reached the parking lot. He opened the door of a low, sleek car, and she slipped inside.

Her skirt rode up high as she tucked her legs in. She laughed. "Whoops."

In the car, his hand found her leg, and she returned the favor. She felt so good. *This* felt so good. She leaned over the console and kissed his neck. He smelled like soap and alcohol. His face was rough, and she scraped her lips across his jaw.

He pulled her closer. She wished she could make the console disappear. It was a barrier, digging into her ribs.

By the time the car stopped, she was desperate for more. She followed him through the back door of a house, and she tripped over an empty suitcase. He steadied her, then pulled her into the darkness. She followed blindly, her needs propelling her.

⌒)(⌒

Sabrina woke to a distant thud. She opened her eyes, then shut them against the bright light pouring into the room. Maybe the thud had been her brain pounding against her skull.

Even closed, her eyes ached. The bed under her felt odd. Soft and not like her bed at all. Then she remembered. Nantucket. The hotel. But that didn't explain the sun streaming into the room.

She forced her eyes open in time to see the door to the room open. Where was she? She'd gone to a bar the night before.

An attractive brunette appeared in the doorway just as a body moved beside Sabrina. A man, bare chested, was awakening.

Sabrina felt a chill sweep over her and realized she was unclothed beneath the covers. She clutched the cool sheet to her chest.

The woman froze in the doorway, her ice-blue eyes widening. She looked back and forth between Sabrina and the man.

The bar. She'd been in the bar. Tie Man. He'd bought her a drink.

"Tracey!" Sebastian sprang up. He stared at Sabrina as if he wasn't sure how she'd gotten there.

"That's _it_, Sebastian. It's over!"

Sebastian jumped from the bed, tugging the sheet with him, wrapping it around his waist, leaving Sabrina exposed.

She grabbed the pillow, clutched it to her.

Sebastian cursed. "It's not—I'm sorry, baby!" He followed the woman—his wife? His lover?

Sabrina wasted no time finding her dress, lying haphazardly on the hardwood floor. Her head throbbed as she leaned over to retrieve it. She shrugged into her dress, sliding on her sandals even as she tugged the dress over her hips. She hopped on one leg, finding balance as she slipped on her second sandal, then scanned the room for her bag.

Then she realized he had driven her there. How would she get back to the hotel? She didn't even know where she was.

The woman was screaming now. "How dare you bring that tramp here! Sleep with her right under my nose!" Her voice wobbled erratically.

She had to get out of there. The voices were coming from across the house somewhere. She crept down the hall. Sebastian was apologizing, pleading. "Come on, Tracey—"

"Don't you touch me!" the woman said.

The back door was within sight. The voices were coming from the living room just beyond the kitchen. She could slip out without being seen. Her feet moved quickly across the linoleum. She opened the back door and escaped into the bright morning.

She walked almost an hour before she came to a main road. She'd asked a bicyclist for directions to town and had walked until her feet were blistered. By the time she'd returned to the hotel, the aftereffects of the tequila and her night of shame put her in bed for the day.

She'd known that night had been a terrible mistake, but she hadn't known until much later that it would ruin her chance with Tucker.

Now, Sabrina turned up the hill and blew out a shuddery breath before setting a punishing pace. If she ran hard enough, fast enough, maybe she could chase the memory from her mind.

Harbormaster: I love the way we talk about nothing.

Sweetpea: I love that I can say anything I want to you. I've never had that freedom with anyone else.

Sixteen

The next night, Arielle went shopping for some things to perk up the loft, giving Sabrina a chance to write Tucker. After she'd sent the first message, he'd replied, and they'd been chatting since.

Are you kidding? she wrote. *Name one good movie in the eighties. Just one.*

She sent it and leaned back, anticipating his answer. She realized she missed being with him on the weekends. She'd gotten accustomed to going to his house, to being with him physically.

She shook the thought, reluctant to spoil her good mood.

His response appeared.

Back to the Future. E.T. Raiders of the Lost Ark. Honey, I Shrunk the Kids . . . I could go on and on.

Honey, I Shrunk the Kids?, she replied.

He knew she wasn't a movie buff. Give her a good book any day. She wasn't even sure how they'd gotten on the topic, but that's how it was with them. They'd leap from one topic to another, and before she knew it, hours had passed.

"Ooooh, who's Harbormaster?" Arielle's voice made her jump.

"Don't sneak up on me like that." Sabrina's heart raced from the scare.

"I wasn't sneaking. You were just distracted." Arielle wiggled her eyebrows. "Is it a maaan?"

Sabrina closed the program before Arielle could snoop. "Yes, it's a man, but he's just a friend."

"A friend, huh?" Arielle tugged Sabrina's ponytail, then set a bag on the floor and sank onto the sofa, still panting from her trip up the stairs. "Does he live on the island?"

She supposed the truth couldn't hurt. "Maybe." She regretted closing the program without saying goodbye to Tucker. She'd write him when Arielle took her bath.

"So, are you, like, dating? Come on, tell all. How long has this been going on?"

"There's nothing going on. We're just writing each other. What did you buy?" Why did her cousin have to be so meddlesome? But then, maybe if Arielle saw she'd moved on from Jared, she'd stop pushing her to attend the wedding.

"Stop changing the subject. When did all this start? I know I'm being nosy, but give a single girl a break. I haven't had a date in months."

Sabrina couldn't imagine that was by anything but choice. "We've been writing a year or so."

"A year! And he hasn't asked you out?"

How could Sabrina explain without revealing everything? "I told you, it's not like that."

"Ha! I saw that look on your face when I came in. You were totally absorbed, and you had this goofy smile on your face."

"I did not have a goofy smile—"

"Did too. Completely goofy."

"Whatever. Don't you need a bath?"

"Changing the subject again?" Arielle raised an eyebrow. Finally, she jumped off the couch. "Fine, fine. Be all mysterious and secretive," she tossed over her shoulder, walking down the short hall.

"I will, thank you very much," Sabrina called after her.

The next week Sabrina had to admit that Arielle had livened up the quiet loft, and coming home to someone was nice, even if it did mean the TV was on too much. She'd bought a new rug and a giant oval mirror that she hung in the hall. That was coming down the instant Arielle left. Sabrina didn't need to see herself every time she came and went.

If only Arielle would stop pressing her about the wedding. If she had a dime for every time Arielle had said, *"But the family will be so disappointed . . ."*

"Order's up, Sabrina," Gordon called from the grill. She hadn't heard the bell. It was unlike her to be so distracted, but Arielle's arrival had discombobulated her. It was as if her two worlds, past and present, had collided. As much as she enjoyed Arielle, she couldn't help worrying that her path would cross with Tucker's. For that reason, Sabrina was eager for her cousin's departure. But she was beginning to think Arielle wasn't going anywhere until Sabrina agreed to attend the wedding.

Well, that wasn't going to happen.

Sabrina set the loaded plates on a tray and delivered them to table fourteen, a four-top by the front window. Outside the glass pane, the morning sun wakened a sky that promised to be clear and blue. The door's bell chimed, and Oliver shuffled in, nodding at her from across the room. She wondered what word he had up his sleeve today.

She went for the coffee carafe, and when she returned to fill Oliver's mug, Arielle was seated at the table diagonal to his. She looked flawless in a pastel-pink T-shirt. Her blonde hair framed her face, and pink lip gloss highlighted her trademark smile. Arielle waggled her fingers at Sabrina.

Panicked, Sabrina glanced at the clock above the door. Nine minutes after seven. Tucker would arrive in three minutes.

Three minutes. She had to get Arielle out of there. Quickly. He'd think he'd found Sweetpea, and then what? Everything would be ruined. And just when she was so close to convincing him that finding her was hopeless.

Sabrina made a beeline to her cousin, watching the smile slide from Arielle's face.

"You've got to leave," Sabrina whispered. She should've told Arielle not to come here. Why hadn't she just said it? Now look what was happening.

Arielle opened the menu. "What? I came for breakfast."

"I know. I can't explain now, but you can't stay." She checked the clock. Ten minutes after seven.

"Sabrina," Oliver said, tapping her arm. "Yesterday I gave one of my employees a vituperation. What do you make of that?"

She glanced in his direction. "Not now, Oliver."

Arielle perused the menu. Sabrina took it from her hands, watching her cousin's eyes widen. "You have to leave. Now. *Please.* I can't explain, but can you just trust me?"

Seeming to read Sabrina's desperation, Arielle eased back from the table and stood. "All right, but you are acting awfully weird, cuz, and I expect a full explanation later."

"Okay, okay." Sabrina ushered her toward the door, praying Tucker was running a minute or two late for once. The clock read 7:11. Her heart was in her throat, a solid lump that pulsated wildly.

The kitchen bell dinged. Table five's order.

Sabrina pulled the door for Arielle, but her cousin stopped on the threshold, coming face-to-face with Tucker.

No.

No, no, no. Her mind spun in a hundred directions as she watched the emotions flicker across Tucker's face. Surprise at nearly bumping into Arielle. Recognition. Confusion. One emotion faded into the other, slowly, as if time was wading through molasses.

Then his eyes found hers. Two furrows crouched between his brows. Something dimmed his eyes. Hurt? Disappointment? But that made no sense.

Tucker looked at Arielle. "What's going on?" he asked finally.

Say something. Think, Sabrina!

Arielle was looking at her, too, her eyes searching for answers Sabrina didn't have.

"Excuse us," a man behind Sabrina said.

They were blocking the exit. Sabrina and Arielle moved outside, letting the man pass.

What could she say? She was caught. There was nothing she could do but introduce them. Her eyes begged Arielle to play along.

She swallowed hard. "Tucker, I'd like you to meet Arielle. I was—I was going to surprise you, but, well, here she is. The woman you've been writing to all this time." In her stomach, an aching hole opened, wide and gaping. The smile on her face felt frozen and stilted. Plastic.

Arielle studied Sabrina a moment, then turned a dazed smile on Tucker.

Tucker looked between them. Finally, as if remembering his manners, he extended his hand. "Nice to meet you." He cleared his throat. "In person, I mean."

Arielle shook his hand. "You too."

Sabrina shrank inside as they touched. What had she done? What was going to happen now? Now that Tucker thought he'd met the woman of his dreams? *You're going to lose him for good, that's what.* The thought awakened an old wound.

A tap on the café window snagged her attention. Char motioned toward Gordon, who gave an exaggerated shrug from the kitchen window. His brows were pulled low in a deep V. It was the same look he had right before he'd fired their last server. The couple at table five was glaring at her. She had to get back in there.

Tucker gave his cap a sharp tug, then stuffed his hands in his pockets.

"I have to get back to work and—uh—Arielle has to be somewhere else . . ." Sabrina looked to her cousin for a confirmation.

"I do. I have to be somewhere else."

"So, maybe you two can catch up later?" Sabrina eyed Arielle, who took the hint and started walking away.

"Sure, later," Arielle said.

Tucker nodded once. "See you."

As he entered the café behind her, Sabrina could swear he was burning a hole through the back of her head. She needed a moment alone like she needed oxygen. She didn't even look at Gordon as she passed the kitchen and headed to the employee restroom. Just two minutes. She closed the metal door behind her and bolted it shut, leaning against it. Her legs quaked. Her entire body had become the epicenter of some horrific earthquake.

What now? What was going to happen? Could she get Arielle to leave? But then Tucker would wonder why she'd come at all.

There had to be some way out of this. *Think!*

She remembered the look on Tucker's face. Not the response she expected from someone meeting the woman he'd been desperately searching for. But then, he'd come to the café expecting coffee and had gotten the surprise of his life instead. Maybe he'd been in shock.

Well, he wasn't the only one. And Arielle must be totally perplexed. But she could deal with her cousin later. Right now, she had to face Tucker, had to seem pleased that she'd located his Sweetpea.

Sabrina closed her eyes and banged her head against the door.

Okay, maybe she could fix this. Maybe she could convince Arielle to spend a day with him and then go home. Then Sabrina and Tucker could continue writing, and everything would return to normal.

Normal. The word had such a nice ring.

She drew a deep breath, let it fill her lungs, then exhaled, feeling in control now that she had a workable plan. Of course, she'd have to convince Arielle to cooperate. And she'd have to endure the knowledge that Tucker was with her cousin. The notion made her stomach twist.

One bridge at a time, Sabrina.

A tap on the door startled her.

"Sabrina . . ." Char's voice called. "You okay in there?"

She straightened. "I'm fine."

"Well, Gordon's not, honey. You've got three orders up, and he wants to know why you're MIA."

"Be right out." Sabrina splashed cold water on her face and tidied her ponytail. *Just go out there and do your job. You'll be too busy to chat with Tucker. Tell him you'll talk to him tonight. No, scratch that. There's no reason for you to go to his house tonight since you've already found Sweetpea.*

The realization hit her fresh, and her spirits deflated. No more evenings at Tucker's. No more impromptu suppers or boat rides. No more sitting close at the desk while he read over her shoulder.

You ninny. That's what you wanted. All these mixed feelings were making her crazy. But she couldn't worry about that now. *Get through the next half hour. Once Tucker leaves, you can figure out everything else.*

She exited the restroom and collected the plates of food. "Sorry about that," Sabrina told Gordon when he glared at her through the window.

She delivered the food to the tables, then took the orders of two new customers. Next she went for the coffee carafe and stopped at Tucker's table first. No sense delaying the inevitable.

"So," he said as she poured the coffee, "you found her, huh?"

Sabrina drew up her lips and hoped for the best. "Surprised?"

He leaned back in the chair. "You could say that."

He was looking at her oddly. Staring. Studying her as if he'd ordered oatmeal and she'd served a bowl of wet sand.

"Well, Sabrina . . ." Oliver said from behind her. "What do you think about that? You know, about my giving an employee a vituperation yesterday?"

"Oliver, I—"

"So, how'd you do it?" Tucker asked. He adjusted his cap, crossed his arms over his chest. His arm muscles bulged against his fists.

A man across the room caught her eye and raised his empty mug in the air expectantly.

Sabrina nodded his direction, then looked at Tucker. "How did I . . . ?"

"Find her," Tucker said. "How did you finally find her?" His words sounded like ice chips, chiseled from a thick, heavy block. His chin rose. He tilted his chair back on two legs.

"I—"

Oliver hooted. "I stumped you, didn't I?"

She turned a glare on Oliver. "It means reprimand," she said just to shut him up.

"She from Ohio, like you thought?" Tucker asked.

Why didn't he seem happier? "Uh, no. Georgia."

The bell dinged as Gordon put up another order. She had to get it together. "I have to get back to work. I'll explain later." Maybe by then she would actually have an explanation.

Harbormaster: Women are so complicated. What do
you people want?

Seventeen

Tucker steered his boat into the harbor, relieved his last tour was
over. The bow sliced through the water, parting it effortlessly. A
wind had kicked up from the east, blowing in angry gray clouds
that reflected his mood more accurately than the cumulus clouds
that dotted the sky earlier.

Every customer annoyed him that day. The forty-something
woman whose coiffed hair required them to move at a snail's pace,
the dad who let his kids riffle through the boat's cubbies and com-
partments, the couple who couldn't keep their hands off each other
all the way to the Vineyard and back . . .

Even Dorothy's bluntness had annoyed him when he'd returned
to the office between customers. *"Boy, you're in a snit today."*

No kidding. What man wouldn't be when the woman he loved
was foisting him on some other woman? And that's what Sabrina
was doing.

He recalled the moment that morning when he'd come face-
to-face with the phony Sweetpea. He'd relived the nightmare a

hundred times, and each time it left him more irritated than the time before.

It stank, and that's all there was to it. How much could Sabrina care for him if she pushed him on some other woman? Didn't the thought of him with someone else make her want to hit something?

And who was this woman, anyway? Some longtime friend of Sabrina's here to play a part? How long would she stay, and was he supposed to see her again? Take her out?

He pounded his fist on the steering wheel, feeling it vibrate under his hand. He didn't want to be with this woman . . . Amber? Arielle? He couldn't even remember her name. He wanted to be with Sabrina. But now that she'd supposedly found Sweetpea, he wouldn't be spending time with her at all. There was no excuse for her to come over now.

So much for Operation Sweetpea. Instead of forcing Sabrina out of hiding, he'd forced her to find a stand-in.

Now he'd be back to stealing moments at the café during coffee refills. Back to pretending to read the paper while he watched her every move. Back to being his old, pathetic self.

Only now he had a new girlfriend to amuse. He prayed she wouldn't stay long. What if she remained the rest of the summer? What if she was moving here?

Please, God, no. His thoughts took every disastrous detour, and by the time he finished ruminating, their old online relationship didn't seem so terrible after all.

Arielle was waiting inside the door when Sabrina returned. "Okay, spill it."

Sabrina closed the door and set her bag down. "Nothing like being bombarded the moment one gets home."

"Nothing like being pawned off on some stranger at seven o'clock in the morning."

"Touché." Sabrina went to the kitchen and poured a glass of iced tea. Her head pounded. All she'd wanted was to come home, curl up in bed, and pretend today never happened.

Arielle had followed her to the kitchen. "Out with it. Who's this Tucker guy, and why did you say I've been writing him for a year?"

Sabrina sighed. "Let's sit down."

"It's that bad?"

"Unfortunately, yes."

They sat at the kitchen table. Sabrina looked out the window, where dark clouds hung low over the ocean. The water chopped and churned beneath them, an angry, moving canvas. Despite the day's beautiful start, a storm was brewing. She hoped Tucker was off the water.

"You're Sweetpea," Arielle said. "Why did you tell that guy it was me?"

"I'll get to that. Sheesh. Let me start at the beginning." It was the only way to make her cousin understand the importance of what she was about to ask.

"This should be good." Arielle crossed her arms and cocked her head.

Not a great start. *Just get it over with.* Sabrina stalled with a sip of tea, then told Arielle about the start of her relationship with

Harbormaster. She told Arielle how stunned she was to discover Harbormaster was Tucker from the café. And then came the first hard part.

"After he sent his own photo, I didn't know what to do," Sabrina said. "I couldn't send my photo or he'd know it was *me*."

Arielle's face softened. "What's so bad about that? He probably would've been delighted. You could've started dating."

Sabrina shook her head. "You don't understand."

"Then explain it."

"I'm not like you. He wouldn't have been delighted. He would've been disappointed."

Arielle started to interrupt, but Sabrina waved her off. "And I didn't want that anyway. I *don't* want that."

"Don't want what?"

"A relationship. I'm done with that."

"You can't be done with relationships, Sabrina. They're part of life."

"Well, they're not part of my life. And I like it that way." *Liar.* Well, maybe *like* was too strong a word. It was safer that way, that's what she'd meant.

"But you have a relationship with him, whether you call it that or not."

"A relationship at a safe distance. I can handle that."

Arielle shook her head. "We'll get back to that later. So he sent a photo and you didn't reciprocate. What happened next?"

Back to that. How could she say it? It seemed so harmless at the time. She never intended for Arielle to know or be involved. How was she to know that—

"Sabrina?"

"Well, I couldn't send my picture, and he wanted a photo and . . ."

"And . . . ?"

Sabrina licked her lips, gone suddenly dry, like someone had sucked all the moisture from the air. "Remember that photo you sent me? The one of you on the beach in Florida . . . ?" Her voice got smaller as the sentence dragged out.

Arielle's countenance changed. Her eyes widened; her jaw went slack. She sucked in a breath and held it, frozen. "You didn't."

"It gets worse."

Arielle's eyes slowly narrowed. "Could it possibly?"

She slumped in her seat. "Unfortunately." How could she have deceived him like that? And yet, wasn't she planning to cover her deceit with another lie? Her Aunt Bev's words danced through her mind: *What a tangled web we weave, when first we practice to deceive."*

"Go on." Arielle was glaring now.

This wasn't looking good. Not good at all. What was she going to do if Arielle refused to cooperate? What possible reason could she give Tucker for bringing the woman here only to have her disappear again?

One step at a time. "About six weeks ago, Tucker approached me after work and asked if he could hire me to find the woman he's been writing."

"What? Why would he ask you?"

"He'd been talking to Renny, and she was raving about how intuitive I am. Of course, she was talking about her stories and how

I help her with the clues. Tucker thought if I read the letters, I could piece together enough facts to locate this woman."

"How ironic."

"I tried to dissuade him for all the obvious reasons. I tried to convince him that if she didn't want to be found, it was best to leave it alone. But he was determined. And I thought—well, if I could pretend to try and find her—me—and fail . . ."

"And he's paying you for this?"

Sabrina felt heat creep into her face. All right, it was wrong. But he'd backed her into a corner. "I've been donating his money to Nantucket Soundkeeper."

"Oh, that makes it all right."

"I know, I know!" Did Arielle have to beat her with it? She already felt like slime. "I didn't know what else to do. He was going to hire someone else if I said no, and I couldn't risk that."

"I don't understand."

"You couldn't understand, Arielle."

"Does this have something to do with Jared and Jaylee?"

"I don't want to talk about that." Sabrina took a swig of tea.

"Everyone gets hurt sooner or later. You have to pick yourself up and have some hope."

Sabrina wasn't going there. She'd already hashed it out a hundred times in her own mind, and it was settled. Besides, there was a far more compelling reason that prevented her from telling Tucker the truth now, but she couldn't tell Arielle about that.

"You don't have to understand," Sabrina said. "Just try and understand that this relationship is special to me. Too special to lose."

"Then let it become all it was meant to be. Tell him who you are."

Sabrina stood, her chair scraping against the ceramic. "No." Her breath caught at the thought of him knowing. At the thought of him realizing who she was and what she'd done. Eventually he would introduce her to his sister, and everything would be ruined.

Arielle took her hand. "What are you so afraid of?"

She had to get back on topic. She wasn't going into this with her cousin. "I've already set the plan in motion. I've nearly finished reading the messages, and I was going to inform him next week that it's hopeless, that there aren't enough clues for anyone to locate her."

Sabrina walked into the living room and plopped on the couch that Arielle had moved against the wall. "I didn't anticipate you coming here, and I certainly didn't anticipate Tucker seeing you."

Arielle approached, sitting on the edge of the sofa next to Sabrina. "I'm sorry for that." Her voice gentled, "But maybe this was God's doing. Maybe this will force you to do what you should have done to begin with."

How did God get in the middle of this? "I'm not telling him who I am." She drove the words home with her eyes. Arielle needed to understand how adamant she was. She wouldn't lose this relationship.

"We write every night. Usually about nothing, but sometimes we talk about serious things. About politics and previous relationships and our deepest fears. I depend on him. I never meant to let that happen." She begged her cousin to understand. "If I tell him who I am, I'll lose him. And I can't bear that. I just can't." Her eyes burned, and she felt tears welling up.

"Oh, honey." Arielle embraced her, rubbing her back.

Sabrina blinked back the tears. She wouldn't have to lose Tucker. She could still salvage this mess if only she could convince Arielle to do this one tiny thing for her.

Sabrina pulled back and wiped the corner of her eye with her knuckle.

"So, what now?" Arielle asked.

Funny you should ask. Sabrina folded her hands in her lap. "I was hoping you'd agree to see him."

Arielle leaned back. "You are not asking what I think you are."

"A few dates and it'll be time for you to leave."

"A *few* dates!"

"It won't be hard. You know me well. Just pretend to be me." Sabrina tried for a grin. "It's not like he's hard on the eyes."

"That's hardly the point!"

Arielle's indignation resurrected the guilt in Sabrina. Not only had she fabricated a lie, but she was asking her cousin to perpetuate it. Arielle had always had a high code of honor. So had Sabrina before all this. Before Nantucket. Before Jared. What had happened? How had her life spun so far off track?

"I know it's a lot to ask," Sabrina said.

"I don't leave for two and a half weeks. How can I go out with this guy and pretend to be something I'm not? I can't do it."

Why couldn't her cousin see how much it meant to her? What had Sabrina ever asked of Arielle? "You mean you *won't* do it."

Arielle stared, eyes wide. "I'm not the one who started this charade."

"And I'm not the one who showed up here uninvited." Sabrina regretted the words the moment she said them.

Arielle's eyes turned down at the corners, a mirror image of her mouth. She slowly stood.

She should say something. Maybe she should apologize, but she was still angry. It was selfish of Arielle not to do this one thing for her. She had to know how important it was.

"I'm going for a walk." Arielle headed out the door, shutting it hard.

Sabrina heard her cousin's sandals thudding down the wooden steps. Across the room, the logo on the screen saver darted across the computer screen. Tucker would expect to hear from her, expect to see her—Arielle. She checked her watch. He'd be home soon. What should she do? What if he called—or worse, came over?

Why did this have to happen? Why did Arielle have to come? Why did she have to show up at the café just when Sabrina was ready to wrap everything in a nice, tidy bow?

Eighteen

Sabrina turned and pulled the blanket over her shoulders. A thick wedge of moon brightened the sky, illuminating the tree outside the window, and a gentle breeze ruffled the sheers. The air smelled of rain and salt from the storm. How long had she been lying here? An hour? Two? She refused to look at the clock for confirmation.

Her only consolation was the squeak of the sofa bed in the living room as Arielle tossed and turned. At least Sabrina wasn't the only one kept awake by the argument. Then she felt guilty for the thought. Really, what had Arielle done wrong? She'd inadvertently stepped into Sabrina's mess.

But would it kill her to help me?

Tucker must be wondering why she hadn't called or written. But if he'd been so eager to meet Sweetpea, why hadn't he contacted her? Surely he was eager to see Arielle. *Especially now that he's seen her in person.*

Maybe she could fabricate a family emergency that called Arielle away. Still, that wouldn't prevent him from wanting to know where she lived. And if she'd come to the island for the express purpose of meeting him, why wouldn't she disclose her address?

She turned again, tugging at the sheet that had bunched around her legs and tangled with her feet. Arielle's words haunted the corridors of her mind. *"Everyone gets hurt sooner or later. You have to pick yourself back up and have some hope."*

If only it were so simple. There was no hope where Tucker was concerned. Not when it came to a real relationship. She'd sealed that fate her first week on the island.

"Sabrina?"

Her eyes snapped open. Arielle stood in the doorway, dimly lit by the moon.

"Are you awake?" her cousin whispered.

Sabrina rolled onto her back and checked the time. She'd been awake for two hours. "Yeah."

Arielle entered the room, and Sabrina scooted over as she eased down on the bed's edge.

"I can't stand for things to be like this between us," Arielle said. She'd stayed out past dark, and by the time she'd returned, Sabrina was in bed.

"Me either."

They sat quietly, listening to the wind rustle through the leaves. Somewhere in the distance, a dog barked. Sabrina loathed the guilt that pricked her conscience, but she deserved it. She'd created this mess. Although she wished Arielle would help, it wasn't her cousin's responsibility.

"I'm sorry I got angry," Sabrina said. "I didn't mean what I said about you being uninvited."

"I'm sorry too."

Thunder rolled in the distance, and raindrops hit the roof, first in loud dollops, then in a steady patter. Sabrina got up and pulled the sash until it clicked in place, then crawled back under the covers.

"I don't know what I'm going to do about Tucker," Sabrina said finally. "But it's my problem, not yours." Maybe it was going to blow up in her face. If she told Tucker Arielle had to leave the island, maybe he'd give up on the relationship. Maybe she'd never hear from him again.

She envisioned coming home to an empty inbox, no letter asking how her day had been. Tried to imagine her evenings without their back-and-forth conversations. Could she go back to that kind of life? That kind of loneliness?

"The thing is, I have an idea," Arielle said.

Hope sprouted a tiny seed. At least someone had an idea. "Let's hear it."

"I don't think you're going to like it."

"Like I have so many appealing options."

"True." Arielle shifted toward her, pulling her feet onto the bed and wrapping her arms around her knees. "The way I see it, we both want something. I was thinking we could make a deal."

It didn't take a genius to figure out what Arielle was saying. "The wedding."

"If you agree to go to the wedding, and *be nice* . . . I'll go out with Tucker."

They'd both have to don some serious acting skills. Sabrina would have to pretend she approved of Jaylee and Jared's relationship, and Arielle would have to pretend to be Sabrina.

She didn't want to go to the wedding. Didn't want to see Jaylee. And she especially didn't want to see Jared.

But what about Tucker? *Is it worth losing him over? Can't you bury your pride for one event? Just hold your head up and stick it out?* Fear was such an ugly thing.

"What do you think?" Arielle asked.

"You know this doesn't change anything. My going to the wedding—"

"I know."

She knew what Arielle was thinking. That if Sabrina saw their family, everything would fix itself. Maybe it would. Maybe that's why Sabrina was afraid to go home.

But in all fairness she was asking Arielle for a huge favor. It was a fair trade. "You'll be here for another two and half weeks. Tucker will expect to see you a lot." As it was, he'd wonder why she hadn't called tonight. "Maybe six or seven dates?"

"*Six or seven?* It's only one wedding."

"It's an entire weekend."

Arielle tilted her head and pursed her lips. "Three dates."

"Four."

The pause between them was filled with the pitter-patter of rain. Finally Arielle extended her hand. "Four."

Sabrina put her hand in her cousin's, and they shook on it. "Deal."

Harbormaster: When I can't sleep, I work.

Sweetpea: When I can't sleep, I write to you.

Nineteen

"Why are you here so early?" Nate asked Tucker as he ducked into the office, out of the rain.

Tucker wiped his face dry and pulled his schedule for the day.

"You look awful."

"Thanks." Tucker had a grand total of three hours sleep. He'd worked until eleven and risen before dawn. He was avoiding the inevitable phone call or email from Sabrina. He'd had his cell phone off since his run-in with the Sweetpea imposter the morning before and hadn't checked his email since. Sabrina must be wondering what was up.

"Something going on?" Nate scanned the schedule. "Business all right?"

If only it were that simple. "Business is fine." Why did relationships have to be so complicated? He'd pursued Sabrina for over a year, and he was farther than ever from winning her.

"Must be a woman." Nate chuckled.

Tucker scowled.

Nate sank into Dorothy's chair and spun around, lacing his hands behind his head. "Women are complicated, man. I'm just glad you've moved on to a real, live relationship."

Tucker had recently confided in Nate about Sweetpea, but had never told him it was Sabrina. She was as real, live a woman as you could get. Unfortunately, she didn't want a real, live relationship.

"You *have* moved on . . ."

Tucker pulled a file and looked over the bills. "Not exactly."

"You're still mooning over some woman you don't know?"

"I do know her." He knew her better than he'd known any woman. Maybe that was why it hurt so much.

"Dude. She could be a man."

"She's not a—" Oh, for crying out loud. "I mean, I really know her. In person."

Nate's eyebrows scrunched under his hairline. "I'm confused. This is that email chick we're talking about, right?"

He made it sound cheap and meaningless. "She's not an email chick."

"Well, when you don't know her name—"

"Sabrina." What could it hurt? Nate didn't go to the café, and there must be a dozen Sabrinas on the island.

Nate smiled. "Ah, she does have a name. So you know who she is. What's the holdup?"

"The holdup is she knows who I am, but she doesn't know I know who she is."

"Come again?"

Tucker exhaled hard. "Stay with me here. I met her . . . where she works. I wanted to get to know her, but she was kind of stand-offish." More like a brick wall, but why put a nasty spin on things. "I found out her email and started writing her anonymously, and that's how this whole thing developed."

"But you said she knows who you are. At least, I think you did."

Tucker clenched his jaw. Thinking about it still caused a jolt of humiliation. "After we wrote awhile, I sent her my picture."

Nate smirked. "Pretty gutsy."

"Pretty stupid. She didn't own up to knowing me."

"Ouch."

"She sent me a photo of some other woman, passed it off as herself."

Nate leaned back in the chair until it bumped the desk. "What, is she, like, homely or something?"

Tucker narrowed his eyes. "No, she is not homely." She just thought she was.

"Just asking."

"She's very attractive. I don't know why she sent some other woman's picture."

"She doesn't want to meet you."

"You think?" It wasn't something he liked to dwell on. He was a decent guy who just wanted to love her. Having that love rejected wasn't the best feeling in the world.

Tucker explained how he'd devised a plan to spend time with Sabrina and how they'd spent the past six weeks working together.

"You're paying her, and she's pretending to help you find her own self."

"Basically."

"You're both nuts."

He was beginning to think so too. "It wasn't going too bad until the other woman showed up yesterday."

"What other woman?"

"The woman from the photo. Sabrina said she'd found my friend and, *voilà*, here she is."

"Dude. That's bad."

Uh, yeah. He checked his watch. Should he go to the café as usual? Would the imposter be waiting for him? He didn't know what to do.

"Who's the woman from the picture?"

"No idea."

"This Sabrina chick must have some reason for not wanting you to know. You sure she's not, like, married?"

He was tired of defending her. "She's not married."

"Well," Nate set his arms on the armrests, smiling. "What's this other chick look like?"

"I don't care what she looks like. It's Sabrina I care about." And he'd been so close to a breakthrough. That last night when he'd driven her home. The way she'd looked at him, her defenses crumbling down to her feet. He felt it. He'd been certain he was making headway. That it was only a matter of time before she admitted who she was.

And then she'd gone and found an imposter to play her part. Had the moment in the car scared her? Made her retreat even further? What was it that kept her away?

"What are you gonna do?" Nate's voice pulled him from his thoughts.

There was the question. So far he'd avoided any possibility of seeing or hearing from Sabrina, but that couldn't continue forever. He'd have to do something. He needed to figure it out soon, though, because Sabrina expected him at the café in fifteen minutes.

"Don't know," he said. "I don't know."

Sabrina topped off Oliver's coffee, then bussed table six for Evan, who'd spilled milk down his apron and gone for a fresh one. Business was slow that morning, the drizzling sky keeping most of the tourists in their hotels.

She checked the clock and saw it was time for Tucker. He hadn't responded to the message she'd sent first thing that morning. She'd awakened early and spent forty-five minutes writing one paragraph while Arielle hung over her shoulder. What was he thinking? Surely he was eager to see Arielle.

The bell above the café's door jingled, and Tucker entered, dripping wet from the rain. From the corner of her eye, she watched him navigate the tables and seat himself in his usual spot.

She grabbed the coffee and headed his way, her heart speeding in anticipation. *Keep your cool. He doesn't know anything.*

He flipped his cup as she arrived at his table. "Morning," he said, then cleared his throat.

She forced a smile. "Good morning." She poured the coffee. "Did you get Arielle's email?" *Well, that was abrupt.* She bit her lip, wishing for a little tact.

He sipped the coffee. "No, actually. I got in late last night, and I was at work before dawn this morning."

Oh. She hadn't figured on that. *Well, don't just stand here with the coffeepot like an idiot.* "She wants to see you, of course."

"Funny, she didn't before."

Sabrina panicked, speechless. *Think of something!* "You're right. I—I had to do some fast talking, and you were right all along. She was afraid of taking the relationship to the next level. But she can explain all that to you later."

He nodded once. "Right."

He didn't seem eager. He hadn't even asked why Arielle hadn't contacted him yesterday.

"She's staying with me."

"Really." His cap was pulled low over his eyes. When he looked down, she couldn't see them at all.

"So you can reach her there. Or email, whatever." At least if he wrote, she'd still have contact with him. *You truly are pathetic.*

"I'll do that." His smile didn't reach his eyes. Why didn't he seem happy? Why were his eyes as dim as the harbor on a moonless night?

The kitchen bell dinged. Table four's order. "Great."

An awkward silence bloomed. "I'd better fetch that order."

"Sure." He snapped his damp paper open to the front page.

She turned toward the kitchen before she realized she hadn't refilled Oliver's cup and he hadn't said a word. How was she going to survive the day? How would she survive the next two weeks knowing Arielle and Tucker were together?

And what if Arielle and Tucker . . .

No. She wouldn't even consider it. Wouldn't allow herself to remember what had happened the last time the man she loved connected with one of her cousins.

Harbormaster: Where were you last night? I missed you. I kept imagining you were out with some hot guy, and he was whisking you off to some fancy restaurant in his convertible. I almost came over there and beat him up when you came home. Oh, wait. I don't know where you live.

Sweetpea: Smart aleck.

Twenty

Tucker turned down the collar of his polo and fastened the bottom button. He'd found Sabrina's email when he returned from work.

I'd love to see you tonight. It doesn't matter what we do.

She'd suggested he email or call to set up a date. He'd replied and suggested dinner out. At least a restaurant would offer distractions, and he wouldn't have to worry about awkward silences.

His cell phone rang, and he snatched it off the table, along with his keys.

It was Tracey. "Hey, sis, how's it going?"

"You're on your way out the door, aren't you?"

"How the heck did you know that?"

"I have my ways. I just called to chat. Want me to call back?"

Tucker got into his car and started the engine. Tracey sounded better than she had the week before. She was going to get through this. "I can talk on my way there."

"Your way where?"

"On a date." That was going to invite the questions.

"Oooh, I'm so happy for you. You're finally getting somewhere with Sweetpea. I think I hear some wedding bells in your future."

He gave a wry laugh. "Not exactly. The date isn't with Sweetpea."

"What? I thought for sure she was the one you'd finally bring home to Mom."

He turned onto Main Street, already crowded with summer people heading to dinner.

He didn't feel like talking about Sabrina and her stand-in. "It's a long story. I'll tell you in later. How's your new job going?" He worried about her starting over in a big city like Atlanta. But if the accident several years ago had revealed anything about Tracey, it was her iron-core strength. He'd never seen anyone fight so hard through rehabilitation.

"I really like it. The people are friendly, and I feel useful—which I needed."

They chatted a few minutes about her job.

"You been eating?" he asked when there was a break in the conversation.

"Yes, Mother."

"Someone has to keep you in line." He turned onto Sabrina's street. "Speaking of which, have you heard from Mom and Dad lately?"

"Only every other day. Sheesh, you'd think I was suicidal or something."

He thought of Sabrina's dad and all the pain his selfish exit had caused. "Don't even joke about that."

"Sorry. You know what I mean though. I am starting to feel like I can breathe again. I found a good church too. I'm thinking about joining the choir."

"That would be good for you."

He pulled into Sabrina's drive and turned off the ignition.

"You're there, I'll let you go."

He smiled. "Am I on hidden camera?"

"Have fun on your date."

"Not likely."

Tracey laughed. "Lucky girl."

They said goodbye, and Tucker pocketed his cell, exiting the car. He was so not looking forward to this.

His good shoes crunched on the gravel of Sabrina's driveway as he approached the steps to her loft. Would Sabrina answer the door? If only he were going out with her. He'd wondered a hundred times if he should call an end to this absurdity. If he should admit he knew who Sweetpea was. But he was in too deep now. To do so would, at the very least, embarrass her, and, at the worst, anger her to the point of excluding him from her life. He was, after all, guilty of gross deceit. Then again, so was she.

In the end, he'd convinced himself to get through the dates.

How long could Arielle possibly stay? A few days? A week at most? Sabrina hadn't said in the email. At least, he assumed it was Sabrina who had written. But maybe not.

He shook his head, frustrated, as he approached the door. *Get it together, McCabe.* He raised his hand and knocked.

A few seconds later, Arielle appeared in a white dress. "Hey there!" Her smile was Julia Roberts wide. "Let me grab my bag, and we're good to go."

As she reached somewhere to the side, he peeked inside, hoping for a glimpse of Sabrina, but the interior was dark and empty.

"All set." Arielle slipped the thin strap of a wallet-sized bag over her bare shoulder.

He led the way down the stairs, opened the car door for her, then slid behind the wheel. He wasn't sure what to say, how to act. Maybe he should save them both a lot of trouble and tell her he knew she was an imposter. Before he could weigh the thought, she spoke.

"It's a gorgeous night, oh, my goodness. Even the rain was nice last night. I love the smell of rain, and the sunshine today . . . I could stay here forever."

She had a soft Southern twang that sounded nice. Comforting. "Summer's nice, but it gets pretty cold in the winter. We year-round residents have to take extra precautions to preserve heat in our homes. Especially the homes on the shore."

"Still, the summer is to die for, and the whole place has great energy. How many people can say they live on an island? It's awfully romantic."

He turned out of the drive, wishing she hadn't mentioned the *r* word, because now an awkward silence filled the car. He turned up the air. If only he'd thought to turn on the radio before he'd arrived. It would've filled the silence, but to do so now would be rude. Would she expect him to hold her hand? To kiss her good-night? His palms grew sweaty and sticky on the leather steering wheel.

"Well," she offered, "I guess since we already know so much about each other, we can skip the small talk, huh?"

"Guess so." He pulled his lips upward and hoped for the best. "Though I don't know what you do for a living or where you live. You've been a little secretive about that." He spared her a quick glance.

She laughed, nervously, he thought. "I live in Georgia, but you probably guessed that by my accent."

"Where 'bouts?"

"Macon. Born and raised there. I teach preschool, which I love. Not for everyone, I know, but those little rug rats are a hoot."

Even if he hadn't known Arielle wasn't Sweetpea, he would've been suspicious by now. She had too much energy, and she talked more and faster than his friend did. It hit him that her job gave her summers off. Still, surely she couldn't stay long on a preschool teacher's salary. Though since she was staying with Sabrina, there weren't many expenses involved.

Arielle related a story of a boy in her class who'd gotten a LEGO stuck up his nose. His mom took him to the ER to have it removed. She chuckled at the memory.

"Reminds me of when I got that Tic Tac stuck up my nose. But you already know all about that." Wasn't *he* feeling ornery tonight.

"Right, right." She fidgeted with her fingernails. "Those kids. Oh, my goodness, the things they say. I could fill a book. One day in the spring, I went home early because I'd developed a fever, and Mia, this adorable little girl, told her mom I went home with a temper! Can you imagine?"

"Must be pretty entertaining." She was nothing like Sabrina. Not that she wasn't nice. She seemed sweet, but she wasn't Sabrina.

He pulled alongside DeMarco's clapboard building and parked, then helped Arielle from the car. The shingled sign over the front windows swung in the wind.

"This looks so quaint. I love Italian."

Tucker opened the door for her, and the host greeted them.

"Hey, Tucker." Brant Morgan shook his hand.

Tucker introduced Arielle, then Brant seated them at a table for two by the front window. The restaurant smelled of seafood and garlic, and Tucker's stomach gave a rumble.

Across the room, he recognized an older man he'd taken to Martha's Vineyard a couple days before, along with the man's wife. The Wescotts were old money—he'd seen all the signs—and Mr. Wescott was a semiretired attorney.

Mr. Wescott caught his eye, a quick look of recognition followed by a crease on his forehead. Before the man could look away, Tucker nodded his chin upward. The guy probably wondered how a boat driver could afford a place like this. Tucker's lips twitched.

Arielle opened the menu, but her eyes took in the restaurant's atmosphere. "It's like a cozy country inn, very intimate. And it has nice flow, which is unusual for a restaurant."

Tucker opened the menu and perused the items, though he knew what he was ordering. "Are you interested in decorating?"

"It's a hobby. I've already rearranged Sabrina's loft. The furniture placement was all wrong. She needs to change the wall color, but I haven't quite decided on a color."

"Well, you just got here."

Her smile seemed to freeze for a minute. "That's true. I've got plenty of time to decide. That olive green is so dark and depressing."

He wondered what she meant by "plenty of time." "How long can you stay?"

She closed her menu. "A little over two weeks. We'll have plenty of time together."

He tried for a smile. "That's great." Over two weeks. How many dates would he have to go on? He'd figured on two or three tops. This was getting worse and worse. Maybe he could email and say the spark just isn't there in person. That was a thought.

The server arrived to take their drink orders, but since they'd decided what they wanted, they ordered their food as well. He wanted the date to be over, and the sooner they got their food, the sooner he could take her home. *Relax. You don't want her thinking you're eager to get rid of her.* He felt a moment's pang at the thought. It wasn't that she wasn't nice, but he was tired of feeling un-comfortable. And it wasn't the stiff shoes.

While they waited for their food, Arielle more than held up her end of the conversation, but service was slow, as was typical for a fine-dining establishment. His faking skills lacked, and he didn't have it in him to try harder. Still, she didn't seem to notice.

"Oh, my goodness, this looks delicious," she said when the server set their plates down. She stabbed a small chunk of spinach leaves and slid it into her mouth.

Tucker placed the white cloth napkin in his lap, said a quick silent prayer, then dug his fork into the capellini. He ate here regularly, and the shrimp-and-pasta dish was his favorite, but tonight his taste buds seemed numb.

"This place is hopping. I'm surprised you were able to get a table on such short notice."

"Fine dining is huge here, especially during the summer. This place books up a week in advance, but Brant's an old friend, so he squeezed us in."

"Is Nantucket the kind of place where everyone knows everyone? The island's not awfully big."

"Yes and no. In the summer the place swells with tourists and summer people. A lot of them own homes and come back year after year, so you get to know them. I have a lot of repeat customers that I've gotten to know pretty well."

They talked between bites of food, her mostly. When the server brought their bill, he tucked the cash inside the leather folder and set his napkin on his plate.

He didn't want her to feel rushed, but she'd finished her salad and refused dessert. Maybe she was ready to call it a night too. Or maybe she'd suggest they go somewhere else. Dread parked itself at the curb and fed the meter.

"You probably have to get up early in the morning," she said. "Maybe we should call it a night."

He exhaled quietly. "I do have an early run. Would you mind?"

She set her napkin on her plate and scooted her chair back. "Not at all. We'll have plenty of time to catch up."

That's what he was afraid of. Tucker walked her to the car and helped her inside, then slid behind the wheel. The evening was warm and dark, the stars dotting the cloudless sky.

"Thank you so much for supper. I haven't had a salad that tasty in years, truly."

"You're welcome."

They talked about his job on the way home, and he told her stories he'd repeated a dozen times to other people. Before he knew it, he was pulling into Sabrina's drive. A light shone from the window, and he thought he saw the movement of a shadow. He put the car in park, turned off the ignition, and helped Arielle out.

As they ascended the steps, his mind spun. Would she expect a kiss? Should he shake her hand? Hug her? Nothing seemed appropriate. None of it appealed.

They reached the small landing, and she faced him in the circle of porch light. Her skin glowed golden. "Would you like to come in for a few minutes?"

His eyes went to the window. He wanted to see Sabrina, but not under these conditions. "Not tonight, thanks. I should get home and to bed."

She touched his arm. "Well, thanks so much again for a wonderful supper."

"You're welcome." Should they make plans to meet again? She probably expected him to, but he couldn't bring himself to do it. He only wanted to get home and write Sabrina.

Sweetpea: When Jared left me for my cousin, I couldn't help but think of my dad and the pain he went through when my mom died. I even wondered if suicidal tendencies were hereditary. Is that crazy?

Twenty-one

Sabrina pressed her face to her bedroom wall and peered through the sliver between the drapes. It seemed Tucker and Arielle had been gone an eternity. She tried to stay busy with last-minute research for Renny's new manuscript, but her mind hadn't left Tucker and Arielle all night.

A glance at her digital clock proved they'd been gone less than three hours, not long for a date. But, oh, those hours had crawled.

When Arielle and Tucker came into view, her mood deflated like a punctured party balloon. They looked perfect together. Arielle in her gauzy white dress that displayed her long, lean legs, and Tucker in his crisp white polo that showed off his broad shoulders. Her sleek blonde hair was the perfect foil for his dark curls. They looked like a couple. Like the wealthy summer people who sunned in the afternoon and dined in the evening at the exclusive restaurants.

They stopped on the landing, Arielle too close to the door to be visible from her position. Tucker was in full view, the cone of porch light a mellow spotlight on him. Would he kiss her good-night? *Please, no.*

She didn't think she could bear it. The image of Jared and Jaylee flashed like a blinding beacon in her mind, the memory so fresh it stole her breath.

She turned, pinning her eyes to the opposite wall, to the shad-owed painting of a meadow she'd bought at a Nantucket gallery the summer before.

Arielle wouldn't let him kiss her, would she? Then again, she'd asked her cousin to play the part. And wouldn't Tucker find it odd if she turned away? *Why didn't I have this conversation with Arielle?*

Unable to resist, needing to know the truth, no matter how much it hurt, Sabrina peeked through the slit. She heard Arielle's voice, muted, then Tucker's. Why hadn't she thought to crack the window?

Her cousin reached out and touched Tucker's arm. Sabrina pressed her lips together. Was touching really necessary? She waited to see how Tucker responded.

But after a small smile, he was turning away, and then she heard the click of the front door closing.

Tucker's footsteps thudded down the stairs, and a moment later his car started.

"It's safe to come out now," Arielle called.

Was it? Did she want to hear about the date? *It's not like you have a choice. You're going to write him, and he's going to find it a little odd if you have date amnesia.*

A tap sounded at her door. "Sabrina? I know you're awake."

"Come in." She plopped on the bed as Arielle entered and flipped on the lamp.

Arielle's dress flared across the bed as she sank down. "Aren't you going to ask?"

"Ask what?"

"You know very well what. He didn't try to kiss me goodnight— not that I would've let him."

Sabrina didn't know how to respond. Admit she'd been worried? Pretend she didn't care?

"In fact, I have to say it was nice to go out with a gentleman. He didn't so much as touch me all night."

Relief flowed through her. Then a second later, she wondered why he hadn't. If he felt as strongly about Sweetpea as he claimed, wouldn't he want to touch her? Hold her hand? Maybe he was taking it slow, afraid of rushing after it had taken so long to find her.

"Did he ask how I found you?" Sabrina asked. They'd invented a story about Sabrina finding Sweetpea on another chat site, just in case.

Arielle frowned. "Actually, he didn't. So much for all that planning and rehearsing."

"Well, he might ask next time." The whole idea of a next time made her want to vomit. "Or the time after that."

Arielle spread out beside Sabrina and rolled to her side. "We went to DeMarco. Have you been there?"

"Not a restaurant I can afford on my salary, but I've heard it's good."

"Oh, my goodness. That salad was heavenly. They brought around this dessert tray, and the panna cotta looked so yummy, but I knew you were waiting with bated breath, so I said I was full, but truth be told, I could have *so* tied into that thing."

Sabrina felt a stab of guilt for the jealousy she'd felt moments ago. "I appreciate that. So, what did you talk about all night?"

"A lot of nothing, really. I told him about teaching preschool and that I live in Macon. You said that was okay, right?"

He would've been suspicious if Arielle had kept her occupation a secret. "Right." Sabrina turned to face Arielle, propping her head on her palm.

"So, let's see, we talked a little about his job and about Nantucket. I told him I'd be here for two more weeks."

He must've jumped for joy. Maybe the whole kiss thing had worked out for tonight, but did she really think a red-blooded man was going to keep his hands off a woman like Arielle for two weeks?

"That was kind of odd, come to think of it. He didn't seem overjoyed, but maybe he's not the expressive type."

"Did you make plans to go out again?"

"Not really. We just said we'd chat on email and left it at that."

They were quiet for a moment, and the hum of the air conditioner filled the gap. Would he write when he got home tonight? Would he say he enjoyed her company?

"He's a good listener. I think I talked too much, but it was so refreshing to be with someone who actually listened, you know?"

He *was* a good listener. Why did it hurt that Arielle appreciated the same quality? No, not hurt. Made her feel threatened.

Tucker is not Jared. And Arielle is not Jaylee.

Yeah, but Tucker thinks Arielle is you.

She squeezed her eyes closed and wished this were over, for time to fast-forward two weeks. She longed for simpler times when she was just Sweetpea and he was Harbormaster.

It had gotten so complicated.

"I wish you'd tell him the truth." Arielle disrupted her thoughts.

"You just want to bail on our agreement."

"I just want you to find happiness."

"Trust me, telling him the truth won't bring either of us happiness."

"Maybe you're not giving him enough credit. He seems like a nice guy."

She'd been through this. But even a man like Tucker had his limits. She couldn't expect Arielle to understand, because her cousin didn't know the whole truth. "Just keep your end of the bargain, cuz, and I'll keep mine."

Arielle sat up and shrugged. "Fine by me. He's not exactly an ogre." She scooted across the bed and bounded onto her bare feet. "Well, I'm going to grab a bath before bed."

"Goodnight." Sabrina lay in bed until she heard Arielle shut off the water, then went to check her messages. Tucker had been home long enough to write. She opened the program, half hoping he'd written, half terrified of what he'd say.

In the end, all the emotions were for nothing, because there was no letter from Tucker at all.

Sweetpea: I went to the library yesterday and spent a lovely afternoon buried in a book of poetry. Are you sure you don't like poetry? Maybe you've just never tried Longfellow.

Twenty-two

When Sabrina returned from work the next day, Renny was pruning the rosebushes by the front walk. She hunched over a bush of pale pink buds, examining the petals of a rose in full bloom. The sun beat down on her back, and beads of sweat had popped out on her forehead.

"Afternoon, Sabrina." She straightened from her crouch, swiping the dirt from her red Hawaiian shirt.

Sabrina pulled her mail from the box and approached. A warm breeze blew in off the ocean, stirring the loose hairs by her ear and carrying the fragrance of roses. "*Gan Eden* is looking lovely. But you picked a hot day to garden."

"Well, the muse always visits while I'm pruning, and after last night, I need a visit."

"Didn't go well?" Sabrina leafed through the mail, bills and junk.

"I wrote two pages in four hours."

When Renny was on a roll, she could write two chapters in four hours. "Sorry to hear that. I'm sure it'll come to you. It always does. Have you heard anything on *Danger in the Night?*"

Renny stretched her back, then swatted a fly. "No, no, nothing good, I'm afraid."

It was early yet. Surely they wouldn't reject that one. Renny's stories were better than many of the books she bought. She shook her head. "It's only a matter of time."

Renny laughed, her leathery skin creasing at the corners of her eyes. "You're good for my ego, that's for sure. How are you doing, *amita?* Having a nice visit with your cousin?"

"She sure livens up the place."

Renny laughed. "I'm glad she came. She's good for you—full of *simchah!*"

"*Simchah?*"

"Joy, full of joy! You need more joy in your life. Your cousin's a believer?"

"How did you know?"

Renny tapped her temple. "I know these things."

Sabrina shook her head and made her exit. Returning to her apartment, she was glad she had no plans. Tucker hadn't written that morning, and she was eager to see if an email awaited her.

The loft was empty, and a hot-pink Post-it was stuck to the computer monitor. *Went for a walk.*

Sabrina set down her bag and opened the email program. Tucker had been quiet at the café. A couple times she'd caught him staring at her with a strange expression, but when she caught his eye, he looked away.

One message waited in her inbox, the one she'd hoped for. She clicked on it.

Hey there. Hope you had a good night's sleep. I checked my schedule when I got home last night and it's pretty full today. Saturdays are crazy this time of year. Would you mind if we didn't get together tonight? My schedule is lighter tomorrow. Maybe a picnic or something? Your call. If you're up late tonight, maybe we can chat awhile.

Sabrina stared at the words until they blurred. He hadn't mentioned their date. Hadn't said what a wonderful time he'd had, hadn't told her she'd looked beautiful. But then maybe he told Arielle that last night.

Not something she wanted to dwell on.

At least he and Arielle wouldn't be together tonight. It was something. Her cousin would be relieved.

She hit Reply and stared at the blinking cursor. He wouldn't get the message until late, but maybe when he returned they could get a conversation rolling.

Before she could formulate her thoughts, Arielle returned, her skin glistening from the hot sun, her hair pulled into a high ponytail. "What a gorgeous day! I think I'll put on my suit and go for a swim. How was work?"

"Okay." She closed the email, deciding to put supper on first. She wondered if Arielle had gone to the grocery for fruit and vegetables. Having a vegetarian in the house changed mealtime.

At least Arielle would be home for supper, though she didn't know yet. "I have good news," Sabrina said.

Arielle rummaged through her stack of clothing, a lumpy pile she'd shoved into the hollow recess of an end table. "You're telling Tucker the truth?"

Sabrina tilted her head and glared at the back of her cousin's head. She refused to give credence to the comment. "You're free for the night. Tucker wrote and said he was booked until late."

Arielle pulled her bathing suit from the pile and stood, frowning. "Oh. Well, okay."

"I'll put something together for supper," Sabrina said.

"I already made a fruit salad for you. I guess I'll be having that too."

Sabrina watched Arielle shut the bathroom door. Not the reaction she'd anticipated. Not that her cousin had seemed disappointed, but for someone set on avoiding dates with Tucker, she sure hadn't seemed relieved.

Harbormaster: I talked to Tracey again today.
Divorce is for the birds. I'll spare you the sordid
details, but I still want to beat the guy to a pulp.
Does that make me a bad Christian? There's all that
"turn the other cheek" stuff, but it's hard when the
person who got slapped is your sister. She's already
been through so much.

Twenty-three

Tucker couldn't stand the thought of faking it today. He had to
pretend to some extent, but after his long day yesterday and another
restless night, the thought of entertaining Arielle, running into
people he knew, introducing them, was too much to stomach.

Which was how he came to be standing at his grill, flipping
steaks. He checked the underside of the T-bones, then flipped them,
hoping Arielle would arrive before he singed them. The potatoes
were done, resting in their foil skins on the table. The broccoli was
keeping warm in the steamer.

He'd offered to pick up Arielle, but she'd replied, saying she'd
walk over. He'd been certain it was Sabrina at the keyboard. It had
been her short, snappy sentences. When he envisioned Arielle's

emails, he imagined long run-on sentences, punctuated with "oh, my goodness."

Now he wondered if Arielle had gotten lost between Sabrina's house and his. She was twenty minutes late. The sun was low on the horizon, but there was plenty of daylight left. She didn't believe in cell phones—he'd learned that on their last date—so he couldn't call. He should call Sabrina and see when she'd left. The idea gelled, an excuse to talk to her more than anything.

He turned the grill to low and dialed Sabrina. She picked up on the second ring.

"Hey there," he said.

The pause lasted so long he was about to identify himself, but then she responded.

"Tucker. Is something wrong?"

He smiled at her immediate assumption. "Does something have to be wrong for me to call?"

"If past experience is anything to go by."

"Come on, now. Isn't it possible I just called to see how your day went? To see if Oliver stumped you with a word yet? To see if—"

"When you're on a date with my—with Arielle—not so much."

Tucker sank into the wicker deck chair. "Okay, you got me. I called to see when Arielle left. She's not here yet." At the moment, he wouldn't mind if she had taken a detour. A very long one.

"Oh. I was out getting groceries, so I'm not sure when she left. I wouldn't worry though—she gets distracted sometimes and tends to run late."

Interesting observation for someone she'd supposedly just met. "You seem to know her well."

"Not really. She just—well, she's been staying here, so you get to know a few things about a person, that's all."

"Right." He didn't want to talk about Arielle. "So, are you going to keep me in suspense?"

"Am I supposed to know what you're referring to?"

He smiled. "Oliver. I believe he'd dropped the word *propinquity* as I was leaving this morning." He'd been late for his first run or he would've stuck around for pure entertainment value.

"It means nearness or proximity."

"You subscribe to Word of the Day or something?"

"Something wrong with that?"

Tucker laughed. "There is such a thing?"

The doorbell pealed. A pang of disappointment ricocheted through him. He wished he hadn't planned this date with Arielle. He wanted to talk with Sabrina all night. Maybe if he ignored her, she'd go away.

"Was that the doorbell?" she asked.

Busted. He entered the house through the sliding door. "Actually, yeah. I guess Arielle made it."

He stopped by the recliner, delaying the inevitable, not wanting to hang up just yet. *Just say it, Sabrina. Tell me the truth, and trust me to handle it, whatever it is.*

"Well," she said. "Have fun."

Not likely. "Talk to you later." He hung up, disappointed and frustrated. *Get it together, McCabe. You're going to scare the poor girl if you open the door with a snarl on your face.*

He took a deep breath and opened the door.

"Hey!" Arielle looked fresh and energized from her walk, her cheeks flushed.

"Come in."

"I love your house. It's so cozy and, oh, my goodness, right on the water. And I do mean *on* the water. Sabrina said you had a boat tied up outside, but I didn't know she meant *right* outside."

He smiled at her enthusiasm. "You can look around if you want while I get the food on the table."

"Sure."

Tucker dished up the broccoli and brought it outside. By the time he had the grill off and the steaks on the plates, Arielle was opening the sliding screen. Her hair was down, and it swung around her shoulders as she turned.

"Your house is so gorgeous. I could help you with the—" Her eyes seemed to stick on the plate of food.

He pulled out her chair. "What's wrong?"

The wicker chair crackled and creaked as she sank into it. "Nothing. I—I was just saying I could help you with the flow of your room. If you want, that is."

He studied her as he sat down. Something was wrong, though she was trying to cover with a smile.

"Yours is well-done, the way you like."

"Thank you."

He handed her the A1 sauce, but she hesitated before taking it. "I have Worcestershire if you prefer."

"No, no. I—I think I'll enjoy it plain."

Tucker dropped his napkin in his lap, breathed a quick prayer, then dug into his steak. It was juicy with a nice tang from the spices he'd used. He remembered when he'd grilled for Sabrina. Had it only been a few weeks ago? He'd had her right there in his house. What if he'd told her the truth? Would she be sitting here now instead of Arielle? Had he missed his opportunity?

He and Arielle made small talk, but conversation became stilted after ten minutes. Tucker wondered how he was going to survive the rest of the night. What had Sabrina been thinking? Arielle was nothing like her. In fact, they were complete opposites. Did Sabrina think he could be fooled so easily?

When they finished eating, he carried their plates to the sink. Upon his return, Arielle's face seemed pale. But maybe the pretense was wearing on her. It was certainly wearing on him.

Her lips turned up as he sat down.

"I didn't know what you might like to do," he said. "I could take you out in the boat. You might enjoy the sunset."

Her face fell.

"Or we could go for a walk or watch a movie. I have a pretty extensive collection—"

"A movie sounds great."

"Good. I'll stick the dishes in the dishwasher while you peruse the selection."

She followed him inside, and he pointed her to the DVDs. He wondered if she'd select a mystery or suspense like Sabrina, or if she'd choose based on her own preference.

When he returned to the living room, she'd chosen *Witness*, one of Sabrina's favorites.

"Ah, an old favorite, huh?"

"Why not?"

He put in the DVD, started it, then settled on the couch, close enough to Arielle but not touching. He fast-forwarded through the previews, and they watched the movie's opening.

Having seen the movie twice before, his mind wandered. Would Arielle expect him to make a move? How many dates could they go on before she realized something was wrong? A man who had feelings for her would've kissed her by now or would at least be looking for the opportunity.

He studied her from the corner of his eyes. Her arms were wrapped around her stomach, and she wore a grimace.

"You okay?" Her skin looked pasty.

"I—I'm not feeling so good." She swallowed, panic lacing her eyes.

He paused the movie, and Harrison Ford's face froze. "Can I get you something?"

Before she could reply, she sprang from the couch and ran down the hall. The bathroom door slammed shut. Two seconds later, he heard her hurling.

In the kitchen, he filled a glass with water, wet a washcloth, then tapped on the door. "Arielle? You all right?" Maybe she had a stomach virus, though it was an odd time of the year for that.

"Yeah." Her voice shook on the word. She vomited again.

He wanted to do something, but what? He felt helpless. Maybe she had food poisoning. Couldn't be the steaks, too soon for that.

Poor girl. Here she was, pretending to be something she wasn't, and now she was ill on top of it. Maybe the stress of pretending was getting to her. What a disaster. All of it avoidable if he'd just admitted the truth to Sabrina when he'd had the chance.

Maybe it's not too late.

A flush sounded; then the water ran. A few minutes later, she opened the door. Her pallor was even worse, a greenish cast ringed her mouth, and smudges of black stuff underlined her eyes.

He handed her the water and washcloth.

Her hands shook as she took them. "Thanks. I'm sorry—"

"Nothing to be sorry for. Come sit down."

"I must have a virus or something . . ."

"I'll take you home as soon as we're sure you're okay." He hoped Sabrina didn't catch whatever Arielle had. Looking at her now, wobbly and shaky, he wondered if she was going to make it through a car ride.

"If you don't feel up to going home, you could stay here."

He helped her to the recliner, and she ran the washcloth under her eyes. "I'm a mess." Her eyes filled, spilling over.

He hovered, uncertain. "Are you feeling worse?" Maybe a trip to the hospital was in order.

She sniffed. "No." But the tears flowed faster.

Maybe it was stress. What if he told her the truth? It would ease her worries about his expectations. It occurred to him belatedly that she may have taken his offer to stay as more than he'd intended.

Her breath wavered on an inhale. "I'm not her." The words shook on release.

She seemed rooted to the seat, so he sank onto the sofa. He wondered if she was aware she wasn't making sense.

"I can't do this anymore." She put her hand on her stomach, her eyes finding his again. "I'm not feeling so good."

He stood. "Why don't you—"

She darted past him, down the hall, into the bathroom. *Slam.*

He grimaced at the violent sound of her stomach emptying its contents. His own gut tightened in response. What if she *was* sick from the pretense? What if it was getting to her? His offer to stay the night hadn't helped.

A few minutes later the toilet flushed and the faucet ran again. This had to go down on record as his worst date ever. He'd never actually made a woman sick before. *Way to go, McCabe.*

The door opened. He helped her back to the living room, a sick sense of déjà vu filling him.

She was weaker and shakier than before. He wondered if this was going to continue all night.

"I feel better," she said after she settled in the recliner. She picked up the washcloth and wiped her eyes again. "That's what I get, eating steak after four years meat-free."

"You're a vegetarian?" He thought back to the night at DeMarco. She'd ordered salad, but that wasn't unusual. If only she'd said something. No wonder she'd eyed the food with horror. He felt like a heel.

"You must be confused, and I don't feel well enough for tact, so I'm just going to say it. I'm not your Sweetpea. I'm not her. I'm Sabrina's cousin from Macon, Georgia, and that's all I am. I didn't write all those letters. I'm sorry."

Sabrina's cousin? The one cousin was marrying her ex-fiancé, so this must be the other one.

"You don't seem awfully surprised." Arielle licked her lips. "Or mad." She was looking better, getting her color back.

"I'm not. I know you're not Sweetpea."

She stared at him. Emotions flickered across her face, starting with confusion and ending with anger. "What?"

"I guess it's my turn to say sorry. I know Sabrina is the one I've been writing."

"You *know*?"

"I know."

She let her head fall against the recliner's back. "If you know and she knows, what in creation am I doing here?"

Tucker folded his arms. "She knows and I know, but she doesn't know I know."

Arielle closed her eyes. "I am not well enough for that."

He explained how he'd fallen for Sabrina at the café and tried to get to know her anonymously online. He explained how he'd hired her in order to get her to open up. He explained his disappointment when Sabrina had brought Arielle instead.

"That's not what happened, just so you know," Arielle said. "She didn't know I was coming."

"She didn't bring you here to pretend to be Sweetpea?"

Her head rolled back and forth against the chair. "She tried to keep us apart, but that one day at the café . . . she just—did what she thought she had to do."

The realization comforted him. At least Sabrina hadn't been trying to pawn him off on someone else. She was a victim in this charade too. Sort of.

What a mess I've made of this, God.

"She's going to kill me for telling you," Arielle said.

Maybe if Arielle knew all this, maybe she knew what Sabrina was hiding from. "Why?" he asked. "Why won't she tell me who she is?"

"Why haven't you told her that you know who she is?" she countered.

Ah, the protective cousin had arrived. She was feeling better. "I'm afraid of scaring her away. She—she means a lot to me."

He looked at the TV screen, gone blank from being paused too long. "Look, I know it might seem like I've strung her along, pretending I don't know who she is. But it's not like that. I—I love her, okay? All those letters . . . hearing her heart, night after night. She's special to me. More special than anyone I've ever met."

Would he ever get to tell her in person? Now that Arielle knew, she'd probably tell Sabrina everything. And where did that leave them? Sabrina would be furious that he'd known all along. *Furious* wasn't the word. She might feel he'd played her for a fool. He'd probably get a lap full of hot coffee in the morning.

"Do you know why she won't admit who she is?" he asked again.

Arielle sat up straighter. "I don't think it's my place to say. Oh, my goodness, she's already going to kill me."

Tucker frowned. "Not going to be too happy with me either." Any chance he'd had with her was gone. She might stop writing him. What was he thinking? Of course she'd stop writing. What was he going to do if he'd lost her for good?

Once again he tried to imagine how Sabrina would feel when Arielle told her the truth. Furious wouldn't be the half of it. Add humiliation to the mix, and you had a concoction that spelled "The End." Done. Finished. *El finito*.

Though he loved Sabrina, he wasn't blind to her faults. She was stubborn as a bull. Look how long she'd harbored anger toward her ex-fiancé and cousin and her whole family for that matter. If she felt Tucker had betrayed her trust, she'd never forgive him. Why hadn't he considered that before?

The dishwasher kicked into a different cycle. A boat engine roared to life outside.

"Unless . . ." Arielle started. Her brows puckered, and she chewed on her lower lip.

"Unless . . . ?"

She locked her gaze on his. "Unless we don't tell her."

The idea didn't sound as fabulous as she apparently thought it was. It would get them both out of trouble, but what good would it do otherwise? At least they could dispense with the date pretense. That was something.

"I probably shouldn't tell you this, but Sabrina cares about you a lot. Maybe you already know that."

Something warm and pleasant swelled in his gut. He'd hoped. He'd even been pretty sure at times. But hearing it confirmed was euphoric. "She hasn't said it in so many words."

"Well, this hasn't been easy on her, watching us go out."

"Really?" It shouldn't make him feel so pleased.

"She was peeking out the window the other night when you brought me home."

She did care. She cared a lot. It must be eating her alive to see him and Arielle together. Especially after losing one man she loved to a cousin. "You're not suggesting we make her jealous."

Her face fell a bit. "That would be kind of mean. Especially after what Jaylee did."

"It's still pretty fresh."

"Oh, my goodness, she would hate me."

It would be cruel to stir up those feelings of betrayal. It might not even work. He imagined Arielle flowing in the door from one of their dates, raving about him. He imagined the letters he could write, the things he could say about their time together.

The look of hurt on Sabrina's face.

"I don't think I can do it," he said.

"It's for her own good. I don't think you'll get anywhere with her unless she's forced into it. She needs a big push."

But Jared had hurt her deeply. He didn't want to do the same. He couldn't believe Arielle was willing to risk her relationship with her cousin.

"I love her, too, you know," Arielle said. "Besides, maybe we can get you some time alone with her."

Now, *that* idea appealed. "How?"

"I don't know. We'll figure out something."

It would be worth it if he could get time with her. He missed having her over. He longed for time alone with her. If Arielle could arrange that, maybe he could show Sabrina how much she meant to him, how special she was.

"Deal?" Arielle asked, her brows disappearing under her bangs.

What did he have to lose? "Deal," he said, hoping he hadn't made another mistake in what was beginning to look like a long string of gross miscalculations.

Twenty-four

Sabrina read the first lines of Tucker's email, her chest muscles squeezing the oxygen from her lungs. Arielle had said little when she'd returned from Tucker's. Only that he'd served steak and she'd gotten ill.

She hadn't looked ill when he'd brought her home. Her makeup was faded, but she had a natural glow and a mysterious smile hovering on her lips. *I'll bet Tucker kissed her*, Sabrina thought, her knees going weak.

Arielle took a quick shower and lay down on the couch. She was asleep within minutes, and Tucker's message arrived shortly afterward.

She reread the first lines.

Hey there. Hope you're feeling better. You had me worried. I hope you're not coming down with something—talk about bad timing, huh?

When you're feeling better I'd like to take you out on my boat. Maybe we can have a picnic on the water and watch the sunset. I always wanted to do that with you, did I ever tell you that? There's something romantic about twilight on the water. The colors are unbelievable.

Write soon and let me know how you're feeling, okay? Until then, I'm thinking about you . . .

Was he really? Or was he thinking about Arielle?

Of course he's thinking about Arielle, you fool. That's who he's spending time with. He's falling for her. Just like Jared fell for Jaylee.

And she had no one to blame but herself.

Her fingers hovered over the keyboard. She wanted to reply. Maybe he was still at the computer. But he thought she was Arielle. What if he went on and on about the date?

As hard as she'd tried to hang on to him, he was slipping away. The thought brought a tidal wave of fear. She poised her fingers over the keys and started typing.

I'm feeling better. It was probably something I ate for dinner—

She paused. Maybe it would be better if he thought it was a stomach virus. That would require a few days to recover. Three days of keeping him and Arielle apart. She deleted everything she'd typed.

I'm still feeling a little nauseated. I'm sure I'm fine. Probably just a stomach virus or something.

She sent the message, then tapped her fingers on the desk, waiting. Behind her, Arielle snored lightly on the couch. She'd thank Sabrina for buying her time. Of course, for all she knew, the effects of the steak might actually last a few days. She hoped not, for Arielle's sake.

After several minutes, she gave up hoping for a reply from Tucker. He must've gone to bed.

She changed into her pajamas and curled under the quilt, tucking the cover under her chin. If they could survive the next two weeks, everything could return to normal. Arielle would be gone, and she and Tucker could continue writing. She could revert to sneaking glances at the café while he sipped his coffee. That was all she wanted.

But if that were all she wanted, Sabrina wondered why the thought of returning to normal carved a hollow spot in the center of her chest.

Laughter was the first thing Sabrina heard when she opened her apartment door. She closed the door, tossed her bag on the desk, and followed the sound of Arielle's soft voice. She found her cousin on the balcony, the phone cradled between her cheek and shoulder.

"That's so true," she was saying. "Oh, hi, Sabrina." She pulled her bare feet from the railing. "Sabrina's home," she said into the phone. "Okay. All right." Another chuckle.

Sabrina went to the kitchen and pulled the pitcher of iced tea from the fridge. She wondered who Arielle was talking to. It could be Aunt Bev, or Uncle Everett, or Jaylee. But Sabrina had a sinking feeling it wasn't any of them. Through the mesh screen, she heard Arielle laugh again.

Sabrina poured a glass of tea and took a long drink. They'd been busy at the café. Evan had called in sick and they hadn't found a replacement, so she'd bussed her own tables.

She heard the beep of the phone being turned off, then the grinding slide of the screen door.

Arielle stopped inside the door, all signs of laughter gone. "You told him I'm sick?"

Sabrina tried to decipher the source of her cousin's anger. "You were puking at his house last night."

"I feel better today. I told you this morning."

"You said you still felt nauseous."

"I said I felt a *tad* nauseous, but much better."

What in the world? Her cousin set the phone in the cradle and passed her on the way to the fridge.

"He has tickets to the community theater tonight," Arielle said.

"And . . . ?"

Arielle tossed her a look. "And now I can't go because he thinks I'm sick. He said I needed to stay home and rest."

"I thought you'd be relieved to avoid a few dates. I thought you'd be pleased."

Arielle surveyed the contents of the fridge.

Cold air washed over Sabrina, raising gooseflesh. Clearly Arielle was not pleased about missing her date. Clearly Arielle wanted to be with Tucker. Sabrina tamped down the fear that perched on the stoop of her heart.

Arielle pulled out a bottle of organic juice and shut the door. "What's done is done, I guess." She passed Sabrina and called over her shoulder, "Oh, I told Tucker you'd accompany him to the theater tonight."

She *what*? Sabrina followed Arielle to the living room, where her cousin had plopped on the sofa and flipped on the TV.

"You told Tucker *I'd* go with him?"

Arielle took a swig of her juice, taking her time, then set it on the end table and smiled sweetly. "I thought you'd be pleased."

Sabrina's own words came back to haunt her, and Arielle seemed to enjoy the fact. "Why can't he just skip the dumb play?"

"His secretary has one of the lead roles, and this is the last night it's showing."

So what? Why did that require him to drag Sabrina along? Her heart was performing a traitorous show of its own. "Can't he go alone?"

"He has two tickets."

"Well, can't he find someone else?" Her voice crescendoed.

Arielle changed the channel, surfing with a calmness that made Sabrina want to throttle her.

"I told him you loved the theater," she said. "And there's no need for his money to go to waste. He's already underwriting the Nantucket Light Keepers," Arielle so kindly reminded her.

Soundkeepers. Sabrina clenched her teeth. That was beside the point. Arielle knew how hard it was for her to be with Tucker. Then again, it was hard to see Arielle with Tucker too. Which was worse? Waiting for Arielle to return from her date or suffering through it herself?

Come on, Sabrina. Suffering?

Okay, so she enjoyed being with Tucker. That was the problem.

"He's picking you up at five."

"Five?" The play couldn't start until seven or eight at least.

"You're going to supper first."

"Supper?"

"Are you going to repeat everything I say? He already had reservations."

Oh, sure, reservations. That made all the sense in the world. Sabrina glared at Arielle, but her cousin seemed oblivious to her distress.

Finally, Sabrina wandered toward her bedroom, seeing her own dazed look in the oval mirror Arielle had hung in the hall. That thing was so coming down.

She was going on a date with Tucker.

You are going on a date with Tucker.

It's not a real date. He doesn't even want to be with you. You're a substitute for Arielle. Keep that in mind.

If she remembered that, she'd be fine. The only question was, could she make herself remember it when she was staring into Tucker's eyes across a candlelit table?

Sweetpea: Little-known fact about me: I haven't worn heels since prom.

Harbormaster: Little-known fact about me: I haven't worn a suit since I dropped out of law school. Little-known fact number two: I have a special appreciation for people who wear choking neckties.

Twenty-five

Le Languedoc was a restaurant and inn located downtown on Broad Street. The building featured cedar shake shingles, white trim, and blue shutters that matched the awning outside.

Sabrina fidgeted with the wispy strings of her belt as Tucker pulled into a parallel parking space. She pressed her lips together, unaccustomed to the sticky feel of lip gloss. *"Just a little,"* Arielle had said when she protested. *"You already have those gorgeous thick eyelashes, but a little color on your lips will do wonders."*

Judging by Tucker's expression when she'd answered the door, maybe Arielle was right.

Tucker turned off the engine, then helped her from the car. They hadn't taken five steps when her heel caught in a crack on the sidewalk. She stumbled forward.

Tucker steadied her, his hands burning the skin on her arms.

Idiot! She couldn't even walk a few steps in these ridiculous shoes Arielle had loaned her. Why hadn't she worn flats? She felt like a little girl playing dress-up in her mother's clothes.

"I should've let you off at the door," Tucker said.

"I'm a klutz in heels."

He laughed, a deep and warm sound. "This from the server who balances five plates of food on a tray, skirting tables and waitstaff without a spill?" He smiled.

The host took them out to the terrace, a secluded garden covered with an awning. Over their heads, white lights twinkled.

They were seated at a blue checkered table in the corner of the patio. Patrons filled the other tables, their chatter creating a quiet clamor. They looked at home in this upscale restaurant with their expensive jewelry and name-brand handbags.

The evening was mild, and the patio shielded them from the ocean breeze. The delicious aroma of garlic and steak filled the patio.

"Have you been here?" Tucker asked.

"No, I haven't."

He looked so handsome in his crisp white shirt and blue tie that matched his eyes. *He's wearing a tie.* She opened the menu, more to occupy her hands than anything. He opened his as well, and when the server came, they placed their orders.

Before an awkward silence could settle, Sabrina spoke, "So, your secretary is in the play?"

He propped his arms on the table, and she noted the sturdy thickness of his forearms protruding from his rolled-up cuffs.

"Dorothy. She's sixty-something years old and half-blind, but she throws herself into whatever she's doing."

"So what's the play we're seeing?"

"*Cinderella*. She plays the fairy godmother."

"Oh, for a fairy godmother! I can see where that would come in handy." She cringed as the sentence ended and took a sip of water. She wished she knew what to say, how to act. It had been a long time since she'd had a date.

"You don't need one tonight. You look especially nice. I like your hair down."

After staring at Arielle, she probably seemed plain as a weed next to an exotic orchid. "You don't have to say that." She immediately wished she could recall the words. He was going to think she was fishing for a compliment.

"It's true."

She glanced at him. His eyes turned down at the corners. She picked at the tablecloth, deciding not to argue. She didn't need someone patronizing her, especially not Tucker. Even Jared had rarely commented on her appearance. She didn't expect flattery.

Sabrina checked her watch, wondering how long the food would take and what they'd talk about until it arrived.

"Bored already?" The corners of his lips turned up.

"No, I just—I just wondered what time the play starts."

"We have plenty of time."

Great. Just what she wanted to hear.

"How was work today?" he asked. "You seemed busy."

She was glad for the trivial subject. "Evan was sick, so we bussed our own tables, which made it pretty hectic."

"Do you like working at the café?"

She shrugged. "I'm good at it, and it pays the bills."

"What about your work for Renny?"

"I love it. I hope someday when she's published and writing a couple books a year, she'll want me full-time."

The server brought their drinks. Sabrina sipped her tea. She'd thought Tucker might question her about Arielle, but he seemed content with casual conversation.

She had a flashback of the night he'd driven her home when it was raining. That night replayed itself often with vivid accuracy. The warmth of his palm on her wrist, his deep, throaty laugh. The woodsy smell of his cologne a breath away. The way he'd looked at her, as if she mattered.

Had Sabrina read more into the moment than there was?

Did it matter? There was no future for her and Tucker. Nothing beyond an email relationship.

And what would happen if Tucker and Arielle fell in love for real?

———

Tucker escorted Sabrina into the United Methodist Church, placing his hand on the small of her back as they navigated the crowd. She looked beautiful in the elegant navy blue dress. Her hair spilled around her shoulders like a dark veil, and it was all he could do to keep from touching it, from running his fingers through it. It had been a task keeping his eyes off her.

He greeted a few people, nodding on their way past. Normally he'd stop and chat, but he wanted Sabrina to himself. They found seats near the middle of the room next to an elderly couple who held hands. He wished he could take Sabrina's hand, but he was supposed to be in love with Arielle.

When Sabrina set her purse on the floor, he sneaked a glance at her. Her hair swung forward, falling across her cheek. She sat back, tucking it behind her ear, and the fragrance of lilacs and something citrusy reached his nostrils. He inhaled deeply. This may be his one and only date with Sabrina. If only he could get her to confess what was holding her back. He couldn't even email the question now. He was supposed to think Arielle was Sweetpea.

"You haven't asked about Arielle," she said, as if reading his mind. Her hands were folded primly in her lap.

"Was I supposed to?" A woman squeezed by with her teenage daughter.

"I thought you might ask my opinion of her."

"What do you think of her?"

She tossed him a look. "She's awfully nice."

What could he say? He had to be careful. "She wears a lot of makeup."

"I thought men liked that." She reached over her shoulder, to toy with her ponytail, he thought, but when she found her hair unbound, she returned her hand to her lap, seemingly oblivious to the jingle of her charm bracelet.

"Some do, I guess. I always liked a more natural look." His eyes took in Sabrina's natural beauty. Sometimes nature couldn't be improved upon.

He cleared his throat. "But you're right, Arielle is nice. A little . . . flighty, but nice."

She frowned at him, as though she were trying to look inside him.

"What?" he asked.

"I thought you liked her."

Was he handling this badly? What did she want from him? Did she want him to want Arielle? Was he supposed to be singing her praises? "I do."

She faced forward, the picture of calm. He would've believed it, except her hands were clasped so tightly her fingertips went pink, her knuckles white.

Ah, it's getting to you, my little Sweetpea. He was torn between tweaking her jealousy and comforting her. He settled somewhere in between.

"She's not exactly what I expected."

"What do you mean?" Her voice sounded squeezed through a knot.

He didn't know how to respond and wondered why he'd said it. The lights dimmed, and Tucker breathed a sigh of relief as the audience quieted.

"To be continued," he whispered.

⌐⌐⌐

Sabrina's mind wandered through the play. What did he mean Arielle wasn't what he'd expected? Was that good or bad? Was he suspicious that Arielle wasn't Sweetpea?

"There's Dorothy," Tucker whispered in her ear a few scenes later. His breath tickled strands of hair and sent a shiver down her spine.

Onstage, his secretary had made her appearance to a disheveled-looking Cinderella. The godmother's sparkly silver dress hugged her thick waist, and she waved a magic wand as she talked. Her brunette wig matched her conspicuous glasses. As oddly casted as she was in the role, she played it well.

As the play progressed, Sabrina forgot the woman was sixty-something and wearing thick glasses. All the actors were talented and, by the time Prince Charming put the glass slipper on Cinderella's foot, Sabrina realized she'd lost herself in the story.

After the actors returned for a curtain call, Tucker and Sabrina followed the throng of people into the darkened night. He ushered her with his hand at her back, and Sabrina's pulse sped at his touch. She could feel the heat of his palm through the thin material of her dress.

When they reached his car, he helped her in, then slid in behind the wheel. "What'd you think?"

Sabrina clutched her bag in her lap. "Bravo. Your Dorothy seems pretty feisty."

"You don't know the half of it." He tossed her a grin.

His right arm rested on the console between them, inches from her own. If this were a real date, would he take her hand? Would he lift it and press his lips to the ridges of her knuckles?

"I realized halfway through the play I left my cell phone on my boat," he said. "Would you mind if I swung by the harbor and got it? They're calling for rain tonight."

"Not at all."

Once they left the theater traffic, the roads were deserted. He turned toward the wharf.

The thought of a few extra minutes with Tucker gave her more joy than was healthy. *Just a few extra minutes. What could it hurt? Tomorrow will be here soon enough, and he'll be back with Arielle.*

She didn't want to think about that. She wanted to live in the moment for a change and not consider the ramifications.

She laid her head against the headrest and closed her eyes. For now, right this minute, Tucker was beside her. If she concentrated, she could hear him breathing above the whir of the car's engine. If she inhaled, she could smell the woodsy fragrance of his cologne. If she tried hard enough, she could imagine the way his jawline would feel against the softness of her fingers.

"You look peaceful."

Her eyes snapped open. He was parked outside his office, the streetlamp shedding a pale yellow glow on his features. How long had they been there?

"What were you thinking?"

A hot flush climbed her neck. "I don't remember."

"You had a little smile."

Remembering the direction of her thoughts, her mouth went dry. He was looking at her like—like he wanted to look at her. Like there was no place else he'd rather be. Like there was no one else he'd rather be with.

Absurd. He was in love with Sweetpea. Or Arielle. She wasn't sure which. She wasn't sure who was who anymore.

She cleared her throat. "You'd better get your cell."

He looked away, out over the darkened water, and removed the key from the ignition. "Come with me."

"Why?" His boat was a short walk down the pier.

"I want to show you something."

In his boat? At night?

"Come on. Take a walk on the wild side. You don't have to get up early tomorrow."

He had her there. "True."

"Come on." He motioned toward the door with his head and exited the car.

Curious, she did the same, then followed him down the lit pier, careful of where she stepped. With her luck, one of her heels would catch between the boards and she'd fall flat on her face.

When they reached his boat, he helped her onboard. "Have a seat back there," he said. "Are you chilly?"

"Are we going somewhere?"

"Don't you trust me?"

"Do you always answer questions with questions?"

He smiled. "Only with you." He untied the boat, then retrieved a thick blanket from a cubby and wrapped it around her.

Tucker sat in the captain's seat, pocketed his cell phone, then started the boat.

Moments later, they were gliding slowly through the harbor, the lights from town growing distant. What were they doing out here? Why did he want to take her out on his boat when he should be eager to get her back to her apartment and see how Arielle was faring?

Why are you looking a gift horse in the mouth?

When they cleared the harbor, he accelerated and the wind kicked up, blowing her hair off her face. She drew the blanket tighter and closed her eyes, letting the cool air wash over her. What would it be like if Tucker were her boyfriend? What would it be like if he were her husband? If everything was different? If everything weren't so complicated?

She opened her eyes and watched him navigate the smooth water of the ocean. The moon lit his white shirt, and the wind tossed his hair. His shoulders looked sturdy and broad, wider than the seat back.

He looked back at her as if to confirm she was still there. They exchanged a smile.

Pretend everything is different. Just for tonight. What could it hurt? Just to be with him and relax and let whatever happens happen.

It wasn't like anything would happen anyway. Tucker was in love with Sweetpea. Or Arielle. Or whomever.

She shook her head, not wanting to work at the fussy knot her life had become. *Forget all that. Just think about now. Right now. Out here. Me, Tucker, and the open sea.*

A few minutes later he slowed the boat and the wind died down. It was dark out on the water. Only the glow of the moon lit their way. The boat drifted to a stop, and Tucker walked toward her.

"You look cute all wrapped up like that."

She was sure she'd never been called cute. Maybe she had a fairy godmother after all.

Tucker sat beside her on the narrow bench. "We're here."

She looked around them. There wasn't a soul or anything else around. Only a blanket of darkness that hid the world from sight. "Of course we are."

He smiled. "You're going to be just like Dorothy when you're about sixty, know that?"

"Alone and feisty?" The words slipped out before she knew they were coming. She didn't like how vulnerable it made her, and she wished she could snatch them back.

"The feisty's a definite."

She could feel him watching her. She didn't dare look. Her eyes fixed on the water off the port side where the moon shimmered on the surface.

"The alone part is up to you," he said.

Not so much, she thought. But what did he know?

You weren't going to think about that tonight, remember? Why was it so hard for her to relax?

Uh, because she had one hundred and ninety pounds of man flesh sitting beside her?

Not just any man flesh. Tucker. And he was looking at her again.

"Why are we here?" Her voice cracked on the question.

He didn't seem to notice. "The second show."

"Second show?"

"Up there." He pointed upward, and she followed the direction of his finger.

Overhead, the sky was a black canvas, smooth as velvet and dotted with what looked like a million fireflies. She'd never seen so many stars. Some as bright as the moon, others so faint she could hardly see them.

"There are so many." She looked up until her neck began to ache.

Tucker placed his arm along the back of the bench. "Lean back." His eyes glowed dark in the shadows. Her heart stuttered.

She laid her head in the crook of his elbow, the strength of his bare arm resting against her neck. Oh, how she'd missed this. Things email could never provide. *Security. Comfort.* She could list a hundred more.

She inhaled the scent of his cologne, not daring to tear her eyes from the night sky. *Smells.*

The boat rocked slightly, a cradle on the water. The wind hummed a lullaby and waves lapped the boat, a gentle percussion.

"Sabrina?" he whispered.

Voices. She swallowed around a dry lump in her throat. *Don't look.* Do. Not. Look.

"What?" she asked so quietly she wasn't sure if he heard.

"Look at me." His voice, low and deep, beckoned.

She turned her head. He was so close. His breath mingled with the salty air and cooled her cheeks. His eyes . . .

His eyes were a deep pool, the color of the ocean at midnight. Had anyone ever looked at her the way he looked at her now? What was there, shimmering on the surface? Longing? Devotion? Desperation? She soaked it up, every ounce.

"What?" she asked, needing to know. Needing words, not trusting herself to interpret his expression.

And then his hand was on her face, his palm cooling her flushed cheek. His thumb grazed the ridge of her lower lip, and she thought her lungs might explode. *Touches.*

He drew closer, and then his lips were on hers, the merest of touches. A butterfly's wings, a baby's breath. It shook her to the core.

His lips tasted hers, teasing gently. *Kisses.*

It had been so long since she'd felt like this. Had she ever felt like this? Really wanted? Needed?

He deepened the kiss, ran his hand through her hair. This wanting, this needing, filled her to overflowing. She breathed him in. Tucker. The man who knew everything about her, the man who knew her every scar, inside and out. The man who loved her anyway.

Only he didn't know he loved her. Didn't know she was Sweetpea.

He was supposed to love Sweetpea.

Why was he kissing her? She felt betrayed. Then she felt silly because he was betraying her with *her.*

Even so, the feeling persisted. If he loved Sweetpea, how could he kiss Sabrina? She felt enraged on Sweetpea's behalf.

She pushed at his chest, breaking the kiss.

Her breaths came hard and short. She saw the confusion in his eyes before she turned. "Take me home."

"What's wrong?"

The answer to that question could fill a book. Did she have desperation written all over her? Is that why he'd kissed her? Wasn't he getting enough action from Arielle? The thought provoked her.

"I've had enough of the second show." She pulled the blanket more tightly around her, but the chill seeped right through.

He touched her hair. She flinched away. A lump the size of Texas lodged in her throat, and she feared she'd really make a fool of herself if he didn't put some distance between them. Why had she come out here with him? What was she hoping to prove?

Her thoughts from earlier washed over her, mocking her. *Pretend everything is different. Just for tonight. What could it hurt? Just to be with him and relax and let whatever happens happen.*

Stupid, stupid.

Now she knew what it could hurt. Her. The ache spread from her throat to her stomach and camped there.

"I'm sorry," Tucker said, still looking at her. "I didn't mean—"

Didn't mean what? Didn't mean to kiss her? Didn't mean he wanted her? Didn't mean to betray the woman he really loved?

She'd never know what he didn't mean, because after he said it, he went to start the boat, leaving her huddled against the cold.

Sweetpea: Kissing is highly underrated. Characters in movies go from first base to home plate in one giant leap. Doesn't anyone value the kiss anymore?

Harbormaster: I do. ;-)

Twenty-six

"So . . ." Arielle bombarded Sabrina the moment she stepped from her room the next morning. "Tell all. How was your date?"

Sabrina rubbed her temples and headed to the kitchen to start a pot of coffee. "I don't want to talk about it." It was bad enough that it kept her awake until all hours of the night. The quiet ride back on the boat. The tense ride home in the car. The awkward goodbye. Her mind had whirled like a hurricane all night.

Arielle followed her to the kitchen. "What do you mean you don't want to talk about it?"

"I mean I don't want to talk about it." Sabrina rinsed the pot and added water to the tank. "As far as I'm concerned, you're fit and healthy again. You go out with him tonight." Even as she said it, a stab of jealousy pierced her.

Thank goodness it was her day off. She didn't think she could face Tucker so soon after—

"I don't understand."

"You don't have to." It was Arielle he wanted to see. She'd only been a substitute last night. Maybe he'd been lonely and desperate or something. Maybe he wasn't the man she thought he was. The Tucker she knew would never have made out with one woman while in love with another.

Maybe he was like Jared after all. Maybe all men were.

She set the filter in the basket and plugged in the coffeemaker, shoving the bracelet up her arm when it got in her way. So much for the tangible reminder of heartbreak. She'd blocked everything sensible from her head the night before. Her head pounded now. She needed caffeine. She needed peace. She needed a new life.

"Did he say something?" Arielle asked.

Sabrina turned toward the living room.

Arielle took her arm. "He thinks I'm sick. This is your chance with him."

"I don't want a chance with him. He's all yours." Sabrina jerked away.

"Sabrina!"

"I'm taking a shower." Sabrina closed the conversation with the slam of the bathroom door, but not before she heard Arielle's growl of frustration.

Renny was potting a plant in the front yard when Sabrina was leaving for the post office. Her shadow fell over Renny's form like a dark cloak as she approached.

"Morning," Renny said. Her bare knees dug into the soil and her calloused heels were propped in the air.

The yard had become a profusion of color over the past several weeks. Sabrina wondered where Renny was going to fit the flowering plant once it was potted.

"*Gan Eden*'s filling up fast," she said. "Are you stuck on your story? Do you want to brainstorm more?"

Renny scooped dirt from the bag into the terra-cotta pot. "No, I don't think so." She brushed her hair from her face with the back of her hand.

"I had some ideas the other day that might work."

Renny put down the scoop and sat back on her haunches. "Listen, I decided to give up writing."

Had the woman lost her marbles? "What?" Of all the zany ideas Renny had, this was the craziest of all.

"Don't worry, I want you to stay in the apartment, and I won't charge you rent. I love having you here; you're good company. More than that. You're like a daughter to me, really. But I'm done with writing. I'm going back to what I know. Gardening."

"You know how to write. You're extremely proficient."

"Not proficient enough."

"I've told you, it's just a matter of time!" The thought of all that talent wasted made Sabrina ill. "Someone is going to want *Danger*, just wait and see."

Renny retrieved the shovel and started scooping. "No, no, I don't think so. I'm tired of trying. I'll never be good enough."

"You're good enough *now*. You'll probably get the call any day."

"No, I won't."

How could the woman be so stubborn? "I guarantee it."

Renny laughed, not the pleasant kind. "I don't think so, *amita*."

There was something Renny wasn't telling her. "What's going on, Renny?" Something wasn't right. Why would Renny quit when she was still waiting to hear from several publishers? Unless she'd gotten the rejections . . .

"Did you—have you heard from the publishers?" Surely not. Sabrina couldn't imagine anyone saying no to *Danger*.

"No, I haven't." Renny patted the dirt with her bare hands, packing it tightly around the gnarled stem.

"Well, see then? There's still—"

"I didn't send them." Renny pulled her soiled hands back and grabbed another scoop of dirt.

"Are you still unsatisfied with the characterization? Do you want to work on it some more?"

Renny stood suddenly, rubbing the soil from her hands. She studied Sabrina as if trying to make a decision. Finally she said, "Come here."

She walked toward the porch, and Sabrina followed onto the brick stoop. They entered the foyer and walked past the airy living room into the dining room, which overlooked the ocean. Renny bent in front of the cherry hutch and pulled out a fat drawer. It settled in place with a squawk.

Renny stood upright. "There they are."

Sabrina looked into the drawer, filled to the brim with stacks of paper. "Your manuscripts?"

"All nine of them."

Renny's words from earlier soaked in. *"I didn't send them."*

That's not what she meant . . . that she hadn't sent them, any of them, to publishers. Was it?

"I never sent them." Renny crossed her arms over the toucan on her Hawaiian shirt. "I didn't mean to lie, but I couldn't do it."

"Why not?" All those years of writing, locked in a drawer? All the work Renny had done, all the work Sabrina had done, wasted? She didn't understand.

Renny went to the sink, turned on the faucet, and pumped some soap. "I was waiting until my writing was good enough. I was going to go back and fix the earlier ones." She shook her head.

Sabrina looked at the drawer of manuscripts. The earlier ones were weak in spots. Pacing problems, weak writing, stale characters. The last three, though . . . she'd wondered why some publisher hadn't snapped them up. Now she knew. Renny had never sent them.

"Why did you do it, then? Why spend all those hours—all those hours, Renny!—writing and brainstorming and researching? Why do all that work and just . . . stick it in a drawer?"

"I don't expect you to understand."

"You're right, I don't understand." Her words wobbled. All those hours she'd spent researching locations and killing methods and police procedure. All those hours reading and editing. She'd been paid for her work, but it felt empty. All for nothing. Where was the faith Renny clung to?

"What about God and his will that you talk about?" Sabrina asked. "How can he do his will when you won't do your part? Send them to your agent now. At least the last three."

Renny dried her hands. "I can't."

Sabrina reached into the drawer. "Then I will." It was a small matter to write a cover letter and stick them in the mail.

"Stop it!" Renny grabbed her arm. "Leave them be. It's not your place."

Sabrina straightened. Renny was right. It was her work. Her decision. She had to know one thing. "Did you ever intend to send them?"

Renny closed the drawer, and it creaked under its load. "I was going to send them when they were good enough."

Sabrina opened her mouth to say they already were, then shut it again. She'd already said it, many times over. One more time wouldn't make Renny believe it.

Harbormaster: Remember in sixth grade when we just had to ask a friend if so-and-so liked us? Life was much simpler then, huh?

Twenty-seven

Arielle was waiting for Tucker when he arrived at the Even Keel Cafe. He navigated the maze of tables and joined her in the corner against the rear wall. The scent of seafood and grilled steak tempted his taste buds, reminding him he'd skipped lunch.

Arielle had left a voice mail on his cell, asking to meet after work. She looked up as he approached, her wide smile absent.

"Hi." He slipped into the chair across from her.

"You got my message, obviously."

"I tried to call you back. Got the machine." He'd expected Sabrina would answer. Had half hoped she would. Maybe she had caller ID.

Before he could grab the menu, Arielle leaned forward, intent. "What did you do?"

"What? Nothing."

"You didn't tell her you knew?"

"No." He wondered why she thought that. Sabrina had been

so quiet all the way home, despite his efforts to initiate conversation. "What did she say?"

"She didn't say anything. And I mean nothing. She's been quiet as a mouse all day."

Was she angry he'd kissed her? He'd hoped Arielle might be able to enlighten him. He'd almost sent Sabrina a message that morning. But he could hardly mention the kiss when he wasn't supposed to know Sabrina was Sweetpea.

"What did you do?" Arielle was giving him the look she probably used on her preschoolers. Her arms were crossed now.

He shifted on the chair. He could say nothing. What was another secret between friends? Then again, what did it matter if he told her?

"I—uh. I might have kissed her."

Her eyes widened. "You *might* have kissed her?"

Was that such a bad thing? A man kissing the woman he loved? He had nothing to be ashamed of. Then why did he feel so rotten?

"Well, she kissed me back," he said in a small voice.

"But that's a good thing," Arielle said.

"You would think." It had sure felt good. It felt good every time he relived it too. Right up until the moment she pushed him away and demanded he take her home.

"Huh," Arielle said.

The server came and took their orders. The restaurant was noisy, the clatter of scraping utensils and the loud hum of too many conversations. It was giving Tucker a headache.

"So, what happened after the kiss, if you don't mind my asking."

"She pushed me away and asked me to take her home."

Arielle frowned. "That's it?"

He decided to skip the part about his heart beating madly. "That's it."

Arielle sipped her tea. "Huh," she said again when she set down her glass.

That's all he got? *Huh*? Weren't women supposed to have insight into each other's souls? They were cousins; she had to know something.

"She thinks you're cheating on her," Arielle said.

"What?"

Arielle took a white bottle from her cavernous bag, unscrewed the lid and dumped green powder into her water. It turned cloudy.

"You're supposed to be in love with Sweetpea, who you're supposed to think is me, and yet you went out with her and put the moves on her." She stirred the water and took a sip.

The stuff looked like algae water. Tucker grimaced. *And steak makes her ill?*

"She thinks you're cheating on her," Arielle said.

"You mean on Sweetpea?"

"Who is supposed to be me."

Tucker rubbed the back of his neck. For crying out loud.

"She feels betrayed."

"By her own self?"

"Think about it. You're not supposed to know she's Sweetpea, so what's she supposed to think when you're in love with Sweetpea, yet kiss her?"

So complicated. When had life gotten so complicated? What sense did Arielle's speculation make? How could he cheat on Sabrina with

Sabrina? Though, in a wacky sort of way, it made sense when you figured Sabrina didn't know he knew. He rubbed his eyes.

"I have a tincture for headaches if you want to try it."

He looked at the disgusting green water. "If it's anything like that, I'll stick to Tylenol, thank you."

She shrugged, capped the white bottle, and tossed it into the cavity of her bag.

"So what now?" he asked. "What am I supposed to do?" Arielle was her cousin. Surely she had some insight, some idea about how to make Sabrina crack.

"You connected online, and that's comfortable for Sabrina. That's your only real connection at this point. I suggest you go back to that."

"I want a real relationship with her."

Arielle gulped down the green stuff, gave a tiny shudder, then followed up with a sip of tea. "You just work on the relationship where she's comfortable." She smiled furtively. "And leave the rest to me."

Sweetpea: Have you ever told anyone about our letters?

Harbormaster: Just my sister.

Twenty-eight

Sabrina heard the ding of a message hitting her inbox and realized she'd forgotten to reduce the volume before turning in. She wasn't sleeping anyway. She crawled out from under the covers and crept into the living room. Arielle, a shadowed lump on the couch, breathed a soft snore.

Sabrina slid into the chair and moved the mouse, awakening the computer. It was Tucker.

Are you awake? he'd written.

Like she could sleep after fretting over Tucker and Arielle all night. Her cousin had returned with a mysterious grin that left Sabrina with an empty ache.

Yes.

Sabrina had wanted to ask Arielle how their date went. But each time the words had caught in her throat. What if she didn't want to know? A new message arrived with a ding. Sabrina muted the volume, then opened the message.

Wanna chat awhile?

Yes, she typed.

What was Tucker thinking about right now? Was he remembering his night with Arielle? Was he thinking about how beautiful she was in her gauzy white shirt and fitted jeans? Another message arrived.

Are you going to answer all my questions with a yes?

She smiled.

Yes.

It had been a while since they'd chatted on email. She missed it. She missed him. Her thoughts turned to the kiss they'd shared on the boat the night before. If she closed her eyes, she could still feel his lips on hers. *You have got to stop this! It's getting you nowhere.* She opened her eyes to a new message.

In that case, I'll have to come up with something more consequential to ask.

Her stomach fluttered. What would he want if he could ask anything, knowing her answer would be yes?

She placed her hands over the keyboard.

I'll ask the questions here. ☺ If you had one wish, anything you wanted, what would it be? Something for yourself—not world peace.

She sent the message and leaned back, ready for a wait. Instead, an email popped right back.

You first.

She smiled. No fair. She wrote the first thing that came to mind.

To be beautiful.

She sent the message, then wished she could reach into cyberspace and retrieve it. He would say she was beautiful because he thought she was Arielle. And Sabrina didn't want to hear him rave about Arielle's beauty.

She opened his reply with trepidation.

You have a lasting beauty, soul-deep. The kind that won't fade with age. Save your wish for something you need.

Sabrina reread his answer. Not what she'd expected. He hadn't raved about Arielle's beautiful smile or her gorgeous hair. His words warmed her.

She poised her fingers over the keys.

Your turn.

She speculated about what he'd say. More time to enjoy life? A family of his own? She realized she didn't know what Tucker wanted most, and that surprised her after all the hours, all the letters. How had they not discussed this before?

His message arrived, and she opened it eagerly.

I want to know you more.

What could he mean? They did know each other well. And he was now seeing her in person, or so he thought. She wanted to ask, but reconsidered.

Maybe you'd be disappointed.

She sent the message, then feared it had been a mistake. Before the anxiety peaked, she got his reply.

Never.

Sabrina closed her eyes. If only it were true. If only things were different.

This conversation was getting out of hand. It was getting scary. She needed to change the subject.

Tell me something about you that I don't know.

Maybe he'd tell her how he'd gotten the scar between the knuckles of his right hand. Or maybe he'd tell her about his first dance or his favorite place to think.

The email appeared in her inbox, and she clicked it open.

I love you.

Her lungs constricted, pinching off her air supply, making her next breath impossible. Her lungs were too big for her chest. Her skin too tight for her heart. The words, blurred on the screen.

The cursor's arrow pointed to the words, emphasizing them. He'd never said it before, when she was just Sweetpea. Why couldn't he have said it before Arielle had come? She wanted full claim on the words, wanted to snatch them up, draw them close like a favorite blanket.

But the words didn't belong to her. They were Arielle's.

Would Tucker have said them if he knew who she was? She didn't have to answer, didn't even want to. Had he told Arielle tonight? Is that what caused her mysterious smile?

Then she remembered the question that had preceded his words. She'd asked him to reveal something she didn't know. He couldn't have told Arielle. But what if he said it tomorrow night or the next? What if Arielle was falling for him too?

Another message appeared. Her pulse raced like a boat hitting the open sea.

I don't expect you to say anything. I just wanted you to know.

The truth was, and she couldn't deny it any longer, she loved him too. God help her, but she did.

You can't tell him. Yes, she knew that too. There was nothing she could say. Her breath came in quick puffs, drying her mouth. She had to put an end to this conversation before she found herself in deeper waters.

She took the mouse, her fingers trembling, and clicked on the X, closing the program before she did something really foolish — like telling Tucker the truth.

Sweetpea: My aunt and cousins keep trying to reach me. If I avoid them, will they go away? Sorry to be so snarky. I was never good at conflict resolution.

Twenty-nine

Only when Sabrina saw Tucker ambling toward his table did she realize she'd been hoping he wouldn't have the audacity to show. But there he was, seating himself at his usual table, looking too handsome, turning that crooked grin on Oliver.

Just the one peek of him with his cap pulled low over his curls sent her traitorous mind back to the boat where she'd been within arm's reach of heaven. *Deep breaths, Sabrina. Deep breaths.*

Resolutely, she grabbed the coffee and headed his way. *It's just another day at the café, another morning pouring coffee for Tucker, pretending I'm just his server.* Never mind his lips had been locked on hers two brief days ago.

Not helpful.

Mercifully, Oliver's mug needed to be topped. Two extra seconds' stalling time. "Thanks, Sabrina."

She drew a deep breath and turned. *Just another day* . . . "Good morning, Tucker." *Pour coffee. Do not make eye contact. Do not pass go. Do not collect two hundred kisses.*

Dollars.

"Sabrina." He nodded, or at least, she thought he did.

"I was wondering . . ." he began.

The kitchen bell dinged. Saved by the bell. "Excuse me." She rushed toward the window, but it was Char's order.

"I'll get it," Sabrina told the server, who was in the middle of making coffee.

"Thanks, hon."

No problem. She had to stay busy. Very, very busy. Her mind rewound Tucker's last words. What had he been fixing to say? *"I was wondering . . ."*

If we could talk?

If I could explain?

If we could go back to the break room and make out?

Bad, Sabrina.

She delivered the tray of food, and when three more tables filled in her station, she nearly shouted with glee. Thank God for summer people. They ran her for ketchup, extra napkins, and refills, and she was happy to oblige.

Her contact with Tucker the next half hour was limited to filling his mug twice, as she passed his table. Then finally, he was checking his watch. *Better go, Tucker. Can't be late for work.*

A few minutes later, the bell over the door jingled, signaling his departure, and Sabrina felt the weight of an oil barge lift off her shoulders.

The day was exhausting. The café hopped, but the tips were worth the hard work. By the time she pulled into her drive, however, she was ready for a brisk jog. Arielle had borrowed her bike to ride the Surfside bike path to the other side of the island so she'd be gone awhile. It was the perfect time to slip away and—

Someone was sitting on the steps to her loft. At the sound of her tires on the gravel, Tucker straightened from his slump.

Her heart found a new gear and, unfortunately, it wasn't Reverse. What was he doing here? He must be waiting for Arielle, but her cousin wouldn't be home until this evening. Why wasn't he at work?

She turned off the engine and exited the car, steeling herself against his boyish charm. Her eyes flickered over his broad shoulders and the thick forearms that rested on his jean-clad knees. Nothing boyish there.

A-hem.

"Sabrina." He pulled his cap off and stood.

"Tucker. Arielle's out for a bike ride, and I don't imagine she'll be back for a while." She moved toward the steps, but a body was in her way.

He put a hand on the railing, further blocking her path.

Sabrina hitched her purse strap higher, impatient to pass. Impatient to hide in her apartment.

"I came to see you," he said. Those eyes said things that held hers captive.

She cleared her throat and tore her gaze away. "You saw me this morning."

"I wanted to talk about the other night."

Oh, boy. She didn't want to go there. "I—uh—I was going to—" *Go for a jog. Wash my hair. Organize my sock drawer.*

"It'll just take a minute." He shuffled his cap in his hands, turning it in clockwise circles. He was nervous?

Well, he should be. He was the one who—

"Sit down a minute? Please?"

At one glimpse of his baby blues, her mouth went dry. So not fair. Her trembling legs gave way, and she settled beside him. His shoulder bumped hers as he sat, and she edged sideways, which put her knees against his thigh. She shifted again.

Get through this. Hear him out. It'll be over in a few minutes, and you'll be pounding the pavement in no time.

"I know this is . . . awkward . . ."

You think?

"But I'd rather address it and move forward than pretend there's no white elephant in the room."

Sabrina clutched her bag in her lap and watched an ant traverse the step below them. White elephants were underrated.

"The other night I—" He raked his hand through his hair like he might find the rest of the words in there somewhere. "I know you must be confused by what happened."

The kiss flashed in her mind, along with all the feelings it had evoked: desire, tenderness, joy. She had to stop this.

"I'm not sorry," he said in that deep voice that made her miss all those other things email lacked.

He was looking at her, but she was not going to look back. She wasn't. She'd be lost if she did. The other night, darkness had veiled her emotions, but now it was daylight, and she didn't know if she could conceal her thoughts. She was weak, fresh from the memory of that kiss.

"Unfortunately," he continued, "I can't explain why I kissed you. But I don't regret it."

The words brought a mixture of relief and fear and confusion. He couldn't explain? It made no sense. If he were in love with Sweetpea/Arielle, shouldn't he be sorry? Wouldn't his actions make him a first-rate jerk? Yet, she knew Tucker, and that description didn't fit. Not by a long shot.

"I'm sorry for the confusion I've caused. I want to be friends, and my only regret is that I've made things awkward between us."

Friends? Is that what they were? And what would happen when Arielle went home? Or would Tucker ask her cousin to stay? What reason could Arielle give for refusing to see him again, and where would that leave their online relationship? Why did this have to be so confusing?

"Sabrina?"

She had to focus. "Yes?" The black ant was hauling a chunk of something half the size of its body. Probably taking it home to feed its family of five.

Tucker bumped her shoulder, playfully.

She looked at him and fell smack into his shadowed blue eyes. As if the sight of him awakened her other senses, she became aware of his musky cologne, of his hip grazing hers. Have mercy. She could almost taste the kiss they'd shared, feel the tenderness of his lips as they brushed hers.

Now, she watched as those lips parted, as if he were fixing to speak. Her gaze flitted back to his eyes. Yes, he was about to say something. Something important.

She felt herself being pulled in, and she went willingly, all her fight draining away.

And then a memory. The smell of cigarette smoke, the taste of alcohol, the sound of a sheet ripping clear of a mattress.

She cleared her throat and broke eye contact. "Everything's fine, Tucker. Thanks for stopping by." She stood and clutched her bag to her stomach like a leather shield. "I'll have Arielle call when she returns."

She brushed past him, her feet taking the steps quickly as if she were late for an appointment. She heard Tucker's quiet goodbye in the beat between steps and wished her own life crisis could be tweaked and reworked like the plot of one of Renny's stories.

Sweetpea: Why is it so hard to get back on track once something has derailed? Your faith journey, your relationships, your career . . . sometimes it seems like the impossible task.

Thirty

Sabrina toweled off, then slipped into her favorite capris and a button-down blouse. She cleared the fog from the mirror and ran a comb through her wet hair. Arielle had been gone when she'd returned from work, probably out buying something else for the loft. The air smelled of paint, and the kitchen walls were still damp.

Sabrina surveyed the pale yellow she'd approved several days ago. It was drying to a nice buttery color. Arielle had worked hard to get it painted over the weekend.

The furniture had been rearranged again too. Sabrina frowned as she surveyed the room. Maybe she would get used to it.

She shook the thought and checked the time. Sabrina thought she and Arielle might go to 'Sconset to see the village and take a stroll along the Bluff Walk. Arielle would love the doll-sized houses in 'Sconset and the tiny picturesque gardens. It was Sabrina's favorite part of the island.

They could make sandwiches and take a picnic up to Sankaty Head Lighthouse. It was the least she could do after all the work her cousin had done. Arielle hadn't seen much of the island and, although she hadn't complained, it seemed a waste. Maybe on her next day off they could go out to Altar Rock for a view of the moors, cranberry bogs, and harbor. It was Sabrina's favorite view from the island.

Sabrina worked her hair quickly into a ponytail. It would be nice to spend time with her cousin. And with Jaylee's wedding looming only a few weeks out, she needed the wedding details so she could mentally prepare.

Between the frustration of Renny's disclosure and her confusion at Tucker's declaration of love, the idea of escaping the house, getting away from work, and hanging with her cousin appealed.

In the kitchen, she fished the deli roast beef from the fridge and made a quick sandwich for herself. She filled a pita with the deviled tofu Arielle made the day before, wrinkling her nose at the tangy smell and chunky texture. A wedge of cheese and a bag of chips rounded out the meal. She bagged it and set it in the fridge; then, as she closed the door, she heard Arielle enter the loft.

Her cousin rounded the corner, her ponytail swinging and her cheeks flushed.

She set a bag on the counter. "It is so gorgeous out there! I found a couple cute baskets at a shop in town," Arielle said.

"Thanks." Sabrina pulled the two Nantucket baskets from the bag, one a tightly woven cane with cherrywood rims, the other a door hanger basket in a pleasant honey color. "I like them." She set the baskets to the side, then poured two glasses of iced tea.

"Thanks." Arielle gulped half the glass at once. "Say, is Renny all right? I saw her on my way in, and she was raking the same patch of mulch over and over. She didn't even respond when I said hello."

Sabrina told Arielle about her confrontation with Renny over the manuscripts.

"She's been stuffing her stories in a drawer all this time? But isn't she paying you?"

"Indirectly. She lets me stay here in return for my help."

"What does that mean for you? Aren't you two pretty close?"

"I'm not worried about the apartment. Renny wants me to stay."

Sabrina rinsed her glass and set it in the sink. "What exasperates me is that she doesn't recognize her own talent. You know I don't dish out undeserved compliments, but that woman can write." Sabrina slapped the counter with her palm. "It's so frustrating. But at least now I know the problem isn't with a bunch of incompetent editors."

"No, it's a crazy writer who doesn't believe in herself."

"Apparently."

"Can't you send the stories?"

"I was going to. Renny went postal on me." She'd thought Renny was going to rip her arm off when she reached for those manuscripts. "And she's right. It's not my place. I can't make her want to risk rejection."

A thoughtful silence settled between them. Maybe with time Renny would find the courage to send her manuscripts. Sabrina had done all she could, and she'd have to let it go.

Enough brooding. They had the whole afternoon ahead of them.

"I have a surprise. I packed a picnic and thought I'd take you up to Sankaty Head and 'Sconset. It's my favorite place on the island. You have to see—what's wrong?"

"I didn't know you were planning something. Tucker asked if I could go for a boat ride to the other side of the island. I just have enough time for a bath and—hey, I have an idea."

"Why am I thinking I'm not going to like this?"

"Why don't you come along?" Arielle said with the enthusiasm of someone who'd just invented fried tomatoes.

"Like I want to be the third wheel of your bicycle built for two. No, thanks."

"Come on. We can bring your picnic. It'll be fun."

"Fun."

Arielle frowned. "It's not like you have anything better to do. You'll only sit here with your nose in a book."

"I like having my nose in a book." But even as she protested, her mind went there. She missed Tucker. She wanted to be with him. Heaven knew she'd relived those moments on the boat a thousand times. But this wouldn't be like that night. Instead she'd be subjected to watching Tucker fuss over Arielle, watching him touch Arielle, watching him gaze at Arielle as if she hung the moon. Same boat, different day.

"Again, no, thanks. The whole idea was for you to put your time in with him, remember? We had a deal."

Arielle stared her down, her jaw jutting out.

Stubborn. Sabrina crossed her arms. Let her stare. It wasn't going to work.

Her cousin finally surrendered. "Fine, be that way. It's not like he's a pill to go out with." Arielle stood, and, with a flip of her pony-tail, exited the room. "I'm taking a bath."

———

"This isn't working," Arielle called over the wind.

Tucker watched Arielle's hair settle on her shoulders as he slowed the boat and shut off the motor. Water lapped the hull as the boat drew to a stop and seagulls called from the beach. In the distance, the red and white of Sankaty Head Lighthouse was barely visible.

"What's not working?" he asked.

"This whole Sabrina thing. We have to kick it up a notch."

The words opened a hole in his gut. He hated this. He was starting to wish Arielle would go back to wherever she came from so he could pick up the pieces of his relationship with Sabrina.

"Are you mentioning our dates in your emails?" she asked. "Details and stuff that'll make her jealous?"

"Not really. I don't want to hurt Sabrina. I hate thinking about how she feels, knowing I'm with another woman. If it were me, it would be driving me crazy enough without the details." It had bugged him just to watch Cody ogling her, asking her over for dinner. He couldn't imagine how he'd feel if she were right next door with another man.

The sun was sinking in the sky, glowing pink behind a thin layer of clouds. Maybe it was time to call it quits. It was getting him nowhere. He wanted Sabrina to tell him who she was, but if she were going to, she would've done it by now. At this point, he just wanted the intimacy he'd had with her on email. Her letters were different since Arielle arrived, guarded. And how could he blame her?

He shifted toward Arielle. "Maybe it's time for a change of plans."

"What'd you have in mind?" A dainty brow arched.

"Have you considered going home early?"

"Tonight?"

"No, I mean leaving the island."

Her mouth parted, then slowly a look of hurt dimmed the light in her eyes. He didn't know what to make of that. It wasn't like they were buddies or something. She was there to help him achieve his goal, to help Sabrina lower that wall.

"This has been harder than I thought," Tucker said. "And we're not making headway with Sabrina."

"We need to give it more time." The hurt look was gone, shadowed by some other expression he couldn't interpret. "What if she sees us together more?"

"You already tried to convince her to come tonight. She's not going to agree to that. Can you blame her?"

"What if I invite you over when she's not expecting it?"

He sighed. "Arielle . . . I don't want to hurt her any more." God knew that was the truth. He had to do something soon before his relationship with Sabrina was damaged beyond repair.

"I love her," he said. He needed Arielle to understand how difficult this charade had become.

That look again. What was up with that?

"Maybe we can arrange for you and Sabrina to be together again, alone," she said finally.

"I don't think she's going to buy another illness." Still, the idea of being alone with her was tempting. If only they could make it work.

"I get migraines sometimes. Sabrina won't think anything is amiss if I have to bail out on a date at the last minute."

Maybe that would work. Still . . . "Last time we were alone, it didn't go so well. Actually it went too well." He grinned, feeling sheepish at his admission. "I seem to be short on self-control where your cousin is concerned."

Arielle looked away, admiring the sunset, he supposed.

"Maybe if we keep it fun," he wondered aloud. "No moonlit boat rides or romantic strolls on the beach."

"Maybe you could do something Sabrina enjoys."

"Yeah, something like that." Hope pried its way in, wedging open the door again. The boat rocked gently in the waves as he racked his brain for an idea. He mentally went through Sabrina's letters, searching for some activity she wouldn't turn down. What was she obsessed with? What activity would she do anything to participate in, even if it meant being stuck with him?

He felt a grin work its way onto his face. "I have an idea," he said.

Thirty-one

The front door slammed and, moments later, Arielle appeared in the kitchen. "Couldn't you have a more interesting hobby?"

Sabrina had tried to read all night. Too bad she hadn't gotten her mind off Tucker and Arielle long enough to finish a chapter. Finally, she'd given up and started a batch of cupcakes. Sometimes a girl needed chocolate.

"You have something against cupcakes?" Sabrina pulled the pan from the oven, and the sweet aroma filled the kitchen.

"Not *that* hobby. The book thing."

What was Arielle carrying on about? Whatever it was, she didn't seem pleased. "What are you talking about?"

"He's taking me to some dead writer's house in Boston. He cleared his schedule for a day, already bought tickets, and now I have to fake interest in some ancient property and probably a zillion artifacts. Booooorrrinnng."

A stitch caught in Sabrina's stomach. A writer's house in Boston? There were many of them, but only one she'd mentioned online. "Who? Which writer?"

Arielle pinched off a piece of hot cupcake and slid it in her mouth. "Henry Fellow Longsworth or whatever it is."

Sabrina's insides felt weighted with lead. "Henry Wadsworth Longfellow?"

"Yeah, that's it. Ugh! Within blocks of all those wonderful boutiques and I'll be stuck in some moldy old house."

It wasn't fair. Sabrina would give her right arm to go there. "Charles Dickens visited that moldy old house, and so did Nathaniel Hawthorne." Sabrina loosened the cupcakes from the pan and set them to cool on a wire rack.

Arielle sighed. "Unless they're interested in having me redecorate it, I couldn't care less about some dumb old house."

Her cousin's acting skills were going to be tested. "Well, you'll have to feign interest. He knows how badly I want to go there."

"No kidding. Hey, these are pretty good."

Sabrina watched Arielle take a hot cupcake and bite into it. Steam rose from the center, carrying the sweet scent, but suddenly she didn't feel like chocolate. She didn't have an appetite at all.

"I think I'll turn in." She didn't have to be up early for work or she would've turned in long ago. Besides, she was too busy fretting over Tucker and Arielle to sleep.

"I'll wrap these when they've cooled." Her cousin took another bite of the cupcake.

"Thanks." Sabrina retreated to her room and slid under the covers, feeling the familiar stab of jealousy.

———)(———

A pounding at the door roused Sabrina from a deep sleep. She checked the clock. It was early. Too early for Renny.

The trip to Boston. Were Arielle and Tucker leaving this early? She hadn't heard Arielle moving around, hadn't heard the water running in the bathroom.

Sabrina peered through her bedroom window. Tucker stood on the landing, his hands tucked in his pockets, bouncing on the balls of his feet like he couldn't wait for the day to start.

"Arielle?" she called, swinging open her bedroom door. The living room was dark, and her cousin was a shadowed lump on the couch.

"Arielle, Tucker's here." She shook her cousin.

"What?"

"Tucker's here. You're going to Boston today, you overslept."

Arielle moaned. "I have a migraine."

Another tap sounded at the door. "Come on, Arielle, he's waiting."

Arielle pressed her fingertips to her temples. "I can't go."

"You're not just trying to get out of this, are you?"

She moaned again.

"Maybe it'll go away if you take something."

"I already did, hours ago."

The cupcakes. Chocolate gave Arielle migraines. She wondered how many her cousin had.

Tap, tap, tap. The knock was louder. She had to answer the door before he woke Renny.

"Tell him I can't go. Apologize for me, okay?" Arielle rolled away as if it were a closed matter.

Great. Not only was Tucker going to be disappointed, but Sabrina had to deliver the news.

She sighed and went to the door, wishing her hair wasn't matted and straggly, wishing she wasn't wearing her pajamas. She gave her hair a futile fluff and pulled open the door.

Tucker's smile was disarming. "Good morning."

"Uh—hi, Tucker." She cast a glare at the lump on the couch. "Um, I'm afraid I have bad news. Arielle has a migraine this morning."

His eyes registered surprise, but the smile hung around. "Oh. Is she going to be okay?"

"She gets them occasionally—I mean, she said she does. She said she doesn't feel up to going today. She asked me to apologize for her."

His smile faltered. "Oh." He looked toward the yard.

Sabrina followed his eyes toward the yard, down the tree limb to where the robin's nest still clung for dear life. She could hear the hum of Tucker's car from the front of the house. She felt bad that he'd cleared his schedule for the trip, and now it was canceled. He looked vaguely disappointed, and she was so tired of disappointing him.

Then he turned his full attention on her. "Hey, I have an idea. You want to go with me? Arielle said you were a fan of Longfellow too."

Her traitorous heart jumped the curb, and she clearly saw a sign marked "Danger Ahead." "Oh, I don't know—"

"Come on, it'll be fun. I already reserved tickets, and I cleared my calendar for the day. I was looking forward to it." He gave her the puppy dog look. So not fair.

Reasons. She needed reasons to say no. She couldn't think of a single legitimate one.

"It's your day off, right?" he asked.

She clenched her jaw. He knew way too much about her. "I

have to go to the grocery. And read. I was going to read today."
Lame, lame, lame.

"You can do that any day. Come on, you're already up. Doesn't
a trip to Boston sound fun? It's a beautiful day for a boat ride. The
Longfellow House . . . Please?"

Tempting, it was so tempting. And it was a beautiful day. Already
the sky was clear blue, and the temperature promised a mildly
warm day. Still . . .

"I'm not ready. I just got up, haven't even showered yet." *Is that
the best you can do?*

"We have time. I'll wait in the car, just come down when you're
ready."

"But—" She had no more words, but it didn't matter, because
Tucker was already traipsing down the steps like a kid just dismissed
from school.

Sweetpea: I think courage resides deep inside of everyone. But sometimes it's impossible to reach because of all the stuff piled on top.

Thirty-two

Sabrina strolled through the gardens beside Tucker. Every now and then his arm brushed hers, especially when they toured the crowded house. The artifacts had been fascinating, and though she knew most of what the guide recited, just seeing the rooms and desk where Longfellow had written had been a dream come true.

The garden showed off its summer wardrobe, a riot of colors and textures. Blue delphinium, pink hollyhock, vibrant purple Japanese iris, and dozens of other varieties crept and climbed the surfaces of the garden. Renny would be in heaven.

"What's that?" Tucker pointed.

Sabrina caught sight of the bronze object nearby. "That must be the sundial. Longfellow's daughter placed it here. She put her father's favorite motto on it."

"How do you know so much about this place? I think you could've led the tour."

She shrugged. She'd never mentioned it in email, so it was

safe to do so now. "I wrote a fifty-page essay on Longfellow in college."

Tucker leaned over the inscription on the sundial. "I can't read it."

"You don't speak fluent Italian?" she teased, then caught herself when he turned his crooked smile on her. "It means something like 'Think that this day will never dawn again.'"

Tucker straightened, and she felt his eyes on hers. She'd felt him watching her throughout the day. On the long boat ride to Boston, over their quick lunch once they'd docked, through the house tour. Did they mean anything, those looks? She was confused.

"Think that this day will never dawn again." She thought it was meant to be inspirational, but today the thought depressed her. She wished this day could dawn over and over for all eternity.

She ran her fingers over the sundial, wondering what Tucker was thinking. A bird twittered, serenading them. Tucker was probably thinking about Arielle, wishing she were here instead. Though he had been a lighthearted and entertaining host. He'd made her laugh repeatedly, and Sabrina realized she hadn't had so much fun in—well, she didn't remember the last time.

Now, though, an awkward silence had fallen. Even the bird stopped his song, as if waiting expectantly.

She had to break the silence before whatever Tucker expected, whatever she hoped for, happened. "It's too bad Arielle couldn't come." The name of her cousin had an instant dampening effect, at least on her.

"I'm having a great time. You're a fun and knowledgeable date." He cocked a grin at her before starting along the path again.

She fell in step beside him. The sun was sinking in the sky, had fallen behind the trees. A mild breeze cooled her skin.

"How about we find an air-conditioned café for a quick supper before we head back?" he said.

"Only if you let me pay my half." He'd insisted on buying her lunch.

"Have it your way, stubborn."

She bumped her shoulder into his arm, delighting too much in the sturdy feel of him.

⌒⌒

Tucker pulled his car onto Sabrina's street. Tired though he was from the long day, he dreaded its end. He'd enjoyed Sabrina. Seeing her in her element, talking about her passion. It made him fall more deeply in love with her. It made him want to end the secrecy between them.

Just tell her you know.

No, I can't risk losing her.

All the way back on the boat, he'd waffled back and forth.

Back and forth, back and forth. He was about to drive himself crazy with indecision. It wasn't like him. But the cold, hard facts were that he'd spent another day with Sabrina, and she was no closer to telling him the truth. Whatever it was, whatever was holding her back, it had her by the heart and wasn't letting go.

Now, he pulled his car into her drive, feeling reasonably settled about the decision he'd reached. He flipped off the ignition and unbuckled his seatbelt.

"You don't have to walk me up. Arielle's in bed already," she said quickly. Sabrina had called twice to check on her cousin.

"I'll see you to the door." He exited the car before she could argue. They weren't done yet; she just didn't know it.

He followed her up the steps, admiring her form from behind, wishing he could set his hand at the small of her back. *You have no right to be looking, much less touching. What would she think if she knew the direction of your thoughts?*

Sabrina fished her key from her bag and aimed it at the knob.

Tucker took her fist in his. "Wait. I wondered if we could talk a minute." They'd had all day. Why didn't he do this earlier?

Because you were hoping she'd do it herself.

"I—I should probably check on Arielle."

"You called an hour ago, and she was in bed."

She looked at the door as if hoping it might open up and swallow her. "I haven't thanked you for today. I enjoyed seeing the mansion and—and everything." She was looking everywhere but at him as she pulled her hand from his grasp.

He leaned against the door frame, conveniently blocking the knob. He saw right through her parting words, an attempt to end the evening quickly. "I'm glad you could go." If she only knew how glad. If she only knew how badly he wanted to prolong the night.

But it was late, and they both had work tomorrow. Still, there was the matter of that one last piece of business. He took a breath, digging deep for courage.

"Sabrina, I feel like we've gotten to know each other pretty well recently." He waited for a response, but got none, save a long swallow.

"I want you to know, if there's anything you need, anything you ever want to talk about, I consider you a close friend."

She tucked in the corners of her lips, a cross between a smile and a grimace. "Thank you."

Her eyes darted over his shoulder, then to the ground between them, then to her hand that held the key. He was pretty sure the words *I've got to get out of here* were tumbling around that pretty little head.

He wanted her to be still long enough to hear him. He wanted her full attention. He nudged her chin up with his finger until she met his gaze.

She was a frightened doe. Those big brown eyes overflowed with panic. Worry lines creased her forehead, and her shoulders were plywood stiff. He regretted his words if only because they'd changed Sabrina back into the Ice Princess.

His hope withered slowly under a scorching light of realization. He didn't know why—why she wouldn't tell him, why she hid behind email, why she'd gone to such great lengths to protect herself.

But if she needed to hide, for whatever secret reasons, didn't he love her enough to wait? In the space where hope had resided, a seed of mercy sprouted. *Ah, honey. I'm sorry I pushed you. You're worth the wait.*

He tried for a smile he didn't feel. "You're tired. Get to bed." He pressed a kiss to her forehead and felt the softness of her hair under his lips, smelled the sweet scent of ocean and lilac in her hair.

He'd scarcely pulled away before her key found the lock, and then she was gone.

Sweetpea: Everyone yearns to be loved for who they
are. Not for what they look like or what they do or
what they've accomplished. I wonder how many
people actually find that.

Thirty-three

A cab waited in front of the house when Sabrina returned from
work. Maybe Arielle was going somewhere.

For three days Sabrina had been lost in thought, remembering
every moment of her date with Tucker. The morning after, Arielle
had quizzed her about the day, and she'd told her cousin everything.
Except the kiss. But it wasn't a real kiss, just a brotherly kiss on the
forehead.

Only it hadn't felt brotherly at all.

She entered the loft and kicked off her work shoes. Arielle was
hunched over her floral suitcase, pushing on the swollen bag, struggling
with the zipper.

A glance around revealed a lack of all things Arielle. The sandy
spot by the door where she usually kicked off her sandals was bare,
the end table where she piled her clothes was empty. Dread welled
inside Sabrina. "Where are you going?"

Arielle gave the zipper one last tug. "Home."

She watched her cousin haul the suitcase off the sofa and set it at her feet. "What do you mean?"

"I've had enough of this charade, cuz. It's time for me to go. I'm catching the ferry, and I booked a flight from Cape Cod."

Had something happened between her and Tucker? This was totally out of the blue and utterly unfair. "What happened?"

"Nothing happened. I have to get back. I just—I can't do this anymore." A flicker of something—fear?—flared in her eyes before her eyelids shuttered them.

Now that Sabrina looked closer, Arielle's face looked strained, her lips tipped uncharacteristically down at the corners, her brows pulled together. What was going on?

"It's only a few more days, Arielle. We had a deal."

"Deal's off. I don't expect you to come to the wedding, so you're off the hook."

What in the world? Arielle had begged her to attend Jaylee's wedding. It was the only reason she'd come. "What reason did you give Tucker?"

A nonchalant shrug. "I didn't tell him. I'm sure you'll come up with something."

"You didn't tell him?" What explanation could Sabrina give? *Sorry, Tucker. The love of your life disappeared as quickly as she'd appeared.* Why was Arielle doing this?

Her cousin was wheeling her suitcase past her, toward the door. Sabrina grabbed her arm, panic building. "Why are you doing this? What are you so afraid of?"

Arielle whirled on her heels. "Don't question *me* about fear.

You're hiding behind some email name because you're afraid to have a real relationship. You're worse than Renny, hiding her manuscripts in a drawer."

Arielle's anger, her words, stopped Sabrina cold. Her hand fell from her cousin's arm.

"Go back to your safe little emails, Sabrina. Never mind that you're missing out on a real relationship with a wonderful man . . ." Arielle's words wobbled as the sentence trailed off.

When the door closed behind her cousin five seconds later, Sabrina knew with sudden clarity why Arielle was leaving the island, why fear laced her eyes, why angry words were spilling from her tongue.

Arielle had fallen head over heels for Tucker.

Sweetpea: I haven't been to church since the Jared/ Jaylee episode. I just haven't been able to bring myself to go.

Thirty-four

Sabrina paced the length of the loft as the taxi pulled away. So, Arielle had fallen for Tucker. Was it any surprise? He was a wonderful man, just as she'd said. It was a miracle some woman hadn't snatched him up already. But did it have to be her cousin? Was Sabrina destined to lose every man she loved to one of her beautiful cousins?

Sabrina kicked the chair Arielle had placed against the wall, and it toppled over, hitting the floor with a *thwack*. It was so unfair. What right did Arielle have stealing the only man she cared about? It had been stupid to encourage those dates. Stupid! Sabrina couldn't have done a better job sabotaging herself if she'd tried.

She reached the windows and turned. Arielle's feelings aside, the relevant question was, where did Tucker stand? He was caught in a triangle and didn't know it. Was he in love with Sabrina or Arielle or some bizarre combination of them both? Sabrina ran her hands over her face. What had she done?

And how was she going to tell him Arielle was gone? What

reason could she give? A family emergency? But what excuse could she give for keeping the relationship online now?

Was it time to admit defeat? To send him a final letter ending the relationship?

She imagined coming home to an empty inbox, facing Tucker at the café every morning with no hope of having that intimate communication again . . .

How her heart ached at the thought!

She couldn't do it, she just couldn't. It was all she had of him. All she could ever have, and it would have to be enough.

And yet, was it fair to tie him down to a relationship that could never go deeper than email? *But he loves you.*

Why, God? Why, of all people, did it have to be Tucker? Why, of all men that night, did it have to be his brother-in-law?

But it was what it was. Begging and praying would change nothing. She had to focus on the problem. She had to decide what to tell Tucker and how to say it. Arielle had left a fine mess, leaving in a snit as she had.

Sabrina stopped pacing, her feet stopping on the braided rug Arielle had bought. Arielle had left Sabrina in a bind, but the fact that she'd left, despite her growing feelings for Tucker . . .

It was so obvious she'd almost missed it. Arielle was leaving for Sabrina. Despite her cousin's testy words, she was removing herself from the picture out of love for her. Leaving so that Sabrina wouldn't get hurt again.

And Sabrina hadn't been nice about it.

She cringed. She'd let her confusion and anger blind her, but everything was clearer now.

A knot of anxiety tightened inside. She couldn't stand that they'd parted on bad terms. Especially now that she realized Arielle was willing to sacrifice a possible relationship with Tucker for Sabrina's sake. She snatched her bag, slipped into sandals, and ran down the steps.

Traffic in town was heavy, and pedestrians littered the sidewalks, waiting to cross the street. Sabrina had to stop pedaling at every crossing, further delaying her mission. As she neared the wharf, the congestion thickened with passengers arriving from Hyannis, exiting the ferry with their fat suitcases and dog-weary grins. Taxis lined the street, waiting to drive tourists to their hotels and rentals.

After parking, she hurried up the concrete dock, dodging pedestrians, feeling like a trout swimming upstream. She hoped Arielle hadn't boarded. She scanned the ferry's rails for a glimpse of her cousin. Someone on the middle deck had long, blonde hair and looked—

Thwack! She slammed into another body and staggered backward. "I'm so sorry." She reached out to steady the woman, eager to move on.

But her eyes caught on the woman's face. On those icy blue eyes she could never forget. They'd haunted her ever since that day. That morning in the house in Madaket.

Maybe the woman wouldn't recognize her. Sabrina averted her eyes quickly, turning her head. She had to get away quickly. "I'm sorry." Giving up her mission to fight the crowd, she turned toward town for a quick escape.

"It's you." The woman's voice rose over the din of voices and footsteps.

Sabrina broke into a run, trying to disappear in the throng. She prayed Tracey wouldn't follow. If she could just make it to her bike . . .

Tucker hadn't said his sister was coming. But why would he mention it to Sabrina? He'd probably told Arielle, and her cousin had no knowledge of that fateful night. Tracey had probably come to meet Arielle. And now Arielle was gone and—

Tucker.

He was probably here to pick up Tracey. Here somewhere in this mass of humanity. He would be parked in the same area as her bike.

Changing direction, she turned up Water Street. She'd go back for her bike later, long after Tucker and his sister left. She hustled up the sidewalk, making a left when she reached India Street. The crowd had dispersed, making her more visible. It was irrational to think Tracey had followed her, especially when she'd been encumbered with luggage. But what if Tracey told Tucker she'd seen her? What if they were both looking for her?

Where could she hide? In the distance, the steeple of First Congregational Church, Renny's church, poked into the sky like a pointy finger. Quickening her pace, she headed toward the building. She would hide there until the sun sank. Then she'd sneak to her bike under the cloak of darkness.

When she reached the church, she darted up the steps, out of breath. An elderly man stood just inside the door. "I'm sorry, the tower is closed for the day."

"Oh." Did this mean she couldn't enter? "I wasn't coming to

climb the tower. I was—" She looked over his frail shoulder into the sanctuary.

Sanctuary. The word had a nice ring. "I wanted to—to pray." It might have been a lie, but Sabrina suddenly realized it was true.

"By all means," the man said, ushering her forward.

She couldn't take her eyes from the altar. It drew her like a magnet. She did want to pray. Like Renny. Like Tucker. Like *her*, before her life fell apart. She *needed* to pray.

Maybe she'd find answers or, at least, solace. She'd missed that and only now realized how much.

She needed to pray because the web she'd become ensnared in was too big, too sticky to escape on her own—it didn't take a genius to see that.

And yet, after seeing Tucker's sister, after the reminder of what she'd done that night, of all she'd done since . . . she felt unworthy.

She stopped at the sanctuary's entrance. It was so . . . white in there. White walls, white pews, white altar and pillars. Did her presence sully the place? Did she have the right to be in a holy sanctuary? In the presence of a holy God? Would the usher have thrown her out if he knew what she'd done?

Would God strike her dead for having the nerve to enter his house? Because she realized with sudden clarity that he did know. Knew everything she'd done, from that first week on the island through her lies and charade. She'd blocked it from her mind all these months, pretending he didn't see or didn't care enough to notice.

Yet, what hope did she have on her own? Would he mind her return if she was seeking his help?

A movement at the altar caught her eye. A woman was hunched

over the bottom step of the pulpit in prayer. There were others dotting the pews. Their presence gave her the boldness to take one step
and then another.

Her courage grew as she neared the altar, but her heart took a
dozen beats for each step down the long aisle. She didn't recognize
the woman at the altar until she was nearly upon her.

"Renny." Sabrina didn't mean to say it aloud, to disturb her
friend from prayer.

Renny raised her head. Her eyes were red rimmed. "Sabrina . . ."

She'd never seen Renny cry. Not even when her beloved pet
bird died suddenly. She knelt by her friend, forgetting her own
troubles. "What's wrong? Did something happen?"

Renny wiped her nose with a tissue that was wadded in her fist.
"I'm fine. I'm here about my stories."

"Your stories?"

Renny nodded, wiping her eyes.

Sabrina waited for her to continue.

Renny laid her hand on her heart. "I've really been fighting *El
Shaddai*—God—on this one."

"What do you mean?"

"I was afraid. So afraid, it paralyzed me. I couldn't send them, I
just couldn't."

Sabrina settled down lower beside Renny. "Oh, Renny."

"Can you believe fear can be so paralyzing? I've been afraid my
whole life, hiding away in my big house with nothing but a view
of the ocean. My fear has been a wall that's separated me from
freedom. It kept me from pursuing my dreams and living a full life.
I'd write a story, intending to send it. Then I'd hit that wall of fear

and decide it was too hard to get to the other side. Too thick, too high. Too scary. Rather than face the anxiety, I'd hide on the safe side of the wall, where it's not so scary."

"But you can change that."

Renny dabbed her eyes. "With God's help, I'm going to do it. I'm going to send my babies out there, all nine of them. If they all come back, I'll find a way to deal with it. He'll help me through it."

"I'm so glad to hear that." Sabrina patted her shoulder, wishing, not for the first time, that she was a hugger. She was sure Renny could use one. Spontaneously, she reached over and put her arms around the woman.

Renny gave her a tight squeeze, then released her a few moments later. "Well, enough of my blubbering. What brings you here, *amita*?"

Sabrina breathed a laugh. "I've been doing a little hiding of my own. I'm so confused." She rubbed her temple.

"I left my scalp massager at home . . . that always clears my confusion." Sabrina smiled, but Renny wasn't joking. "Well, never mind that. Want to talk about it?"

Before she could lose her nerve, Sabrina spilled the whole story. Renny already knew about Jaylee and Jared, but Sabrina had never told her friend about the night of her transgression or the charade with Arielle. She finished the story with the moment on the pier that now seemed like hours ago.

Renny listened, offering nods of encouragement and sighs of sympathy. When Sabrina was finished, Renny pulled a clean tissue from her pocket and handed it to her.

They'd shifted and now they sat on the altar steps, their backs to the pulpit. The others who'd come to pray or think had left.

"I'm tired of doing this alone," Sabrina said.

"Doing what alone?"

"I turned on God after Jaylee and Jared betrayed me. And then I committed adultery with another woman's husband and felt too ashamed to return."

"Ahhh . . . The same sin that separated you and God, separated you and Tucker."

"I never thought of it that way, but you're right. I have a wall just like you, and it's right between me and God. I don't want it there anymore."

"Oh, honey, it doesn't have to be. He's received many a prodigal child, myself included. Just come back to him. It's called *teshuvah*. Returning, a repentance of sin."

Was it that simple? Would he receive her after she'd rejected him? After she'd committed that despicable act?

She'd royally messed up. She'd done to another woman what Jaylee had done to her. She felt ashamed and unworthy. Unworthy of freedom and happiness. Unworthy of God's mercy. Her wall *was* too thick. Too high.

"What I did was so—I still feel dirty. I knew better, and yet I . . ."

"God is standing at the top of the wall with a rope. You only have to take hold of it. You can trust him, Sabrina."

Can I, God? "But, I've got this huge mess . . ."

"He knows that. And he's not going to wave a magic wand and make it disappear, but he'll help you do what's right. Help you overcome your fears—just like he did mine."

Sabrina thought of Renny's years of hard labor. "You've been fighting that one a long time."

Renny grinned. "Okay, so it took me a while. You're a faster learner than I am."

Sabrina was tired of hiding on this side of the wall. Tired of the limitations when the other side offered so much freedom.

All right, God, I'm grabbing the rope. Are you okay with that?

"He loves you, Sabrina. So much, *amita*."

Sabrina stared into the darkened sanctuary, feeling calm for the first time in months. The wall was still thick. It was still high. But Jesus held the rope, and he'd help her over it. Somehow, some way, he'd get her safely to the other side.

Sweetpea: I hate being the bearer of bad news. Once, Jaylee double-booked herself for prom. I had to tell the guy who came second that she'd already left with someone else. I'll never forget the look on his face.

Thirty-five

Dear Tucker,

Sabrina typed the words, then stared at the blinking cursor until it mesmerized her. She'd emailed Arielle as soon as she'd returned from the church. She'd apologized for her harsh words and said she understood why Arielle had left. She'd even managed to thank her cousin. Arielle would get the message when she returned to Macon, and they'd undoubtedly settle things over a phone call.

But her letter to Tucker . . . What could she say? She tapped her fingers on the keyboard. He would expect her to give some reason for leaving the island. And she had to let him know she couldn't see him again.

She wanted to tell him that she and God were back on speaking terms. Maybe she could include that too. He'd be thrilled for her.

But first, how could she explain Arielle's departure without telling another lie? She was adamant about avoiding more lies. All that deception had gotten her nowhere.

Tucker's words from the week before popped into her mind. *"Unfortunately, I can't explain why I kissed you. But I don't regret it."*

That's what she would do. Offer no explanation and ask him to trust her.

The phone rang, and she was grateful for the disruption. Probably Renny calling to set up a brainstorming session now that the creative neurons were firing again.

"Hello?" Sabrina tucked the phone into her shoulder and swiped away cookie crumbs Arielle had left behind.

"Sabrina?"

Tucker. She dropped the crumbs in the trash and rubbed her hands together. Was it too late to hang up?

"Yeah." She could hit herself for not writing Tucker as soon as she'd returned.

"Hey, how's it going?"

"Fine." *Except everything is fixing to fall apart.* She covered her face.

"I was wondering if I could drop by tonight. My sister's visiting for the weekend, and I wanted her to meet you. I mean, you and Arielle."

This cannot be happening. "Uh . . . Arielle's not here." Sabrina paced across the room.

"Will she be back soon?"

Here goes. Sabrina swallowed the dry lump in her throat. "I—I have something I need to tell you."

"What's wrong? Are you okay?" The concern in his voice about broke her.

"Arielle left. I mean, she left the island." She gentled her voice, stealing herself against the pain she was causing. "I—I don't think she's coming back." Her heart hurt for him. She wanted to coat the words with chocolate or something to make them go down easier, but there was no way to sweeten them.

"She left?"

Sabrina heard the surprise in his voice. "I'm sorry, I—I don't know what to say." An understatement. A huge understatement. *Please don't press for details.*

"Did she say why?"

A question she could answer honestly. *Thanks, God.* "Not really. She was packing when I got home from work, had a cab waiting. I'm sorry she left without an explanation. I'm sure she'll be in contact soon." *She's in the middle of writing you as we speak.*

A silence ensued. A long one that made her wonder if Tucker was still on the line. Then finally, he spoke. "It's okay, Sabrina. I think I understand."

He did? Had something happened between Tucker and Arielle after all? Had he kissed her? Told her he loved her?

Please, no. She couldn't bear the thought of him whispering those words into her cousin's ear, of seeing Arielle wrapped in his arms the way Jaylee had been in Jared's. She scrubbed the image from her mind.

"Sabrina?"

He didn't sound hurt or depressed. She was confused. "I'm here. Just be watching for that email."

"I will."

"Yeah, so I'll—uh—see you bright and early, then."

"See you tomorrow."

She turned off the phone and set it in the cradle, their final words ringing in her ears. She couldn't go to work the next day. Or even Sunday. What if Tucker brought Tracey? She could ruin everything with just one word.

Sweetpea: My dad whistled when he was happy. That was before my mom died, so I was little, but I still remember the tune, the way his lips puckered, and the way it made the whole house cheery.

Thirty-six

The next morning there was no email response from Tucker. Sabrina puttered around the house, cleaning and reading all day, hoping the time would pass quickly, eager to hear from him. She'd taken two personal days and asked Char to fill her spot so Gordon would have no cause to complain.

When evening arrived, she opened her email again. In her message, Sabrina had said as little as possible about her departure from the island. Arielle's departure, she corrected herself. She'd spent most of the email expressing her joy at finding peace with God. She knew Tucker would rejoice with her.

While writing the letter, Sabrina also had come to grips with her anger toward Jared and Jaylee. How could she hold a grudge against her cousin after God had forgiven her? It was time to let it go. She'd told Tucker that too.

Now, she opened her email program and smiled when she found Tucker's reply in her inbox. Finally.

I'm so happy for you. I sense a new freedom in the tone of your message, and I couldn't be more pleased. Isn't it amazing how God accepts us right where we are, regardless of where we've been or what we've done? It's such a foreign concept in this world that it's hard to fathom.

I'm also glad you've found it in your heart to forgive your cousin and ex-fiancé. I can't believe you're going to the wedding—I'm so proud of you. I'd love to go with you, if you'll have me. I admit that it relieves my mind to know you're able to put Jared behind you completely. Does that make me a selfish jerk?

I want to talk with you more about all this, but my sister, Tracey, is visiting for the weekend so my spare time will be limited for a couple days. Know that I'm thinking about you and missing you.

Sabrina couldn't keep the smile from forming. She reread his letter and noticed he hadn't said anything about her leaving except that he missed her. Obviously he couldn't go to the wedding, still a few weeks away—but, oh, how she wished he could be there with her.

She sighed. He'd probably be out of touch until Sunday night when his sister left, and until then, she had only one goal.

Stay out of Tracey's sight.

———)(———

Sabrina felt like singing when she awoke early on Monday. She'd survived the weekend without running into Tracey, and her relief was tangible.

When she exited the bathroom, her eyes caught on her own image in the oval mirror Arielle had hung there. She stopped in front of it. Well, her cousin was gone now. Sabrina grasped the maple frame in her palms, ready to pull it from its spot, but something stopped her.

She uncurled her fingers, releasing the frame, and stepped back from the mirror. The honey color of the wood contrasted nicely with the sage color Arielle had painted the hall. The mirror had a beveled edge that was simple and elegant, and the face staring back from the middle of it really wasn't so bad.

Sabrina watched herself grin. Maybe she could live with the mirror after all. Happy with her decision, she turned toward the kitchen, but when she rounded the corner, she bumped her leg on the end table. Straightening, she surveyed the room with fresh eyes. She really didn't care for the way Arielle had arranged the furniture. She preferred to face the window looking over the ocean, not the TV.

Before she knew it, Sabrina was scooting the table, sofa, and recliners into new positions. As she gave the sofa one last shove, her bracelet caught on the fabric. She worked the heart charm loose from the material and straightened.

Why was she wearing this stupid bracelet? That part of her life was over. Sabrina unfastened the clasp, walked to the wastebasket, and dropped it inside. It landed at the bottom with one last jingle.

Turning, she surveyed the living room critically. It was good. She didn't know why she hadn't thought of the arrangement before. She liked it much better. Not only did it open up the room, but it seemed brighter and cheerier somehow. Giving a satisfied nod, Sabrina used the extra few minutes before leaving for work to peruse *The Inquirer and Mirror*.

When she reached the back section, a help-wanted ad drew her eye. It was for an editorial position at Mill Hill Press, right here on the island. Maybe it was time she did something with that literature degree.

But if she weren't working at the café, she wouldn't see Tucker every day. The thought put an ache in her stomach.

But she'd still have the email relationship. Was it worth the trade-off? Maybe it would be easier not seeing him all the time. Anyway, she might not even get the job. She'd put in her application and see where it led.

The thought put an extra bounce in her steps as she exited her loft. Dark clouds obscured the sun, but not even a gloomy day could dispel her good mood. The lyrics from "It's a Beautiful Morning" hung in her head like harbor fog on a warm spring morning.

Once she was at her station, Sabrina tied her apron and tucked an order pad in her pocket.

"What's with the mysterious smile?" Char asked as Sabrina made fresh coffee.

Sabrina shrugged. "Just in a good mood."

All was well. She and God were hanging out again. Arielle was gone. The charade was over. And she'd survived the weekend without running into Tucker's sister. Oh, yeah, life was good.

"Oliver's trying to get your attention," Char said. "Probably wants to stump you with another word, poor man. He'll never give up."

The kitchen bell rang, and Sabrina trayed an order, collected a couple refills of milk and juice, and headed to the corner table.

⁓⁓

"Promise you won't say anything," Tucker said. He loaded the last of his sister's luggage and closed the trunk.

Tracey limped to the car as the first drops of rain fell; then Tucker slid behind the steering wheel and turned the key. "Tracey . . ."

"What?" She flashed wide baby blues at him.

"We're not going unless you promise."

"Let's get this straight. This is the woman you love, the woman who's stolen your heart"—she covered her heart—"who gives breath to your very—"

"I'm waiting."

Tracey sighed, still in drama mode. "Oh, all right. Party pooper. I came here for nothing."

"Who asked you?"

"You did."

"Yeah, well, I didn't know you were going to be such a pain in the patootie."

"Are you going to get this thing in gear? We'll have to skip the café if you don't hurry. I'm not missing my ferry."

"Maybe that's not such a bad idea."

"I promised to be a good girl. Now, let's go. I have to see this shining example of womanhood."

Now that Tracey's divorce was final, her life was settling down. She'd lost the emaciated look she'd had since she and Sebastian split, and she was starting a new life in a new city. Her new job as a hospital dietician was giving her a purpose and allowing her to meet new people. He was starting to see her trademark steel will reappear.

"I still don't understand why you don't just tell her who you are."

"I told you, she's been hurt. Did I ask for your advice?"

"I'm your sister, honey. You don't have to ask." She patted his shoulder. "I'm always here for you."

"Your generosity overwhelms me." Tucker backed from the drive and put the car in forward gear. The weekend had passed quickly. He'd assigned some of his trips to Nate to make time for Tracey, but his sister didn't seem to mind hanging around his house while he worked.

"All joking aside, bro, I had a great time this weekend. After the lousy start, that is."

Tracey had been upset after running into the woman she'd caught Sebastian with, but she'd been determined to stay. And when Tracey was determined, nothing stood in her way. Tucker's goal had been to keep her so busy she didn't have time to dwell on it. Besides, the island wasn't that small, and presently it was crowded with summer people. Chances of running into the woman again were slim.

As Tucker pulled to the curb and parked diagonally, a butterfly or two fluttered in his stomach. "Not one word."

"I promise! Sheesh."

"Or look."

"I'm here to see her, Tuck."

"You know what I mean."

Tracey rolled her eyes and reached for the door.

Tucker hit the lock button, and all the locks snapped downward.

Tracey glared.

He couldn't believe he was so nervous. It wasn't like Tracey was a blabbermouth. She could be a brat when she wanted to but she'd never hurt him.

"She means a lot to me, Trace." *Everything, actually.*

Tracey's face softened, and she laid her hand on his. "I get that. Relax. I won't do anything to draw undue attention, okay?"

Tucker gave a sheepish grin and hit the button, unlocking the doors.

They ducked through the drizzle, slowed by Tracey's uneven gait; then he opened the door for Tracey and ushered her to his table. Oliver was already at the neighboring table with his steaming mug of coffee.

He introduced the man to his sister, and they made small talk as they settled in. He handed Tracey a menu.

"How am I supposed to see her when I'm facing the street?" she whispered.

"Stop whining. She'll be around soon with coffee." Sabrina was loading a tray at the kitchen window. Her uniform was still spotless as far as he could tell, and her ponytail was caught in her collar, but he knew one flip of her head would set it free.

"Bacon and eggs are good, and so are the pancakes if you're in the mood for them."

"I'm starving," Tracey said.

It was good to see her appetite back. She'd lost too much weight the last year. "Get the Hungry Captain then. It has a bit of everything."

Sabrina delivered food to a table at the back, then retrieved the coffeepot as Oliver drained the last drop in his cup.

"Okay, here she comes," Tucker whispered to Tracey, feeling his heart pounding into his throat. "Act natural." He turned his mug over and settled back in his chair, striking a casual pose.

Sweetpea: Did I mention I hate surprises?

Thirty-seven

Sabrina's mind was so occupied, she was at Oliver's table before she felt Tucker's presence behind her. Was it that late already?

She filled Oliver's mug and removed the empty creamers from his table. He had a word coming, she could smell it.

He didn't disappoint her. "Did you hear about the *opprobrious* behavior of the students here on summer break?" Oliver asked.

Someone squeezed between the tables, and Sabrina leaned forward to let them by.

"Hey, Sabrina," Tucker said after they passed.

She turned with a bland smile, steeled against Tucker's charm.

She met his gaze and was extending the coffeepot when she became aware of the other person at the table.

Her eyes collided with the blue gaze of Tucker's sister.

She was supposed to be gone. She'd come for the weekend, and it was Monday. She should be far, far away by now. Sabrina's nerves rattled like a stack of dirty dishes on a rickety table.

The woman's friendly smile turned down, and the twinkle in her eyes turned as dull as old ice.

The pot shook in Sabrina's hand. Mechanically, she poured the coffee. The stream of liquid shimmied dangerously close to the rim.

Please, God.

"*Opprobrious* behavior, I'm telling you." Oliver's voice was a dull buzz somewhere in the distance.

Sabrina finished filling the mug.

"Sabrina, this is my sister, Tracey," Tucker was saying. "She came all the way from Atlanta to—What's wrong?"

Sabrina couldn't move. Couldn't tear her eyes from Tracey's rigid face. A rush of dizziness hit her like a rogue wave, sudden and debilitating. "I—I have to—"

Leave.

Now.

Before Tracey tells you.

She couldn't be here when he found out. And he would find out. The look on Tracey's face confirmed it.

Sabrina wavered under the dizziness, then took a step toward the kitchen. Char blocked the path with a large tray of food.

"Sabrina." It was Tucker's voice.

Could she dash out the front? A family of five clustered around the entry, waiting to be seated. She was trapped.

"*Tucker.*" His sister's whisper was like the slicing wind of a hurricane, harsh and angry.

She had to leave. Sabrina spun, sloshing coffee over her wrist. The burning pain was a welcome distraction. She bumped Char on her way by.

"Sabrina . . ." Char scolded, but Sabrina kept going. She heard Tucker calling her name and prayed he wouldn't follow. But no, his sister was no doubt informing him who she was, telling Tucker she was the one responsible for breaking up her marriage.

She dropped the pot at the station and darted to the back. Grabbing her bag, she exited through the rear door. She should've told Char or Gordon she was leaving. She'd never walked off a job, but she couldn't go back now, couldn't go back and see the look on Tucker's face when he learned the truth.

Tucker watched Sabrina skirt the tables and exit the room; then his gaze swung to his sister. Between Sabrina's panic and Tracey's— what? anger? hurt?—he didn't know what to think.

"Was it something I said?" Oliver's befuddled voice barely registered.

Tracey's nostrils flared twice. She wrung the napkin until it split in two.

Dread clogged Tucker's throat, but he squeezed the words out. "What is going on?"

Her gaze bounced off his. "Not here."

Oliver watched them with interest and, across the room, Char cast a curious glance their way.

"Come on." He stood, taking Tracey's arm. He ushered her outside, through the drizzle and into his waiting car.

Tracey's breaths came heavily, fogging up the windows. "It's *her.*" She peered through the passenger window. "I can't believe it's her, of all people."

The dread spread downward, a thick ball of trepidation. "Tell me, Trace," he said, but suddenly wasn't sure he wanted to know. He watched a raindrop trickle down the windshield, collecting others in its path, growing larger.

"The woman I found Sebastian with is your Sabrina, your *Sweetpea*." She drilled him with a look.

No, it couldn't be. She was mistaken. He shook his head, a firm denial.

"Did you know?" she asked, pricking him with darts of accusation.

"No, I didn't know. I can't believe you said that."

"Well, I'm a little freaked right now!"

Freaked didn't come close to what he felt. Tracey was wrong. She had to be. Sabrina wasn't the kind of person who would—

"Look," Tucker began, "calm down and let's think this through. It was probably dark that morning you found Sebastian. And it was over a year ago . . ."

"It was *her*. You think I can forget the face of the woman I found my husband in bed with? And she ran off, didn't she? Clearly she recognized me."

He needed a little healthy denial right now. He ran his hand over his face. This couldn't be happening.

He thought he'd known Sabrina . . . Sweetpea. She'd never said anything that indicated she was capable of something like this. She'd mentioned mistakes in the past. But this—this went beyond anything he'd imagined.

Suddenly his words from a letter resurfaced. He'd told Sweetpea about Tracey finding Sebastian with another woman and eventually about the divorce. Tracey had been in anguish at the discovery of his affairs, and he'd felt so helpless. He'd vented with

Sweetpea. He'd said harsh things, knowing she wouldn't judge him for it.

The realization kicked in.

"That's why." His whispered words barely penetrated the patter of rain on the rooftop.

He'd been ruthless in his summation of the events, his feelings toward Sebastian and the woman Tracey had found her husband with—had he called her a whore?

Oh, God. That's why she wouldn't meet me, isn't it? Why she wouldn't admit who she was. She knew what she'd done to my sister and pronounced herself unforgivable.

It was making sense. The refusal to meet, the photo she'd sent, the charade with Arielle. It all made sense when viewed in light of this new piece of information.

"I need to get out of here." Tracey laid her head back, closing her eyes as if she wanted to forget the whole mess.

And he was right in the middle of it. "Maybe you should stay awhile. We could talk. We can get you on a later ferry."

"I think I've had enough of Nantucket. No offense."

Tucker squeezed her hand, then started the car and pulled onto the street heading toward the wharf. Why did this have to happen now, when Tracey had just recovered from Sebastian's betrayal?

Betrayals, he noted the plural. The discovery of Sabrina and Sebastian was just the eye-opener that revealed his other affairs. But his sister didn't need that reminder. He wasn't pouring salt in the wound.

"I'm sorry, Trace." *And what are you going to do now? How can you choose between your sister and the woman you love?*

He thought of Sabrina, no doubt panicked and devastated, and he felt torn.

But Sabrina knew. She knew what she'd done, who his sister was, and she'd let him fall for her, opened up to him and let him in.

When he reached the parking lot, his sister waved him off. "No, just drop me at the wharf. You need to get to work."

"I can wait with you."

"I need to be alone, Tucker." She crossed her arms over her chest, avoiding his eyes, and he knew she felt he'd betrayed her somehow.

A defense rose on his lips, but he held his tongue. She knew he was innocent, but feelings could be deceiving sometimes. Time would sort it out. He only wished he could be there for her while she did the sorting.

When he pulled the car close to the terminal, he helped Tracey with her luggage. He didn't want to leave, felt like he was dumping her at the curb. "Are you sure you don't want company? I can call Dorothy and—"

"I'm sure." Her eyes were bloodshot, but her shoulders were back, her head up.

He felt like a heel. Helpless, he put his arms around her and drew her into a hug. "I'm sorry, honey."

She stood stiffly for a few seconds, then embraced him, her face turned into his T-shirt. "It's not your fault. I know that. I just need some time to work through this."

Forgiving Sabrina seemed impossible, but he knew Tracey was capable of the impossible. If she could prove the doctors wrong and learn to walk again, she could forgive Sabrina someday.

He kissed the top of her head. "You got it." He hated the timing, hated that she was returning to a big city where she hadn't yet established close friends.

"Go on, now. I'll be all right." She straightened and grabbed her luggage.

It was only as he was pulling away from the terminal that he realized his relationship with Sabrina, everything he'd fought for, everything he desired, was now in jeopardy.

Sweetpea: Some mistakes can't be undone.

Thirty-eight

Sabrina had to get out of there, off the island. She had to leave. What other choice did she have? She grabbed a suitcase from the closet and began jamming it with clothes, then realized she needed to call a cab.

Before she took two steps, she stopped. It was pouring rain. Every tourist in town would be calling for a cab, and she didn't have an hour to wait for one. She'd have to ride her bike. Realizing the suitcase was too big to transport, she pulled a smaller one from the closet and dumped the contents into it. Her hands shook. Her body trembled.

Pajamas, socks, toothbrush . . . What else? She pulled the rubber band and ran her hand through her hair. She couldn't think.

Tucker. *Oh, God, the look on his face.* The confusion, the concern. And his sister. She didn't even want to think about the accusation in those eyes. And Sabrina deserved all of it.

Toothpaste. Yes, she needed that and her vitamins. She was getting a pounding headache, the kind that required one of Arielle's nasty tinctures.

A knock rattled the front door.

She sucked in a breath and stared at the white door like it might bust off the hinges and assault her.

But reality was worse, because Tucker could be on the other side of that door. Would he do that? Would he confront her with his sister's accusations?

A sudden thought brought another wave of panic. What if his sister was with him? What if—

Another knock sounded, harder this time. She wouldn't answer. The blinds were drawn; maybe they'd think no one was home. But her bike was out front.

Look through the peephole, Sabrina. Just check.

She made her feet move by force of will. She approached the door and leaned in, careful not to touch it. Maybe it wasn't Tucker at all. It might be—

Renny. The sight of the woman's face, distorted in the glass, brought an exhale that fogged the peephole. She caught her breath, then opened the door.

"I did it!" Renny spun in a circle, a one-woman party, her fluorescent orange Hawaiian shirt blooming at the waistline. "Wahooo!" She waved her hands, oblivious to the rain trickling down her face.

"Did what?"

Renny singsonged her answer and accompanied it with a little jig. "I sent off my manuscripts, my manuscripts, my manuscripts . . ."

Sabrina allowed a tiny smile at her friend's exuberance. "That's wonderful, Renny."

"I saw you ride up the drive and just had to come tell you. Can I come in? I have to celebrate, I feel so . . . free!" She spun her way past Sabrina. "Why's it so dark in here?" she asked when she finally stopped.

Sabrina had forgotten to turn on the lights. She flipped the switch and shut the door.

"Why are you home so early?" Renny asked. "And what's this? I didn't know you were going somewhere. Did you change your mind about your cousin's wedding?"

Her suitcase sat open and full on the same sofa where Arielle's had sat only three days before. So much had happened since then. Some of it good, and some of it bad. It was the bad part that was eating her lunch.

"Sabrina?"

"I'm fine. I'm just . . . taking a trip." And she was still shaking. With fear? Anxiety? Desperation? It was impossible to separate the emotions spiraling through her.

"What's wrong, *amita*?" Renny had finally curbed her excitement enough to notice something was amiss. She laid her hand on Sabrina's arm.

Sabrina didn't have time for explanations. She had to leave before Tucker actually did come knocking on her door, possibly bringing his sister just for fun.

She grabbed her light sweater off the hook by the door and folded it hastily into a lump. "Nothing's wrong. I decided to take a vacation." A permanent one.

"Where to?"

She hadn't gotten that far. Hadn't thought beyond the ferry that would take her off the island. She could go home to Macon, but the thought of seeing her family . . .

She rejected the idea with unwavering certainty. She needed time to digest her feelings before she went home for the wedding.

"Something's wrong, I can see it on your face."

Sabrina shoved the sweater in the suitcase.

"You're shaking, Sabrina. Sit down and talk to me."

Sabrina didn't argue as Renny led her to the chairs in the corner. Rain drizzled down the window behind Renny and pattered on the roof.

"Now, what is going on?"

"I have to leave for a while. Something happened this morning. That's why I'm home early."

"What happened?"

At the question, the scene at the café played in slow, horrifying motion. The memory was like a punch to the stomach. "It's Tucker. He brought his sister to the café this morning to introduce her to me."

Renny sucked in a breath. "The twin sister? The sister that—"

"Yes." If only there were another.

"Maybe she didn't recognize you."

Sabrina gave a wry laugh. "Oh, she recognized me all right."

"What did she say? Did she tell Tucker?"

"I didn't stick around long enough for that special brother/sister moment." Her sarcasm was alive and well. Good to know.

Why was she sitting here when every moment heightened the possibility of a confrontation with Tucker?

"I have to finish packing." She jumped from the sofa and pulled her sandals from the floor.

"Wait, child. Where are you going? Let's think this through."

"There's nothing to think about, Renny. I can't stay here now that he knows. He'll hate me."

"Well, he might hate Sabrina, but he won't hate Sweetpea."

Sabrina set her shoes in the suitcase. That was true. It was something, at least. But she couldn't face him every day at the café, knowing what she'd done and what he thought of her.

"You still have your email relationship."

Thank God for that. It was salvaged at least. Maybe she should write him now. But no, that would slow her down. And she was supposed to be at work and he'd wonder why she was—

Another realization dawned. He was going to write tonight and tell her about his discovery. He would tell her exactly what he thought of Sabrina. She was going to hear every vicious thought running through his head—not that she didn't deserve it.

But she couldn't bear to know what he thought of her now.

"Or maybe . . ." Renny was massaging her scalp with all ten fingers. "Maybe you should tell him everything."

Renny had missed the point. "He already knows everything."

"Not *everything*." Renny's eyes were wide as she nodded her head slowly.

Sabrina sighed. "The only thing he doesn't know is—no. No, I can't tell him I'm Sweetpea."

"Why not, *amita*? What've you got to lose?"

"Tucker." Well, not Tucker, but Harbormaster. Sabrina shook her head. Such a mess. She grabbed a novel from the end table and stuffed it in the suitcase. Like she'd be able to read.

She had to make a plan. She could take her bike on the ferry, but she'd have to rent a car in Hyannis. Thank God money wasn't an issue. She didn't make great money at the café, but she spent little of it since she didn't pay rent.

Renny laid a hand on her arm. She hadn't even noticed the woman approach. Renny's sympathetic expression contrasted with the wildness of her hair after her "massage."

"All you have is a correspondence with the man. If you love him, tell him the truth. Maybe there's *tikva*."

"English, Renny."

"Hope. Maybe there's hope."

Sabrina was already shaking her head. "You didn't see his sister's face. She was livid. I wanted to die on the spot."

"That's her. Not Tucker."

"You don't know how close they are. You don't know the things he said when he was telling me—telling Sweetpea—what happened with his sister and her husband. He used a word to describe that other woman—me, Renny!—that I don't even want to repeat, much less think of being!"

She had to go, had to finish packing. Renny was only holding her up.

"What about honesty? What about doing the right thing and trusting God to work things as he wills? You're strong enough to do the right thing. You've already come through so much." She shrugged. "I'm just trying to be the voice of reason here."

Ha! There was nothing reasonable about that plan. She had to think. She needed to take her address book, her cell phone and charger, what else? She saw the paper on the counter, opened to the editorial ad. So much for that new job.

"Sabrina, stop for a moment and think."

"I can't think with you hounding me, Renny." She regretted the snap of her voice as soon as the words were out. "I'm sorry. I'm just—feeling a little scattered." She walked toward the door. "Thanks for telling me about your manuscripts. I'm happy for you, really. I know there are wonderful things in store for you. But I need to finish packing now."

She wondered for a minute if Renny was going to take the hint. Renny finally lumbered toward the door, but she wasn't quite finished.

"One more thing and then I'll leave."

Sabrina sighed heavily.

"Last spring I was eager for gardening season, and I started some seeds indoors. A few varieties, but among them were sweet peas."

Sabrina barely kept from rolling her eyes. "I feel a metaphor coming on."

Renny ignored her comment. "The seeds have a hard coat that can cause the plant to sprout slowly or unevenly. Before you plant them, it's recommended that you chip away a piece of the shell. Once they go through that, they sprout quite nicely and will even survive a hardy frost."

Sabrina checked her watch. The meaning wasn't lost on her, but she didn't have time to psychoanalyze herself.

"Okay then. I'll let you get back to your packing." Renny turned on the landing, her eyes wet. "I'll be praying for you. Call me when you find a place tonight and let me know you're all right."

Hearing her gentle words, Sabrina really regretted the tone she'd taken. She nodded. The woman loved her, was only trying to help. "I will."

Renny patted her shoulder and left. Sabrina started to close the door but stopped when her eyes settled on the branch outside her door. She followed the length of it once. Twice. Finally settling in the empty crook where two branches met.

It was gone. The nest had finally given way to the wind and fallen. When had it happened? The emptiness that filled her defied all logic.

She closed the door and returned to the task at hand. After changing out of her uniform, she went to the bathroom and gathered the shampoo and a few rubber bands. She chucked the things in her suitcase, then went to the kitchen for her vitamins, checking her watch again.

A pink patch blotched her wrist from the spilled coffee. It still burned, but there was no time for such trivialities. She was going to be too late for the early ferry, but she could catch the next one. Hopefully there was space. She should call and reserve a spot.

The light was flashing on her machine. Char, no doubt, calling to say Gordon was in an uproar about her MIA status. Ignoring the pulsing light, she looked up the number for the fast ferry and dialed.

As she punched in the last numbers, a knock sounded. Renny must've massaged out another metaphor and was back to give her another reason to stay. The line rang while she went to the door.

She was going to tell Renny she didn't have time for this. She'd call her from the ferry or something. They could talk it out then.

On the other end of the phone, a woman picked up. "Hy-Line Cruises, how may I help you?"

Sabrina swung open the door, signaling just a minute with her finger. But her hand froze in the air. Her fingers tightened on the phone.

"Hello?" the voice on the other end of the phone said. "May I help you?"

Sabrina needed more help than the woman on the phone could offer, because the face she was staring into wasn't the pudgy face of her eccentric friend, but the strained, rain-dampened face of the man she loved.

Thirty-nine

"Hello?" the woman on the phone repeated.

Sabrina stared at Tucker, watched as rivulets of rain ran down his face. His hair hung in wet strands, matted to his head.

The other end of the phone went dead, but Sabrina didn't know what to do. Invite Tucker in? Slam the door and lock it?

He made the decision for her, squeezing past, out of the weather. When a recording came on the line, Sabrina turned off the phone.

Tucker took a few steps into the room. The lighting suddenly seemed as bright as a spotlighted stage, and the bulging suitcase, square on the sofa, was the star of the show.

The doorway, still open, beckoned. If only she could dart through the door. How could she face him now?

But she needed her suitcase. She needed her purse, lying on the table across the room.

Tucker turned, looking her in the eye.

What was he thinking? She couldn't tell, couldn't read the features that were normally so easily discerned. Unable to meet his gaze any longer, she turned and closed the door.

You deserve everything you get. Just face it like a woman. Straightening her shoulders, she turned, though she couldn't bring herself to meet his eyes.

"Tell me everything." His words were barely discernible over the pattering of rain.

"I think you pretty much know everything now."

He took one step closer, then stopped as if his sandals were glued to the floor.

She wanted to melt into a puddle and pour through the floorboards. To think he knew what she'd done. That she'd behaved so loosely, that she'd slept with a married man—his sister's husband, no less. It was what Jaylee had done to her. Worse, even.

"I want to hear it from you."

"Do you doubt your sister?" Was he giving her the benefit of the doubt? Surely not. And yet, why would he care about her side? She'd done it, she was guilty.

"I don't doubt Tracey. I want to understand."

Sabrina laughed bitterly. "I have no excuse, Tucker. Everything you're thinking about me is true."

"How do you know what I'm thinking?"

"Because anyone would be thinking it!" She crossed her arms over her heart as if she could protect it from the coming pain.

"I'm not just anyone. And neither are you."

"I'm the woman who slept with your brother-in-law. The whore who broke up your sister's marriage." The phrase slipped out, and she recognized her blunder.

He winced, looking away. She watched the straight line of his back as he walked toward the patio door and looked out.

Did he remember his own words sent to Sweetpea all those months ago? But he knew she'd read the emails right there in his office. He just didn't know she'd originally read them as Sweetpea.

His broad shoulders hunched as he crossed his arms. She couldn't believe he was so calm. Why didn't he just have his say and leave?

Because he was Tucker. That's not who he was.

But his words from that long-ago email pricked her. He'd been angry when Tracey had told him about that morning, about Sebastian's infidelity. He'd been ready to hunt the man down and beat him to a bloody pulp. He'd made no secret what he thought of the woman his brother-in-law had been with. What he thought of *her*.

"Tell me what happened." He was facing her again.

Her mind went back to that night. Back to the depressive state she'd been in when she'd come on her solo honeymoon. He wanted to know everything, and what could it hurt? It didn't excuse what she'd done, but Tucker deserved to know the whole story.

But she had to be careful. Tucker knew Sweetpea's story. She had to be vague.

"I was going through a—a dark time when I came here. I was alone and depressed. Barely made it out of my hotel room for days. I—" She could hardly find words to describe her desperation, to describe how the pain of betrayal had swallowed her whole.

"Go on." His gentle tone spurred her on.

She picked at the cuff of her blouse where it had frayed. "After a while I found an effective, if not necessarily brilliant, way to escape my sorrows. I went to a bar and got drunk." Shame flooded her face as she recalled the way the night culminated. But she was going to be woman enough to admit in broad daylight what she'd done under the cover of night.

"There was a man across the room. He was nicely dressed, and he was looking at me. I—I couldn't believe someone who looked like that could find me interesting, but he bought me a drink." Her eyes sought out his, testing the waters. But Tucker was silhouetted by the light from the patio door.

"I went home with him. I don't remember everything. I never even noticed his ring . . ." Such a feeble excuse.

"I didn't realize until the next morning when his wife—when Tracey—came in." Mortification cloaked her. Her hand went to her throat. She was so dirty. And admitting her transgression to the man she loved was beyond humiliating.

And yet, it didn't compare to what Tracey had suffered.

Nothing she said would rectify or justify it. Jaylee's words, spoken the night she'd discovered her with Jared, haunted Sabrina now. *"We didn't mean for it to happen—didn't mean for you to find out like this."* They were empty words that changed nothing.

Sabrina had still been betrayed, just as Tracey had been. Sorry didn't change a thing. Tracey's marriage was still over.

The air felt heavy, unbreathable. Sabrina needed to get out of there, she wanted to run as far away from this place, away from Tucker and his steady gaze, as she could. She could send for her things later. There was no returning, she knew that now.

She rushed to her suitcase and closed it, pulling the zipper.

"What are you doing?"

She hauled the case off the couch and set it on the floor. Her purse was beyond Tucker. She went for it.

He took her arm. "Sabrina."

She shrugged out of his grasp and grabbed her things. "I've got to go."

"Where?"

Sabrina pulled her suitcase across the floor. It snagged on the rug's edge, and she jerked it loose.

Tucker grabbed the handle.

"Let go!"

"Tell me where you're going."

"Out of here, away, what does it matter?" She tugged the suitcase from his grasp and pulled open the door.

He followed her down the steps. Rain poured down her face and soaked her clothes within seconds. The suitcase was heavy and awkward.

"You're running," he said. "Where are you going to hide? You can't hide from what you did."

The accusation stung. She blocked out his words, pretended the rain washed them away. There was nothing he could say to make her feel worse, was there? And yet, his presence convicted her, made her ever more cognizant of her offense.

She reached the bottom of the steps. Tucker caught her arm. The suitcase slipped from her wet palm and tipped, landing on the gravel with a thud. Her purse fell to the ground afterward.

Before she could stop him, Tucker snatched it.

He had her purse, and where could she go without money? She felt trapped, and it wasn't a feeling she liked. "Give it back." She glared.

"Not until we talk."

"We have talked."

"No. You've talked and I've listened. Now it's my turn."

Her eyes burned. She wanted to cover her ears with both hands. She didn't want to hear what he had to say. It would hurt too much, and she was tired of hurting. Maybe it was selfish, but she wanted to go away and forget everything that had happened. She wanted to start over fresh someplace where she hadn't done so many wrong things, hurt so many people.

"Give me the bag." She reached for it, but he held it away. Thunder cracked.

"Five minutes," he said. "Let's get out of the rain." He took her arm.

She jerked it away. How dare he hold her hostage. "I want my purse!" A stare-off ensued. Tucker's eyes looked dark under the storm's shadows. Dark and stubborn.

"Fine. We'll do it right here then." He tightened his fist around the strap of her bag.

She crossed her arms, a futile act of defiance. He could have his say. She didn't have to listen, didn't have to respond. He wanted to settle the score. Let him say all the awful things he could, call her all the names she deserved.

At the thought, a whimper rose in her throat, but she strangled it before it escaped.

He was quiet so long she wondered if he'd changed his mind. But no, he was only waiting for her to look at him. Rain trickled down his face like tears. His spiked lashes framed eyes that were full of something that contradicted her expectations.

"I know you're not the woman who did that dishonorable thing."

She searched his eyes, confused. "What? Yes, I am—"

He put his fingers over her mouth. "Shush, it's my turn." When she quieted, he spoke again. "I know you did it, but it doesn't define who you are. It was one night, one mistake."

He was letting her off the hook? It didn't make sense. Somehow it angered her. Where was the justice in that? The justice for Tracey.

"Don't make excuses for me. Of all people, you shouldn't be defending what I did. You should detest me on your sister's behalf. What I did destroyed her marriage."

Tucker gave a sad smile. "You were one in a long line for Sebastian. Tracey discovered the truth after that morning. She would've been able to forgive him the one indiscretion, but he has a problem that goes beyond that one night with you."

There'd been others? The divorce hadn't been her fault alone? The news removed a bit of weight from her shoulders. Still, how could Tucker be so . . . so . . . ?

"I don't hate you, Sabrina. I—"

She wished she could pull the words from his tongue. But they seemed stuck there. His gaze roamed over her face, making her conscious of her own state of dishevelment.

Sabrina wiped the rain from her cheeks.

"I forgive you." His words washed away every other thought. "You don't need to leave. Nothing needs to change. Don't go."

It was so tempting, everything he said. But could she continue with the way things were when he didn't know the truth? Forgiving Sabrina the café waitress for her perfidy was one thing, but could he forgive Sweetpea for the same crime? Could his sister ever forgive her?

Of course not. It was more complicated than Tucker dreamed.

And she was weary of the pretense. Weary of loving a man who thought she was someone else. The relationship that meant everything to her was nothing but a lie because Tucker was in love with an illusion.

"Sabrina?"

She looked at the man she loved and knew with sudden clarity that he deserved more than she'd given him. More than she could ever give him.

It was over. All of it. She would tell him the truth and let the chips fall where they may. Then Tucker would hate her. Then Tucker would gladly return her purse and let her leave the island.

The thought carved away a section of her heart, the part where courage resided. She didn't have the guts. Didn't have the strength to face him when he learned who she was, and found her profoundly lacking in integrity and basic morality. She wasn't at all who he thought she was.

Renny's words played back. *"What about honesty? What about doing the right thing and trusting God to work things as he wills?"*

But what if . . . what if she couldn't handle it? What if it cut her to the core?

Do you trust me? The small, familiar voice came from somewhere deep inside.

"Sabrina, talk to me."

She took one last look at him as he was now, savoring the compassion in his eyes for a moment longer. He was a good man. He deserved better than she could offer. He deserved someone who wasn't dragging her past around on a heavy chain. Someone like Arielle. The thought appeared out of nowhere.

Of course.

Sabrina had been nothing but selfish through the entire relationship. She could do this one selfless thing. It would hurt, but it
was time to let Tucker go, set him free. It was time to tell him
everything.

She whispered a quick prayer for courage. "Okay, you've had your
say. Now I need to have mine." She suddenly felt shy, remembering
all the words she'd said, all the letters she'd written. He knew more
about her than anyone. To tell him the truth was to expose herself,
to be vulnerable. All the things she'd thought she was done with.

"Go on."

"I—" *Dear Lord, how can I say it? Give me the words.* He looked
so innocent, and she was going to hurt him. She hated that more
than anything.

He wiped a trickle of rain from her cheek with the back of his
fingers. "Go on," he said again.

She closed her eyes against the touch, then forced them open.
"I—I have something to tell you that may come as a shock. I've
done something—I'm afraid it's going to hurt you and—" Tears
burned at her eyes, clogged her throat with a lump the size of a
boulder.

"Just say it." His tender look was about her undoing.

He was going to hate her afterward.

Do you trust me?

"I'm not who you think I am, Tucker. I—" *Just say it.* "I'm
Sweetpea." Once the boulder came loose, she couldn't stop the flow
of words. "I've been her all along, since the beginning and—"

"Sabrina."

"—when you sent the photo, I was afraid because—because I had feelings for you, and I didn't think you could possibly love someone like me, and then later I realized what I'd done, that Sebastian was your brother-in-law—and then you asked me to find her—to find *me*, and I didn't know what to do, so I pretended to look for her—"

"Sabrina."

"—but I felt so guilty taking your money, so I donated it to Nantucket Soundkeeper, and then Arielle showed up—she's my cousin—and then you saw her and—"

"*Sabrina!*" He dropped her bag and took her face in his hands. "Would you just shut up?"

Her thoughts spun slowly to a halt, like a vacated merry-go-round.

And then her mind began spinning slowly again, this time with questions. Why was he touching her so gently? Why was he looking at her like that—with such tenderness?

"I *know*." He looked at her as if to drive each word home. "I know who you are," he repeated in a whisper.

He knew she was Sweetpea? But how, and when? And why did he hire her?

"Aw, honey, I've waited so long for you." His thumb grazed her cheek, sending a shiver down her arms.

"But how—when?"

"From the beginning. I sought you out."

"But why?"

"I wanted to know you."

"But you hired me . . ."

"To spend time with you. I wanted to be with you. I wanted you to tell me who you are."

His words filled the empty places in her heart. "But Arielle . . ."

"I wanted to knock you silly when you stuck me with that woman. But then Arielle told me she wasn't Sweetpea, and I told her I already knew who—"

"You knew all along?" Sabrina felt dazed. He wasn't in love with Arielle? She remembered his letter that night. *"I love you,"* he'd written. And she'd thought the words were for her cousin. But the words had been for her alone.

She remembered their date, the boat ride. "The kiss . . ." she said.

One side of his mouth tilted in a grin. "The kiss."

He'd let his feelings run away that night. He'd wanted to be with her, not Arielle. He'd wanted to kiss her, not Arielle. Could it be true? Even now, she was afraid to believe.

That morning suddenly rushed to the front of her mind. It seemed so long ago, though it had been an hour at most. She'd seen the look on his face, the look on his sister's face. He hadn't known that part. She stepped back now, needing distance. His hands fell away from her face.

"What's wrong?"

How could anything come of their relationship when they had that between them? Even if Sebastian had made a hobby of sleeping around, could Tracey ever forgive what Sabrina had done?

Her lip wobbled, and she bit it still. "Tracey."

For the first time since her admission, his face sobered. A rivulet of rain traced a path down his temple, his jaw.

"How could she ever forgive me?"

"Same way I did."

"But I don't deserve it."

Tucker pulled her against him. She curled into his wet torso and hid her face in the wall of his chest.

"None of us do, Sabrina. You think I haven't made mistakes?" His words rumbled in her ear. He lifted her hand and kissed the tender flesh of her wrist where the coffee had spilled. "You think Tracey hasn't made mistakes? She's a strong and compassionate woman. She'll come around in time because she knows how much I—"

The sentence hung in the misty air, but Sabrina was enjoying the heavy thud of his heart too much to leave the comfort of his embrace.

But she felt Tucker's hands on her arms, felt him pushing her away. Felt him looking at her with eyes that spoke all the words she needed to hear. "She knows how much I love you." He squeezed her arms firmly and gave her a little shake. "*You*, Sabrina. No one else."

She soaked it up, all his eyes had to say, all his words meant. If she heard it a million more times it wouldn't be too much. The words turned her legs to noodles and warmed a path clear to her heart, seeping into all the dark crevices. The journey had been long and hard, but the destination was worth the trouble. More than worth it.

Tucker.

He lowered his head, and his mouth tested hers. She was sure he could feel her heart banging against his stomach, but soon, she forgot about her heart. All she could think of was the way his lips felt on hers, soft as a feather's touch. When he pulled away, she wanted to protest.

"Our first kiss." He brushed her wet hair from her cheek.

"Second," she corrected.

He grinned. "That one didn't count. You thought I was a two-timing creep."

Her thoughts returned to the uncertainty, the confusion of that night. "No, I didn't."

He gave her a look.

"Maybe a little."

"I couldn't help myself. You were so beautiful sitting there on the water, with the moonlight on your hair. You must've been so confused." He dried her face, the rain and tears, with the back of his hand. "Don't be confused about this, though, Sabrina. I love you with all my heart, and nothing's going to change that."

Were lovelier words ever spoken? She wanted Tucker to feel the way she did now. She wanted to tell him the rest of it, the part that mattered most.

"I love you, too, Tucker. So much." Emotion closed her throat.

"I've waited a long time for those words," he whispered, then dropped a quick kiss on her lips. After a pause, he was back for more. Sabrina wrapped her arms around his neck, ran her fingers through the curls at his nape. She couldn't get enough of him. He smelled like Tucker and tasted of heaven.

His lips were strong and gentle all at once. His touch sent a shiver of pleasure down her spine into the farthest reaches of her heart. When he ended the kiss, it was only to gather her closely in his arms.

"I meant what I said about going to the wedding with you. If you'll have me."

She smiled. "I'd love that." Peace enveloped her, and she remembered Renny's words from weeks ago. *"God will give you peace on
this. I know it."* Now Sabrina knew it too.

She was all wrapped in Tucker's embrace, a chick under his wings.
She could get used to this, she decided. The rain pummeled them,
but they were already drenched and she wasn't going anywhere.

"Not in a hurry to get out of the rain after all?" she asked.

"What rain?" he whispered. And with one last grin, his lips closed
over hers again.

Dear Friend,

I hope you enjoyed your brief journey to Nantucket through the characters of Sabrina and Tucker. My goal in this Nantucket series has always been to show the love of Christ through the relationship of the hero and heroine. Writing it has made me think long and hard about Christ's love for us and the human response to it.

You may have noticed that Tucker loved Sabrina in a God-the-Father kind of way, that he sought out the relationship, pursuing her until she was ready to come to him fully. Conversely, Sabrina was intent on hiding, shamed by the sin she committed "against" him. She's not so very different from us!

I'm so thankful to have a God who seeks me out, one who persistently pursues me—despite my efforts to hide and build walls—and lavishes love on me like I'm his only child. I hope you've discovered that same kind of love on your own faith journey and that *Seaside Letters* has somehow given you a fresh view of Christ.

Blessings!
Denise

Reading Group Guide

1. Sabrina hid behind the facade of the Ice Princess because of past suffering. What are some of the events that caused her to withdraw from relationships?

2. Sabrina was unattractive as a child, and though she grew out of it, she still viewed herself as homely. What baggage (words, attitudes, or actions) from your childhood do you hang on to even though it's not necessarily true?

3. What were some of Tucker's characteristics and actions that reflect Christ?

4. Tucker knew Sabrina was Sweetpea from the beginning. How did his activities at the beginning of their relationship reflect God's actions toward us?

5. Things began to spin out of control for Sabrina after she told her first lie—sending the photo of Arielle to Tucker. Have you ever found yourself getting deeper and deeper in your own pit of deceit? How did you extricate yourself?

6. When Sabrina asked Tucker what he wanted most, his reply was that he wanted to know her more. Do you think God feels this way about you? Why or why not?

7. Why did Sabrina use email to keep Tucker at a distance? What do you use to keep the ones you love at a distance? What is preventing you from true intimacy? Do you keep God at a distance? How does our sin create a wall between us and God?

8. Isaiah 43:25 says, "I, even I, am he who blots out your transgressions, for my own sake, and remembers your sins no more." What does this mean, and how did Tucker's actions reflect God's reaction to our sin?

9. Renny didn't mail her manuscripts for fear of rejection. What are you most of afraid of? How has fear affected your actions? What steps can you take, with God's help, to overcome it?

10. Renny couldn't quite believe she was a talented writer, despite Sabrina's encouragement and compliments. Do you have a God-given talent you aren't using? What's stopping you?

Acknowledgments

Every author knows it takes many people working together to make a book happen. I'd like to give a shout-out to all those who put up with me, helped me with research, double-checked me, and encouraged me along the way.

I have to start with the Thomas Nelson fiction team. I'm so honored to work with this creative, hardworking, and dedicated team of publishing professionals: publisher Allen Arnold, Amanda Bostic, Jocelyn Bailey, Kathy Carabajal, Jennifer Deshler, Natalie Hanemann, Chris Long, Ami McConnell, Heather McCulloch, Becky Monds, Ashley Schneider, Katie Schroder, and Micah Walker.

I have to give an individual shout-out to Ami McConnell, who amazes me with her insight. Her editorial advice makes me look so much better than I am. I also owe a debt of gratitude to Jessica Alvarez, my second editor on this work—see, it takes two of them to keep me in line.

My agent, Karen Solem, intercedes, encourages, and does all that annoying contract stuff. Melissa Hankinson graciously offered to read the manuscript with an eye toward getting the Nantucket details right. Thanks to Joy Geiger for her help on research—we'll keep the specifics to ourselves.

My best buds from Girls Write Out (www.GirlsWriteOut.blog spot.com), Kristin Billerbeck, Colleen Coble, and Diann Hunt: God knew what he was doing when he put us together.

My family is a constant source of joy, encouragement, and research material! Thanks, Justin, Chad, and Trevor—you impact my writing in more ways than you know. And Kevin, my partner in crime. I can't believe it's been twenty years!

Lastly, thank you, friend, for joining me on this journey to Nantucket. It's a real treat to share my stories with others, and I'd love to hear from you. Send me an email at Denise@DeniseHunterBooks .com or visit my Web site at www.DeniseHunterBooks.com.

About the Author

Denise Hunter is the award-winning and best-selling author of several novels, including *Sweetwater Gap*. She and her husband are raising three boys in Indiana.

Author Photo: Amber Zimmerman